amal
twit
fren

VALLEY GIRLS

A NOVEL BY

MARK S. LUCKIE

Sara—
Happy reading!

ISBN 978-0-578-77856-3 (Paperback)
ISBN 978-0-578-77857-0 (eBook)

www.marksluckie.com

*To Ms. Lewis and Mrs. Carter, for showing me
how to use my voice to help others find theirs.*

VALLEY GIRLS

ONE

This was the perfect opportunity for a selfie.

The California morning light filtered through the glass walls of the magnificent lobby where Kelsey Pace was seated patiently. It was the nervous young woman's first day as a communication manager at Elemynt, the hugely popular social media app and one of the hottest tech companies in Silicon Valley.

Since it was founded eight years prior by tech industry icon Troy McCray, Elemynt had become a household name with tons of users around the globe. The exquisitely modern décor of the company's headquarters was the perfect reflection of the millions of beautiful photos posted every day to the platform. The possibly hundreds of photos she saw daily were a fraction of the astounding total on the app.

The range of people who used Elemynt was truly remarkable. The best celebrities and influencers with millions of followers each shared glamorous images with adoring fans. One follow of an Elemynt account and Kelsey could see photos of fantastic architecture in Paris or chefs in New York City creating gourmet meals from scratch. The President of the United States regularly posted messages from the White House. Even the Pope shared daily prayers to his official account. It was amazing to witness one app uniting the world.

Pretty much everyone was on Elemynt. It was more of a curiosity for someone to not be on the app. The platform included the option for people to keep their profile in private mode so that users were required to request to see the account's posts. A lot of people took advantage of that. But to have no profile at all was just plain weird.

Kelsey checked herself out in the camera of her phone. She adjusted her natural blond locks and double-checked her lipstick and lashes. Kelsey's role as a public relations professional was to help companies define their image. In her field, how she presented herself was equally important. If there was ever a time to be on point, this was it.

The new recruit would soon meet with her manager Jonathan Sykes, the vice president of communications at Elemynt. They were set to have a quick welcome chat over coffee before the start of her new hire orientation. The meeting was the first stop in the exhilarating day to come.

Kelsey and her friends always shared photos of themselves in the coolest moments of their lives. Whether it was a night out with the girls or a landmark moment in her career, if Kelsey saw an opportunity to seize a captivating photo, she took it. As a woman who loved seeing and doing new things, she was contributing to the awesomeness of the platform in her own unique way.

Kelsey's thousands of followers were rooting for her and her brand-new position. It still hadn't sunk in that she was actually working for the company that she and countless others adored. She was nearly bursting inside with happiness. Kelsey had to share the experience right as it was happening.

The Elemynt app gave users the option to add a caption of up to 500 words and one #hashtag of their choice. Lots of space to write out for Kelsey to write about how her dreams were coming true. How she could possibly encapsulate in words the thrill in her heart would be an unexpected challenge. Also, she needed to get her first photo just right.

Kelsey looked around the gorgeous lobby for inspiration. The extra-friendly receptionists behind the wide marble front desk said a cheery "good morning" to the employees trickling in, ready for the day's work. A security guard stationed near the glass doors that separated the lobby from the wonderful world on the other side watched as they swiped their badges at the card reader. The temporary badge bestowed upon Kelsey was draped close to her chest. The lobby that was full of color and life made for a sensational background.

Kelsey positioned the camera at the perfect angle and snapped several photos, one right after the other. The newbie smiled more brightly with each snap, overjoyed that the resulting post would be the first representation of her new journey.

Right as Kelsey was deciding which of her pictures she wanted to share, the front door of the lobby swung open with a jolting crash. A horde of reporters and cameramen burst into the room barreling toward the startled professional like a runaway high-speed train. The mass of people jammed every inch of the once peaceful lobby. They spoke loudly over each other and angled microphones and recording devices while photographers darted around in a snapping frenzy.

Kelsey shot straight out of her seat in a panic. Her mind raced thinking of whether they were there for her or if she had done something wrong. Kelsey was on the Comms team, but it was impossible that she would be the target of their attention. Even the receptionists were unsettled by the abrupt intrusion. Kelsey instinctively began thinking about what to say when the unruly group reached the seating area she occupied alone.

As the crowd of media types forced their way into the space, Kelsey noticed that they were not headed in her direction. Instead, they swarmed around a tall bearded man doing his best to reach the reception desk. Reporters hustled around him, shouting questions and feverishly jotting down notes. The throng of photographers jostled for closer proximity to their subject.

At the opposite end of the room, the glass door leading to the Elemynt campus glided open. An ombré-haired, twenty-something woman in a blazer and audacious high heels approached Kelsey.

"What a circus, right?" she chuckled.

Kelsey recognized the woman as Sarah Fields, her new colleague on the External Communications team. The two met during Kelsey's lengthy interview process and got along right off the bat. Sarah's porcelain skin was made more radiant by the camera flashes of nearby paparazzi. Her impeccably manicured eyebrows raised in delight as she greeted Kelsey.

"Is this... did I come at a bad time?" Kelsey asked, still shaken from the unexpected ordeal.

"Oh, don't worry about that," Sarah said in amusement. "That's the president of Turkey. Anyway, we have bigger issues right now. Ready to go?"

Kelsey barely had time to scoop up her purse before Sarah caught her by the arm to take her away from the commotion. With Sarah in the lead, they powered through the room, wading through the cacophony of cameras.

The two flashed their badges at the smiling security guard and swiftly crossed the threshold toward the employee-only area of the building.

The selfie would have to wait.

Sarah and Kelsey raced past the labyrinth of glass walls that populated the interior landscape of the buildings. A kaleidoscopic sequence of artwork in primary hues framed rows of faces working diligently at their craft. Brilliant minds pored over digital displays packed with green and purple lines of code. The employees of Elemynt scribbled complex theorems on whiteboards and hunched over laptops personalized with assorted stickers. Those who weren't at their desk moved swiftly from one colorfully furnished meeting room to the other.

Kelsey took in as much of the office environment as possible in their sprint toward a destination unknown to her. Sarah's windswept hair served as a beacon for Kelsey to follow through the endless corridors. Kelsey ran half-marathons before but never through a stream of highly-populated office buildings.

"Are we going to meet Jon?" Kelsey asked between breaths.

"You should know our boss is a world traveler," Sarah said. "He's rarely at headquarters because he's always flying to other Elemynt offices to develop communication strategies for different markets. He should be here later this afternoon, I think."

"So where are we going?" Kelsey asked.

"The Bunker," Sarah replied as if Kelsey knew what she was referring to.

Sarah made a swift left, then another, and came to a sudden stop in front of an unmarked door. She wiped away the lone bead of sweat that formed on her brow. Kelsey's composed colleague held her employee badge to a reader by the door handle and knocked twice. Together, they entered a dark room illuminated solely by the glow of computer screens and television monitors.

Kelsey's eyes adjusted to the activity happening under the cover of darkness. She found herself in a compact, windowless room with twenty monitors arranged on a wall lined with sound-proof material. About a dozen people were positioned at workstations that, from the labels affixed to them, showed they were monitoring for anomalies on the platform, including downtime, latency, and DDOS attacks. Additional monitors cycled in live video feeds of various corners of the Elemynt campus.

Organized chaos permeated the isolated space. Men typed feverishly at their keyboards and spouted questions at each other in technical terms Kelsey did not recognize. All hands were on deck for the Elemynt employees who furiously attempted to solve some urgent problem.

Sarah took the covert operations in stride. Kelsey, on the other hand, tried her best not to show how startled she was by the sensory overload packed into the dim room. Her heart thumped wildly.

The deep baritone voice of a man at the center of the room cut through the din.

"Do we have an approximate location?" he yelled.

The man's lacquered ebony complexion was silhouetted by the monitor before him. The furrowed contours of his face were more clearly defined when he drew closer to the moving digital map that captured his attention.

Sarah hovered over the man's shoulder. "Please tell me this isn't going to get out to the media. One wrong move and I'm dealing with questions from reporters all day. I'd like to spare us from having a conversation with the executive team explaining why Elemynt is on every news site and cable TV news channel."

"That won't happen if I can help it," the man said without taking his eyes off his work.

Sarah returned her attention to a very confused Kelsey. "This is Leon, our vice president of Global Security. He's the lead on efforts like making sure company data stays secure or going after people trying to take down the app for whatever reason. He's got his own C.I.A. in here. And a whole squad of security officers on and off-campus."

Kelsey did her best to remember as much of the rapid-fire information as she could.

"Triangulating his position!" someone called from the corner.

Leon gestured toward his team. "We make situations go away before they become major problems. Are you going to tell me who this is, Sarah? Another problem for me to deal with?"

"Kelsey is the latest addition to the External Comms team and my newest colleague," Sarah said proudly. "It's her first day here."

"Shouldn't she be in orientation?" Leon eyed Kelsey with suspicion.

"Yes, she should but there's no better way to learn about the company than to see how it works up close and personal. They start with ice breakers anyway so it's not like she's missing anything."

Leon espied the paper badge dangling from Kelsey's lanyard. "This is the most secure room on the whole campus and you brought a new employee with a temporary badge in here?"

"I'm a jump right in kind of girl," Kelsey smiled reassuringly. "I promise I'll get it as soon as possible."

Sarah finally explained the reason for the ongoing ruckus. "One of the engineers on the mobile development team left a backpack in a bar and, surprise, it was stolen."

"We're chasing after a bag?" Kelsey asked.

"No, the company property in it," Leon said. "A MacBook laptop, specifically. The employee was working on one of our confidential new products and we think whoever stole it has been targeting other company property for months now. We're using the GPS embedded in the computer to track its location."

"There's no telling what this guy is trying to access," Sarah said. "New product plans... access to internal accounts. It only takes one stolen file or two and our business plans are in the hands of bad actors or worse, reporters who would write every detail about it the second they got a hold of it."

Leon returned to his diligent monitoring of the screens, ignoring the presence of the Comms ladies and concentrating on the active hunt for the stolen technology. He hurled directions at his charges in the room.

The role of the External Comms team of which Kelsey was now a member was to build, protect, and maintain the public perception of the company, Sarah explained. A good reputation translated to a strong relationship with the app's users, which led to more growth and their continued engagement with the platform. A bad reputation resulted in people using the app less and the collapse of everything the company built over the years.

"We want to have as much positive news about the company as possible out there," Sarah said. "Not whatever this is."

"The data of hundreds of millions of users is contained in the app," Leon added. "We need to respect that and keep it safe."

Kelsey was simultaneously frightened and titillated by the issue at hand. The potential breach was indeed cause for concern. But working for a company that cared extensively about protecting the interests of users made it that much more inspiring. A week before her first day, the rep from Elemynt human resources emailed Kelsey and every new employee that came before her a large set of digital documents to sign, including several lengthy non-disclosure agreements. They boiled down to two things. We have secrets. Don't ever share them.

"Leon, I don't mean to tell you how to do your job," Sarah said.

"But you will," he said without looking up.

"We can remotely erase lost employee devices if someone gets a hold of it to keep them from accessing company information. Why don't we do that?"

"Because we don't want to lose him," a husky female voice interrupted.

Kelsey was startled yet again, this time by a woman standing against the rear wall who had been hiding in the shadows of the room. Her shoulder-length hair fell haphazardly around her scrunched face. Her clothing choices — an Elemynt T-shirt and cargo shorts — were slouchy. It was evident from their fadedness that they were overworn staples in her wardrobe. Kelsey guessed that whoever the woman was, she did not spend much time in the public eye.

"We need to keep him on the computer so we can track him," she said. "If he figures out the computer is wiped, he's ditching it. We'll lose him forever."

Sarah halted her questions for Leon to introduce Tai Zhang, Elemynt's head of internal communications.

Tai's wardrobe was spartan but her knowledge of the inner workings of the company was deep. She was one of the earliest employees at Elemynt. The quiet force began her career tenure as a securities mobile developer for Android before moving up the ranks to product manager. She was incredibly skilled at translating the company's mission and goals to engineers who spoke in code. As a result, Troy asked her to lead internal comms for Elemynt.

Sarah, Kelsey, and Tai shared the same goal — to highlight the best of the company. Because of their roles, they accomplished it in two different ways. Tai shaped the messaging for employees about the company's direction and latest developments. Sarah and Kelsey made use of relationships with journalists to circulate positive stories about Elemynt in the media. What they unfortunately had in common was a potential breach on their hands that could completely upend all of their work. Tai would be left to craft explanations to employees and Sarah would scramble to counteract stories that put the company in a negative light.

Kelsey extended her hand to Tai in a greeting of understanding.

"Sorry, can't talk right now," Tai said curtly. "You know with this crisis and all. Making sure we cover our ass? Leon, what's the latest?"

Kelsey pulled her hand back in surprise. Not the time.

"He's in Palo Alto!" one of the techs yelled. "We've tracked him to a 100-foot radius of Sand Hill Road near El Camino Real."

"It's not a residential neighborhood," another offered. "He can be at any one of the businesses over there."

"Where are you, dude?" Leon grumbled to himself.

"Hold on, I think I know!" Sarah exclaimed. "There's a coffee bar over there where the techie people hang out. I go there for my chai lattes. If he's on that corner, I bet he's in there."

"Dispatch one of the Elemynt security officers to that location," Leon said to his team. "We need to get there before he leaves. And have them get me a live audio feed from their phone too. We're not letting this guy get away."

"Patching in to the nearest officer," a team member confirmed.

The anxious group in the bunker listened to the audio streaming through the bass-heavy speakers affixed to the walls. The sounds of a crowded café filled the space while they stood by helplessly.

How the security officer would find the guy among a restaurant full of Silicon Valley types was beyond Kelsey's understanding. He needed to do what he could in the abbreviated time he had. It was an urgent matter that needed to be solved immediately to procure the stolen property. Kelsey's heart raced watching the chase unfold.

"You're looking for a silver MacBook," Leon reiterated.

"There's a million people with MacBooks in here," the male voice on the speakers said under his breath.

"We can't go through each one," Leon grumbled. "It'll tip the guy off and then he's outta there."

The teams in the bunker volleyed ideas back and forth in an attempt to nail down a feasible solution.

Kelsey could have hung back in the shadows of the increasingly cramped room. It was her first day at Elemynt and jumping into a crucial conversation was likely not wise. However, Kelsey was not the type to fade into the background when there was a solution she had a strong gut feeling would work.

Kelsey spoke up over the mounting back and forth. "Leon, do you have a photo of the laptop that was stolen?"

"Employees at Elemynt all get the same laptop," Tai responded tartly.

"Completely understand that…" Kelsey said. "but if the guy had a sticker on it you'll know which one is his. That'll make it easier to find."

The lightbulb went off in Leon's head. "Somebody get me archived video from the employee's desk ASAP! See if we can get an image of the top of his computer."

In less than a minute, one of the men on the Security team posted an image of the employee's desk on one of the largest screens in the bunker.

"You're looking for a MacBook with an Iron Man sticker!" the employee yelled.

"Roger that," the security officer on the phone replied.

Heavy footsteps and the trudge of moving chairs could be heard as the officer wound his way through the table in search of the branded laptop.

"I have a visual!" he said through the speaker.

There was a panicked rush as the officer hurried through the noisy café. It was now or never for him to get the stolen laptop back. He came to an abrupt stop. Kelsey held her breath.

"Sir, you are in possession of stolen property," he could be heard saying. "Release it or we will call the authorities."

The voice of a stuttering young man in search of an explanation was followed by the sound of panicked running, the gasping of café patrons, and a slam of the front door. Radio silence filled the room when there should have been an update.

"Did we get it?" Leon said with excitement in his voice.

There was no response.

The assembly in the bunker feared the worst. They managed to track the guy down to a specific location, the equipment was within reach, and yet he somehow managed to escape with the computer and its confidential information. He was free yet again to pilfer employee property at will.

"Do we have the laptop?" Leon growled angrily.

"Equipment secured," the guard confirmed.

The bunker erupted in cheers and hearty self-congratulations for the completion of a mission that, for a second, seemed doomed for failure. The apprehension of the property saved them from weeks of headaches, meetings, and whatever sanctions Elemynt leadership would have in store for the stakeholders involved. Kelsey took pride in knowing that her observation in the minute or less she spent navigating the hallways led to a huge win for the team.

Kelsey's first instinct was to jump up and down in cheerful victory. However, she made sure to maintain her poise. Through ups and downs, she always maintained her cool.

"Well, how about that?" Sarah high-fived Kelsey. "External Comms team undefeated! Guess this little incident won't be on the cover of the New York Times after all!"

Kelsey reveled graciously in the round of thank yous delivered by her colleagues. It was the first hour of her first day at Elemynt and she was already a hero.

"Welcome to the team, Kelsey," Sarah smiled. "I think you're going to do alright."

* * *

Kelsey entered Elemynt's storied orientation room to find a hundred of her new colleagues buzzing in anticipation of what was to come. Her adrenaline from the events in the bunker was swapped with a communal rush of excitement. Kelsey had first days at other companies before, but this was *Elemynt*, the mecca of innovative thinking. The smartest minds in the tech industry passed through the distinguished doors. She was joining an elite group of thinkers starting off their paths toward further greatness.

Posters in a rainbow of colors proclaiming the values of Elemynt adorned the lively space. Her favorite among them was a kelly-green sign with "Don't Hesitate, Innovate" splashed in white, cursive letters. Words to live by.

At the front of the room, ahead of the many rows of chattering employees, was a stage awaiting whoever would lead the activities of their first day. Above it was a large screen on which the words "Welcome Noobs!" was projected. Just below them was the Elemynt logo, a green leaf inside a perfect green circle.

Most of the new employees in the arrangement of chairs were in their 20s or early 30s clad in T-shirts or decked out in full business attire. Kelsey introduced herself to the people seated next to her — a software engineer working on machine learning and a global sales manager soon to be based in Dubai. In the orientation room were people from every corner of the globe speaking a variety of foreign languages.

No matter which of Elemynt's 30 plus offices around the world they would be stationed in, the company flew every new employee to headquarters for their first week. The goal was for them to become acclimated with the culture at HQ before they went their separate ways. Whether they were from one of the larger offices in London or Mumbai or the smaller counterparts in Chicago or Johannesburg, Elemynt employees began their journey in the esteemed orientation room.

Up to the stage hopped Heather, a ray of sunshine sporting a green Elemynt polo shirt. The company logo was embroidered in white stitching above her heart. Her gregarious energy further elevated the spirit of camaraderie in the room.

"Oh my gosh, you all look so good today!" Heather said with a rapturous smile. "Let's start by giving yourselves a big round of applause for being here! Yeah!"

The enthusiastic applause in the room was as resounding as a sports stadium during a championship game. The shared thrill of becoming part of the Elemynt family could not be contained.

Heather was part teacher and part evangelist, introducing the newest recruits to the wide world of Elemynt. She told of how she held previous positions at other tech companies and that Elemynt was absolutely the best company she ever had the pleasure of working for.

"We have 900 million people on the app around the world," Heather said. "Can you believe it? Almost a billion people!"

The number was indeed an extraordinary feat for what used to be a startup with less than a hundred users. The Elemynt app began as a scrappy tool for a group of friends to communicate and blossomed into a worldwide phenomenon. Kelsey was still in awe that she would be a part of the company's legacy.

"You guys, we literally have hundreds of people apply for every single Elemynt job post," Heather beamed. "People here are the best of the best!"

Kelsey was proud to have earned her place at Elemynt. Her previous role at UltraTalk, a smaller tech company based in Boston, could not compare. Unlike Elemynt which focused its platform on connections between individuals, the company centered its focus on online communities devoted to specific interests.

UltraTalk had a reputation for being a robust platform with legions of devoted users. However, it hit a wall in growth because the tight-knit communities were seen as not welcoming to new users. In order to sustain the platform and attract more advertisers to it, the company needed to change its reputation. As the public relations lead, Kelsey had to be ambitious to give the media positive newsworthy moments to report on.

Kelsey proposed what her then colleagues said was impossible to do — get people from the internet to meet in person and have fun doing it.

Kelsey smartly assembled internal teams at UltraTalk to launch meetups for users in some of the most popular categories on the platform. The company sponsored regional car shows where people behind the screen names showed off their coolest rides with their fellow internet denizens. They also launched a crafting convention where makers created fantastic works using a variety of tools supplied by the company. One of their most popular activations was a series of parenting meetups in various cities with the most active users acting as discussion moderators. The offline interactions for online communities were a huge hit.

Ultimately, the media did her work for her—portraying the company in a highly favorable light and as a place where real people made real connections. The earned media Kelsey was able to generate turned UltraTalk around in the minds of reporters and the public. Engagement on the app spiked dramatically and new user sign-ups were through the roof.

It was a big surprise when, out of the blue, Kelsey received an email from a recruiter at Elemynt. They saw her enormous success and invited her to apply for an open position. Kelsey was over the moon to receive recognition for a series of campaigns that she was extraordinarily proud of.

Kelsey impressed her way through several rounds of intense interviews, confident that her background and skills were impeccable. Fast forward one month later and she was officially seated in a coveted spot at Elemynt. A million people wanted to be where she was at that moment.

Her dreams of one day becoming the head of a Fortune 500 company would be possible with the lessons learned from Elemynt. Her love for communications brought her into the pivotal role at the unparalleled company and would carry her through to her ultimate goal.

"We're not just creating a product here," Heather said to eagerly listening ears. "Elemynt is changing the world. This app changes people's lives. You are changing people's lives."

Another huge round of applause echoed Heather's admirable statement. The new employees in the room and those across the campus were a part of something much larger than themselves. Their ability to change the way people communicated with each other was unlike any other position they would ever have.

"Okay, now we have something special for you guys," Heather smiled. "We have a message from some of the senior leadership at Elemynt just for you. You ready?"

The group in the room nodded agreeably in confirmation. The lights dimmed and the screen transitioned to a warm white light with the Elemynt logo at the center. A second later, Troy and his legendary smile appeared via video to the exhilaration of the watchers.

"Welcome to the Elemynt family!" he said brightly.

A close-up shot of the tech icon with his A-list movie star looks and incandescent blue eyes filled the screen before them. Bouncy, upbeat music accompanied his exquisitely lit visage that looked directly into the camera. A graphic that read "Troy McCray, Founder and CEO" appeared below his face. As if he needed an introduction.

"Congratulations on your decision to join Elemynt!" he said. "There's never been a better time to be at the company. We're charting a new course for the world through the digital experiences created right here."

Troy spoke with pride about the now legendary founding of Elemynt. The video was interspersed with clips of the happiest of employees and Elemynt users on their phones, snapping photos, and smiling with friends and family members.

When Kelsey was first approached about the position, she watched and read interview after interview to get a feel for her potential new boss. Watching in chronological order, the media coverage framed a young upstart transformed into a top-tier CEO.

Troy famously wrote the bulk of the original code that powered Elemynt while studying computer science at Stanford University in Palo Alto, not far from the current Elemynt campus. The young college student believed in the power of visual images to bring people together. He wanted a tool that would make it easy for people to share with friends and loved ones in an intimate digital setting that forewent the global nature of social networks at the time. Troy dropped out of school to pursue the creation of Elemynt having learned more on his own than a degree could teach him.

Elemynt succeeded at an accelerated rate because rather than chasing after traditional big names in top industries to join the platform like other social media companies did at their tipping point, Troy sought out up-and-coming talent. His mission became to woo burgeoning social media stars to switch over to the app he created with their needs in mind. He hosted fun-filled and photo-ready summits in global locations where he asked the influencers in attendance one question: "If you could build the perfect social media app what would it be?"

Elemynt developed the platform at a rapid rate in response to the feedback from those creators. Troy was always game to try out ambitious ideas, keeping whatever was most popular with users. And so Elemynt became known as "the people's app." Many social influencers used it regularly and encouraged their followers on other platforms to join them as well. Makeup artists, comedians, college sports stars, gamers, and a variety of young talent across a wide spectrum of disciplines turned Elemynt into the place to be.

When Elemynt became the new, hot thing, suddenly celebrities who were household names joined the platform too, making its reach soar astronomically.

Troy saw an opportunity to turn the fun tool into a legitimate business. He hired many of his college buddies to come on as staffers and made himself chief executive officer. The change required Troy to transition from engineer to business mogul.

He set out to pitch the platform to as many listening ears with deep pockets as possible. In turn, he received tens of millions of dollars in funding from investors who saw the potential for Elemynt to become a global success. Blessed with a slew of money in the bank, Troy hired scores of teams and built the foundation of the headquarters at which Kelsey was now based.

The company made Troy the king of Silicon Valley and Elemynt was his crown jewel. Troy was seen as an innovator following in the steps of tech luminaries like Steve Jobs and Bill Gates. His Elemynt account was packed with pics of him with the most famous and influential people. Photos of himself with rock stars at music festivals were posted next to meetings with heads of state at global conferences. Across the spectrum, the famous faces used Elemynt religiously to connect with their audiences.

Troy prided himself in swapping out who he followed every month with a new batch of people from a notable group of his choosing. One month it would be rocket scientists or mommy bloggers, the next it was horticulturists or extreme sports players. The goal was to see the platform from different perspectives and continue to iterate in ways that benefited all communities while maintaining the intimacy of the platform.

At the end of the month, Troy wrote a post about his learnings on the official company blog along with insight into what he was thinking about for the future of the company. The writings had a devoted following, from tech aficionados and internet enthusiasts. Each line was dissected in message boards and in writeups by the press lauding his openness. USA Today called it the mark of a genius. Forbes dubbed Troy the "King of Communication." Free publicity at that level was priceless.

"Our mission is to use technology to make the world a better place," Troy said from the screen. "We're able to do that because of smart people like you. Thank you for choosing us as your new home."

The faces around Kelsey were rapt while watching video of the head of the company addressing them. They shared a gratifying sense that he was talking to each of them personally, outlining what their future could be like. It didn't matter which department they worked in, Troy said. The teams were aligned on a common goal.

The bubbly music continued as the screen transitioned to a video message from another central figure at Elemynt — Catherine Rowe, chief operating officer. Kelsey reeled with elation at the sight of the head of business operations at the company and one of the foremost women executives in tech. As one of the few female executives in the tech industry, Catherine was instantly an exemplary figure that women looked up to. She was strong. Powerful. Smart. A great decision-maker. A mom and a terrifically talented businesswoman. Kelsey adored her to no end.

"We congratulate you on your first day," Catherine said. "Elemynt is a community and we encourage every person here to learn from the people around them. We are stronger when we work together."

Catherine Rowe was already a huge name in the corporate world even before joining Elemynt. She rose to the top through sheer force of will, leading business operations at Fortune 500 companies for years.

At a pivotal time of growth for the company, Elemynt was in need of the brainpower of a chief operating officer of her caliber. Troy's mind for innovation needed to be counterbalanced with an executive who could focus on revenue and making Elemynt profitable. Troy courted Catherine for months with an offer to shape her role at the company, to which she eventually said yes.

In her first year, Catherine developed a comprehensive plan to achieve year over year growth. It was just what the company needed to propel itself to financial success. With the CEO and his unending knowledge of engineering at the helm and the skillful COO at his side, the company could actualize any goal they set for it.

Most notably, Catherine's background prior to Elemynt stood in contrast to Troy's fabled early departure from Stanford and his ongoing bachelor status. The longtime executive was a graduate of Wharton School of Business and was married for ten years before a tumultuous and very public divorce. Her husband left her alone to rear their juvenile son and daughter while she simultaneously led business operations for some of the nation's leading companies. It was an unexpected upending of life as she knew it.

The hard times turned out to be a blessing in disguise. Catherine thrust herself into writing as a means of reckoning with the events of her life.

The result was two books: "Mom in Charge," a memoir on parenting, followed a year later by "Boss Lady," a manifesto for the modern working woman. It was her second tome that propelled Catherine into global superstardom. "Boss Lady" spent months on bestseller lists and was required reading for any woman working in the corporate world.

The lessons imparted by the inspirational book instilled a confidence in Kelsey that taught her not to be afraid of her own voice. Society had for centuries mired women in discrimination, sexual harassment, and a supposed "inferiority" to men. To achieve the success they deserved, women needed to take on a boss-like mentality and project that in their workplace. Women could forge the careers they wanted for themselves when they were in control of their own image and outspoken about their capabilities. The lessons were a major reason Kelsey was seated in the Elemynt chair.

The publication of "Boss Lady" transformed Catherine into a feminist icon almost overnight. Catherine's openness about what it took to be authentic at work encouraged others to do the same. Women gravitated toward the message of being in control of their destiny.

Catherine was also highly regarded for the dinner parties she hosted at her home where influential women discussed ways to further the advancement of their shared gender. The gatherings and the book inspired Kelsey to found a social group in Boston for women to come together and learn from each other. Kelsey wouldn't have the rewarding career she enjoyed to date if it weren't for the nurturing group and, by extension, Catherine Rowe.

Her fellow female employees in the orientation room were also especially thrilled to see Catherine's face on the screen. The number of role models for women in business unfortunately paled in comparison to their male counterparts. Catherine Rowe was a rare female figurehead whose outsized impact opened the doors for them to step into the highly-competitive positions they currently occupied.

"Your success is important to us," Catherine concluded. "We've created an environment where anyone with an idea can see it realized. Use this moment as an opportunity to focus on your passion and to do the most meaningful work of your life."

The video continued with more interviews with various higher-ups and employees lauding the spirit of Elemynt. When the lights went up, Heather led the group in a well-deserved round of applause for those featured in the video. Kelsey clapped along in delight.

"Alright, I'm so excited to bring to you our first guest speaker today!" Heather said with a thrill. "Here to talk about how we're making Elemynt a place that's inclusive for everyone is our Head of Diversity Comms, Daniela Vasquez!"

The room warmly greeted the curly-haired, olive-skinned woman assuming Heather's place at the front of the room. She moved with an aura of regality in her casual T-shirt and jeans.

Kelsey perked up because another person in a Comms role at Elemynt would be addressing them. She intended to glean as much information from Daniela's the speaker's presentation as she could.

"I have a question for you all," Daniela said to the gathering. "How many of you know what 'Chicana' means?"

A few hands popped up in the audience, nearly all of whom were Hispanic. Kelsey never heard of the word and from the looks of the people around her, most of the other employees had not either. Kelsey's quick perusal revealed that the majority of her compatriots at orientation were either White or Asian and mostly male. Daniela was gratified to see at least a few acknowledge they did know of the term.

"Yo soy Chicana," she pointed to herself. "I am a Latina born here in the U.S. whose family is originally from Mexico."

The new employees listened closely to see where she was heading with her story.

"I went to a school in Florida where I was one of the only Latinas and the kids there would make fun of me for my curly hair," she said, gesturing at her auburn locks. "My classmates' hair was straight or wavy and I was made fun of for it constantly. After dealing with that for almost a year, I wanted straight hair too so I could be like the other girls."

Daniela described how she would repeatedly venture to the salon for a blowout or wrap her hair with clips and a bandana at night so she could have straighter hair by the morning. But her hair would never last in the aggressive Florida humidity.

"I would cry all the time, praying that I could have the same hair as everyone else," she said. "My mom would comfort me and tell me 'Tu pelo es tu corona. Your hair is your crown. Be who you are, mija.' I started embracing my curls because they weren't a flaw...they are what make me special. My hair connects me to my heritage, to my mom, and to my family."

Daniela playfully bounced her hair for extra effect. The woman before them was fiery and passionate but also spoke with a broad inviting smile that encouraged the room to absorb her remarks. Kelsey leaned it to hear more from the Comms professional before her.

"At Elemynt, we want you to know that having diverse perspectives is what makes this company successful," Daniela said to the enraptured audience. "Different backgrounds mean different ideas. So, we want you to bring your full self to work and wear your crown!"

Daniela landed a heartfelt plea for her new co-workers to respect diversity on and off the platform. Rousing applause followed the speaker's exit from the stage, the loudest coming from the Hispanic employees in the room. Their commendation of her message caused the rest of the crowd to clap louder. Daniela's words, plus the anticipatory energy in the room, created an exponential wave of appreciation for her encouragement.

Kelsey loved the cute story. Seeing a woman with the power to inspire a group of people in an earnest way was phenomenal. She hoped one day soon to meet Daniela and gain more insight from her experiences at the company.

Throughout the afternoon, more speakers were cycled in and out of the orientation stage. A manager from engineering came in to outline the algorithms that powered the app. A member of Leon's team discussed security protocols they needed to be aware of as new employees. A representative from the human resources team outlined the healthcare and benefits they would receive (of which there were many).

Heather again fronted the room with a sincere appreciation for the enthusiasm of her flock. She encouraged them to maintain a strong work-life balance — making sure they took ample time away from their company duties to enjoy the lifestyle Elemynt afforded them. She concluded the orientation with one last round of motivation.

"Remember, the success of this company depends on you," she said with vigor. "You *are* Elemynt. Can't wait to see what you achieve together!"

When the new recruits exited the orientation room, they were greeted by a lineup of green-shirted employees eager for their arrival. The welcoming committee stood ready to outfit them with the official Elemynt gear laid out on the long table before them. It was a rite of passage that each new employee had the pleasure of participating in. Like Christmas in the spring.

The first order of business was to replace their visitor's badge that signified that they were a foreigner on the campus. Kelsey accepted with glee a glossy new employee badge with her picture and name imprinted on the front. She held the laminated white card tightly in her hand. It was a prized possession she would forever cherish.

Further down the line, Kelsey was bestowed with an Elemynt branded backpack that contained her very own gleaming MacBook laptop and an accompanying iPhone with service one hundred percent paid for. In the front pocket of her new bag was a laptop sticker that underscored Heather's charge. "You Are Elemynt."

Kelsey was officially a "Myntor," the title bestowed to employees of Elemynt. She emerged from the orientation with tremendous satisfaction in working on behalf of technology that made a difference in the world. She couldn't wait to share the story of Elemynt with the public. Kelsey wanted people everywhere, whether they were on the platform or not, to feel the same feeling she experienced at that moment.

* * *

When Kelsey and the new Myntors emerged from the building into the cool California afternoon, Sarah was there waiting to welcome her. The moment Kelsey anticipated since she first signed on the dotted line had arrived. She would finally see the storied headquarters of Elemynt first hand.

The breathtaking campus was a sprawling 10-city block fantasyland spread over a wide swath of Palo Alto. The tapestry of buildings punctuated with splashes of color was a joy for the eye. Behind the glass doors of every structure, magic was underway. From the engineers drafting the code that made the app possible to the tinkerers powering the next evolution in technology, there were more than ten thousand employees who populated the company headquarters. More than a hundred departments were housed in its walls — from design and marketing to platform operations and data science.

Myntors casually strolled the beautifully landscaped pathways, badges swinging from their waists, and talking animatedly about the day's events. Her new colleagues were mostly clad in khaki shorts and hoodies in varying colors or T-shirts emblazoned with the Elemynt logo or that of previous employers. Quite a few represented their prestigious alma maters — Stanford, UC Berkeley, MIT, and more.

Kelsey and Sarah's traditional office wear and heels were in stark contrast to the laid-back outfit choices of most of the employees they passed. Kelsey wondered quietly if she was perhaps overdressed. Her dad, who was a practical man, would want her to be comfortable for sure. However, her mother always underscored that she should be at her most presentable when she stepped out of the house.

"You never know who you might see or who will see you," she would say.

And so Kelsey's heels would continue to be a staple of her wardrobe. She might throw on a pair of sneakers on Fridays just to keep it fun and fresh.

Sarah proudly listed the incredible perks Elemynt offered: nine restaurants of varying cuisines serving free breakfast, lunch, and dinner; a beauty salon and spa for on-site rejuvenation, two full-sized gyms, a centrally located bar offering hand-crafted cocktails, plus wine fridges and fully-stocked wet bars tucked in various buildings. And that was just the beginning. Employees were treated to free unlimited drop-off laundry and dry-cleaning services, electric cars that they could borrow for a few hours at a time, a library, a music room, a woodshop, and a yoga studio with free classes daily.

Kelsey did her best not to faint from the extravagance. There was such an abundance of amenities that Sarah had to pause in the middle of her explanation to snag a refreshing beverage from the nearby pizza stand.

Kelsey watched Myntors zoom by on the neon green bicycles available to them at stations across the campus. The parade of visitors winding through headquarters were in awe listening to their respective employee hosts describe the incredible workplace. Moms, dads, small children, friends, and former coworkers stopped every few steps with their mouths agape. They were stunned by the vending machines dispensing free technology accessories, amazed at the bustling sushi restaurant, wowed by the 3D printing room, and enchanted by the sweet smells wafting from the on-campus bakery. No expense was spared to make Elemynt the best place to work.

Kelsey and Sarah checked out the arcade which was packed with wall to wall pinball machines, shooter games, Dance Dance Revolution, and a range of popular gaming consoles and their various iterations.

Surrounded by the constellation of lights from the pinging machines, Kelsey had one lingering question for Sarah: Why all this? The size and scale of the incredible number of perks were more than any employee could ever want. No need or desire was left unmet.

"Really, it's because Silicon Valley is one of the most competitive job markets in the world," Sarah said. "Tech companies want to hire the best talent out there. Who you have working for you can make or break a business. When the best of the best join the Elemynt family, which they do, Elemynt wants to give them every reason to stay."

"The paychecks are nothing to sneeze at either," Kelsey laughed.

Working in tech was hardly a vow of financial celibacy. Most employees were pulling in, at minimum, a six-figure salary and the numbers climbed when other financial incentives were factored in.

Kelsey was startled when she received her offer letter from Elemynt. The $50,000 a year pay increase over her previous salary in Boston, plus stock options and bonuses based on her performance, was an offer she couldn't refuse. As if she would ever dream of it. With all the amenities lavished on her fellow employees, the only reason Kelsey would ever need to leave the campus was to sleep.

"And by the way, we have nap rooms in a bunch of buildings if you ever need to catch some quick ZZZs," Sarah said, almost reading her mind.

Kelsey was so caught up in the beauty of the campus she forgot to take pictures of it to share on her Elemynt account. Sarah was kind to let Kelsey retraced her steps to snap pics of the breathtaking features along the way. Kelsey made sure to tag her location in each of her posts. She didn't want to leave any doubt that she was at *the* Elemynt headquarters. The faves and comments on her posts rolled in with her friends congratulating her and sending best wishes.

"So proud of you!"

"Love you, Kelsey!"

Just as Kelsey began to catch her breath from the fabulous tour, Sarah ushered her toward the building where their workspace was located. At the entry, Sarah showed Kelsey how to flash her badge on the scanner adjacent to the marble front desk.

"Welcome to Elemynt, Kelsey!" the receptionist exclaimed. "Enjoy your first day!"

"How'd she know it's my first day?" Kelsey smiled. "You told her?"

"It's that new employee glow!" Sarah said as she opened the door for her colleague. "J.K.! Your name and face pop up on their screen when you badge in. It also shows where your desk is and your start date at the company."

Further into the reaches of the building, warm daylight from the floor to ceiling windows blended with the cool fluorescent lighting that hovered from the industrial ceilings. The expanse was a million times larger than Kelsey's old office. All of her coworkers at UltraTalk could fit in one floor of the building and still have room to spare.

Scattered about the space were lounge areas with relaxed seating for impromptu meetings. They were ideal locations for people to brainstorm big ideas or discuss their latest ventures with their colleagues.

Sarah paused briefly to show Kelsey one of the campus' many "micro-kitchens." The spaces, which were as large as some people's living rooms, were outfitted with a line of refrigerators and racks of snacks from around the world. She eyed the wasabi peas and chocolate-coated Pocky from Japan, tamarind candy from Mexico, and stroopwafels from the Netherlands. An array of a supermarket's worth of cereal was arranged neatly in clear plastic containers. The refrigerators stocked with drinks of every variety and level of caffeine and/or sweetness were flanked by an espresso machine and towering urns of exotic coffees.

Kelsey was somewhat taken aback by the rows of bottled water cooling in one of the fridges. The Elemynt campus had a reputation for being eco-conscious. The copious amount of plastic was not in line with a push for sustainability. A moment later, she saw next to them taps for an array of waters: still, hot, cold, and sparkling. Kelsey grinned to herself. Of course they had them. Why she doubted the company for a second, she would never know. The place was fantastic. Perfectly perfect.

The areas between the lobby and the nearby conference rooms were like mini-museums of modern art. Kelsey admired the colorful, large scale artwork on the various walls.

"The office buildings around the world all feature work by local artists," Sarah said. "Our People team who does the design of the offices connects with them to bring the vibe of the city into where we work."

Intermixed between the site-specific installations were posters of varying colors and designs with the credos of Elemynt: "Connect Communities." "Stay Focused." Kelsey resolved to do her very best to embody the encouraging mantras.

Sarah and Kelsey wound through a corridor, passing by conference rooms where Myntors met in glass-walled spaces. The rooms were named after groups like candies, birds, local neighborhoods, and even conspiracy theories. The "Elvis Isn't Dead" room must have housed some pretty interesting conversations. There were a huge number of conference rooms in Elemynt offices around the world. It was a genius way to bring fun and order to naming conventions.

Sarah demonstrated for Kelsey a Wayfinder, one of the interactive touchscreens found on the walls of buildings throughout campus. The maps they contained would help her identify the location of the desk of anyone in the company.

"Each desk has a code on it," Sarah said. That code is specific to you. How about we check out your new home!"

* * *

Beyond the collection of conference rooms was the sprawling main area for employees to work and thrive. The open floor plan was filled with long stretches of white desks unencumbered by walls or cubicle partitions. The workspaces were outfitted with the requisite monitor and keyboard and yet each one had its own personality. Myntors were accompanied by stacks of books or action figures or impressive collections of cans of Red Bull energy drinks.

The desks were all different and a reflection of the owner. Still, there was a sense of peace and order to the space. A small number of people talked among themselves but only loud enough for the person next to them to hear. People with phone calls they needed to take ducked into empty meeting rooms or one of the enclosed phone booths built for one.

"And voila!" Sarah said. "Here's your new place of business."

Sarah gestured to the gleaming, six-foot-wide desk and ergonomic chair that were now all Kelsey's. Sitting atop the desk was a spectacularly large bouquet of flowers in various shades of lilac and blush. A note was attached.

On it was a handwritten "Congrats!" followed by Jon's name. Kelsey nearly tipped over the vase containing the flowers when she saw what lay beside it — a brand new, glossy copy of Catherine's book "Boss Lady." Kelsey eagerly flipped the book open to the first page. There Catherine inscribed it "To our newest #BossLady" and her signature written with a flourish.

"Catherine knows who I am?" Kelsey gasped in shock.

"Jon probably arranged it for you," Sarah said. "How cute is this!"

Kelsey already owned a copy of the title but this wasn't some random book off a shelf. It was signed by Catherine, on the desk at the company they now both worked for, and it was addressed specifically to Kelsey. The newbie was overwhelmed with joy and humility at the treasure given to her.

Kelsey needed a breather. Her head spun unexpectedly from the sensory overload from the wonders of the day. She politely excused herself to the ladies' room to calm the jittering excitement bubbling within her.

"I'll be back, one sec," she said.

The spread of hygienic accessories Kelsey encountered on the other side of the door marked "W" was unlike anything she'd ever seen in a company restroom. The bathroom was stocked with toothbrushes, floss, and mouthwash as well as tampons and maxi pads in colorful wrappers. All free. In the rear of the bathroom were full individual showers for morning joggers and bike commuters. The generosity of her employer was evident at every turn.

The lighting of the vanity mirror above the sink made Kelsey's skin glow and eyes sparkle more than they ever had in her life. She stared deeply at the woman in the reflection. Her new reality was a workplace paradise that she could not believe she was a part of. She reminded herself that she was indeed worthy of the experience.

Kelsey worked tremendously hard to get to her level of achievement. She was being rewarded for years of diligence and exceptional skills. She would return the trust in her by giving Elemynt the best she had and then some.

Kelsey exited the restroom, more rejuvenated than before. She thought through all the angles she could snap a picture of the charming bouquet of flowers to post to her Elemynt account.

"Hungry?" Sarah asked.

Kelsey was so intoxicated by the sights and smells of the various food offerings that she did not realize she hadn't eaten anything that morning.

"Starving," she replied with a smile.

* * *

The warehouse-like dining hall boasted a dozen stations with heaping servings of specially crafted dishes. Pork ribs, mashed potatoes, shakshuka, Russian stews, tabouleh, lamb chops, fire-roasted chicken, and more were there for the taking. A salad bar spanned half the room and a carving station with succulent meats and roasted tofu was patronized by a line of hungry guests.

On the other side of the serving trays of piping hot delicacies, a row of chefs chopped and diced away in a top of the line kitchen to keep the fresh food flowing. It was a remarkable production to ensure the sumptuous platters were never empty.

At the dessert station, delectable hummingbird cake and Mexican wedding cookies on white platters were available for employees to snag at their leisure. A frozen yogurt machine churned next to an assortment of sweet and crunchy toppings.

Around her was more food than Kelsey could ever eat in her lifetime. And no cash, credit, or debit card required.

Hundreds of employees shuffled in and out of the food mecca for a late lunch, most of them portioning their selections into compostable takeout containers. Others enjoyed their meals at one of the pristine picnic-style benches that filled the north side of the space. Lines moved speedily as employees helped themselves to whatever they wanted. They laughed and talked with their colleagues about what they would indulge in that day.

"They bring in guest chefs sometimes too," Sarah said, pointing to a dedicated station.

One of the specials that day was a la minute tuna tartare seasoned with cracked black pepper and surrounded by snow pea shoots, enoki mushrooms, and saffron aioli. The offering next to it was a bright yellow bowl of coconut curry soup topped with rice and nori sculpted to form a winking emoji.

"Like, how do you even decide?" Kelsey said in wonder.

"I start by doing some light reading," Sarah replied.

Sarah pointed to the detailed color-coded labels above each dish. "Green means it's good for you which is usually what I go with. Yellow is like, eh, you'll be alright. Red means you'll be in the campus gym until next Friday."

Each dish was also labeled as gluten-free, vegan, vegetarian, or dairy-free wherever applicable. Kelsey didn't have any dietary restrictions but if she did, she would be in good hands.

While her coworkers busied themselves with heaping plates of chicken tikka masala or their choice of the four available kinds of pizza, Kelsey headed directly to the salad bar. The range of delicacies did tempt her to break her diet. However, she didn't want a few mouthfuls of awesomeness to lead to the undoing of her waistline. Kelsey accompanied her leafy greens with a fresh-pressed juice from the rainbow of colors before her.

The seating area was a high-volume blend of animated conversations and the clanging of trays and silverware. Sarah and Kelsey placed their trays on a bench table with just enough room for them to sit across from each other. To her left, a group of college-aged engineers gabbed in speedy Korean over a heaping stack of waffles draped in whipped cream and strawberries. To her right, a bunch of scruffy engineers were engaged in conversations so technical, they would require the Rosetta Stone to translate.

"The UX sophistication is almost at an optimal state. Our PM is giving us more resources to show granular value at scale."

"Shift priorities from data aggregation to product adoption and that's what you get. Bro, pass me that syrup?"

Kelsey's eyes danced around the room absorbing the hub of activity. Above the tables, TV screens announced in bold graphics upcoming campus events. There were Q&As with thought leaders in tech coming up that week, a half marathon along the Bay on Saturday, and on the following Tuesday, a Dungeons and Dragons tournament. An ongoing series of fun and camaraderie amongst her fellow Myntors.

Kelsey turned her attention back to Sarah who was taking bites of grilled shrimp with kaffir lime salsa.

"What do other employees think about the Comms team?" Kelsey asked.

"The funny thing is most people at the company don't know we exist," she said. "Just executive leadership — we call them the Dream Team — and the press. The closest a regular employee comes to knowing who we are is when they see a news article about Elemynt and it has a quote from 'a company spokesperson.' Of course, that's me or Jon and now you."

Sarah explained that for a while she was the only person leading External Comms for Elemynt. After her three years on the job, Jon, who had been working at the company for a year as Director of Growth, was appointed by Troy as VP of Comms and Sarah's new boss.

"Jon's a smart guy," Sarah said. "He has solid ideas. We're lucky to have him and to have you too."

There were two other women in Kelsey's role before her, but they both left separately to pursue careers in other industries. Following their absence, Jon was working to build out a new era for the Comms team that aligned with Troy's mandate from Elemynt's board of directors. The esteemed group of advisers that represented shareholders' interests was particularly keen on keeping public sentiment high.

"When people love us, investors are happy," Sarah waved her fork. "We keep that up through the work we do every day."

"What you're saying is we've got a lot of pressure on us," Kelsey smiled.

"Not necessarily," Sarah thought out loud. "But what we do makes a big difference in the company's success and that makes us the coolest kids on the block."

"You're going to be late to the all-hands," Kelsey heard Tai say from far behind her.

Tai approached the two dining colleagues unannounced, lugging a takeout box filled to the brim with pizza. Kelsey wondered if her coworker had a recurring habit of sneaking up on people. In the brighter light outside of the bunker, Kelsey noticed that the photo on Tai's badge was a much younger version with her hair colored violet. She considered whether Tai had always been brusque in the way she talked with people face to face.

"You know being on time is kinda important here," Tai said.

"What's all-hands?" Kelsey asked Sarah.

"Uh, only one of the most important meetings of the week," Tai said. "Duh."

Sarah sighed patiently. She explained the concept that Tai had not given her the time to speak to Kelsey about just yet. There was a lot for them to cover and it had been less than a day since her colleague had become an official employee.

All-hands, Sarah said, was a meeting the company held every Monday at 4 p.m. when every employee gathered to hear from Troy about the latest big picture news. A select few higher-ups from around the company would also give an update on the state of affairs, internal-only information about upcoming plans, and new products under consideration. Myntors in global offices dialed into a video feed of the all-hands. Those in headquarters would gather at the campus auditorium.

"Tai leads the planning for all-hands because she heads up Internal Comms," Sarah explained. "Our girl is responsible for creating the messaging from executives to our fellow employees. She's good at 'speaking Elemynt.'"

"Man, sometimes I wish I had it as easy as you guys," Tai interrupted snarkily. "You announce a product, send a few quotes to reporters and then, bam! All the news sites are repeating it, no questions asked. Employees...they're the ones with the real questions."

"Sit down with us," Sarah gestured with a smirk. "Have a salad."

"Ah, gotta go," Tai said with an upturned nose. "Some of us are real busy. Gotta double-check the messaging that's going out to 20,000 employees plus the 100 that started with you this week, Kelsey. Enjoy your meal, folks."

Tai carted her soggy to-go box out the door and disappeared as quickly as she came. Sarah was unswayed by Tai's interruption. The tension between the two looked to be one-sided. Perhaps Tai needed to relax more. Kelsey admired Sarah's ability to take daggers and potential disasters in stride.

"She really is hilarious, isn't she?" Sarah chuckled. "20,000 employees asking a few questions. I get it. How about billions of people around the world who have tens of thousands of questions and just you, me, and Jon to answer them. She may think she has the bigger responsibility. However, I think the math is on *our* side."

Kelsey didn't want to say anything to offend either of her co-workers. She offered a simple head nod and "okay."

"Anyway, she is right about one thing," Sarah said. "We need to get over to all-hands. Don't want you to miss out on seeing Troy on your big first day!"

TWO

The uptempo pop music that served as the score to all-hands could be heard from several buildings away. The bass emanating from the other side of the auditorium doors thumped in time with Kelsey's elevated heartbeat. It was her first official meeting at Elemynt and an unspeakably cool moment in her life.

Kelsey and Sarah floated into the queue of employees swiping their badge at the security check-in near the auditorium doors. Signs around the entrance indicated that no cameras or recording of any kind were allowed in the internal-only gathering. All-hands was one of the rare times when posting to the app about an event at Elemynt was a big no-no. Kelsey kept her phone securely in her pocket.

The two Comms ladies positioned themselves in the rear of the bustling auditorium where they soaked in a panoramic view of a thousand employees restlessly taking their seats. The glow from laptops and phones illuminated faces working to wrap-up last-minute emails and project details before the kickoff. Troy McCray would have their undivided attention.

A stage ten times as large as the one in the orientation room dominated the front of the space. Behind the platform was a video screen two stories high displaying the circular green Elemynt logo. The vast auditorium was filled to capacity which meant there were many thousands more watching on their laptops around the world. It was a monumental moment of the week that employees were sure not to miss. Kelsey knew that she would be working alongside a large number of other employees. To see what equaled to a small portion of them filling the vast room took her breath away.

"I remember when all the employees at the company could fit in here at the same time," Sarah glanced around the room. "That was only three years ago, maybe. Now you can barely fit the culinary staff in here. This place has grown so fast. It's incredible when you think about it, right?"

At 2 p.m. exactly, the weekly all-hands meeting officially kicked off with a surge of introductory music befitting the arrival of the man in charge.

"Hello, Myntors!" Troy said as he strode to the stage to immense fanfare.

His piercing green eyes sparkled under the stage lights as the rows upon rows of elated employees lauded his presence. Like his product that captured the attention of the world, Troy drew in the room with his charm and effortless cool. He was a rock star and all-hands was his concert. A mic tucked in his ear and around his perfectly square jaw allowed him to speak freely with nothing between him and his troops.

The Elemynt CEO was clad in his signature black T-shirt and a pair of casual denim jeans. When Troy showed up, people knew what look to expect from him. Troy's footwear though was a constant surprise. Vintage Jordans, limited edition Adidas, and designer pairs collectors would die to get their hands on were included in his rotation. His wardrobe overflowed with so many options that it seemed as if he never wore the same pair twice.

"First, let's give it up for our noobs who joined today!" Troy exclaimed.

"That's you, newbie," Sarah patted Kelsey's shoulder excitedly.

Kelsey glowed with appreciation of the acknowledgment from her new colleagues.

The badge photos of the people in her orientation class flashed on the screen. The display was a ceremonious debut that was lifted higher by her welcoming peers.

"Noobs, you came at a great time!" Troy said. "What a week for Elemynt! Thanks to everyone's hard work I am proud to announce…we now have one billion people on the app!"

The screen behind him blasted the words "1 BILLION" in huge letters backed by digital floating confetti. The audience of Myntors celebrated their collective achievement with self-congratulations and cheers of accomplishment. Kelsey was in awe of the astounding feat. One billion people directly affected by her work!

"It wasn't that long ago that we were a tiny office by the Bay," Troy grinned. "Now we're a 20,000-person strong production. And we're planning to double that by next year. Not bad for our tiny little start-up in Palo Alto."

The audience chuckled at the cheeky underestimation. A Silicon Valley institution with offices in many of the world's major cities wasn't exactly a startup. Troy's frame of mind was intentional. Thinking like a smaller, nimbler company kept it open to new ideas and its growth accelerating.

Troy spoke of his vision in soundbites, pausing for a brief second between sentences to allow the previous one to digest. He walked across the stage at a steady pace, gesticulating occasionally with each movement underscoring his point. Every word he said was important. Everything was filled with an idea.

"I'm excited to say we're on track to have 1.25 billion people on the platform by the end of the year," Troy said. "It's going to take every one of you here to make that happen. If anyone can do it, it's us!"

Kelsey gleaned why the talented workforce stood behind Troy's goal-setting. The founder of Elemynt had a confidence in his vision that encouraged people around him to believe in it as well. It was an honor for employees to hear directly from a real-life hero.

"Thinking big picture about the future is what's always going to get us that exponential growth we need," Troy said. "I'm going to bring up the best product guy in the biz to talk more about the new technology on the way. Give him a round of applause, everybody!"

In Troy's place on the stage came Gary Rao, the visionary VP of Product at Elemynt. They greeted each other heartily as they swapped places at the front of the room. Gary had the posture and fleece vest of a dad and the enthusiasm of a young programmer straight out of college. Gary's zeal for developing innovative new features for the company was matched only by that of its founder. He humbly led a team of thousands of engineers whose work he represented weekly at the all-hands.

"Thanks, Troy!" he said. "We launched live video last year which enables people to share their moments in real-time from wherever they are in the world. We now have an average of 25 million people going live every day. Who needs TVs when you have the Elemynt app?"

"Not me!" someone yelled from the back of the room.

"Hey, I like you!" Gary shouted to the anonymous person. "Give them a raise! How about our new Elemynt VR headsets? How many of you guys have one now?"

A score of hands shot up. The company-branded virtual reality headsets were flying off the shelves and into the hands of millions, including Kelsey's fellow Myntors.

"I see my fellow nerds out there!" he smiled. "Not getting out much are ya?"

The crowd giggled with love at the endearingly corny jokes Gary tossed their way. His infectious optimism was fueled by his position to share the results of the outstanding work of the people who reported up to him.

"As all of you know, Elemynt is constantly on the lookout for ways to create technology that makes life easier for people. The next way we're doing that is with the newest iteration of virtual shopping!"

Gary described a new system under development in which users linked their Elemynt account to their VR device to get access to a virtual store that replicated a real shopping experience. Clothes, shoes, accessories...it was all there. The best part was the user could try on the items on display in a virtual mirror with an avatar that represented their exact weight and body type. Once they selected the items they wanted to purchase, they used the payment option on file for them to have the clothes delivered right to their front door.

"We're giving people access to the stuff that makes them happy and saving them money and time in the process! What do you guys think?"

The audience applauded with the excitement of children turned loose in a candy store. Myntors contemplated with each other what stores they wanted to see in the VR world and what clothes they would buy. Kelsey loved in-person shopping, but this was next-level.

"A huge thanks to our VR teams and to everyone for working to make this a reality! Let's give them some applause!"

While everyone showered their colleagues with due praise, Kelsey's mind snapped back to her official duties. The system Gary discussed was not public knowledge. He was revealing sensitive internal-only information to tens of thousands of people at once.

"Is the press going to hear about this?" Kelsey whispered to Sarah.

"We don't say anything at all-hands we don't mind leaking," Sarah responded. "Actually, we kinda expect it. It's part of building the hype for new info we plan to put out officially anyway. If the press gets a hold of the 'secret plans' before we announce them, they feel like they're getting a scoop. That means they're more likely to cover whatever it is we wanted them to cover in the first place."

A series of presentations from different Elemynt leads was followed by the question and answer portion of all-hands. Each week, employees were encouraged to submit or to vote online for questions to be asked of Troy at the coming all-hands. If employees received one of the top five votes in the ranking, they would receive a notification that they could pose the question live in front of their colleagues or via video conference. The democratic system was designed to encourage participation from across the company.

Questions could be posed to Troy about whatever employees desired — the latest product developments, his outlook on events surrounding the company, his favorite breakfast foods. Keeping in mind that the whole company was watching, Sarah emphasized.

Kelsey spotted Tai across the way intently eyeing the Myntors lining up behind the mics set up in the aisles of the auditorium. If there was time left in the Q&A for additional questions, Troy would answer as many as he could.

The dialogue between Myntors and the founder was an important part of the company's culture. An exchange of ideas instilled a trust on both sides that the entirety of the company was moving the company forward together.

The Myntors in line gushed as they one by one posed questions to their leader. Most were congratulatory in nature for recent achievements by Elemynt and its teams. A few were suggestions for ways to improve the various parts of the company.

Troy responded to each questioner with a warm sincerity that made them feel like the most important person in the room. They walked away giddy inside that they received singular acknowledgment from the chief executive. The room applauded after the close of each answer, proud of their counterparts and equally proud of Troy's endearing responses.

A Myntor who was more solemn in disposition than those before him approached the microphone stand. The pre-voted questions were exhausted and the Q&A had become an open mic. Kelsey was nervous about the gravity of what he may ask. The whole affair had been exceedingly positive so far.

"Have we considered letting users select the type of information they share with our advertisers?" the Myntor asked hesitantly. "Like maybe they want to share their age or gender but not their location?"

"Thank you for that question...we're thinking about it," Troy said in earnest contemplation. "We do everything in our power to protect account privacy by using the most advanced security technology possible. As the platform keeps growing, we'll be doing more of that by always thinking of people first."

The attendees in the auditorium clapped in response, satisfied with the answer. Kelsey was impressed that Troy handled the question deftly. The response was broad for sure but it indicated that the leader of Elemynt always had his finger on the pulse of his creation.

Several more questions and Troy's time on stage neared its close.

"You all rock!" Troy exclaimed. "Thank you, Myntors!"

The CEO exited the stage to a wave of adoration. Troy was even more charismatic and thoughtful in person than Kelsey anticipated he would be. She was proud to be a Myntor led by an outstanding visionary.

"Check this out," Sarah whispered. "This is my favorite part of all-hands."

Elemynt's Head of People, Melissa Cooperston, ascended to the stage like a radiant ball of optimism. The California blonde with the sun-kissed complexion oversaw employee relations and set the overall vibe of fun that was a part of the company culture.

"Hey, cool kids!" she smiled. "You all know every week we have our 'Community Spotlight' where we feature a story of how Elemynt is bringing the world closer together. This week, I'd like you all to meet Susie! She's six-year-old from Billings, Montana. Let's watch!"

A video appeared on the auditorium screen of a plucky little girl handing out cups of lemonade from a homemade stand. In front of it was the cutest hand-drawn poster adorned with unicorns drinking lemonade and the price — "50 cents." The camera panned to show a long line of smiling people waiting to be served. Accompanied by uplifting music and sunny clips, the video told how Susie saw a story on Elemynt about kids who went hungry because they didn't have access to food. She was inspired to do her part to help out. Susie, with help from her mom, whipped up gallons of lemonade and set up a stand in the family's front yard.

"Kids shouldn't be hungry and everyone helps me because it's the right thing to do, I think," Susie said between pours.

When Susie's parents posted about her stand on Elemynt, people from near and far came out to support. They posted photos of themselves on their account holding cups of the sweet and satisfying lemonade along with the hashtag #SweetForEats. The stand turned into a viral sensation almost overnight. By the end of the month, Susie raised $1,500 with every dollar going to charity.

"I'm so proud of her," Susie's mom said while hugging her beautiful daughter. "Thank you to everyone at Elemynt for making it possible. We love you."

"Thanks, Elemynt!" Susie cheesed.

The auditorium beamed with oohs and aahs and cheers of support. The love in the room for the little girl who demonstrated the power of what was capable through the app warmed the hearts of the individuals watching. Employees commented to themselves how they too could help her cause. Kelsey watched as they navigated in droves to Susie's account to lavish her with lots of new followers.

"This is the kind of story we want to land in the press," Sarah said to Kelsey. "Other comms reps in the tech industry are out there pitching stories about their product and what it can do. Which is okay, don't get me wrong. But reporters get those boring pitches all the time and it's not really what news consumers want to read. They like stories about people doing inspiring things. And that's what we put in our media partners' laps. Our product just happens to be a part of a larger human-interest story. Easy sell."

Kelsey was intrigued by the golden PR strategy. There were countless stories like Susie's that surfaced on Elemynt. It would be a snap to share stories of how her colleagues' work affected the world in inspiring ways. The foundation of her role at the company could not be easier.

At 4 p.m. on the dot, Kelsey's first all-hands came to a close. The bouncy music continued to pump the speakers as Myntors made their way to the rear of the room. Frozen margarita machines with both the virgin and alcoholic variety were set up for their refreshment. Employees sipped the delicious icy goodness and nibbled on house-made tortilla chips while talking excitedly about Troy's proclamations. Their motivation to go forth and do phenomenal work filled the space with an infectious can-do spirit.

* * *

When the dynamic duo returned to their workspaces, Jon was there waiting to welcome them back. Their manager was a vision of Silicon Valley executive excellence. Jon's sculpted hair with no trace of gray was becoming of a career guy in his late 30s. He sported a navy polo shirt and tapered khakis — the uniform of a man who would rather be wearing a suit. His casual-cool look was effortless with a laidback demeanor to match.

"Our new recruit!" Jon said. "It's been quite a day for you."

"The best first day I've ever had by a longshot," Kelsey agreed.

"If you want to cut out early, we'll start bright and early tomorrow. It'll be a long day. That work for you?"

Kelsey agreed to his proposal, already thinking about what could possibly be in store for the following day. Her first order of business was to find out where on the closed campus she should call for a rideshare car. Elemynt picked up the expenses for Kelsey to have her Audi sedan shipped from Boston to California. An immense help that made transitioning to a new state a simple affair. Problem was, the car wasn't scheduled to arrive until later that week.

Kelsey previously read through the portion of her orientation packet that described the free Elemynt shuttles that transported employees to the various corners of the Bay Area from early morning to night. The dedicated rides journeyed to and from the hubs of Oakland, San Jose, and San Francisco to as far as Pleasanton thirty miles east and Marin County two hours' drive to the north. The set stops were selected to be within a few blocks of the bulk of employees' homes. The shuttles also stopped at BART train stations in case riders wanted to have their cars waiting for them in the adjacent public parking lots. The incredible offer was further proof of the extraordinary lengths to which TC would go to meet the personal needs of its staff.

As amazing as the perk was, on her first day Kelsey opted to skip it altogether. She didn't want to possibly be late for her orientation because she mistakenly missed her shuttle ride. Starting on the wrong foot was an absolute no-no. Kelsey welcomed Jon's help in locating her way home.

"It's pretty simple once you get the hang of it," he said, reaching for his work phone. "Open up the employee app like this. Then enter your address. There we go. The next bus leaves at 5:30. Station A."

Kelsey noted that Jon went out of his way to help his new team member. Most other managers would point in a general direction and tell her to figure it out herself. In spoke volumes that Jon would navigate the shuttle guides with her.

"Jon, I—" Kelsey piped up, looking for the right words.

"What's up?"

"I appreciate you letting me a part of this team," Kelsey exhaled.

"We're glad to have you with us," he replied warmly. "And make sure you take some snacks home with you. You'll need your fuel for tomorrow."

* * *

The shuttle buses lined up in their designated spots like majestic steel carriages waiting to whisk employees away. Each one announced its destination in a digital display above the driver. Occasionally, they flashed adorable messages like "Have a nice day!" or smiley face emojis.

The bus driver greeted every single person who swiped their badge as they entered the stairwell. Kelsey waved a thoroughly cheery hello in response.

This wasn't the yellow school bus Kelsey saw in the movies. The ride was outfitted with free wi-fi, leather seats, privacy curtains for each of the windows, and two electrical outlets per seat to charge devices. There were also comfy chairs in sets of four facing each other with a collapsible desk between them for casual meetings on the way home. Two high-definition screens built into the walls of the shuttle were in place for small groups to share presentations if they desired. This was luxury Silicon Valley living at its finest.

Kelsey settled into a row to herself with full views of the world outside of the broad window. Most of her co-workers pored over their laptops or were entrenched in their phones. A few talked quietly to each other about the business of the day. Kelsey began to open the brand-new company laptop that she couldn't wait to check out for herself. Instead, she cradled it tightly in her arms. She wanted to revel in the peaceful moment.

As the shuttle pulled away from the depot, the sunlight danced on the endless rows of parked cars in the surrounding lots. Within moments, the bus was on the highway, the glass buildings of Elemynt fading into the distance behind it. One of the most exciting days of Kelsey's life was coming to a close. Part of her didn't want it to be over. The sequence of events was like an unreal dream from which she was about to wake up. But for her to have a good second day, the first would have to come to an end.

Like all new employees stationed at headquarters, Kelsey was offered a signing bonus of several thousand dollars to live within seven miles of Palo Alto, save for a few neighborhoods. East Palo Alto, a poorer area and primarily Hispanic community that bordered the wealthy city Elemynt called home, was off-limits. Elemynt didn't want to be seen as disrupting the community, she overheard someone say at orientation.

Whispers abounded of East Palo Alto being higher in crime which explained in part why the rent was much less pricey than other areas. There was no need to move to that specific location anyway. The salaries Elemynt provided to its employees gave them a wide swath of Bay Area neighborhoods to choose from. And no living in the unincorporated nearby mountains either. Not if they wanted the bonus.

Kelsey would have preferred to stay a short distance to the campus whether or not the bonus was in place. She opted for a gorgeous apartment in Foster City, a neighborhood on the Bay approximately halfway between San Francisco and San Jose. She fell in love with the lagoon-adjacent roads and the feeling of serenity that surrounded it. Foster City also featured one of the best bike and jogging paths in the country which extended the entire perimeter of the city and along the water. Kelsey very much intended to spend most of her free time there. A good run always rejuvenated her spirit.

Kelsey's laptop remained closed but she couldn't resist opening up her personal phone. She spent most of the shuttle ride home posting more pics from the day on Elemynt and responding to messages from friends and family.

Moving to the West Coast meant leaving behind her mother and father who resided in one of Connecticut's stately suburbs. Her parents were as excited, if not more, about Kelsey's new job. She signed them up for Elemynt accounts two years prior and they took to it instantly. Her father, a retired software engineer, posted images from his nature walks. Her mother, a superintendent for the local school district, loved following her favorite politicians and news personalities.

Kelsey's parents always took good care of their cherished daughter and continued to encourage her to pursue her dreams. It was important to Kelsey that she made them and the various people who aided her in her career proud. She wanted to live up to her standing as a symbol of excellence. Kelsey's cheerleading squad was behind her rooting for her every step of the way. Each fave on the Elemynt app was a pat on the back letting her know she was loved and supported.

* * *

The exterior of Kelsey's apartment building was beautifully landscaped with leafy gardens and a koi pond that together evoked eternal tranquility. Inside her apartment, however, was just short of chaos.

The jungle of towering cardboard boxes that dominated her living room desperately called out to be unpacked. The movers graciously set up her bed and situated her couch when she first arrived. Those were pretty much the only items in place. The rest was buried under miles of packing tape and Styrofoam peanuts. The sole piece of décor was a framed photo of her mom and dad placed on the marble kitchen counter.

After the eventful day, Kelsey was ready to rest. Her home would be picture-perfect once she got her bearings in the new city.

Just as she was beginning to unwind, Kelsey received a video call on her personal phone. Brad, her former boyfriend and one-time love of her life, was undoubtedly calling to congratulate her on her first day. This was the call she was waiting for. Kelsey could not resist the all-American guy with the five o'clock shadow and the seductive blue eyes.

"How's the new president of Elemynt?" Brad asked jovially. "Making million-dollar decisions yet?"

"It's my first day," she laughed. "And that's not my title but one day maybe."

"I see it for you now. Kelsey Pace, global superstar."

"That's some jump," Kelsey giggled.

"When you put your mind to something, baby, you get it. Look at you now. A big timer in Silicon Valley."

Kelsey's heart fluttered at his doting words. The enchantment of the moment was interrupted by what sounded like several motors running at once. Kelsey scrunched her face at the phone.

"Where are you?" she asked. "And what's that noise?"

"Oh, that? Those are llamas. I'm in Peru."

Brad's left bicep flexed as his muscular arm held the phone out in selfie mode. Behind him was a pastoral scene of lush fields with the braying of animals just out of frame. He moved the camera to show more of the scenic view. Sure enough, a flock of friendly llamas roamed the area near him.

"That's how they say 'hello'," he smiled.

Brad was an exceptionally adventurous world traveler. There was no telling where he would be when he called.

In the years since they first met, Brad had always been a different kind of guy in the best way. Their very first encounter was when Kelsey was waiting outside her Boston University dorm for her rideshare car to arrive. He pulled up to the curb in a silver Tesla, not the normal car for a driver from the app.

She struck up a conversation with the handsome man behind the steering wheel. He was a computer science major and talked with great zeal about his plans to enter the tech industry and create the software that would change the world.

From his disposition and the fancy ride, Kelsey gleaned that he didn't need the money that driving around fellow college students provided. When she asked about the car, Brad responded with words Kelsey would never forget.

"I thought it'd be an awesome way to meet new people," he said with an intoxicating wink. "I'm lucky to have someone as cool as you to ride with."

Since that moment, Kelsey was head over heels for the guy. He sparked joy in her life in a way no one else could.

It was his sense of adventure that made Kelsey love him more. Dates around campus turned into weekend trips to Montreal or quick getaways to Puerto Rico. The pair talked about the exotic destinations they wanted to visit together. They imagined themselves on camel-back trips in Dubai, safaris in Africa, drinking margaritas in Cuba. What they had between them was what most people wanted in a relationship — endless love and mutual support.

The two were inseparable until after their senior year of college when their burgeoning career paths called them to different cities. The decision was tough but ultimately necessary to move forward with their ambitions. As fate would have it, they reunited years later at UltraTalk where Brad was hired as a systems engineer around the same time Kelsey came on as the Communications Manager.

Their love hit an obstacle when the company management decided to "streamline" its teams to focus on the core product. They fired many of the engineers working on "special projects," including Brad who was one of their most dedicated employees. To have his dream job suddenly taken away from him traumatically bruised her love's ego.

Brad fell into a heavy depression, shutting himself off from the world, not answering his phone, and never leaving the house. His sense of focus in life was gone. Nothing Kelsey did or said could convince him that he was the star she knew him to be.

Brad one day had a sudden epiphany that would draw him from his stupor. Rather than taking a new position elsewhere, Brad set off on a journey to see as much of the world as possible. With his family's best wishes and Kelsey's supportive farewell, he set about traveling from country to country leaving his life in the United States behind.

Since his ongoing excursion began, Brad treated his Elemynt account like a full-time job. He snapped jaw-dropping photos on far-flung trips to the French Alps, the Galápagos Islands, and the hinterlands of India. In the 12 months after he'd been let go, Brad traveled to 23 countries across five continents documenting the stunning sights along the way on the Elemynt app.

If there was cell reception at his destination, he would check in with a video call to Kelsey. Otherwise, she'd follow him on the Elemynt app which he used with increased frequency. Brad amassed tens of thousands of followers with whom he shared his incredible adventures.

Brad was a wandering man, but he wasn't exactly roughing it. He spent days in the mountains or trekking through forests but he'd end his jaunts with a few days at a palatial Intercontinental Hotel suite or a five-star resort that cost more than the GDP of some small countries.

Plenty of female admirers posted adoring comments on his posts. However, Brad's heart belonged to Kelsey. In infinite calls and private messages, he professed his continued love for his college sweetheart which she warmly accepted. Thousands of miles and many trips stood between them but their love for each other was a fire that being apart could not extinguish.

That said, what the two had between them currently was not what Kelsey would consider a "relationship." She didn't believe in long-distance relationships, especially when the distance changed every week. Brad was literally the one who got away. Kelsey had no choice but to let him. She would not stand in the way of what made him happy.

"My girl is a big-time PR lady," Brad said flirtatiously over the sound of llamas.

"Oh, I'm your 'girl' now?" she laughed. "Girlfriends don't see their boyfriends once every six months."

"You have another guy you're calling to tell about your big day?"

The answer was no. Brad may have been the love of her life but that was by default. Kelsey was too entrenched in work to chase after new romance.

Kelsey recounted to Brad the highlights of her first day at the amazing company. She described the endless amenities and how Elemynt treated its staff like kings and queens. The most forward-thinking work in the tech industry was underway at the company. It was a far better environment than UltraTalk and possibly a job that Brad would love.

"I wish you could come see the campus," Kelsey said with a spark. "Elemynt seriously has some of the best coders in the world. You'd fit right in."

Deep down, Kelsey hoped that Brad would change his outlook on life and settle into a regular job again. Kelsey looked forward to the day when they could possibly build a life together, perhaps in Silicon Valley. She was well aware that the notion would take some convincing.

"I'll get there as soon as I can," Brad said. "I have a couple more stops before I hit the States. I'm rooting for you baby."

The loving message was a perfect way to end the evening. After several kisses at the camera and vows to call each other again soon, Kelsey excused herself to go to sleep. Another wonderful day awaited her in the morning.

THREE

The fifteen-foot tall recreation of the Elemynt logo at the main entrance of the campus glinted in the morning sun. The sign was a preeminent symbol of the wonderful imagination and innovation just beyond the security gates. Tourists flocked to the illuminated landmark to snap their photo in front of the Silicon Valley version of the Hollywood sign. For them, it was an opportunity to show off that they saw the venerable institution in person, for themselves.

Kelsey watched from her shuttle bus window as early morning visitors took turns posing in front of the beckoning sign. A few looked to be discussing how they could see the rest of the campus. However, if they were not official guests, the eager visitors wouldn't make it past the security checkpoints the employee bus navigated its way through. Elemynt was a public app but also a private company with real people who worked there. Kelsey was glad to be among them.

Kelsey and her new coworkers poured out of the white chariots to head toward their various destinations at Elemynt HQ. Smaller shuttles and rows of Elemynt bicycles were available if they needed to journey to one of the further reaches of campus. Most Myntors made a beeline toward one of the bustling cafeterias or headed to the gyms for early morning workouts.

After some consideration, Kelsey tried to bring herself to wear a T-shirt to match the wardrobe of the majority of her coworkers. However, she could not shake the fact that she was far more comfortable in heels and a blazer. She was assured in her choices knowing that she worked on the Comms team, one of the company's more public-facing roles. In that regard, standing out was a good thing.

The stretches of open desks surrounding Kelsey's workspace pulsated with the murmur of keyboard taps and mouse clicks. Cable news networks on the screen above her desk announced the breaking news of the day. Her friendly colleagues buzzed to and from conference rooms clutching coffee and chatting with their teammates. Those who opted for breakfast toted piping hot omelets, sugary pastries, and fresh-pressed orange juice.

Kelsey watched as a uniform-clad member of the horticulture team tended to the array of plants that added liveliness to the office. As she set out her new company laptop, Kelsey reflected on a nearby poster emblazoned with the words "You are Elemynt." Yes, she was.

Never one to settle for a blank white space, Kelsey set up her desk with vibrant pink orchids, a vintage brass banker's lamp, and several framed photos of her family and friends back home. The personal touches made her area shine. A good work environment was an absolute must.

Kelsey's work calendar that came pre-installed on both her MacBook and iPhone was already half full with slotted meetings. She was scheduled to attend the weekly gatherings of a wide range of teams, including product, design, business development, and platform engineering plus half-hour, one-on-one meetings with names she didn't recognize but couldn't wait to connect with.

Kelsey's email inbox was surprisingly filled with a litany of messages from reporters representing news media around the world. She had been added to the External Comms teams' public group email address one week before she started by either Sarah or Jon. While the influx of notification was daunting initially, Kelsey was thrilled to take on the challenges the email and calendar invites represented.

"Life's so much more interesting when you're your own secretary," Sarah said, announcing her arrival.

"Without a doubt!" Kelsey said cheerily.

Sarah stood over Kelsey's shoulder and pointed at the crowded inbox. "I see you've found our bread and butter."

"Just getting a jump on the day," Kelsey nodded.

Sarah placed her purse on her desk and settled in next to her colleague. "It's like being the popular girls at school. When you're one of the most successful companies in the world, you're going to have reporters reaching out constantly."

"Which is what we want, right?" Kelsey asked.

"Totally. It's up to us to filter through the inbox and find reporters who work for the media where we want to land our stories."

"And keep an eye on everyone else before we leave them on read."

"The lady catches on quickly!" Sarah brightened. "Most of the people just want comment for their story from an Elemynt spokesperson. We'll either forward them to the company blog which is where we make our announcements or skip it if it's not important."

"Question for you," Kelsey paused. "I was looking at news stories about Elemynt and they never say 'no comment'. It's always—"

"'Spokesperson could not be reached for comment'" Sarah said definitively. Yes, and that's how we like it. Why waste your fingers writing 'no comment' when not replying at all works just as well?"

A time-saver, Kelsey thought. Elemynt's trademark efficiency at work.

"We do need to keep an eye out for stories that might be a bigger deal for whatever reason and we'll need to be proactive on. Some journalists don't take 'no comment' for an answer."

Kelsey understood that firsthand. Reporters could be a pushy bunch when they wanted a "scoop."

Sarah detailed the system the Comms team put in place to sort through incoming requests.

"If it's a rando journalist you can just move it over here to the archive," she said, highlighting a folder on Kelsey's screen. "Go ahead and put a yellow flag on the email if it needs the team's attention but it's not an emergency. An orange flag means we need to get the immediate team together at some point to meet about it. Red flags are for full-blown fires."

Kelsey's heart jumped at the thought of an issue so bad it would be considered a fire. "Do things get that drastic?"

"Don't worry, we rarely get any kind of red flag email," Sarah said reassuringly. "Most of these you'll be able to sort through yourself."

Sarah scrolled through the inbox, giving Kelsey an opportunity to mentally sort where the emails would go. Archive. Archive. Forward to the blog. Maybe a flag? Archive.

A curious number of messages from a "Tim Westbrook" with a Washington Chronicle email address caught Kelsey's eye.

"Oh that guy," Sarah rolled her eyes. "Ignore him. He's assigned to cover Elemynt and he's always trying to dig up dirt. He can't write a word if we don't give him anything. Go ahead and put him in the archive."

Kelsey had no problem prioritizing away unnecessary tasks. Goodbye, Tim.

"On to the fun stuff," Sarah said. "Let's get to know our co-workers, shall we?"

Sarah navigated to a bookmark in Kelsey's internet browser marked "Commynt." On the other side of the link was a multi-faceted portal of communication created exclusively for employees.

The core features were very similar to the Elemynt app. People could post photos with captions about happenings like product announcements from their teams, thoughts on the latest developments in the company, pop culture moments, and more. There was an option to fave or share each post just like on the Elemynt app.

Every Myntor in the company had a profile page from which they could post whatever they desired. The people Kelsey followed on Commynt would appear in her feed, a stream of posts organized by the most recent submission.

"You like running, right?" Sarah asked.

"It's my jam," Kelsey said proudly. "My goal is to run a full marathon once I get settled here."

"Cool! Go, Kelsey!" Sarah said excitedly. "So, Commynt has groups which are kind of like discussion boards. See, there's one for marathon runners."

Photos of Myntors at the finish lines at races, training tips, and an announcement of an upcoming 10K were among the liveliest discussions in the group. It was one of the hundreds of Commynt groups dedicated exclusively to Myntors' shared interests. Wine connoisseurs. Wakeboarding. New parents. Cosplay. Employees over 40. There was also a large internal group for all company announcements.

"I'll let you take a look at that while I check my email," Sarah said. "It can get overwhelming, so don't spend too much time on it."

Kelsey navigated her way through Commynt. It was a compelling reflection of the employees who made up the vast company and their individual personalities.

Each Myntor's profile was filled out with cool information like their hometown, alma mater, companies they worked for previously, and their hobbies. Kelsey could click on the points and see everyone within the company who entered the same keyword. Myntors who indicated they were a fan of activities like skiing or operas or multiplayer video games appeared on a generated list with their faces. There were many alumni from Boston University and a ton of Myntors from Connecticut. Seeing other people with her same background made Kelsey's day. She wasn't operating as solo as she thought.

In the sidebar of the main page of Commynt were "Trending Posts." There was a team celebrating a milestone launch. The post received a ton of faves from their colleagues. Special cookies were available in the kitchen of Building 6. Someone announced their engagement with a photo of their beautiful beau. The number of faves and shares on the post was in the hundreds.

Kelsey clicked into the number one trending post on Commynt: "A Safe Place for Doggos."

"If we had health insurance for our pets too, it would increase employee productivity," the person's post read.

The comments were filled with colleagues in full agreement. Myntors spoke boldly about reasons why not having pet insurance was detrimental to the company. They called on Troy to consider the proposal expediently.

"People can really talk about this stuff here?" Kelsey chuckled.

"That's part of an open culture," Sarah said from her desk.

Built into Commynt was eChat, an internal communication system where employees could send direct messages to or video chat with one another. Kelsey noted that it would come in handy for communication that needed a speedy response. She had one message. Jon wanted to meet her in the micro-kitchen near the front lobby in ten minutes.

Kelsey showed up early. Punctuality was her strong suit.

Myntors popped in and out of the busy compact food area, grabbing drinks from the rows of refrigerators and selecting from the range of available types of milk to add to their coffee or cereal. They took turns thumbing through the multitude of options for snacks before settling on the perfect bite.

Kelsey was unsure whether every other employee in the building had the same idea at the same time Jon did. The hustle in the micro-kitchen might have been a common occurrence. Either way, it was awesome to mingle with her colleagues in the vibrant location.

Jon maneuvered his way into the space wearing a sharp blazer which he promptly tossed over his left arm. His snappy outerwear was likely due to a previous formal meeting. He was ready to return to the casual, polo-wearing style more in line with the workplace atmosphere.

Kelsey told herself to relax as well. No need to be jittery in her first meeting with her manager.

"The team's all here!" he greeted Kelsey with a handshake. "Glad you made it back."

"I was up as soon as the sun was out," Kelsey confessed with a smile. "I would have been in earlier but I didn't know if people would be in the building."

"Elemynt never sleeps," Jon laughed. "That's why I help myself to as much coffee as they'll let me consume. You want anything?"

While Jon joined the queue to use the espresso machine, Kelsey perused the impressive rack of twenty or more teas. They were neatly arranged in alphabetical order from almond rooibos to white pomegranate. She opted for white Ceylon tea, a variety she had never heard of before. There was no better time for Kelsey to step outside of her comfort zone than her first week on the job.

The External Comms team's goals rolled up into the company's goals, Jon explained as he prepared his morning brew. Other departments were tasked with doing the same but approached the mission in different ways.

"Let's say, for example, the company wants to add 500 million more users, which it does," Jon said. "Engineering needs to build the features to attract and retain those people. Sales needs to bring on more advertisers that match with the different demographics. We all get there together. It's our work that's the most important of everything that happens here."

"Why's that?" Kelsey asked curiously.

"No use building great products if no one knows about them," Jon said. "You see, most employees here will never interact directly with the public. We do it on their behalf by promoting their work. We are their storytellers. What we say, the people hear."

Jon's outlook on the company was a reflection of Troy's for good reason. Jon shared with Kelsey that he and Troy were buddies since their undergraduate days together at Stanford. Jon served as a sounding board for Troy back when Elemynt was a few lines of code and a big idea. Their paths diverged when Troy dropped out to further develop Elemynt and Jon went on to pursue his law degree at Georgetown University.

Jon was at the height of his career as a well-regarded tech sector lobbyist in Washington, D.C. when Troy came calling. Troy believed his friend's background made him the ideal person to build out presences in countries where the use of Elemynt was gaining steam. The CEO appointed Jon his director of growth and tasked him with leading the company's foreign efforts.

Where Troy was able to make Elemynt a hit in the States, Jon elevated it into a global phenomenon within a year. He expanded on Troy's strategy of seeding the app with influencers on the cusp of global fame.

Nearly every tech company maintained a presence in international capitals like London, Paris, and Berlin to work with celebrities based there. Influencers living outside of those few major cities rarely received the same level of attention.

By collaborating with key stakeholders in the second largest cities rather than the saturated markets, Elemynt was able to grow interest in the platform at a faster rate. When the number of users in the country reached a predetermined threshold, Elemynt devoted resources to establishing a fully staffed office there.

Jon's dynamic work led to him being bestowed with the broader title of VP of Communications and a team to support him. Kelsey hoped to carry on the legacy of significant achievement he set for the team.

"I'll send you an email that outlines your KPIs... that's key performance indicators," Jon said. "Those are the goals you'll be held accountable for each quarter. You'll mostly be measured on your placement of positive stories about the company you arrange through your media contacts."

"I think you're going to love the ideas I have for media campaigns," Kelsey said. "I promise we'll knock it out the park!"

Jon was warmed by the enthusiasm of his new team member.

"Kelsey, we had hundreds of applications for this job," he said. "An inbox full of very impressive resumes. You know why you stood out?"

Kelsey shook her head no, hanging on his every word in anticipation of the answer.

"Because of your passion," he said. "That matters a great deal to this company. What you did at UltraTalk required the dedication we like to see here."

Kelsey thought of the many late nights, meetings, and phone calls that it took to make the UltraTalk PR campaigns a reality. The payoff was that new and existing users attained a greater understanding of how the platform bettered their lives. Kelsey grew from the experience as well, becoming a stronger communicator personally and professionally.

"I appreciate you seeing that in me," Kelsey said appreciatively.

"Thank you for sharing it with us," Jon paused to sip from his cup. "This isn't a clock in, clock out place and you'll be traveling a fair amount. Still comfortable with that?"

"Of course!"

"Do you have a husband or boyfriend that will mind?"

"No, just an ex," Kelsey said. "He's... taking time off to travel right now."

"I'm sure he's not doing it on a corporate card," Jon grinned. "Make sure you request one from the Finance team. Also, start thinking about when you want to take personal time off. PTO is the key to work-life balance."

Domestic and international travel were pastimes Kelsey enjoyed greatly since she was young enough to carry her own passport. She couldn't wait to see where her work trips carried her. The photos she took in exotic destinations for her Elemynt account would be spectacular. Having time off from the pressures of work as needed would be equally welcome. Kelsey's initial impression that Jon was looking out for her well-being was right on. He would be a great manager as well as someone to learn from.

"By the way, you're meeting Troy today," Jon said. "You're going to be his mouthpiece. I want you to get face time with him."

"Troy?" Kelsey gulped in astonishment. "That's amazing but...it's my second day. Is now the right time?"

"His executive assistant says he has an opening in thirty minutes. That is very rare. The man has a company of 20,000 employees to manage and leaders of the free world gunning to meet with him. We should take advantage, don't you think?"

Jon may have overestimated her ability to jump right in. Kelsey fought back the creeping doubt. It was better to be underprepared for an opportunity than to miss it completely.

"No, no, that's fine," Kelsey said, fighting back jitters. "I like jumping in the deep end as soon as possible."

"That's the spirit!" Jon said. "I want you to head over to...wait... you're new here. Hold on a sec."

Jon reached for his phone to send a message on eChat. Moments later, Sarah strode into the micro-kitchen.

"Sarah, can you accompany Kelsey to Building 50?"

Sarah's face brightened with exhilaration. "You're serious? Building 50?"

"Yep. Better hurry or you'll miss him."

* * *

Sarah and Kelsey were confronted by an unmarked building with no visible windows and a solitary black door. The distinct charm of Elemynt architecture Kelsey had come to know was displaced by a slab of dull, gray cement. There was also no badge reader. Whatever the building was supposed to be, it was a big deal. Kelsey was increasingly uncomfortable with what lay ahead. A disembodied voice from a video doorbell buzzed the ladies in.

What lay before them was much more than anything Kelsey could have ever imagine. Inside the cavernous space was a Hollywood caliber soundstage filled with detailed recreations of family rooms, kitchens, studio apartments, and more. The faux living spaces were illuminated by rows of stage lights descending from the ceiling. A group of engineers crowded around one of the sets watching a person idling around the space with a virtual reality headset nestled over their head. They watched intently, scribbling notes on their laptops and entering data points into spreadsheets. Across the room, another group was stationed around a glowing geodesic dome that resembled a sort of alien igloo.

Troy emerged from the vivid white light of the structure with a megawatt smile. "Hey there, Kelsey!" he said. "Our rising star. Welcome to Area 51!"

In the middle of the nondescript warehouse, home of a futuristic technology hub, stood the brains that made all of it possible. The stage lighting shone down on Troy McCray, chief executive officer and hero to many.

Troy stood taller than he appeared onstage or in the endless videos of his public appearances that Kelsey reviewed. On the other hand, it could have been the natural swagger the CEO evoked with ease. Up close, she could see that Troy's signature T-shirt, which some people mistook for the kind that came wrapped in plastic packs of three, was made of premium cotton. Comfortable luxury. The mark of a man who was truly focused on his work.

Even without the aid of a stage or large screens, Troy maintained a larger than life aura. Kelsey reminded herself that she was no shrinking violet. She was capable of holding court with people of all types, world-renowned executives included.

"Why do you call it Area 51?" Kelsey managed to ask through her nervousness.

"Technically it's building number 50, but I thought Area 51 sounded better," he laughed. "Sarah, always good to see you. You've been in here before, right?"

"I can't say that I have," Sarah smiled. "It's an exciting day all around!"

"Always an exciting day at Elemynt," Troy said. "How about a tour?"

Kelsey was over the moon at the invitation to explore the technical marvels that lay before them. Hearing from Troy directly about his projects was the icing on a very thrilling cake.

"By the way, ladies," Troy paused. "I have to ask you to not tell anyone about this place, not even your fellow Myntors."

"My lips are sealed," Kelsey promised.

"Great!" Troy chuckled. "We don't want our lawyers to have to make a friendly visit to your desk. We're constantly inventing things here that will blow people's minds."

The warehouse and the wealth of imagination it contained were so secret that a fraction of a percentage of employees had access to it, Troy explained. Entrance to the hidden facilities usually required a lengthy additional non-disclosure agreement for the rare few who didn't work in the building to set foot in the door.

Troy strode toward the luminescent dome followed by Sarah and Kelsey who stared in awe at their surroundings. The researchers and technicians cleared the way for Troy to explore his million-dollar project.

"We're working on creating 3D avatars for our new VR product," he said. "You go in here and the cameras capture you from every angle at the same time. These guys load the images into software to get a composite image and out comes a perfect 360-degree simulation."

"Users are going to love this!" Kelsey exclaimed.

"Hold on. Not 'users.' People," Troy corrected her. "Elemynt affects the lives of real people every day. We can't forget who we're building this platform for."

Troy believed wholeheartedly in the company's mission to connect the world. His commitment to creating products that positively impacted the lives of those who interacted with them was one of the top reasons Kelsey joined the Elemynt team. If more tech companies operated with people top of mind, they would be much more beneficial to society and not just random tools or moneymakers for their founders. Kelsey took in with wide-eyed admiration the natural charmer brimming with charisma.

"See these sets?" Troy gestured. "We use 'em to get a sense of what it looks like when people use our products in their homes. Lots of trial runs where we get real people in here."

Troy talked proudly of his outstanding ventures. The CEO had more financial resources than he could spend in one lifetime. And yet, that didn't seem to be his motivation. Troy loved being at the head of his brainchild that hundreds of millions of people used daily. If given the choice between ten billion dollars or ten billion people using the Elemynt app, he would happily choose the latter.

"I know you're thinking to yourself 'how can we afford all this'," Troy waved to the room. "When we generate revenue, that's more capital we can invest in building out new technology. You're familiar with how advertising works on Elemynt?"

"It would be great to hear your perspective on it," Kelsey said.

Kelsey was thoroughly familiar with it. However, she couldn't resist the chance to hear Troy explain the system he built himself.

"We do online ads better than any other platform," Troy said proudly. "When people first join the app, they give us permission to use information from their account to show them ads they'll be most interested in. When you use Elemynt, you post, fave, share, add captions, and follow other people, right? Each of those actions is a marker that Elemynt collects. So, for example, if a lady starts following bridal accounts, we can connect her with wedding planners and cake makers and things like that."

"That's how my fiancé found my engagement ring," Sarah smiled. "An ad on Elemynt."

"Right on," Troy said. "The data from each account lets us create a detailed profile of a person. We always keep in mind that privacy is important to us and to the people who use the app."

Troy described how accounts were grouped into audience segments for security purposes. An advertiser could therefore target a group of people like moms in California, but not a specific account. Elemynt's advertising felt individualized to each person on the app because it only served ads that people would be interested in.

Local coffee shop owners could offer specials to potential customers in their area. A non-profit could promote a leukemia fundraiser to those interested in helping the cause. It was a far better system than ads on TV or on the internet that couldn't possibly be relevant to everyone who saw them.

Tens of thousands of businesses relied on Elemynt to connect directly with the customers most likely to purchase their products. People on the app were shown ads for items or services they were likely to or intended to buy anyway. Ads on Elemynt were a win for everybody.

The lasting connections businesses made with people were as valued as those made from person to person, Troy emphasized.

"And the ads are what keep Elemynt free," Kelsey added.

"Bingo!" Troy said.

"Rumor is the Ad Tech team is working on something bigger?" Sarah said.

"You're a smart cookie, Sarah," Troy smiled grandly. "In the meantime, Kelsey, you want to check out the latest and greatest? Give our 3D capture room a spin?"

Kelsey said yes before Troy could finish the sentence. While she was doing a great job maintaining her poise so far, inside Kelsey was fangirling hard. If Troy asked her to make one of the sets her home for a week, she would have packed her things posthaste and swiftly obliged.

She stepped inside the structure to find a fascinatingly complex framework of hundreds of tiny cameras pointed at the seat in the center. Once she settled in, the technicians outside called to her to evoke a range of emotions with her face.

"Let's see happy!"

Kelsey grinned from ear to ear. A flash of light.

"Excited!"

Big smiles from Kelsey. Another flash. So far, so good.

"Now do sad," the technician called out.

Kelsey tried her best to dampen her happiness.

"Sadder, please!"

It was hard for Kelsey to manage a "sad" face given her excitement but she tried her absolute best. Flash!

A gamut of emotions later, Kelsey emerged from the igloo with her face given the workout of its life. A few keystrokes and clicks later, a three-dimensional image of Kelsey appeared on the monitors. The flawless replica of her entire head completely floored her.

"That's awesome!" Kelsey said. "People are going to be all over this!"

Kelsey and Sarah congratulated Troy on another soon to be success. He excitedly ran through the details of how it was built and when it would go to market.

"There's no limit to what we can do with this," Troy said.

"Once it's ready, we'll have it on every news site and blog around the world," Sarah said.

Kelsey was chomping at the bit to make sure Sarah's forward-thinking proclamation came to life.

"Playing with the toys, I see," the unmistakable voice of Catherine said behind them.

The Boss Lady entered the warehouse unexpectedly followed by a pair of attentive assistants. Kelsey couldn't help but gasp. Years' worth of following Catherine's career made it a surreal experience to see the mogul standing right in front of her.

Kelsey unconsciously straightened herself up to match Catherine's impeccable posture and a chin held high with well-earned confidence.

The tailored blazer, collared shirt, and heels Catherine sported were out of sync with the dress of the technicians and engineers around her. Her elevated style served to put her on a higher plane than the rank and file Myntors. She was the chief operating officer... the boss. Her presence let those around her know as much without her ever having to say a word.

Catherine introduced her two executive assistants, Andrew and Jessica. The pair of fresh-faced Myntors was eternally grateful to be at the side of one of the world's most prominent executives. It was an immense honor that many people would give their left foot for. They held their phones at the ready for any requests the COO may have had. Kelsey surmised that it would take one slip-up for either to be replaced with another eager up-and-comer.

Catherine circled the 3-D capture structure. "The board will be very happy with the new potential revenue opportunities that emerge from this."

Troy agreed. "When they see what people do with this technology...how it changes how the world... man, they're gonna love it."

"Speaking of tech," Catherine said. "Product and Biz Dev are meeting this week to determine how to expand the staffing in the Live division so that we can have the necessary resources to stay on track for quarterly growth goals.

"Hire as many people as we need," Troy said.

"I'll pass that on to the Recruiting team," Catherine said. "Andrew, write that down."

Andrew, who had scribbled notes furiously since they entered, obliged. In the meantime, Sarah and Kelsey stood to the side witnessing the exchange between the two executives.

Seeing both Troy and Catherine in person in one day was a double whammy Kelsey had not mentally prepared herself for. They were the most iconic of industry icons. Two of the most celebrated thought leaders in tech. Where Troy was a visionary of life-changing innovations, Catherine was the business savant that could transform any idea into a profitable venture. The synergy and conflict between them served to make Elemynt the social media behemoth that it was. Kelsey was astounded seeing their collaborations unfold in real-time.

Sarah stepped in to formally greet Catherine. "Can I introduce you to Kelsey? She's new to the Comms team."

"Catherine, it's such an honor to meet you," Kelsey gushed.

Kelsey restrained herself from completely fawning over her shero. The eyes of the staff in the space were squarely on her.

"You are too kind," Catherine said, taking Kelsey's right hand in hers. "It's the support from my fellow women that motivates me to do more."

"Is it possible to get time on your calendar to talk through your vision for the Comms team?" Kelsey asked.

Kelsey took a gamble in asking for a private meeting with one of the busiest women in Silicon Valley. If there was any chance to talk with Catherine face to face, this was it. Kelsey hadn't advanced in her career by not taking risks. It was an audacious move that left Kelsey wondering whether she had crossed the line between employer and employee.

Catherine looked over her shoulder. "Andrew, what's next on the calendar?"

"You have the meeting with Legal at 4 p.m.," he said.

"Ravi had something came up with Biz Dev," Jessica added. "He'll need to reschedule."

"What about my 3 p.m.?" Catherine asked.

"On schedule in the executive conference room," Andrew replied. "I've called a campus car to meet us here at 2:50."

"That's ten minutes then?" Catherine said. "Kelsey, how would you like to meet now?"

The affirmative response was completely unexpected. Kelsey imagined that if Catherine said yes it would be for some time in the future. The newbie would have an opportunity to prepare notes or research questions or come prepared with a bit of experience under her belt to draw from. Kelsey's mouth instantly went dry.

"Go!" Sarah mouthed silently.

"Yes, now is perfect!" Kelsey said gratefully.

"Troy, I'll catch up with you soon," Catherine said with a wave. "Make sure you take good care of our property."

Catherine ushered Kelsey into a full recreation of a typical suburban home complete with furniture and details like bookshelves and artificial food stocked in the kitchen. Windows looked out at artificial views of a picturesque San Francisco while studio lights poured warmth into the ceiling-less room. They sat on the couch and armchair across from each other. For a minute, Kelsey felt as if she was invited into Catherine's home.

The assistants closed the prop door behind them.

"I wanted to ask..." Kelsey stumbled. "from your perspective... I mean. What's the best way to tell the story of Elemynt?"

Kelsey panicked slightly. She wondered if she put her words together correctly. Did Catherine think she was an idiot? Would she stop her without bothering to give an answer?

"Look within yourself," Catherine said sincerely. "Right now, you're feeling the same excitement I did when I began at Elemynt. There's possibility and opportunity wherever you look. You have to sort through that inspiration to find the best approach that feels right for you. Don't stray too far from the voice inside you."

"Hold on to that spark," Kelsey nodded. "Is that how you got to be an executive at the companies you've worked for?'

"You know, I pride myself on being a woman of action," Catherine said. "There's a world of people out there with dreams and ambitions. The difference between me and them is I make the plans to execute them and follow each step until I reach the goal. Making viable business strategies is one step. Following through is how you get to the top."

Catherine listened and spoke to Kelsey in a way that the newest Myntors had not experienced with other executives in the history of her career. Whereas most would be checking emails on their phone or consumed with unrelated thoughts of future meetings, Catherine engaged Kelsey in a deeply personal conversation. The COO's focus was exclusively on Kelsey and her needs. It was girl talk with one of the most powerful women in the country.

"I'll give you the secret to success here," Catherine said. "At Elemynt, you are measured on impact... how you affect the overall success of the company with your individual work. You are in External Comms. Your priority is going to be to get stories out that highlight our work here. What you need to do is to find a way to make your projects larger than life. Take routine processes to the next level with your ingenuity. How you go about that is up to you to figure out."

"Is that how you became the Boss Lady?" Kelsey asked.

"Being a woman in an industry dominated by men means we have to be smarter and achieve more than them," Catherine smiled knowingly. "There's quite a few who want to hold us back from operating at their level. Sometimes unconsciously, sometimes not. What's important is that we never forget how strong we are and that we have earned our place at every table."

There was a knock at the door. Andrew poked his head in.

"The car's here," he said.

Catherine acknowledged his update with a nod. She returned her attention to her enraptured colleague.

"Kelsey, remember to always trust your instincts," she said. "And if you find yourself falling short, remember we have massage therapists on call in Building 12."

With an earnest wave and reassuring smile, Catherine made her way out of the labyrinth of technology.

Kelsey was overwhelmed with joy that she, an employee with just a day and a half of work under her belt, had the opportunity to have a private audience with *Catherine Rowe*. Kelsey received a game plan for success directly from the COO, an incredible woman through and through. Catherine was not only the second-highest-ranking person in the entire company but the Boss Lady herself. Catherine genuinely wanted her to succeed.

Anyone else would have to rely on the words in Catherine's books to guide them. Kelsey was bestowed with personalized advice directly from the messenger that would inevitably fuel the rest of her career. She would treasure the invaluable advice forever for the rest of time. Kelsey could not wait to get started putting it to good use. She had to calm herself down and reorient before standing up from the couch.

When Kelsey returned to the open space outside of the home, she found Troy and Sarah speaking with Gary, Elemynt's VP of Product. The dad of two in the Patagonia fleece vest oversaw the team in the warehouse, in addition to the industry's finest product managers, engineers, and designers.

"I hope I didn't miss anything," Kelsey said to the engaged group.

"We're celebrating birthdays!" Troy said.

"Oh, is it your birthday?" Kelsey said exuberantly. "Happy, happy birthday!"

The trio laughed with each other at Kelsey's response. Kelsey was shaken with brief embarrassment. She was either not in on a joke or there was some miscommunication that flew over the head of the new girl. She had been doing so well.

Gary thankfully averted the awkward moment with an explanation. "Our in-product birthday feature... it's getting some upgrades. We want to up the number of people adding their birthdate to their profile so we have a better understanding of who's using our platform."

Elemynt's existing birthday feature was one of Kelsey's favorite parts of the app. If a person added their date of birth in their settings, the app showered their profile with digital confetti on their big day. It was a super cute way for the birthday guy or girl to share the happy moment with their followers. The feature was also a lifesaver. Like many others, Kelsey was guilty of forgetting friends' birthdays until she saw the confetti or they posted pics of them celebrating.

"You're gonna love the changes," Gary said to the group. "Instead of just the confetti, we're going to deliver a custom digital birthday cake in their inbox! We'll use special algorithms to determine what their favorite color is based on the colors that show up most often in the pictures they post."

"Okay, now that's pretty cool," Sarah said with Troy and Kelsey in complete agreement.

Gary excitedly continued describing what his teams had in store. "Second step is the app will identify their selfie with the most faves, put some balloon graphics around it, and push the photo to their follower's feeds. There'll also be a prompt under the image for people to send the account holder a birthday message. If they do that, the sender will get a digital slice of the birthday cake in their inbox."

"Geniuses," Troy said. "I have a bunch of geniuses working for me."

"Why thank you good, sir!" Gary laughed heartily.

Sarah was equally enthused. "If you have a birthday and you don't share it on social media, did you actually have a birthday?"

Kelsey could get behind the spectacular idea 100 percent. The best part of Elemynt was the connections people made by sharing their cherished moments. There was no better time to send love than on the biggest day of a person's year. The warmth and adrenaline rush that came with friends sending messages of congratulations would be welcome by the app's users.

"This is going to be very important for us," Troy said jovially. "When people put their birthday in their profile, we can do better at matching them with advertisers. We don't want retirement home ads being sent to teenagers or anything like that."

"And no acne cream for the elderly," Gary added.

"I'm thinking that's not something they'd be into," Troy laughed. "Advertisers will love it because they'll be able to target potential customers in specific age ranges with more accuracy. You want to sell to women in their 30s in Iowa? We got you covered. 18-year-olds in Pacoima who are fans of rock music? Hey, concert promoters, we got you too. We need to make sure that when we launch this product it gets the wide adoption we want to see."

As Troy outlined his vision, the wheels in Kelsey's head spun with ideas. They needed an ambitious press push that would match the scale of the new feature.

She wanted to make the all-important impact Catherine mentioned.

"What about celebrities?" Kelsey jumped in.

"What about them?" Sarah asked curiously.

"We encourage celebrities with upcoming birthdays to make sure they have the date added to their profile settings. If people see their favorite celeb using the new feature, they'll want to add their birthdate to their account too."

"I'm liking where this is going," Gary smiled.

Kelsey replayed the conversation in her head. She had to work harder, push further. Imagine what hadn't yet been created.

"It would be a full circle win!" Kelsey said excitedly. "When the celebrities' followers send them birthday messages, it will make them want to post more on the app because they're getting all this love. They become more active and their followers who want to see what they're up to will check in on the app more often. We do a whole press push about the biggest names who used the birthday feature and how Elemynt is connecting them with their fans. People see those news stories and they'll want to get it on the fun too!"

The cheers for Kelsey's idea rang through the expanse of the warehouse. Troy was the most pleased out of everyone.

"What did I tell you?" Troy said. "I have geniuses working for me."

"I'll say," Sarah concurred.

Troy and Gary stood off to the side to discuss how Kelsey's idea could sync with the product team's progress so far. Sarah had her own advice for Kelsey.

"If we're going to make this happen, you'll need to work with Jade Yamamoto, our head of media partnerships."

"Okay, what?" Kelsey gasped. "The Jade Yamamoto? Oh, my god."

Jade was a huge influencer on Elemynt with well over a million followers, including some of the most powerful players across multiple industries. She was one of the brightest social media stars to ever exist. Apparently, she now led a team at Elemynt. Kelsey was having a tremendous run of meeting luminaries to the point where she was almost dizzied by the experience.

"You can't go around her on this idea or you'll be in more trouble than you want," Sarah said. "Reach out to her E.A. and put time on her calendar if you can."

It took lengthy finagling with the assistant and two calls from Jon to get a meeting on Jade's schedule, but Kelsey was able to do so after days' worth of prompting. Kelsey had a game plan that started with a crucial first step.

* * *

It was immediately clear which desk belonged to Jade. Absent were the stark white workspace and the bulky black computer monitor that were standard issue for every Elemynt employee. In their place was a desk draped in turquoise sari fabric topped with dazzling mementos, awards, gold plaques, and a selection of framed photos of Jade with the most famous names in Hollywood. There was only one thing missing — Jade.

The area in the orbit of Jade's desk was far busier and more frenetic than the other buildings Kelsey visited up until that point. Unlike engineers, who sat at their desks quietly typing at code, the members of the team were actually talking to people. They hurriedly entered and exited meeting rooms and juggled multiple phones while holding conference calls with TV networks and entertainment executives.

Striding amongst the bustling Myntors was the woman in charge. Jade was a delight for the eye in her sleeveless, tangerine jumpsuit matched with cream and black Chanel sneakers. The outfit was more fabulous than anything Kelsey had seen in her time so far at Elemynt.

"Hi, gorgeous!" Jade said with outstretched arms. "I appreciate a girl who wears heels on a weekday. You are here to *work*, darling!"

The two women exchanged air kisses and a first-meeting hug. Two seconds in Jade's presence and Kelsey was completely enchanted by the woman before her. She was the embodiment of her all-star social media presence.

"Don't mind me, I'm a slouch," Jade said.

She was anything but. The bauble necklace draped across her clavicle glinting in the fluorescent lights told a different story.

"Is now still a good time?" Kelsey asked.

"It certainly is," Jade said. "My E.A. told me you'd been calling and if there's one thing I admire, it's persistence. You do understand that we'll have to walk and talk?"

Kelsey could see why getting a meeting with Jade was difficult. As Elemynt's Head of Global Media Partnerships, she was at the helm of the company's ongoing efforts to court celebrities and influencers to use the platform. Her team of partner managers worked to build and maintain relationships with the brightest stars in the social media universe. Her calendar was full with amazing conversations and enviable deals.

The weighty role was perfectly suited for Jade considering she was born into the entertainment life. She inherited the stage presence and timeless glamour of her actress mother, a darling of Japanese cinema turned film auteur. Her father was a music executive who transformed unknowns into worldwide superstars. Her three siblings all worked in Hollywood in some capacity. Jade was destined to be a star in her own right.

At a young age, Jade set her career in motion with a well-placed internship at a Southern California movie studio. She worked diligently through a succession of roles over a decade before stepping into a lead position at Creative Talent Agency. The legendary entertainment and media company represented the industry's most illustrious names. Jade was at the top of the institution, building and accelerating the careers of a wide spectrum of talents.

As Elemynt blossomed into a favorite among mainstream celebrities, Troy needed an executive who was well regarded in the entertainment industry to be the ambassador for his platform. To say it was the role of a lifetime was an understatement. Jade was handed the opportunity to rocket the overwhelmingly popular app into another stratosphere.

Kelsey followed Jade as she traveled from desk to desk doling out the day's marching orders to each of her team members. Her directives were capped with an encouraging smile that affirmed that she wholeheartedly believed in their capabilities. Elemynt was packed with incredible women.

"We help politicians win voters," Jade said of her team's responsibilities. "We get musicians number one albums. We fill stadiums and arenas with fans who document the experiences on the app which, of course, creates more fans out of their followers. A lot of those clever ideas you see out there from the most engaged talent on the app? They came from this area."

"And Elemynt does all this for free?" Kelsey asked in bewilderment.

"Yes, of course!" Jade exclaimed. "We're here to inspire them to be their best selves on Elemynt. Every partner we work with strengthens our collective knowledge about what works best on social media. These wonderful people here think through a range of possible strategies and come up with tailored suggestions for each partner we work with."

"How do you even keep up with all the partners?" Kelsey asked. "You're talking a huge number of people."

"We organize them into verticals. There's music, movies, sports, news, celebrities, politics, online influencers, and…" Jade counted her fingers. "Ah, civic influencers. Don't tell those guys I forgot about them. That includes your activists, civil rights organizations, thought leaders… people involved in offline and online communities."

Details of the most influential people in social media were kept from the public. Information regarding the actual behind-the-scenes work of the Media team was a closely guarded secret. Time was ticking in Kelsey's meeting with Jade but she wanted badly to know more about how the operation worked. Jade was open to sharing with her colleague as long as they kept moving.

"My Music leads work with the reps of every artist who's been on the Billboard or iTunes charts. Sports has every major league and the players in them. Celebrities? Well, that's an insane amount of people."

"I can't imagine!" Kelsey said. "But how do you figure out who's a celebrity?"

"Excellent question. We have this grading system that works wonders for us. The partner managers rank the talent from 'A' to 'D' based on their latest projects, buzziness in the news, and, a lot of times, gut instinct. Where people are in their career fluctuates so every now and then we go in and reassess the rankings."

"To make sure people are getting the right amount of attention."

"It's hard work but we're up for the challenge."

She picked up a magazine from a nearby desk and flipped through it.

"Obviously if you're J-Lo or Beyoncé, you're going to be an 'A+.'," Jade explained. "If you're on that level, the Partnership team will drop whatever they're doing to help you out with anything you need. If your team calls at 3 a.m., we're picking up the phone with a smile. If you're a 'B,' you might have a new album or movie out, but you're not super A-list. You'll get invites to our cool events maybe or access to new products. A 'C' grade is like okay, we have your agent's contact info. If we get an email from them, we'll get to it if we can. But that's a big if. You should see our inboxes! If you're a 'D', so sorry, but you're probably not going to get an email back, if you even have our email at all."

"Wow, that's harsh," Kelsey said.

"True. But also so necessary, darling," Jade sighed. "We're a small team and we have every influential person in the world looking to work with us. It's terrible, I know, but there are people out there we won't be able to help. Oh and P.S. don't share my email externally unless you absolutely need to."

Kelsey wouldn't dream of upending the relative anonymity of Jade's true reach. Kelsey was tickled knowing that they were on different sides of the communications spectrum. Her email was full of journalists requesting quotes and exclusive insight. Jade's was filled with agents and talent managers seeking exclusive partnerships that would set their clients apart from the rest. Either way, Elemynt and its employees were hot commodities. They were women in demand.

"There's also this lovely process called verification," Jade said while peering around at her team. "A blue checkmark we put next to their username. It's to keep people from impersonating the famous accounts. You see the checkmark, you know you're following the right person. I'm sure you've guessed by now there's something in it for us too."

Jade retrieved her laptop from her desk. Kelsey looked over her shoulder at the thousands of lines containing the most famous names in the world. The letter grade adjacent to each verified account told the story of the person's fame with a single character. Following that were stats like how often they engaged, the last time they logged in, and how many photos they posted in a month. The existence of that level of information was jaw-dropping. There was no way possible it would be allowed to get beyond the walls of the company. The world would freak.

"Yes, we're swimming in data," Jade said, reading her mind. "I can't tell you how much it helps us know where we should focus our efforts."

Elemynt was first and foremost a tech company. It made sense that there would be data-driven muscle behind every facet of its operation. Kelsey was proud to be a part of a company using its cutting-edge technology to decide how to empower people.

"Verification used to be about making sure people weren't being impersonated and it's still very that," Jade said. "But it's become this big thing having a checkmark. Everyone wants their fame acknowledged. Where people got the idea that a little check is the difference between being famous or not, I'll never know. People are telling my team all the time 'I have this many followers' or 'somebody made a fake account with my name'. But it's not about the number of followers you have or how many accounts are impersonating you."

Jade stopped short of detailing what the exact requirements for verification were. Some secrets she had to keep within her team.

Kelsey would have loved to be verified but she wouldn't admit that to Jade. She was just meeting her and didn't want to come off too strong out of the gate. Besides, Kelsey had a bigger question to ask Jade that, with all the confidential hoopla, she still hadn't been able to get to.

The crux of their work was splashy partnerships around tentpole events like album releases, award shows, elections, and championships. For new product and feature launches, the partner managers matched influencers with what they'd be most interested in before it went to market. Minor issues like mitigating loss passwords and hacked accounts were fast-tracked to admins in another department to resolve. In total, the partnership strategies provided a holistic relationship with the talent who drove much of the engagement on the app.

"It's a win-win-win situation," Jade said. "The celebs are happy because they get to use a fab product that gets them more visibility. The fans are happy because they get closer to their favorite celebrity. Elemynt wins because the exchanges and engagement are happening on our platform."

The breadth of the Media team's influence was far deeper than Kelsey imagined. What began as what she thought was a simple request — get some celebrities evolved in a press campaign — turned on to be the tip of a glacier with further ramifications hiding beneath the surface.

Jade paused at the entrance to an unoccupied hallway. "I'm sure you have a ton of places to be today but before you go...come with me."

What was on the other side of the unassuming door almost caused Kelsey to faint. A closet the size of a bedroom was packed to the brim with rows of jewelry, perfumes, home accessories, and beauty products set on mirror-backed shelves. Dresses from a range of the most recognizable names in fashion were draped artfully on hangers. Racks of shoes in every hue of the rainbow were meticulously organized by color. A collection of designer sunglasses that rivaled the cases of major department stores was on display next to luscious evening clutches, sparkling minaudières, and luxurious handbags in every conceivable color and texture.

In the middle of it all was a vanity mirror with the most impeccable lighting. A pair of luxe white leather and chrome chairs were placed alongside it for soaking in the breathtaking view of the wondrous display.

"Welcome to my little slice of heaven!" Jade said proudly.

The lavishness of the space took Kelsey completely by surprise. Kelsey's closet at home was by no means lacking but this was magnificent and in the recesses of the otherwise nondescript building at a tech company of all places.

"I know you're asking yourself why would this crazy woman build a closet for herself in the middle of an office building with questionably beige walls?" Jade said, gesturing toward the world outside the closet door. "Elemynt, for one. Two:

my followers."

Jade's highly visible presence as head of Partnerships at Elemynt and the span of her career before joining garnered her more than one million followers to date. They praised her unique fashion sense and she was known to stay ahead of trends. One photo of Jade in an up-and-coming designer's outfit or wearing a newly released shoe and her comments were filled with people asking where she got it. Her selections were copied by other influencers on Elemynt and featured in fashion websites or magazines.

The range of items housed in the closet was the result of various PR companies looking to promote new products and retailers. One photo sent to Jade's more than a million followers and the item was likely to sell out.

"Anyway, the people on my team were tripping over steamer trunks filled with shoes and there was enough La Mer to cause a fire hazard. Troy wanted me to have a space to keep everything. I came in one day and there's this. Cute right?"

"Very!" Kelsey said cheerfully.

"I know they think I'm the influencer when truth is, I'm here to make the influencers shine. Also, most of it I give away to the interns."

Jade regarded herself with humility and yet knew full well that she was one of the most influential people in the world. She deserved the closet and much more.

Jade handed Kelsey an Elemynt branded tote bag. "Fill it up with whatever you'd like."

"Are you serious?" Kelsey exclaimed. "Thank you so much! I don't... like where do I start?"

Kelsey reeled back her enthusiasm so she didn't look too silly in front of Jade. She scanned the rows of shoes before selecting a pair of black slingback heels. She selected from an array of makeup palettes in shimmering colors on the dresser and wonderful scented candles. She also added a pair of cat-eye sunglasses and a brushed leather handbag to match. Though she wanted to stuff the entire room in the tote, Kelsey was careful not to be too greedy. Keep it professional.

While Kelsey made her selections, Jade reached for a gilded photo frame under the vanity mirror.

"The most important people in my life," Jade said. "Worth more than all the jewelry in the world."

"Aw, your family!" Kelsey said as she took a seat next to her.

On the left side of the photo was a fair-haired gentleman who would fit right in in Connecticut.

"This is my husband Todd," she pointed. "And these are my twin daughters Sophie and Stella. They're the loves of my life."

Kelsey recognized the cute twosome from Jade's posts on the app. "They're social media stars too!"

"On Elemynt, it's never too early to be a superstar," Jade smiled. "Mommy runs their account for them. If it were up to them, they'd post hundreds of pictures a day!"

Jade spoke wistfully of how she balanced work, two children, and a home life. A lot of dedication went into Jade's accomplishments at Elemynt. She made sacrifices of her own time and work-life balance to elevate the digital lives of thousands of people and by extension the millions of people who followed her.

Kelsey didn't want to interrupt — all of what Jade said was a life lesson wrapped up in fabulosity. However, Kelsey was aching to ask her to help involve her celebrity connections in an Elemynt birthday campaign. Without Jade's involvement, Kelsey's big idea would go unrealized. She had an excruciating decision to make. Get to know one of the coolest people on campus or get straight to the point.

Kelsey seized a chance to jump in. "If I could just—"

"I'm so sorry!" Jade scrolled through incoming messages on her phone. "All this time and we didn't get down to business. And I am running behind. Let me see when we can schedule another sync, okay?"

"This will only take a second, I promise," Kelsey said eagerly.

The thought of losing out on the opportunity that she fought hard to get cracked Kelsey's heart in half. Jade could see the anguish in her face. She seemed to admire Kelsey's spunk and tenacity, two traits that she perhaps saw in herself as well.

"I'll give you two minutes, darling," Jade responded.

Kelsey rattled off a speedy but very coherent pitch tailored to Jade's current strategies. Encouraging talent to engage around their birthdays would in turn net them tons of engagement from their fans. The campaign was a win for Elemynt and Jade's team because it would increase the number of celebs using the app. Finally, connecting with celebrities on a personal level would inspire people who followed them to use Elemynt in similar ways. The ask was an easy lift and sufficiently scalable. All Kelsey needed was Jade's blessing. She hoped to heaven she would get it.

Jade pondered Kelsey's pitch. The team was stretched thin as it was. The ask would require a significant time commitment. Whether it would add to their existing partnerships or distract from them was a serious consideration.

Finally, Jade smiled.

"Get me a list of everyone you'd like to see be a part of this," Jade smiled. "Feel free to think big."

"Fantastic!" Kelsey said with delight. "I'll categorize them by their number of followers if that makes it easier for you to decide who to pitch."

"And rank them by who you want the most," Jade said. "The more streamlined we can make this process, the faster the partner managers can get these asks through."

"Oh my gosh, Jade, thanks for your time!" Kelsey said. "And for the gifts!"

"Wait one second," Jade stopped her. "One more thing before you go…"

Kelsey earnestly hoped that it wasn't bad news or a crazy caveat.

"We have to take a selfie!" Eva exclaimed.

Kelsey breathed an imperceptible sigh of relief. Of course, she had time for a selfie!

The ladies hugged and snapped a photo together to commemorate what Kelsey estimated to be a newfound friendship. Two women with similar goals and passions working side by side.

Jade expertly breezed through the steps of posting the pic to the Elemynt app. Almost instantly, Kelsey received a deluge of notifications on her phone of new followers thanks to Jade's post.

Kelsey felt a sharp pang of panic. The realization of the sudden spotlight she cast herself under made her question whether she made a foolhardy choice. In pursuing her idea, Kelsey took on an ambitious project for a major product launch complete with big-name stars and a global rollout. She was told by several seasoned Myntors that she would need two months or more to get acclimated to the Elemynt environment. Kelsey was ambitious right out of the gate. If the campaign wasn't successful, it could jeopardize her future projects at the company and her reputation with her colleagues.

It was too late to turn back.

FOUR

Kelsey breathed in the crisp morning air that blew across Elemynt's stunningly picturesque roof deck. The greenspace was meticulously landscaped with gorgeous foliage and swaths of perfectly manicured grass. Trees blew graciously in the wind next to vibrant plant life. The oasis spanned a stretch of connected buildings and was as long as several city blocks.

The view from several stories up was an uninterrupted vista of the rooftops of Palo Alto on one side and, on the other, the still waters of the San Francisco Bay meeting the sky-blue horizon. Despite the peaceful surroundings, Kelsey attempted to shake off her nerves. Her big idea had run into a major snag.

Kelsey hewed closely to Jade's suggestion, drafting a list of celebrities with coming birthdays that could be a part of the Elemynt campaign. She designed it to be as easy to read as possible to reduce drag time miscommunication could cause. Before she delivered the requests to the Head of Partnerships, she shared the list with Jon and Sarah to review.

"This is fantastic, Kelsey!" Sarah responded first. "One thing though. I'm seeing a lot of white people on this list? Can you add some black or Hispanic or Asian names? Make sure they are celebrities with fans that are mostly from their same ethnic background. Minority markets are important to us."

"Yes, think on that if you can," Jon replied to the email thread. "We need to use every opportunity we can to show we care about these communities."

The unexpected additional task threw Kelsey off. She understood why Jon and Sarah would add the extra requirement but didn't know where to start. She diligently began her attempt to extend the list by typing out the names of celebrities from different races that she could think of. However, despite her best attempts, she kept coming up with famous names that didn't specifically cater to the communities of their same race as Sarah said they should.

Kelsey tried using a search engine to find black celebrities who made movies for black people. Hispanic music stars who sang in Spanish. The results were helpful but not really. Kelsey didn't recognize most of the names. She needed to know if they were legitimately famous before she passed the list on to Jade. Her colleague was already extraordinarily gracious with her time. Adding unnecessary steps to the process would lessen the likelihood the campaign would get off the ground. Getting it right the first time around was critical.

A eureka moment led Kelsey to an obvious solution. She sent a message on eChat to Daniela, the Head of Diversity Comms, who she heard speak at orientation. The personal story she shared about her hair and her Hispanic background was lovely. Kelsey had been meaning to connect with her anyway since that day. And thus, Kelsey found herself on top of a roof gazing at the morning sky.

Daniela's Commynt profile listed that she loved running, a passion the two shared. Kelsey surmised that a brisk morning walk would be a step above any meeting room on Elemynt's campus.

"Ready for a 10K run?" Daniela kidded as she jogged up to Kelsey.

"I have my shoes laced up!" Kelsey laughed. "Let's go for it!"

"There's plenty of space for it up here, right?" Daniela said with a nod to the breathtaking expanse. "Let's start with a light walk though and see where the day takes us. How about it?"

The warm confidence Daniela exuded at orientation was magnified in the halo of the morning sun. Her natural curls were pulled back with a hair tie which framed her exotic features. She was picture-perfect amongst the greenery around them.

"This place is fantastic," Daniela smiled. "Like a tropical getaway. No passport required!"

"If they mentioned a roof deck at orientation, I would've been here on day two!" Kelsey said happily.

"There's no place like Elemynt!" Daniela said.

The ladies began their walk along the path past the small enclaves of chairs with employees working on their laptops. A small gathering of Myntors practiced the lotus pose on an arrangement of pastel yoga mats atop the verdant lawn. Every plant, rock, and tree selected by the Horticulture Team contributed to the mosaic of tranquility in the middle of Silicon Valley.

Daniela's Commynt profile gave Kelsey a basic understanding of her colleague's background. Undergrad at American University where she double majored in communication and women's studies. Master's degree in organizational communication from New York University followed by a role at a public relations firm in Chicago.

Most of Daniela's family lived in South Florida, including her architect father, her mother who was a corporate interior designer, and her one brother and two sisters. Daniela's earliest photo in her Commynt feed was of her proud family at a festive send-off for her first day at Elemynt. Since her start at the company two years prior, she continually shared exuberant photos that included Myntors from a range of nationalities and ethnicities, possibly as part of her role as Head of Diversity Communications.

Kelsey anticipated, given her role, that Daniela would be open to helping incorporate a diversity component into her proposed birthday campaign for the app. However, Kelsey was worried that her request would come off as racially insensitive. Petitioning her new colleague to suggest diverse celebrities was an awkward ask on their first meeting. Rather than barrel in head first, Kelsey did what made the journalists she spoke with most comfortable before she made her pitch — getting to know them on a personal level first.

"Your speech at orientation was so moving," Kelsey said as they paced along. "I know everyone else in the room was as excited to hear it as I was."

"Aw, thank you!" Daniela said cheerily. "I sometimes sub for the Head of Diversity at orientation if he's busy. Scott usually speaks in front of every incoming group of employees but he couldn't make that week."

"I'm sure he's great but, wow, hearing you remind us to bring our true selves to work was a great way to start a first day."

"You're too sweet!" Daniela beamed. "Scott is fantastic though. He does a lot of our public-facing things like media interviews and speaking on conference panels. His main responsibility is advising the Dream Team. The execs are looking to build out more programs here focused on diversity and inclusion."

"And your role is to share with the public what the Diversity Team is doing," Kelsey confirmed.

"Mostly that, yeah," Daniela said. "My team's main focus is creating a welcoming environment at Elemynt for people from all backgrounds. They also collaborate with community leaders on events for underrepresented groups and direct resources to nonprofits dedicated to diversity. The stories I pitch to the press are usually about that last part."

"Sounds like a lot of fun!" Kelsey said.

"Girl, I wish it was," Daniela shook her head. "Diversity is literally one of the most controversial issues going on at this place. We get pushback from the public who says Elemynt isn't a diverse place to work... which it isn't compared to the diversity of people on our platform. On the flip side, we get flak from employees and managers who think diversity is unnecessary or shouldn't be a priority."

Kelsey was taken aback that having a workforce with people from different backgrounds would be a heavy topic at Elemynt. Kelsey thought she may have been in the harder role between the two of them since she took on communications for the whole company. But her responsibilities were by no means controversial.

"We're trying to strike a balance when it comes to representation," Daniela explained. "The research team here did a study recently. It showed that Black and Hispanic people are overrepresented in terms of the number of people on the app. What's interesting is they also engage two to three times more than any other group."

"I had no idea!" Kelsey exclaimed.

"Most people don't," Daniela shrugged. "The goal for my team is to make sure the people who use the app represented internally. I wish I could say that was going smoothly. Look around you. What do you see? Mostly white and Asian guys, right?"

Sure enough, the Myntors scattered about the roof-deck were similar in demographic. Kelsey couldn't help but stifle a laugh. There were ten guys in hoodies within a stone's throw. Kelsey could see Daniela's point.

"We're doing our best to bring some more color here, I promise," Daniela said optimistically. "The unfortunate thing is we keep running into is the company is made up of employees who mostly went to the same schools and worked at the same companies and live in similar neighborhoods. That makes it hard for diverse candidates to break through those social circles and land a job if they don't have a connection in the same way. It's hardest for Black and Latinx applicants, which is part of the reason why there's so few of us here."

"So, your team wants to change the way Elemynt works on recruiting talent?" Kelsey said.

"Something like that," Daniela mused. "I look at it this way. You know how there are lots of different plants up here on the roof deck? Imagine if there were only two types of plants. Wouldn't be too bad, probably. It would still be pretty. What makes this place beautiful is that there's a huge variety of plant life. Diversity makes the mundane spectacular. But it takes work and cultivating to make that happen."

Daniela spoke with an ease that came from caring about the mission of her job. She was passionate about it on a personal level, probably because she was Hispanic. Being from an underrepresented background drove Daniela to help people like her.

As they continued along the path, Daniela confided in Kelsey the difficulties of pitching stories to journalists about diversity at Elemynt. The general consensus from the public was that Elemynt was a "white bread" company. Senior leadership was eager to dismantle that sentiment quickly. Elemynt was only as good as its reputation. In response, the Diversity Team received what amounted to a blank check to launch internal and external programs that amended existing perceptions.

The support from higher-ups created an ideal scenario for Daniela. The efforts of the team increased the number of positive stories she could seed with the press. There was still the matter of changing internal attitudes, which sounded to Kelsey like an uphill battle.

"There's too many people think of affirmative action when they hear 'diversity'," Daniela said. "It's not about numbers or quotas. We just want our hiring managers to put a little more effort into being inclusive across different categories of underrepresented people."

Kelsey wasn't sure they should be talking about heavy issues right out of the gate. The sun was shining, the birds were chirping. The other employees around them were having a fun, relaxing morning. Still, what Daniela was saying was important to her so Kelsey continued to listen.

"Elemynt has hired a lot more women lately," Kelsey said. "Congrats on that."

"Thanks! It's exciting right?" Daniela said. "Women+, which is our group for female employees, and Pride+ for LGBTQ Myntors are our largest employee resource groups. Right now, a third of the employees at Elemynt are women. That's ways less than men, obviously, but at a company of 20,000 people, that's a lot of women to support each other. We have a ways to go in our other categories, but I love a good challenge."

Kelsey wrinkled her nose at the thought of having to deal with the complexities of Daniela's position. She tackled both internal and external advocacy on a contentious issue that required tailored messaging for every side. A tall order for any Comms professional. Daniela seemed to handle it with grace which Kelsey found infinitely admirable.

"Our big thing right now is connecting our ERGs with popular celebrities and influencers on the app that share their background," Daniela said excitedly. "Black celebrities with black employees and so on doing community events and partnerships. We get good press out of those. The only thing we have to be careful about is not making it seem like we're pandering to either side."

Therein lay the conundrum for Kelsey. For her birthday campaign to take off, she needed the celebrities who weren't white to be a visible part of it. She also didn't want to intrude on minority communities. Kelsey was just about to ask Daniela for her suggestions for people that she should include, but if there ever was an inopportune time to do it, following that statement was it.

Daniela and Kelsey continued their stroll, talking and laughing and getting to know each other more. Daniela was a genuine spirit who Kelsey found herself wanting to get to know more about. The pair arrived at the furthest end of the roof deck where a glass-enclosed juice bar welcomed them. Kelsey eyed the many options of fruity favorites and shot cups of ginger and wheatgrass. Like everything at Elemynt, the price was one swipe of her badge.

After brief consideration, Kelsey opted for one of her favorites — kale and green apple. Daniela clasped an electric yellow blend of mango and banana, accented by a polka-dot paper straw.

"It's my girlfriend's favorite," Daniela said. "I work long hours so if I'm missing her, I'll have something that reminds me of her."

"How cute is that!" Kelsey said.

"Sorry, I'm a sap," Daniela chuckled.

"No, no, we all are sometimes. What's her name?"

"Ro, short for Rosalind," Daniela smiled, a wash of happiness over her face. "Mi princesa Dominicana."

Daniela spoke lovingly about their first encounter at an art collective show in Oakland where Ro was the DJ. Daniela watched her expertly spin the turntables, pumping up the crowd. She described how the glow of the laptop highlighted Ro's chiseled features and bronze West Indian complexion. Daniela was instantly smitten with the gorgeous woman. She couldn't help but lock eyes with Ro from across the room. In return, she received the occasional smile in return while the music pulsed along.

"I didn't know what to say," Daniela shrugged. "All I could think of was to request a song from her."

Daniela kept coming back to the monthly event, each time requesting a different tune from the DJ before returning to the opposite side of the room where her friends waited. Neither woman made the first move. After the fourth event in a row with the same result, Ro finally rushed up to Daniela outside the venue as she was leaving. Ro confessed that she was too nervous to say anything more than "okay" to the beautiful woman who came to the party every month. Ro finally asked her out on the date that Daniela hoped for since they first laid eyes on each other. A series of romantic excursions followed and within a short time, they became inseparable.

"And she's my girlfriend to this day," Daniela beamed. "It's good to come home to someone who loves you."

"Oh, I totally agree." Kelsey said. "Cheers to that!"

They clinked their plastic cups to toast each other. Kelsey loved romance and it was clear that her colleague was all in. She ruminated on the story while Daniela snagged a ginger shot for the road.

An older woman behind the counter clad in an Elemynt green apron and hairnet waved her way. "Hola, Daniela! Que tal?"

"Estoy disfrutando esta deliciosa bebida que hicieron," Sarah responded in quickfire Spanish.

The lively exchange between Daniela and the worker went on for several minutes, leaving Kelsey confused. Her only option was to stand by idly watching a conversation underway in a language she did not speak. Kelsey sipped her dwindling juice until the exchange concluded.

Daniela waved her goodbyes to the woman behind the counter. "Muchísimas gracias, bella!"

Kelsey and Daniela navigated to one of the sets of patio chairs that overlooked the easternmost part of campus to rest.

"A friend of yours?" Kelsey asked.

"She's literally one of the coolest people I know," Daniela said.

Daniela paused. Kelsey sensed a sudden hesitancy from Daniela as if she was burdening their friendly talk with more not so great news.

"What is it?" Kelsey asked.

"Luz and I met about a year ago," Daniela said. "A group of Myntors got together to talk about how to get more benefits for contractors. We're doing what we can to change it up. It's not much of a fair system we have right now."

Daniela explained that contract employees at Elemynt often had comparable

①amalgamation of diff tech cos
—google, Fb, Insta

roles and responsibilities to their full-time employee counterparts. The defining difference was that contractors were hired through third-party agencies for six months to a year at a time. Because of the dual system at Elemynt, contractors were frequently paid lower salaries for similar work and were not afforded the same benefits as FTEs. They were excluded from receiving high-quality health insurance, paid family leave, and access to company-wide meetings like all-hands. Contractors' work agreements were also being renewed for years on end with promises from managers that they would ultimately be converted to full-time.

The main issue of concern according to Daniela was the outsized volume of contract workers at the company. About forty percent of Elemynt employees were contractors, a number that did not include the many more workers in facilities, food service, security, and transportation. Hispanic Myntors made up less than one percent of full-time employees but 35 percent of contractors.

"It can be hard for a lot of my brown brothers and sisters here but we keep a tight community going," Daniela said with what Kelsey came to understand was her trademark optimism. "The Latin+ group has get-togethers and happy hours all the time so we can stay connected and have a little fun outside of work. We also put on some of those community events I told you about. We're a family within a family."

Hearing more stories about minorities and the problems they faced made Kelsey increasingly uneasy about making her pitch. She continued to dance around the question until Daniela broached the subject with no hesitation.

"By the way... your campaign? It's okay to just ask," she said.

Kelsey brightened at the opportunity. "It would be great to have some of the diverse people you talked about being a part of it."

"I'm cool with it as long as our partners don't end up feeling like they're being taken advantage of," Daniela underscored. "People of color know when companies are using us for our skin color."

"Nothing like that at all," Kelsey said. "It's like you said. The more diverse plants, the better."

"Why don't we do this?" Daniela chuckled. "I can give you some names of influencers to add to your list, no problem. After you make the connections, I'll follow through to make sure we're establishing lasting relationships with them. Whatever we can do to promote the diversity on the platform, I'm all for."

"We're in business then! You and Jade are the absolute best!"

"When you have amazing co-workers, anything's possible," Daniela smiled.

* * *

Kelsey found herself bouncing with joy down the hallways and walkways of the Elemynt campus. What started as a simple idea weeks ago — encourage celebrities to use and promote the app's new birthday feature — turned into a worldwide phenomenon.

With Jade's help, 20 different big stars from a range of verticals shared their digital celebrations with their fans. The big names gushed about the delightful graphics, the custom virtual cake, and the ability for people to send them birthday messages. As Kelsey predicted, scores of their followers added their birthday date to their profile's settings so they too could enjoy the fun on their big day.

What Kelsey did not expect, however, was for the press coverage around the new feature to take off as fast as it did. Nearly every major news publisher in America gushed about Elemynt's adorable new surprise. The stunning response from the media led to a 400 percent increase in people entering their birthday on the app. Not only that, the data teams discovered that Elemynt users who added their birthday information were found to be twice or three times more engaged with the app in the following weeks.

The success was more outstanding than Kelsey could have possibly imagined. She was overwhelmed with pride in herself and her ability to execute her fresh idea. Kelsey came to Elemynt to excel and she had done so by knocking her first major press campaign out of the park. The achievement represented well her commitment to a company that empowered ordinary people to create exceptional moments.

The feedback Kelsey received from her colleagues also contributed to the spring in her step. Her manager Jon lauded her accomplishment in meetings big and small. Jade and Daniela effusively congratulated her for a job well done on an extraordinary collaborative effort. Receiving the adoration of her colleagues made Kelsey feel like even more of a winner.

With encouragement from Jon and support from Sarah, Kelsey forged a path to further place Elemynt on the top of a media pedestal. Kelsey's position on the influential External Comms team allowed her to flex her PR muscle in ways she never had before. When Kelsey came calling with pitches, journalists responded immediately, grateful for the elusive access to the company's spokespeople.

Kelsey continually landed stories in the press about new products and the visionary minds at Elemynt. She negotiated with culture magazines to write trend stories on the evolution of the app. A front-page article on teen influencers becoming overnight success stories on Elemynt was a viral hit online. Cover stories featuring Gary as the preeminent thought leader in product and Catherine as the woman who had it all were accompanied by glowing reviews of the star company.

Kelsey's influence was everywhere, from digital publications to TV to long-standing print media. She poured herself into her work and the results were nothing less than amazing.

Taking the time to ramp up toward success would have been fine for anyone else. Kelsey was content with diving in headfirst and making the biggest splash right away.

Whenever possible, Kelsey sat near the center spot of conference room tables during meetings to maintain a strong physical presence among her peers. She was always ready with some way of contributing to the conversation, either with suggestions or a thought-provoking question. Kelsey took notes on technical concepts she didn't understand, then later researched details to elevate her knowledge of the matter. The next time the concept came up in conversation, Kelsey could talk about it fluently as if she had always been well-versed on the topic.

Kelsey established mutually gratifying working relationships with journalists hungry to speak directly with a company spokesperson. They adored that she rationed access to executives for their interviews. In turn, the press wrote favorable stories about Elemynt to maintain the access that separated their reporting from that of their peers.

Kelsey was an email machine, using her best asset - time management- to sort through tasks and requests at lightning speed. Her ability to nail down many different projects at once was the result of ruthless prioritization. She rolled out press campaigns with an acumen that matched Sarah and Jon's years-long skill set.

In every video conference with the team, Jon went out of his way to congratulate Kelsey on her work.

"Let's see how far we can push it," Jon would say. "We win when we think bigger."

Kelsey was able to scale her efforts more easily than she anticipated. Rather than reach out to hundreds of news organizations for smaller but important company announcements, she and the team made increased use of Elemynt's official blog. Each missive was carefully crafted to include quotable tidbits from start to finish. Media outlets copied and pasted the words, no comment from the Comms team necessary.

Elemynt was set on growing its engagement numbers, yet it didn't purchase a single advertisement. It didn't need to. The media did all their advertising for them by publishing scores of stories about the cool new platform that everyone needed to be on. There was barely a publication on Earth that didn't mention the company's genius.

The press campaigns led to increased visibility of company efforts, positive media placement, and upward engagement from people on the app. Kelsey owed a large part of her success to Elemynt for being a fantastic product. It wasn't a hard sell to get first-rate coverage of the company when everything it did was captivating and exciting.

Weeks at Elemynt turned into months. The more time went on, the more Kelsey felt like an old pro. Each energizing day was better than the last.

Kelsey couldn't have reached the level of success she had in her role without the continued support of Jon and Sarah. Jon, while frequently on international trips meeting with local movers and shakers, was always communicative via email or video chat. They held regularly scheduled one-on-one meetings where Kelsey bounced story ideas off of her manager. He responded with ways to make them better or gave her the go-ahead to execute, with few questions asked.

Sarah was always by Kelsey's side to offer advice or tag team on specific projects. In the few cases where Kelsey couldn't figure out which direction to take, Sarah filled her in on the institutional knowledge necessary to push through. Sarah was a sensational colleague and a sister.

Kelsey took satisfaction in doing so well, so quickly. At the start, the new Myntor did not know for sure how she would fare in a company many times larger than her previous employer. The additional boosts of support from Daniela and Jade during their hangouts together imparted confidence in all areas of her life. Kelsey gave herself occasional pep talks to remind herself of her ability to accomplish anything she set out to do.

* * *

After another long day of communicating with press, Kelsey decided to finally take advantage of the campus' amenities. She was long overdue for a relaxing mani-pedi. Kelsey was thankfully able to snag a last-minute reservation at the

Elemynt spa in Building 12. She would return to work with fresh hands and a winning attitude.

Kelsey invited Jade to join her for the indulgence. The always-on-the-go manager and her newest friend responded "yes" without hesitation.

Kelsey stood at the reception desk in awe of the full list of services offered on the menu board. The spa was more than manicures and massages. Blowouts, eyelash extensions, and diamond facials were among the free and discounted options. A door across the hall led to a top-of-the-line barbershop for the men of Elemynt to receive haircuts and beard trims.

The time of their appointment arrived and Jade had not responded to any of Kelsey's recent messages. Rather than miss the coveted time, Kelsey followed the receptionist through the top-notch facility. They cruised toward the row of spa chairs where Myntors were having their nails buffed and beautified. Kelsey settled into her reserved seat with its ample cushioning and built-in massage functions. A technician in a pristine white smock greeted her politely.

Kelsey delicately slipped her feet into the warm water of the basin. The nail tech, an older Hispanic woman with decades of experience in the trade, gently added essential oils and rose petals to the liquid heaven. The treatment was made more surreal knowing that just outside the door was a typical work environment with Myntors at the rows of desks.

It must have been a pleasure for the technician to work at Elemynt, Kelsey thought. She could be at a run-of-the-mill nail salon elsewhere but she was employed at the coolest company and one that cared deeply for its employees.

"How do you like working here?" Kelsey asked.

The nail tech lifted her head responsively as if she were ready with an answer to a question she was asked several times before.

"It's such a good time with being at Elemynt," she said sweetly in broken English. "Thank you for enjoying the services today."

Kelsey expected her to say more. There were endless facets of the company that deserved praise. The glorious mani-pedi carried her away from pressing the question. Kelsey let her mind slip into a heavenly trance as the tech whipped her fingernails into shape with precision and care.

Kelsey's phone buzzed with a text from Jade. "Sry work emergency. B right there."

There was an unexpected rustle in the otherwise serene spa. Kelsey looked up to see Jade striding toward her. Jade's eyes were set on the phone in her hand while somehow simultaneously navigating the maze of manicure tables with ease. She relinquished her stare at the device to seat herself in the empty spa chair next to Kelsey. Jade appreciatively declined a menu of services from an approaching technician.

"What's the emergency?" Kelsey asked. "Something I can help with?"

Jade waved her phone dramatically. "You know Lili Skye, don't you?"

"She's like the hottest thing right now," Kelsey said. "Her songs are on repeat on my phone."

There was hardly a person in the Western hemisphere who didn't know who Lili Skye was. Singer. Songwriter. Three-time Grammy winner. And it all started when she was discovered on Elemynt several years ago.

The young talent recorded a song in a makeshift studio in her bedroom and uploaded it to the app. The catchy track went viral shortly after thanks to her captivating lyrics and heartfelt performance. Record companies scrambled to be the first to sign the online sensation.

Twelve million followers and two albums later, Lili Skye made a name for herself as the music industry's "it girl." Because Lili's beginnings could be traced to the app, it was no surprise that Jade would be in contact with the star.

Jade finally set her phone down in the chair's cupholder. "Some random employee got her email from a friend of a friend or God knows who and told Lili they could get her a meeting with Troy. I am the only person who arranges those sorts of meetings with him and celebrating and trust me when I say they are hard to come by. No one who isn't on my team should be emailing her behalf of the company. That, darling, is the emergency."

"Troy doesn't know about this, does he?" Kelsey asked.

"Well, here's the situation," Jade replied. "Lili is one of our 'A' partners and her manager has other 'A' clients too. We can't get Lili a meeting with Troy right now but we also don't want to cause unnecessary drama here either."

Through Jade's description of the situation, it was evident that she cared about Lili on a personal level as well. The superstar with the incredible rise to fame epitomized the phenomenal possibilities of the Elemynt app. Lili's story was a model for new and existing entertainment figures to aspire to. Jade wanted to keep Lili as happy as possible. However, she needed to do so within the boundaries of her role at Elemynt.

"Have we called to apologize?" Kelsey asked with concern.

"I wish it was that simple," Jade said. "Some people do not take kindly to bad news. You okay if I jump on a call now?"

Kelsey nodded yes. Most of the other employees had completed their appointments and floated back to their workspaces on clouds of bliss.

Jade looked to the nail technician for her approval. The woman flashed an okay sign as she worked efficiently to wrap up Kelsey's pedicure. It likely wasn't the first emergency call to happen in the chair. Nail technicians were required to sign company NDAs too.

"Hi Peg, it's Jade calling," she said into the speakerphone. "I hope you got my emails? One of our employees went rogue, which is understandable to some degree because we love Lili here."

"Very unprofessional," Lili's manager responded coldly. "I assume you'll be firing them?"

Jade rolled her eyes. "That would be up to our Human Resources team but I will be sending an email to the entire company reminding them of our policies."

"That's not enough for me, Jade," Peg said. "Lili is set on coming to your headquarters while she's on tour. What can you give us?"

"When are you all here?"

"Friday."

"This Friday?" Jade said with a furrowed brow. "Well, I hate to say this but he's not here then. Maybe you could meet him at the Glastonbury Festival in a few weeks?"

"That's a possibility," Peg mused. "But she was told she could meet him now."

Jade tapped through her phone. "Looking at Lili's tour schedule… I'm thinking we fly you and your team out to Palo Alto after you play Vegas. Travel and accommodations covered, of course. If Lili does a Q&A and performs a few songs, we'll promote it on our official Elemynt page which has 300 million followers now. We reserve it for our most valued partners only."

"What about a tour of the campus for Lili?" Peg asked. "I know you can do something there."

"I'll escort her personally and I'll arrange for behind the scenes access."

"One more thing…" Peg insisted. "Lili also wants her dog verified."

"That can be arranged," Jade said, looking at her nail beds. "I'll connect you with our Music Partnerships lead and we'll get you sorted out."

The call ended with an exchange of pleasant greetings and promises to follow up via email. Jade jotted down notes in her phone as the tech dried Kelsey's pampered feet.

"Whatever they say, never tell them they can meet with Troy," Jade said. "I have the biggest names in the world going bananas trying to get a meeting with him. Heck, it's hard for me to meet with the man."

Kelsey felt more fortunate than ever that she met with Elemynt's head honcho twice already. She was without a doubt on the road to the impact Catherine described.

"Wait, back up a sec," Kelsey said. "Do we verify dogs?"

"We sure do, darling," Jade said as she sent a blitz of emails to her team. "Let's see… there are about 50 dogs with verified accounts on Elemynt. Maybe a hundred, who knows. A lot of these dogs have more followers than I do."

"I thought verification wasn't about the number of followers?"

"It's not, but did you know how easy it is to impersonate a famous pet? This is Elemynt we're talking about here. We don't want counterfeit chihuahuas on our platform. People need to know they're following the right pup."

"They'd probably prefer a doggy treat over a checkmark," Kelsey said.

"There's a giraffe that's verified too," Jade went on. "I'm not even sure what *they* eat. Okay, we have two days to put on a Q&A in front of the whole company that will be broadcast live to the rest of the world. Luckily, I've done it in less time than that."

"We have some work to do," Kelsey said.

"Yes, and I can't imagine doing it without cute nails," Jade said, calling to the technician. "Can you squeeze me in for a gel manicure, please?"

* * *

Word of the arrival of Lili Skye spread quickly. A crowd of geeked Myntors amassed behind the glass doors of the lobby of Building 10. Safely on the other side near the reception desk was an imposing entourage of security guards, a suitcase-toting glam squad, and one confident manager. At the center of the group, was the guest of honor.

Lili waved to the eager onlookers from behind tinted cat-eye shades. The blue streaks in her hair set against her pale skin and the studded black leather jacket draped over her shoulders gave her a classic rock-and-roll vibe. Lili had graduated from young lady playing tunes in her bedroom to full pop star status.

Jade and Kelsey waded through the employees gawking from a respectful distance to meet the guests. The normally even-keel receptionists behind the desk were also doing their best to keep their cool in the presence of the celebrity.

Peg, a forty-ish woman with a phone firmly gripped in each hand, greeted Jade like they were lifelong friends who hadn't been going back and forth days earlier.

"Beautiful place you have here," Peg said with feigned nonchalance.

The manager could not hide her fascination with the impressive surroundings. She spun in a slow circle, taken by the artistic lobby and the kaleidoscope of cool just beyond the glass doors. Lili and Peg had witnessed firsthand the range of grandeur Hollywood had to offer. However, it was no match for the larger than life allure of Silicon Valley. They were in the epicenter of the tech industry where work and play were intertwined.

Jade was familiar with the enchantment a visit to Elemynt cast on first-timers to the campus. She was content the first impression would take at least some of the edge off the visit.

"We've rolled out the red carpet for you, love," Jade said to Peg.

Lili's emotions were hard to read behind the cover of her sunglasses. Hopefully, she would be satisfied with what lay ahead as well.

Security escorted Lili past the fawning lobby crowd in the direction of the VIP green room. Lili blew a kiss to the fans trickling into the corridors to catch a glimpse of her. They cheered and waved, their excitement at a fever pitch.

Jade and Kelsey showed off Elemynt's most captivating sights along their route, including the game rooms, nap pods, and photo installations bedecked with the Elemynt logo. Lili snapped a hundred selfies a second.

"You can take a picture of everything, except for employee computer screens," Jade politely instructed.

As they journeyed through the color-splashed hallways, Lili suddenly halted at one of the many fully stocked micro-kitchens. The tantalizing rows of snacks and treats were a showstopper for the uninitiated.

"Okay, this is amazing!" Lili said. "People who work here get all of this for free?"

"This and more," Jade smiled.

Lili marveled at the options for several minutes before snagging a bag of Flamin' Hot Cheetos for herself.

Kelsey was taken aback by Lili's unexpected move toward the snacks. Her manager requested ahead of their visit that they prepare for her a vegan lunch of seitan tacos, steamed vegetables, and a special kind of water that required them to send the culinary team on a city-wide search to find.

Watching Lili's wide-eyed wonder, Kelsey completely understood the sensation the wall of free snacks evoked. They weren't just chips, they were Flamin' Hot Cheetos at *Elemynt*. There was a specialness to them that came with being on the campus of one of the world's most popular social networks.

"Celebrities like free stuff too," Jade nodded to Kelsey.

Lili rushed over to a beverage dispenser calling to her from a corner of the kitchen. "Is that rosé on tap??" she exclaimed.

"It's eleven in the morning…" Kelsey whispered to Jade.

"We can put orange juice in it and call it a mimosa," Jade said.

Lili had no interest in adding anything more than the bubbly to her cup. She filled up a tumbler to the rim as if it were a travel size vessel from a stop-and-shop convenience store.

"Please tell me she's at least 21," Kelsey said quietly.

"God, I hope so," Jade thought it over.

The thankfully 22-year-old talent coolly admired the sights as they continued their jaunt through the halls of Elemynt headquarters.

When the group arrived in the meticulously cool, photo-ready green room, Lili and crew instinctively set in motion their pre-public appearance routine. Lili positioned herself in front of the supersized vanity mirror while her glam squad unfurled an impressive array of products to touch up her makeup and hair.

Kelsey and Jade stood by to answer questions Peg might have.

"What do you think about verifying my account?" the manager half asked, half demanded.

In Peg's mind, she needed to be assertive if she was going to nab the coveted checkmark. Her position as Lili's manager meant Elemynt risked future high-level partnerships if the company didn't acquiesce to her request. There was the question though of whether Peg actually met the qualifications.

Jade, the ringmaster of the verification circus, answered in the affirmative.

"Check your account again at the end of the day," she smiled.

Lili, who used the time to snap selfies under the perfect glow of the vanity lights, cleared her throat.

"What time is he coming?" Lili said, taking a sip from her tumbler.

"Who?" Peg cocked her head.

"Troy…the guy I'm here to see. When do I get to meet him?"

Jade and Kelsey exchanged confused glances with each other. They paid for her expenses to come with the implicit understanding that the manager would placate Lili and dampen her request. Peg, sensing that she and her client might lose a very important partnership, turned to the Myntors for a response.

"He's traveling this week," Kelsey offered.

In reality, Troy was in his office a few buildings away. The two guests did not and would not know that.

"He'll be at the MTV Awards so we can schedule time then," Peg offered.

Lili was less than thrilled. "We're not meeting Troy which is what we came for so... what are we doing here?"

The assembly in the green room was suddenly still. The main responsibility of her crew was to keep Lili happy. They were failing at it. The glam squad backed away, brushes and curling irons in hand.

"It's good promo for the album," Peg said.

"I'm playing sold-out arenas on a worldwide tour," Lili deadpanned.

"Let's think about it this way," Jade said, placing one manicured hand on the back of Lili's chair. "Madison Square Garden...a fabulous venue. Legendary. Superstars only. How many musicians have played there?"

"Hundreds."

"Thousands, darling. Do you know how many of those incredible talents are jealous of you right now because you're sitting in this chair about to go on stage at Elemynt headquarters?"

"All of them."

"Every single one. This is the big ticket, honey. The most exclusive venue talent will ever get to play. And you. are. here."

Lili wrestled with Jade's assessment. She downed the remaining sips of rosé were left in the cup and threw the crumpled bag of chips in the trash.

* * *

The auditorium that usually housed weekly all-hands meetings was filled to capacity with restless Myntors. They bobbed about anxiously waiting for their pop idol to take the stage. Countless more were just outside the auditorium doors hoping to stretch the limits of the number of people the venue could hold.

Lili Skye, worldwide phenomenon and global music sensation, was at their workplace, soon appearing right in front of them. The excitement that came with that reality could not be contained. The two empty plush chairs on the stage awaiting Lili and Jade could not be filled fast enough.

Kelsey joined Sarah, who took the scene in stride, and Daniela, who was pretending to take it all in stride, at the back of the room.

"Elemynt blows my mind sometimes," Daniela said happily. "Random celebrities popping up on a Friday? Just wow. This place is the best."

"We need to get this event going soon or we'll never make it out of here on schedule," Sarah said with a clenched smile. "What is up with this delay, anyway?"

"We had some, um, technical difficulties backstage," Kelsey said.

Kelsey did her best to not look riddled with anxiety in front of Sarah and Daniela. The showdown in the green room left her with doubts that the Q&A would be the carefree event Jade planned.

It was imperative that Jade got Lili to say all good things about Elemynt. A squad of video cameras with lenses trained on the stage would stream live to the hundreds of thousands of followers of the company's official account. Inspirational statements would generate positive headlines in the press and also be a big motivator for employees. Or, if things went haywire, the complete opposite could happen. There was no telling what the conversation between Jade and a perturbed Lili had in store.

"We've done this a million times with no problems," Sarah said. "What could possibly—"

"Oh look, there she is," Kelsey pointed.

Jade stepped onto the stage, microphone in hand, speaking the highly sought-after words. "Please welcome to Elemynt... Lili Skye!"

The usually strait-laced employees instantly transformed into rabid fans. The room vibrated with thunderous applause and wild screams as Lili took her place next to Jade. They both paused for a beat while the room full of Myntors thrust their phones in the sky to capture an image of the superstar.

Jade and Lili finally took their seats, a signal to the mesmerized crowd to contain themselves and allow the conversation to begin.

"Lili, people have described you as an icon for this generation," Jade said into her mic. "You went from singing in your bedroom, which we loved, to taking selfies at posh Hollywood parties."

"Oh, I take selfies wherever," Lili smiled. "I'll be brushing my teeth or hanging on the couch and I'm like 'Photo!'"

The audience laughed with understanding. They too were prone to snapping impromptu pics.

The conversation was off to a good start. Jade's words in the green room did wonders to improve Lili's attitude. However, the tumbler of rosé had not left her possession. Lili sipped from the freshly refilled cup that rested at her feet.

"Is she seriously drinking on stage?" Sarah asked. "Can we get that cup away from her?"

"Not without making a scene," Kelsey said.

Kelsey hoped the emotional support beverage looked enough like soda to not arouse suspicions. Since Lili was a larger than life personality, it didn't appear that those watching noticed she was teetering on erratic. To the audience, she was being funny, engaging, and real. But Lili was one slip-up away from uttering a career-ending statement. Not for her though. Whatever cheeky aside she made would be a cute relatable press moment for the darling of entertainment. It was the Comms teams who would be in hot water.

"Tell us what it's like interacting with your fans on Elemynt!" Jade said.

"I love my fans!" Lili grinned from ear to ear. "Y'all make me who I am!"

A rousing whoop emanated from the audience who counted themselves among her biggest supporters.

"How do you deal with this new life in the social media spotlight?"

"People out there are quick to hate on social media, but we need it because it spreads so much positivity."

"That's what we love!" Jade encouraged applause from the audience.

"I used to read every comment on every single picture or video I was tagged in," Lili shared. "People would say 'she's too sexy' or 'she's not sexy enough' or 'this other singer over here is better.' But guess what? The haters won't stop me! I'm in it to win it and I'm not going anywhere so suck it, haters!"

The audience roared with uncontrollable laughter. The trio of Comms women observing from the sidelines gasped in collective shock. The Q&A was going far off-script, the frightfully candid exchange spelled disaster for the stakeholders involved.

"Can't say she's not passionate," Daniela said.

"She's a freaking ticking time bomb," Sarah hissed. "We need to get her off that stage right now or someone's going to get fired and I don't know about you but I don't want it to be me."

"Jade's got this," Kelsey said. "She's a pro."

Kelsey attempted to convince the others as well as herself. Her faith was shaky but it was all she had to go on.

Jade double blinked from her perch onstage. She needed to turn it around. Fast.

"So, tell us about your new album!" Jade said, deftly bringing Lili back to the conversation.

Lili looked out at the crowd, a surprising tear welling in the corner of her eye.

"I never thought in a million years that this would happen," she said. "I love what I do. I love music. And 'cause of Elemynt and what y'all created for us, I can share it with the whole world. Hopefully, I can keep making good stuff for you!"

The auditorium of Myntors sent waves of love and appreciation Lili's way. With a few short minutes left in the scheduled time, Jade effectively turned the conversation into a soul-stirring moment. The testimonial of Elemynt's uplifting effect on people was exactly what everyone — from the fans to the Comms team — could hope for. All Jade needed to do was put a bow on it.

"Lili, tell us what's next for you," Jade said.

"More Hot Cheetos and rosé!" Lili exclaimed. "And go get my new album!"

After a brief acoustic performance of her most popular hits, Lili bowed ceremoniously to the audience in the venue and those watching from home. The reception in the room to Lili's presence was wildly appreciative. Her conversation touched the hearts of many, including the wary women of Comms who could finally exhale.

Kelsey was sure the buzz online about Lili's surprise visit to Elemynt headquarters would circulate quickly. The media would report on the rise of a superstar and, most importantly, how the Elemynt app was a key factor in her continued success. A quote or two from Jade and an undeniably enticing story were at the ready for journalists to snap up.

Sarah was the most thrilled of everyone. She called together the group, including Jade, following the conclusion of the event.

"Hey ladies, here's what I'm thinking," Sarah said. "We need to celebrate! The weather's supposed to be fantastic this weekend...how about we go for a spin on my yacht? Just us Comms girls?"

"I'll bring the rosé!" Kelsey smiled.

FIVE

The women of Elemynt set sail under San Francisco's luminous sky for a relaxed day on the open California waters. Sarah instructed the ladies to wear all white to match the splendid white yacht. Daniela, Kelsey, and Jade obliged by donning chic outfits perfect for an afternoon on the bay.

Tai, however, sat across from them bucking the request wearing a pilling gray hoodie with the Elemynt logo and criminally oversized cargo shorts. She looked...comfortable.

However they were dressed, Kelsey was happy to be in the company of friends for the excursion. She wasn't sure what her social life would be like upon arriving on the West Coast. She felt fortunate to have found new friends in her amazing co-workers.

Sarah wasted no time opening bottles of champagne and setting out the charcuterie their captain brought on board.

"There's nothing better than seeing San Francisco by sailboat," Sarah said. "Everyone should experience it at least once in their lives."

"You're not going to drive the boat for us, Sarah?" Jade said with a wink.

"Ladies, I think it's better if we're on top of the water and not in it," she laughed in return.

The convivial group held onto their glasses while the boat sliced through the bay. The soundtrack to their afternoon was a yacht rock playlist curated by Sarah. The smooth 70s and 80s hits by Christopher Cross, Steely Dan, and Hall & Oates trickled through the craft's speakers. The cresting waves gliding past its sleek hull sent a spray of water jetting behind them. The gulls nesting on the nearby piers watched them on their journey.

Kelsey gently the change of scenery. She could step out of Palo Alto for a while and see the world outside of Silicon Valley. Being out in the open water gave her a freeing sensation that anything was possible.

Kelsey took in the vista while nibbling on one of the delectable olives. "Sarah, is this what working at Elemynt for five years will get you?"

"The IPO is coming soon," Sarah said, tossing her hair back. "You may be cruising in your own ride a lot sooner than you think."

Kelsey suddenly understood what was previously a fleeting mystery. The initial public offering was the big change at the company Catherine referred to in their first meeting.

An IPO was an epic transition from a privately-owned company with a relatively small number of early investors to a public company that sold shares on a stock exchange to outside investors. "Going public" would net Elemynt billions of dollars in financial capital for the future expansion that Troy desired for his brainchild. In addition to being a boon for Elemynt, an IPO would expand the bank accounts of its stock-holding employees as well. Previous initial public offerings by other Silicon Valley companies minted millionaires of their staff overnight.

When Kelsey first signed on to come to Elemynt, she, like other Myntors, was awarded a number of restricted stock units based on factors like seniority and start date. She had the opportunity to be granted additional RSUs depending on her level of performance at the company. The incentives to bring her "A" game were stacking up.

RSUs differed from traditional shares in that Kelsey and her fellow recipients were required to work at Elemynt for a year at minimum to start receiving ownership of them. They were granted portions of the stock in quarterly increments over the course of four years until they had access to every share they were promised at their hiring. Following the IPO, employees could cash out their equity in Elemynt for a life-changing windfall.

Sarah and Tai were among the early employees who received an extraordinary number of shares at their start. They were gifted the Elemynt stock in exchange for lower salaries consistent with the pay of nascent tech startups. The large quantity of RSUs in their possession meant the two would be set for life. They were lucky to be in the right job at the right time.

The IPO would also net a big payday for Troy, the largest shareholder in the company, as well Elemynt's early investors. However, taking a company public was about more than selling stock or generating funding. An initial public offering sent a message to the world that the company was no longer an aspirant startup. It matured into a full-fledged business that could weather complex government regulation and ongoing scrutiny from investors on its golden road to increased financial success.

Kelsey imagined that very few people at Elemynt knew for sure when exactly the IPO would happen. It was widely accepted though that the landmark moment was an inevitability for a tech company whose size and reach grew every day. Wall Street analysts estimated that when Elemynt did eventually go public, it would be one of the largest IPOs in the history of the stock market.

Whether they stood to make $50,000 or millions, every employee at Elemynt needed to continue striving to do their absolutely best work. The value of the company was directly tied to their diligence and commitment. For Kelsey, Elemynt's financial worth was a reflection of its social value. If regular people found value in the app, so would outside investors whose financial support would keep the company booming.

"That's where Comms comes in," Sarah said. "There's so much great stuff happening on the app that people need to hear about."

"I agree one hundred percent," Daniela said. "Isn't it crazy how the fate of a billion-dollar company depends on what we say?"

"Also, hello...I have two future college tuitions to fund," Jade quipped. "Mama needs to pay for Yale."

The ladies sipped rosé in honor of Lili and to the future of the company. Tai had to be different. She drank from a craft beer Sarah brought on board especially for her and buried herself in her work phone between sips. Tai was mostly disinterested in the ladies' discussions. Their colleague wasn't ignoring them per se but she was certainly not contributing to the conversation in one would expect on an outdoor excursion.

On their side of the boat, Kelsey quietly whispered to Daniela. "Why did Sarah invite Tai if it's looking like she doesn't want to be here."

"Tai loves the company a lot..." Daniela replied.

"Don't we all?" Kelsey asked.

"Yes, but she hates External Comms and feels like Sarah is a huge thorn in her side," Daniela said quietly. "Myntors severely dislike reading about the latest company developments in the media first. It goes against this open culture that we have. Tai feels like she has to clean up after Sarah a lot when news gets out before the Dream Team has a chance to speak to employees first."

"Which happens from time to time," Jade added.

"Tai's here because Sarah knows she needs to keep her as an ally or else it makes Sarah's work even harder."

"Seriously, don't worry too much about Tai," Jade whispered optimistically. "She's having fun...just in her own way."

Kelsey instinctively moved to rope Tai into the conversation whether her colleague wanted to be present or not. It was perhaps Kelsey's time on the social scene in Connecticut or following in her mother's genteel footsteps that wouldn't allow her to let a guest sit alone.

"Tai, how long have you been at the company now?" Kelsey asked.

"Eight years," Tai piped up. "Since the beginning."

Jade raised her glass. "She may not be the most public figure but she's one of the most powerful women at the company."

"Yes, she is," Daniela smiled.

"Your family must be really proud of you," Kelsey said.

"Not really," Tai cradled her frosty beer. "I mean they are but my parents are pretty traditional, you know? They always wanted me to get into an Ivy League school and become an engineer. I did but they felt like I let our family and our community down when I took the Comms role. It's cool. I'm still going to be good at my job whatever I'm doing."

Kelsey inferred that Tai's background may have been part of the reason for her ongoing grumpiness. Sarah and External Comms were at odds with her drive to live up to her potential. Kelsey hoped Tai could put her personal issues aside and understand that ultimately they shared a common goal.

"Women rock!" Kelsey said encouragingly. "I mean, hello! There's a reason the Comms teams are mostly female. We get things done!"

"Tell that to the guys at Elemynt," Daniela laughed. "A lot of them think we're dumb, ditzy California girls who only care about shopping and taking men's jobs. More of them need to realize that we're grown women who work twice as hard as they do."

"My God, you should see how they treat Catherine," Jade shook her head. "That's why I find it so funny when the men at this company blame her the minute something goes wrong."

"Why would they do that?" Kelsey asked quizzically. "She's a boss!"

"Because she's a woman at the top," Daniela said. "An issue could come up because of a mistake another executive made and a lot of these ground-level

Blind

guys will still say it was Catherine's fault. For whatever reason, they find a woman in power an offense to their existence. It's so tragic."

"You all have seen the comments they make about her on Mask, right?" Sarah said.

"What's Mask?" Kelsey asked. "An internal tool?"

Tai's shift in tone was as frigid as her beer. "It's an app," she said. "Not ours. You sign up with your Elemynt email to verify you work at the company. Then you get to have anonymous discussions with other employees about whatever. Lots of talk about what Elemynt's doing right."

"And wrong," Sarah pointed out. "It's a lot of dudebros with fake names making judgment calls from the sidelines about company politics."

"Misogyny is a bummer," Daniela winced.

"We work in the tech industry," Jade snickered to herself. "If I haven't pissed off men with my very presence then I'm not doing my job."

"That's why we have to stick together," Kelsey said.

"And support our Boss Lady," Jade responded. "You all are going to the gala, right?"

Catherine was slated to receive an award from Code XX, a non-profit dedicated to increasing the number of women and girls pursuing careers in science, technology, engineering, and mathematics. The honor was well-deserved.

The COO personally donated $2 million to fund the STEM programs at universities with the highest concentration of female engineering students. She was one of the driving forces behind Elemynt's increase of the number of women at the company. And, of course, her book "Boss Lady" was a universal motivator for women to claim their rightful place in the workplace. The event would also double as a fundraiser for Code XX. All the Comms ladies were expected to be there.

"I'm prepping media interviews for Catherine before and after the gala," Daniela said. "She should get great press coverage from this."

"Have you spoken with Inc. Magazine and Vogue?" Jade asked. "They might be interested in feature pieces."

"Can we have one conversation that isn't about Elemynt?" Sarah groaned dramatically. "I just want to cruise on the water and eat my grapefruit."

Sarah held up the large fruit in what was a not so subtle bid to show off the sizable engagement ring on her finger. The up and down motion of the boat made it dazzle under the California sun.

"Alright, Sarah. Let's see that ring of yours," Jade said.

The soon to be newlywed flashed her six-carat diamond solitaire ring with pride. Kelsey was stunned by the size of the rock.

"Pretty soon I'll be wearing a veil on a gorgeous island!" Sarah said wistfully. "The thing I keep thinking about is how hard it's going to be with being a new wife and also doing this job that's pretty much more than full-time."

"That's a feeling that comes and goes, darling," Jade said. "You know me... I'm always traveling to this destination and that. It's been an adjustment, especially since Tom and I had the girls. But we find our ways to make it work."

"How does he feel about you being away all the time?" Sarah asked.

"Todd is a wonderful guy," Jade said lovingly. "The very best. Being out here reminds me... on our first date we were surrounded by water too. Picture it... the pier in Santa Monica sharing cotton candy under the Ferris Wheel. It's been years since that and we're still by each other's side. Me, him, and our two precious ones. I've found that with love, anything's possible."

"I love you and him together," Kelsey said sweetly. "Tai, what about you? Is there someone special in your life?"

Sarah made a panicked slicing motion across her neck in an attempt to halt Kelsey from pursuing the question. There was nothing she could do about it though. The question was out there.

"I'm an equal opportunity employer," Tai said as she knocked back more of her beer. "Some days I'm like 'hey, girl.' Other days I'm like 'sup, dude.'. Depends how I'm feeling that day."

Tai's communication was so dry that Kelsey couldn't tell if she was being serious or not. Jade and Daniela's amused, yet supportive expressions indicated that their colleague was indeed having an honest moment.

Sarah scrambled to change the subject away from Tai's less than traditional approach to romance. "You have a guy back home, Kelsey?"

Kelsey was conflicted about how she should describe to the group her current relationship with Brad. It would have been nice to say he was her boyfriend. But she was a long way from getting him to settle down in one place and be there for her as a romantic partner.

"No. Not really. I mean..." Kelsey stumbled over her words. "There's this guy, Brad. He's traveling the world right now."

"That's wonderful!" Jade said. "We love a man with frequent flyer miles."

"You'd think that would be a plus, but the rest of the world will always be his priority," Kelsey said. "I'm not sure what he loves more — me or the idea of me waiting back at home for him."

"Men!" Jade scoffed dramatically. "We love 'em, we hate 'em, we love 'em some more."

"Daniela, you lucked out being a lesbian," Sarah laughed. "Things would be so much easier being with a girl."

"You think so, huh?" Daniela smirked. "Let me tell you dating women isn't exactly perfect either. Lesbians *love* to love. Friday night you have a date and by Monday morning you look up and you have a wife and her toothbrush is in your bathroom."

"Babes, it took my husband three years to propose!" Jade laughed.

"Lesbians get married in three weeks," Daniela chuckled. "That's one of the reasons I loved Ro from the start. We decided early on to take it slow."

"Don't get me wrong, I love my man," Sarah said. "What I'm saying is men can sometimes be womanizers, emotionally withdrawn, hard to read..."

"Leave their dirty underwear everywhere," Tai said.

"Yeah some of them are gross for sure," Daniela agreed. "But I guarantee you whatever awful habits men have hardwired in their brains, there are women out there doing the same things. I will say I'm grateful to be with someone I love who also puts her unmentionables in the hamper."

"OMG Daniela, you're so spicy!" Sarah exclaimed.

"Gracias," Daniela said.

She turned her attention to the water, sipping her champagne and mumbling something to herself about Punta Cana.

Kelsey and the squad finally sat back and enjoyed the unparalleled views of San Francisco from their position in the Bay waters. They watched with delight the sea lions soaking in the rays on nearby Pier 39. Further down the shore, onlookers packed the touristy Fisherman's Wharf area where the scents of sourdough and clam chowder wafted in the air. The yacht drifted past the iconic Coit Tower and the monuments to industry in the Financial District that gave way to the Bay Bridge and the nearby industrial shore of the Port of Oakland. Tai again sat off the side of the boat, which was fine. Her self-isolation kept her from interrupting the enchanting moment.

The ladies prepared their cameras for the portion of the trip they had all been anxiously waiting for. They were nearing the iconic Golden Gate Bridge and the ultimate photo opportunity. The towering reddish hued structure shot up from the water in glorious splendor.

The ladies commenced an exuberant round of selfies with the bridge and city skyline behind them. They then assembled in front of Jade's phone to go live to her Elemynt account. Jade shared with spirited commentary the majesty of their aquatic adventure. The stream of hundreds of comments from watchers echoed how magical the experience was. For Kelsey, it was a precious moment she would cherish forever.

* * *

Kelsey was awakened out of her nighttime sleep by the sharp ringing of her phone. Brad's name and smiling photo filled her phone's screen. When she answered, her face was bombarded with excessively bright daylight.

Kelsey rubbed her eyes. "Tell me I'm dreaming and you're not calling in the middle of the night."

"Guess I didn't check the time zone," Brad said. "You stop doing the math when you're on the road."

"There's an app for that right there on your phone," Kelsey said.

"My bad, babe," he smiled. "I saw your boat pics and I thought maybe you were treading on my territory."

"Just me and the girls," Kelsey sat up. "No big adventure. We got to talk more about Elemynt and it had me thinking... you should give the company a shot. They have jobs for everything here."

"Babe, you know I'm not sitting around a hotel room ordering room service all day," Brad chuckled. "Me and my buds, we're out exploring these epic places and we document the whole thing. That's why the people love following me on Elemynt. They get to experience it with your boy."

"You can't do this forever," Kelsey said sleepily.

"If I wanted to, yeah, I could," he said defensively. "Maybe I'm not living the way everyone thinks I should but it's my life, you know?"

There was no dissuading Brad from his ambitions or lack thereof. Listening to him go on about the freedom he enjoyed from his travels made Kelsey realize more how much she loved her current position. She was a part of something bigger than herself. Elemynt was a company that touched hundreds of millions of lives. Because of her, many more people would join the app and share their passions with the people who followed them. There was a spiritual satisfaction that came from being a Myntor.

If Kelsey was going to operate at full capacity, she needed adequate rest.

"I have to go," she said into the phone. "I have work in the morning."

"Hold on a sec!" Brad waved at her. "What do you think about getting me verified?"

"Good night, Brad."

* * *

A black-tie affair fit for the queen of Silicon Valley was underway at the landmark Metreon building in San Francisco. Supporters and well-wishers filled the venue in support of Catherine and the non-profit for which she was a dedicated advocate. The room was graced by women in evening gowns draped in sparkling jewelry and men in dapper tuxedos conversing under the bluish glow of the event lighting.

Beyond the guests congregating at the entrance were rows of tables clad in crisp white linens and topped by gilded china. Centerpieces of tiger lilies and bougainvillea were nestled in tall glass cylinders. A raised platform where the distinguished guest would be honored spanned the head of the room. A string quartet played charming melodies that added to the high spirits of the gala while servers circulated with trays of canapes and flutes of champagne.

Kelsey arrived exquisitely dressed for the gala in her favorite evening wear — a midnight-blue, bias-cut dress that hugged her lean shape. Her selection was no match for Jade who slinked toward her wearing a silver beaded gown that flowed from her sapphire necklace to her four-inch stilettos. Jade's jet-black hair draped beautifully around her face in a soft wave.

"A thousand important people in this room and here comes number 1,001," Jade said to Kelsey. "Hello, darling!"

The pair embraced each other, followed by a double air-kiss.

"This place is gorge!" Kelsey exclaimed. "This is all for Catherine?"

"Technically it's for the non-profit," Jade said. "But can you imagine Catherine doing an acceptance speech at a Holiday Inn? Not to mention my diamonds wouldn't match the decor."

"And half of this guest list probably wouldn't attend," Kelsey laughed.

"Let's take a peek around and see who's made an appearance tonight," Jade said.

The duo moved about the room while Jade pointed out the famous faces. Jade had a task for Kelsey and Daniela that night: help her convince the most well-known attendees to join Elemynt or to step up their engagement.

The attendees in the room loved Catherine but a significant share of them did not use the platform at the level they could. The three Myntors would pull double duty that night, celebrating Catherine and doing their part to foster the growth of Elemynt. Kelsey thought the night might have been a laid-back time. Instead, she was going to work. Not that she minded. The gala was a great opportunity to court movers and shakers. And the opportunity to celebrate the esteemed executive was a moment Kelsey would always hold close to her heart.

While Jade and Kelsey surveyed the finery of the evening, Ro and Daniela approached with locked arms. The radiant pair was like the top of an LGBT wedding cake. Ro's fitted tux complimented Daniela's satin draped gown that featured her bare shoulders. Ro's honey-colored braids were swept back into a sculptural chignon. The four women exchanged warm hugs and hellos while admiring their glammed up looks.

"How about this lovely couple!" Jade exclaimed.

"Isn't my baby looking handsome in her tux?" Daniela said, tugging playfully on Ro's lapel.

"Only the best for my girl," Ro blushed. "She made me leave the combat boots at home."

"We might need them to get through this crowd," Jade laughed. "Though we should have prime seating, I believe."

Elemynt procured three tables at the event at a cost of $5,000 each. One would be for executives, another for Catherine's family and friends, and one more for members of the various Comms teams. It was both a gesture of support for the COO and a donation to a cause dear to her heart.

"Ever wear evening gowns for work before?" Daniela asked Kelsey as they navigated toward their designated seats.

"No, only to debutante balls and trips to the grocery store," Kelsey nudged her jokingly.

Kelsey recognized the lone figure already seated at their table. Daniela's manager Scott Kinley, the head of diversity, would be joining them. Scott was one of the most active people on Commynt and one of Kelsey's new favorite follows. He often posted photos of the company's diversity events as well as his home life in the Castro neighborhood of San Francisco.

Scott was more tan than he appeared in his profile photo, likely from the fabulous outdoor activities listed in his profile. His crisp tailored suit highlighted the physique sculpted by religious visits to the gym with his husband.

"Ladies, are we ready to celebrate Catherine tonight?" Scott said with a shining smile.

An extended chorus of yeses from the group confirmed the shared enthusiasm.

"I'm a big fan, obviously," Scott said. "She's always been a huge advocate for our team, you know what I mean? The work we do wouldn't be possible without her."

"Where's Troy at?" Ro looked around. "He's not coming?"

"It's Catherine's night," Jade said. "He didn't want to distract from that. But look who else is joining us tonight!"

The sea of conversing partygoers around them parted to reveal Sarah wowing the room in a strapless silk-chiffon gown.

"Comms teams representing tonight!" Sarah laughed.

A chorus of whoops and raised hands celebrated the gathering of the talented minds of Elemynt.

While the rest of the room found their way to their seats, a mass of white-coated waiters flooded the large hall. They scurried between tables with precision, delicately placing elegant dishes at each setting. When the guests were all served, the waiters departed with the same efficiency as they entered.

The house lights dimmed.

A single spotlight shone on the podium centered on the stage. Their mistress of ceremonies, Yoanna Beaumont, the president of Code XX, emerged to greet the attendees.

"Our honoree tonight is not only the chief operating officer of Elemynt, one of the most impactful social platforms in the world, she is also a philanthropist with a heart of gold. Her work enables young girls and women everywhere to step up and say 'Yes, I can'. Ladies and gentlemen, the Boss Lady herself… Catherine Rowe."

Catherine was showered with several rounds of enthusiastic applause at the announcement of her name. The grateful emcee greeted the executive with outstretched arms as she approached the podium with the elegance of a highly-regarded honoree.

Catherine flashed her million-dollar smile to the crowd. She paused to take in the sight of the women in the room who stood in appreciation of her work. The crowd was thrilled to be in the presence of *the* Catherine Rowe. It was a moment their friends would ask them about at social engagements for months to come.

"Thank you, Yoanna," Catherine said, her voice filling the attentive room. "Each of us knows that women have made incredible strides in the workforce. We have increased our representation in an industry that by and large has historically sought to exclude us. That said, it is an unfortunate truth that we have much farther to go."

The room listened intently to the sage observations coming from the podium. Catherine spoke of the plight of modern women with an impassioned demeanor. Her words flowed with sincerity.

"Whatever stereotypes people want to cast on women as a group does not change how valuable we are to this world," she emphasized. "We must show up for ourselves and to advocate for the many more women knocking on the door of opportunity. Everyone in this room has the power to come together and break through the prejudices of society that aim to stop us from living our true potential. Our success will be measured by the path we forge for future generations."

Catherine's speech came to a close with a roar of inspired applause. The audience was wholly inspired by her challenge to continue to revolutionize the tech industry and beyond. A crescendo of orchestral music underscored a much-deserved standing ovation.

Catherine descended from the stage to the ballroom floor where she was greeted by a throng of well-wishers. The honoree shook a line of appreciative hands while making her way over to the Elemynt table where the group waited to congratulate her.

"Thank you for coming, friends," Catherine said with charm. "Having the home team rooting for you makes this moment that much more special to me."

The Myntors showered her with kudos for being an exemplary boss and a tremendous advocate. After a beat, Catherine was ushered away by the host, leaving Team Elemynt to talk amongst themselves.

Jade signaled for Daniela and Kelsey to join her at the rear of the ballroom.

"You remember the plan, yes?" Jade said. "We're convincing potential partners that they should step up their presence on Elemynt. We'll get around to more people if we do it separately. You ready?"

"I'm going to bring Ro with me, if that's cool," Daniela said. "I don't want her to think I abandoned her."

"Happy couples inspire happy partners," Jade winked. "Go for it!"

The trio shared a laugh before heading in separate directions. It was game time.

A great range of important people filled the gala hall. Wealthy socialites mingled with government officials. CEOs mixed with heads of global non-profits. Kelsey eased her way into conversations, introducing herself as a ranking employee of Elemynt. The faces of the guests lit up when she shared where she worked.

Kelsey regaled them with stories of what she knew they wanted to hear most. She spoke of the amenities, the perks, and what it was like to be surrounded by some of the most brilliant minds in the world, Catherine chief among them.

Sharing the greatness of her employer was Kelsey's entry point into suggesting dynamic content the guests could post to Elemynt. Her encouragement was well-received. Many had simply fallen out of the habit of posting to the platform. Kelsey's recommendations inspired them to share the most deeply fulfilling areas of their lives with their followers.

From across the room, Kelsey spotted a legendary figure in American U.S. politics. Senator Deniece Layne, the Congresswoman from California and one of Kelsey's longtime sheroes, was chatting with a small group. Kelsey knew instantly that she had to speak with her about her Elemynt presence. However, Senator Layne was the biggest deal. The thought of speaking with the prominent figure sent nervousness racing through Kelsey's body.

Senator Layne was most notably one of the few women in Congress and a strong advocate for the African-American community she came from. Like Catherine, she translated her natural charisma into an uncanny ability to rally people behind her for the causes she believed in. Her team made unparalleled use of Elemynt during her re-election campaign for grassroots organization of first-time voters. Her digital strategies reshaped how other politicians engaged on social media.

However, since the election last year, the Congresswoman barely used the app. When she did, her account was populated by screenshots of press releases and staid photos of her at news events. There were no personal touches or enticement for her followers to engage with her. It was unclear why the change happened. Kelsey was determined to find out.

If Kelsey was going to gain the confidence of the Congresswoman, she needed Catherine to make an introduction. Senator Layne was a regular attendee of Catherine's legendary all-female dinner parties. The Senator was one of the women in a wide variety of careers who came together to dine and discuss how to advance the standing of women in the world. Making the pitch would be much easier to if Catherine was part of it.

Kelsey tracked down Catherine to find her engaged in a lively conversation with a group of the nonprofit's largest donors. The honoree excused herself at Kelsey's pressing request.

"I can certainly make the introduction," Catherine said to Kelsey. "The rest is up to you."

Catherine and Kelsey approached the esteemed legislator who was more than happy to step away to say hello to her dear friend.

"That speech was magnificent," Senator Layne said, clasping Catherine's hand in hers. "Women would be unstoppable if there were more Catherine Rowes in the world."

"Your kindness knows no limits," Catherine smiled. "You are carrying the torch for all of us. If I can, I'd like to introduce you to someone who recently joined our staff. This is Kelsey Pace from our External Communications department."

"A pleasure to meet you, Ms. Pace," Senator Layne said, greeting Kelsey with genuine warmth. "You're a lucky woman to work for Elemynt. There's no company like it."

Kelsey was determined to not let her awestruck reaction to the Senator's close proximity get in the way of her mission for the evening. She buried her jittery enthusiasm under a thick layer of confidence. Catherine returned to her rounds at the party, leaving the two to talk it out alone.

"Thanks for taking the time, Congresswoman," Kelsey said in her most professional voice. "I love your Elemynt account! I noticed you've been posting on less than you used to. How are things going with it?"

"I adore the app," Senator Layne said. "I'm sure you know how useful it's been for connecting with my community. I also have had a lot on my plate recently that's taken me away from using it."

"Completely understand," Kelsey said, doing her best to remain confident. "I read about you working on pushing through legislation to end the wage gap."

"It's my topmost priority," the Senator said. "Women deserve to earn the same salary as men for the same work. It's a shame that it's not happening in California or in the country. Something has to be done about it."

"Can I make a quick suggestion?" Kelsey said. "I think you can use the app to encourage your constituents to support what you're doing. you share the stories of real people and families who are affected by the wage gap. You can post video clips of them talking about how their lives would be better if the law's passed. We see a lot of real-world engagement on the issues when real people share real stories. And you already have the followers ready to get behind you."

"I wish I had the time, Ms. Pace," Senator Layne responded. "Washington D.C. keeps my staff and I very busy."

"A few posts a week make a huge difference," Kelsey said, restraining herself from full-out pleading.

"There's also the matter of the comments on my previous posts. They get heated on both sides of the issues."

"People are passionate on Elemynt," Kelsey said. "That's why people love you... because of your passion."

Kelsey got the feeling that the Senator was essentially being polite with her for Catherine's sake. She was not budging. But what was at stake was too great for Kelsey not to land her pitch. The increased engagement on the seasoned politician's account would also activate her hundreds of thousands of followers to interact more with the app too. Kelsey employed a strategy she hoped would seal the deal.

"If you share the stories of your campaign on the app, the Comms team can seed a story with the press about the social media momentum behind the bill. We'll tell them how you used the app to help generate support from communities in your state. They'll love it! Media attention will lead to more support from fellow Congresspeople or at least that's what I've seen."

Kelsey held her breath in anticipation of the response. Her heart fluttered wondering if the sell was enough. A yes would also mean the world to Kelsey as an admirer of the exemplary female leader. Senator Layne was thoughtful while she considered Kelsey's suggestion.

"I'll have my staff give it a go," the Senator finally said. "A 30-day campaign to raise awareness of the issue. How does that sound?"

"That sounds perfect!" Kelsey said with overwhelming excitement. "Let me know if there's any way I can help. And thanks for talking with me!"

Kelsey was thrilled by what was without a doubt one of the most significant accomplishments in her lifetime. The situation — negotiating with a United States Senator— was previously unfathomable and certainly one that she didn't think she was capable of pulling off. Kelsey was dizzy with barely contained happiness. Rather than faint in front of a room full of influential guests, Kelsey stepped out onto the rooftop terrace that spanned the length of the venue.

Kelsey's weighted sigh of relief blended with the brisk San Francisco air. From her elevated vantage point, she could see the comings and goings of the people on the streets of the city. She wondered if in the last minute they did anything half as cool as what she just accomplished.

While she was ruminating on the moment, a male figure approached her.

"Kelsey?" he asked. "Hi, it's Tim Westbrook from The Washington Chronicle. I cover technology out of our SF bureau?"

Tim stood several inches shorter than Kelsey with thick-framed glasses teetering on his nose. She noted that they were more functional than an aesthetic choice. The stubble on his face suggested a man whose tuxes were sourced from a rental store. The undone collar and lack of tie would have been a faux pas for anyone not in his chosen profession.

"I thought I recognized you," Tim joined her by her side. "I've been emailing you about a story you're working on."

"You did? I must've missed it."

Kelsey was fully aware of the numerous emails he sent their way. They were not about projects the team planned to launch a campaign for. The unsolicited press coverage did not warrant a reply.

"Can you get me a one-on-one interview with your boss?" Tim asked. "That speech in there was great."

"I'm sure you can use some of it for quotes for your story."

"I'd rather talk with her directly."

Kelsey's moment of accomplishment was being dulled by a pushy reporter. She wanted to tell him to go hide under the rock he crawled out from. That, however, would not be a proper response at a black-tie affair.

"Tim, this gala is $5,000 a table," she said tensely. "I hope you didn't spend that to get a quote from Catherine."

"The owner of the Chronicle sponsors the foundation that's being celebrated tonight."

"Isn't that unethical or something?"

"We're sponsoring the foundation, not Elemynt or your executives," Tim said. "He believes in their mission. Speaking of ethical...Elemynt has a lot of data on its users. How are you feeling about the security precautions being taken to protect it?"

"No comment," Kelsey said, returning her attention to the view of Mission Street below.

"A billion people use your platform. I think they have a right to know how their information is kept safe."

Tim's beady eyes were determined to pressure Kelsey into a response that she would never in a million years give. The glitz and glamour of the evening did not deter him from turning the gala into an unrequited work meeting.

Sarah thankfully breezed on to the balcony to come to Kelsey's rescue. Sarah's equal disdain for Tim was couched in professionalism.

"Tim, that's enough of that," Sarah said. "I told you yesterday we weren't giving out comments tonight."

"I can respect that," Tim said. "Talk to you tomorrow then. Have a good one."

Kelsey returned with Sarah to the embrace of the gala where her fellow Myntors danced the night away. She refused to let the exchange with Tim lessen the beauty of the night.

SIX

Kelsey sipped her kale and green apple smoothie from what she decided was her favorite juice bar at Elemynt. The delicious blend was the perfect accompaniment for her Monday morning click through her email inbox.

There were the usual emails from members of the press seeking replies for this and that. Some of them Kelsey flagged for Sarah to take a second look at. The messages asking for comments on stories they hadn't pitched themselves she moved to the archive. Two emails from Jon outlining what their goals would be that week came through over the weekend. Those would be Kelsey's priority.

Sarah settled into her workspace adjacent to Kelsey's. She too was toting a freshly-made juice.

"Have you recovered from our night of glam?" Sarah asked playfully.

"Yeah, but it's kind of a letdown I can't wear an evening gown to work," Kelsey kidded. "At least not without being stared at."

The ladies' post-weekend small talk was interrupted by a jarring voice coming from the nearby television.

"Breaking news this morning," a TV anchor said to the camera. "The social media company Elemynt in hot water today..."

Sarah and Kelsey both darted toward the screen at the mention of their employer. There was no way an unexpected news alert about the company could be good.

"The Washington Chronicle is reporting that access to the private information of all of Elemynt's one billion users was for sale online," the anchor said.

He described with shades of disbelief how anonymous accounts on the dark web sold login credentials to Elemynt's internal system without the company's knowledge. For $50 each, shady buyers were granted full administrative access to data for any Elemynt account. The alarming amount of private information available through the portal included passwords, emails, phone numbers, and direct messages between users.

Sarah was aghast at the onscreen revelation. "If those people got access to our backend system, they could see way more than that."

Sarah rushed through an explanation of the existence of a back-end portal used by the company's engineers to review the history of any Elemynt account. It was also used by a squadron of platform moderators to resolve account issues like violations of the terms of service. Through the dashboard, they could view the history of an account's posts and direct messages, contact information entered into the app, the date the account was created, the images and profile pictures they uploaded, including drafts, and a list of the people they blocked on the app.

The portal also housed the data points used by Elemynt to categorize the account for advertising purposes, Sarah said. Through facial recognition algorithms, the system could estimate with near-perfect accuracy the age, gender, and race of the account holder. It determined a person's home and work location down to the city, street, and often address based on the geolocation of photos they posted even if the account holder didn't tag the location themselves. The information was matched with known residential versus business location data to separate the difference between the two.

The platform also contained graphs that tracked the account's number of posts, shares, faves, and followers over time and a tool to calculate the degrees of separation between the person and another account. Separate algorithms calculated their hobbies and purchase histories to categorize accounts into buckets for advertisers to choose from. All of the data housed in the system was in addition to voluntary information like the person's date of birth.

Sarah indicated that she never used the dashboard herself but did see it a few times while looking over Leon's shoulder. It required special clearance and direct approval from the Security team to use. In short, they were facing a public relations disaster.

Kelsey's heartbeat raced thinking of the repercussions of a large-scale privacy breach. The data that most people would guess the app kept about their account was apparently a fraction of what the company actually retained. People entrusted Elemynt with their information.

Kelsey instantly worried about the safety of her account and those of her family. She urgently thought through what private information her own that she never anticipated would be at risk for being exposed publicly.

As expected, a deluge of emails poured into Kelsey's inbox with variations on the same subject lines. "Privacy Breach." "Quick Chat." "Comment Needed."

The story was picked up from the Chronicle site by every news media outlet in the world. "A BLOW TO THE SOCIAL MEDIA PLATFORM." "ELEMYNT LOSES USERS' TRUST." News pundits filled the airwaves with lengthy rants about Elemynt's collection of personal data. Critics shouted from proverbial rooftops why people shouldn't trust the opaque platform. They decried the lax security and signaled that a company at its level should have a slew of safeguards in place to prevent similar events from happening.

"We are posting our lives on the internet," one on-air journalist said. "Strong online security has become a basic necessity. We're not seeing that here."

"Lest we forget advertisers have access to this information already," another added. "Elemynt has become immensely wealthy selling users like herds of cattle to the highest bidder."

A suited panelist agreed. "Most people have never in their lives stopped to think about what Elemynt does with their data. What did you think was gonna happen when you put all your info on the internet?"

Jon's voice came through loudly on the speaker of Sarah's phone. "I'm a mile out from the San Francisco airport. Canceling my flight. I'll be there within the hour."

Kelsey rushed to her laptop to pull up the Chronicle story. It was 1,500 words of damning evidence of a massive breach at Elemynt punctuated with quotes from anonymous sources. The details were information only an Elemynt employee would know. The story was filled with admonitions of the company and its senior leadership.

"User privacy has taken a backseat to the companies' desire to collect as much data as possible," an anonymous employee said.

The byline at the top of the article was listed as Timothy Westbrook, the nuisance from the party. Kelsey suddenly regretted downplaying the unheeded requests. But that's what she had been told to do when reviewing the Comms team's group email.

Kelsey pulled up Tim's last message to see if he had indicated the severity of what he was writing. There it was in her archives — an email describing criminal access to Elemynt's backend systems and a request for comment. She missed a message that should have been immediately flagged to Sarah and Jon.

The explosive news story ballooned into a five-alarm fire. Kelsey frantically racked her brain for ways to combat the growing onslaught of media attention on the company's privacy policies. Engagement numbers and new account sign-ups would plummet if lack of confidence in Elemynt became widespread.

Kelsey trekked through her inbox to get a sense of what questions reporters were asking. There were so many it would take a ridiculous effort to collate.

"There's no way we're responding to all these inbounds, right?" Kelsey said to an equally frazzled Sarah.

"Not until we nail the messaging on this," she said.

"Should we get a draft blog post going?"

"Let's hold on that until Troy says what to do."

Kelsey started jotting down notes anyway. The faster they could get up outbound communication and quell the mob of reporters, the better. Kelsey toiled to have multiple options of messaging to choose from depending on what Troy required of them.

Through her scrambling, Kelsey could not ignore the chaotic back-and-forth discussions happening both internally and externally. Commynt was a mess with hundreds of replies from Myntors across several internal posts. Local TV news stations were picking up reports of the effects the ill-gotten account access had on individuals in their communities. A woman in Minnesota had a bomb threat called into her workplace after an online disagreement. A man in Seattle had his explicit messages to several women forwarded to his wife. A young girl whose private nude photos were leaked to her classmates was missing. Several people were terminated from their jobs for sending direct messages with racist language. Teenagers were outed for being gay along with screenshots of private conversations. The number of insane stories went on and on.

"Elemynt knows about your whole life," a pundit said on the still going television. "We're seeing what's possible if your data got in the wrong hands."

A smirking talking head agreed with his fellow contributors. "One mistake makes it online and you'll never be able to live it down."

* * *

Sarah and Kelsey were the first to enter the "War Room," a secure conference space in a hidden location away from the prying eyes and ears of Myntors. Digital clocks that lined the north wall displayed the ticking minutes in multiple time zones. The highest quality video conferencing equipment on the market was built into the walls and into the centerpiece table that spanned the length of the room.

As the representatives of the External Comms team, the two women needed to be abreast of the company's plans for resolving the issue as they were decided. Waiting for information to be relayed to them could spell the difference between a one-day news story and a crisis that would haunt the company for months to come.

The next to enter the War Room was a dapper gentleman who Kelsey had never seen on campus before. His classic handsome features, sculpted hair, and blindingly white smile would be right at home on a magazine cover. The man's impeccably tailored suit was worth more than the wardrobes of a floor full of engineers. He was also the only person Kelsey had seen on campus wearing a tie.

"Kelsey, meet Wyatt Schumacher, our general counsel," Sarah said. "He's the top legal eagle at Elemynt."

Wyatt shook Kelsey's hand assertively. "Looks like we're going to need a lot of my advice today."

"That's a hell of an understatement," Sarah replied.

Kelsey learned about Wyatt in passing in her pre-employment research. As general counsel, he led the company's team of attorneys and was the go-to figure for a wide range of legal issues. The Palo Alto native was a veteran of the U.S. Department of Justice antitrust division, a position he took following his time at Stanford with Troy. Wyatt was considered to be a D.C. power player with friends in the highest echelons of the seat of government. He was inspired by Elemynt's trajectory to trade his bureaucratic position for a seat at the table at what he believed was destined to be one of the most influential tech companies in the country.

"Wyatt here is going to help get us out of this sticky situation, aren't you?" Sarah said, patting him firmly on his shoulder.

"Without breaking a sweat," Wyatt said coolly. "And when I'm done cleaning up, you can write your press releases."

"I love how you forget we're working side by side on this," Sarah smirked.

"In that case, the three of us together are gonna accomplish big things together," he smiled.

Wyatt spoke with a confidence that Kelsey hoped he could back up with a skillset that matched the size of his ego. The extent of his legal acuity in matters related to security breaches had yet to be revealed.

"When I'm not in D.C., I have a desk in your building," Wyatt smiled at Kelsey. "Swing by next time I'm in town."

With a farewell wink, Wyatt took his seat at the table at what would be Troy's right side. Kelsey sat on a bench on the perimeter of the room stifling her unintentional amusement at her colleague's haughty demeanor. What wasn't funny was the privacy breach that loomed over them. The thought of the unresolved disaster brought her back to the daunting task at hand.

Sarah had long since ignored Wyatt. Her focus was on Kelsey sitting next to her.

"About that conversation with Tim at the gala...you didn't tell him anything did you?" Sarah asked.

"Of course not," Kelsey said. "I shut him down as soon as he walked up."

Sarah searched Kelsey's face for a trace of untruth. Kelsey had nothing to hide. If her exchange with Tim revealed the tiniest hint of what was to come, she would have informed Sarah and Jon without hesitation.

Catherine and Jon's arrival halted the exchange between the two colleagues. Moments after, the War Room was packed with other members of the illustrious Dream Team. Troy wasted no time pummeling the room with unrestrained anger. The brunt of his verbal lashing was directed at Leon, his VP of Security.

"There was a breach that you're just now discovering because a journalist wrote about it??" Troy vented. "In what world does that make sense!"

"It's not as bad as the media is making it sound," Leon said. "If we had social security numbers and financial records exposed like other companies did, it would be a bigger deal. Folks have dealt with way worse than this."

"Is that supposed to make me feel better?" Troy seethed.

"Can you please explain to us how this happened?" Catherine asked in a steady tone.

Leon laid out the timeline of a hacker who was able to gain administrator privileges to the dashboard using a backdoor. They accessed the network by searching for unused admin accounts with an easy to crack password. Once they were inside the system, they created hundreds of accounts tied to false identities without being logged by the systems administrator.

"A trigger alert is sent to Security when a user requests access to the dashboard, like when a new hire comes on for instance," Leon said. "Because the system didn't require them to send actual requests, my team never got alerts."

Catherine was far from pleased. "What you're saying is we've built a fortress, someone got the keys, and was letting people in through the back door while we were doing... what?"

"We shut down access to the framework from new accounts created after the date of the initial breach," Leon said in his defense. "We've set it up so everybody at the company has to re-request credentials. We're making sure access tokens match employee ID numbers."

"Shut it all down," Troy said. "No one gets access to that dashboard until I say so."

"For how long?" Leon asked.

"Until we sort this mess out," Troy grimaced.

"Have we sent a message to the people whose accounts were compromised?" Jon asked.

"We forced all the affected accounts to reset their passwords," Leon said. "That'll keep bad actors who got a hold of their old credentials from logging in as them. But if one of these black-market buyers already accessed their info on the dashboard before the reset and saved it somewhere, there's not a whole lot we can do."

Leon unleashed an array of precautionary measures following the breach, but his team's efforts weren't enough to satisfy Troy or Catherine. Troy launched a one-sided verbal attack on Leon in demand of answers to the failures of the Security team.

"How many people are we talking here?" Troy growled.

"Only a small percentage of accounts were affected," Leon said. "No more than two percent."

"That's a lot of people!" Catherine fumed.

"Twenty million goddamn people!" Troy said.

"Not to mention the many, many more who are discussing the breach as we speak," Catherine said.

"If word gets out how about much info we keep on each account, people will lose their shit!" Troy said. "We're talking hundreds of data points each. This could kill our advertising model!"

Kelsey watched as the execs fought over the precise impact of the breach. Too little, too late proclamations of how it could have been prevented were hurled across the table. The crippling incident potentially put the company's existence in jeopardy, a fate no one wanted to see.

Kelsey was stunned, not so much by the virulent anger on display, but rather because no one mentioned how the breach would affect the lives of the people victimized by it. There wasn't a single acknowledgment of the stories emerging of offline tragedies caused by the exposure of private information.

The newest Myntor wanted to speak up on their behalf but stopped short. She was not a member of the Dream Team. It wasn't her place. So she watched as Catherine and Troy traded barbs about the next steps. Once he took a moment to breathe, Troy convinced himself the negative reaction from the public was a temporary problem that would blow over.

"People aren't going to just stop using Elemynt," Troy said assuredly. "Everyone uses it. Their friends, their family. There's also the crazy number of influencers on our platform that they look up to. If we lost a million users, we could get that number back in a week."

Catherine was perturbed at the assessment. "Our investors, on the other hand, would *undoubtedly* notice."

"Employees are gonna feel some kind of way too," Tai piped up. "When negative news that pops up, it tanks morale and productivity goes down."

"We could be opening ourselves up to class action lawsuits too," Wyatt said. "The only thing worse than an angry mob is one led by a team of lawyers."

Mumbles around the table agreed with Wyatt's assessment.

"I'm advising we don't say anything about the nature of the leak," Wyatt continued. "The more we say publicly, the more it'll be used against us."

"We know the media loves the platform," Jon said. "If we give them nothing, the story dies and we're right back in their good graces."

Catherine was unmoved. "Not making a statement can lead to more speculation from the press."

"In that case, we put a blog post up on a Friday," Jon said. "We wait until right before the weekend. Journalists aren't writing stories at the end of the week and people sure aren't reading them. We go that route and no one can accuse us of being silent on the issue."

"We're not laying out exactly what happened are we?" Wyatt asked.

Troy shook his head vigorously. "No one knows how many people were affected. Just us."

"Do it and keep the blog post brief," Catherine said.

Wyatt agreed. "Jon, you get a draft going and my team will make sure there's nothing in there that will get us sued."

Kelsey sighed with dismay. Elemynt always prided itself on being a company for the people and here they were working to cover up the breach instead of notifying the public. They could offer people more ways to protect themselves or instructions on how to notify authorities if the leak caused them personal trauma. Some extension of goodwill that recognized that actual lives would be affected by Elemynt's lapse in security. A meager blog post didn't seem like the honest way to go.

"What are we doing about employees, again?" Kelsey said from the bench. "They're going to want a deeper explanation. A press release may not be the best way to go."

Tai glared at Kelsey for treading on her territory. "They can see the blog post when it's up. We follow it up in all-hands with a short talk from Troy. We have contingency plans for emergencies. If you want to talk about it, we can take this offline."

Kelsey said nothing further. Minutes later, the meeting came to a close. They had their assignments.

Jon rallied the External Comms team to begin their execution of what would be a delicate task. Resolving the issue with the breach would require a strange reversal of thinking for Kelsey. For the first time, she was taking defensive measures for a company, not proactively reaching out to media. Reporters were chasing after her rather than Kelsey hounding them for story placement.

Jon was, in contrast, fairly unshaken by the ordeal. Kelsey resolved to rely on her manager's understanding of how to move forward. All things considered, she was still a newbie at Elemynt. She would carry out the orders he handed down to the best of her ability.

The finished blog post about the incident, a result of several rounds of editing by various teams, was published before dawn on the appointed Friday. Titled "Protecting Your Privacy" and attributed to Elemynt's Head of Trust and Safety, it was an inoffensive and somewhat vague promise by the company to do better in the future.

"We take the security of Elemynt accounts very seriously," it read. "We worked quickly to solve the issue and have taken further steps to make sure nothing like this will occur in the future."

The post was free from comments from executives and included a conservative estimate of 40,000 accounts affected by the breach. It was capped with links to where people who used the app could review currently available security features.

Kelsey hoped the blog post would be enough to satisfy critics for a while. She needed a break from the drama.

* * *

A continuous flow of high-energy music powered through the speakers of the gym's morning spin class. The thumping beat served as the cadence for Kelsey and her fellow cyclists to sync their bodies with the rhythm. Kelsey forced the pedals of the spin bike into their circular motion. Her blonde tresses were pulled back into a ponytail and away from her face. Her sports bra clung tightly to her sweat-drenched chest.

Kelsey wanted badly to shake off the aftermath of the privacy breach that threatened her inner peace. Her heart stopped every time an email alert pulsated her phone. Feeling on edge was her new normal. She found herself coming home and curling up in a ball and not doing much of anything. Getting out of the door and onto the spin bike was her first step toward reversing the negative energy.

The perky instructor at the front of the class grunted into the microphone strapped over her ear. "Keep those legs moving!" she yelled.

The rows of women pedaled furiously. Kelsey charged faster. Breathe. Push.

Spin class was the reset button that always made Kelsey feel more control of her life. The rush of adrenaline. The fire burning through her muscles. They were the fuel for Kelsey to push her body to the limit. The sweat dripping from her torso was the prize for a job well done. She would rather torture her body than her brain.

Kelsey gripped the handle tighter. Fight through the weakness. Never give up. Ever.

Kelsey pedaled will all her might. Her heartbeat drummed against her ribcage with each rotation. She dialed the knob to increase resistance to a higher level.

"You are strong, ladies!" the instructor called out to the room.

Small hiccups at Elemynt would not defeat Kelsey. She came to the company to be excellent. To do the best work of her life. There was an unexpected twist in her path, but it would not take away from the brightness of her future.

"Last climb!" the instructor yelled. "Give it all you've got! Make it count! Ten! Nine! Eight…"

The wheels of Kelsey's bike spun furiously, outpacing everyone around her. Nothing could truly stop a strong woman except herself. She would always keep pushing.

* * *

Kelsey ventured off to a sprawling area of the campus where a row of food trucks served tasty lunch bites to hungry employees. She surveyed her options. A kosher truck offered falafel and shawarma, a barbecue station served heaping platters of smoked meats and sumptuous sides. The popular Vietnamese food truck endowed Myntors with delicious bánh mì sandwiches and fresh spring rolls.

Deciding on what meal to have should have been easy for Kelsey. However, days' worth of emails in her inbox regarding the breach clouded her ability to think beyond her immediate concerns. On the plus side, the rate at which they came in was dwindling.

Kelsey stepped into the queue for deli sandwiches behind two chatty guys on break from the slog of the day. In the brief time following its occurrence, the privacy fiasco was still on employees' minds, including theirs.

"They put shipping the breach patch at the top of our work list at the daily scrum meeting," one said as he swiped his badge to receive his lunch. "But it was fixed by ten other teams by the end of the day."

"Troy has got this covered, man," his friend responded. "It was a big deal but kinda not, you know?"

"Can I get a ham on rye with extra honey mustard?" the first said to the waiting cashier.

"Make that two."

Kelsey needed a table to herself. While she sat alone cutting into her chicken salad sandwich, the Myntors around her happily gabbed among themselves over their lunch. There was no denying that for most people at Elemynt, it was back to business as usual. Kelsey hoped to get there soon as well. She instinctively picked up her phone to accompany her during her meal. A text from her father sat atop her notifications.

"Did you see this?" it read. "All the guys I follow are talking about it."

At the end of the text was a link to a video post on Elemynt. Since she joined the company, her dad was prone to sending her links to his favorite interesting posts. Total dad moves. Kelsey pressed play.

The shaky video captured an older, white woman on a barely audible rant in what looked to be a fast-food restaurant. The bystander panned the phone's camera to show a pair of distraught Hispanic women being subjected to a verbal attack.

"Speak English!" the irate woman yelled at the two. "This is America!"

One of the women was rattled, but undeterred by the woman's outburst.

"Ma'am, why is it your business if we're speaking Spanish or not?" she said. "Why are you in our conversation anyway? We were talking to each other, not you."

In the periphery of the video, Kelsey could see other patrons of the restaurant were befuddled by the loud exchange. Kelsey was as well.

The aggressive woman whose skin was reddening with anger yelled to the onlookers. "These illegals are bringing drugs into our country! They're doing crime and spreading disease!"

"You're spitting in my face, ma'am," the Hispanic woman said resolutely.

"Go back to Mexico!" she retorted.

The second woman stepped in between the two. "First of all, we are Puerto Rican, not Mexican. We are citizens of the United States. Secondly, we were enjoying our lunch before you came over here bothering us."

The unidentified woman continued to lash out at the two, wagging her finger in both of their faces and threatening to "call immigration." It was an unsettling scene that Kelsey had no desire to continue viewing. She wanted to have a meal in peace, not watch a showdown at a lunch counter.

Before she clicked away, the video showed who Kelsey assumed was the manager of the restaurant firmly escorting the still screaming woman out of the front door. A round of applause from the bystanders celebrated her departure. The two women were left shaking their heads.

"Apparently, we look 'illegal'," one of them shrugged.

Kelsey ended the video. Beneath it was the number of views. More than 175,000. One of those being her father and now her.

Watching an unhinged woman was not how she planned to spend her brief lunchtime. She didn't need the negativity in her life.

The worn-out Myntor sighed and put the phone down. This was not her day. She dug into the sandwich and stared into space.

* * *

As the shouts of criticism against the company evaporated into whispers,

Comms and the Dream Team were left to put flowers on the gravestone of a dead issue. Kelsey pitched Gary and the Product team on an idea for a campaign guaranteed to instill goodwill back into the hearts of users — "International Friends' Day." They could pair the holiday with a visual celebration on the app that highlighted the heartwarming connections between friends. Kelsey hoped it would remind people of the reason they likely joined Elemynt.

The Product teams took Kelsey's suggestion and ran with it. To sweeten the mass appeal of the feature, they built in an algorithm that identified pairs of people who followed each other on Elemynt for a long time and consistently faved each other's photos since they first connected. Using facial recognition tools, a photo was programmatically selected in which the two account owners appeared together smiling. The image would be placed in both of their feeds along with exuberant graphics marking the celebration of "Friends' Day."

To avoid inadvertently tagging exes or the deceased, one of the engineers added a layer of code that would only deliver the custom graphic if both accounts faved a photo from the other in the previous two weeks. With Jade's help, Kelsey also arranged for celebrities to post their own friendship photos along with the hashtag #FriendsDay.

Within hours of its launch, the feature was used by tens of thousands of people on Elemynt. The message of the importance of personal connections rang true throughout the app. The press covered the feature in detail, even sharing their Friends' Day photos on their individual accounts.

There was no feeling more special feeling to a person working in PR than having a killer idea being turned into a wildly successful global sensation. Kelsey was in awe that, so far, she was able to do it twice.

While the sentiment from people using the Elemynt app was at an all-time high following the campaign, employee confidence had not returned to its pre-breach levels.

Following the lingering sting of the incident, Myntors voiced their collective concern about Elemynt's role in the lives of individuals who trusted the platform. Tai came up with the brilliant idea of creating a "hack week" focused on privacy. Anyone in the company — engineers and non-engineers included — with a compelling idea of how to strengthen privacy at Elemynt would come together for a few days to turn their ideas into prototypes. The top selections would be presented directly to Troy for judging. The CEO would decide which of the best to put into production.

The hack week turned out to be a tremendous success with Myntors across the board. The can-do spirit of the company was back and the camaraderie could be felt across the campus.

The remaining piece of the puzzle left to solve was the general public that did not use the app ad thus did not fully understand its power to connect. Because of the onslaught of negative news coverage, Elemynt was more likely to be associated with the breach than the wonderful social media platform its devotees knew it to be. Troy was a folk hero to many, but that love was not translating to the app itself.

To increase the number of new sign-ups, Elemynt had to change public consciousness. In came Jon to the rescue.

Their intrepid VP of Comms arranged for Troy to participate in a nationally televised interview on a major network that would be seen by millions. The interview would frame Elemynt as an American success story and a thinker who made his dreams reality.

The person who needed the most convincing to participate was Troy himself. The company lead rarely gave interviews because he much preferred to focus on the engineering of his product. Jon conferred to him that not participate would further disrupt his ability to maintain that focus. The team needed Troy to invoke every iota of his rock-star charm to turn critics into fans.

The news organizations Jon spoke with predictably strove with all their might to be the one to land the exclusive interview with the highly-regarded figure. An appearance by the tech founder on their network would reap stratospheric ratings and a career-high for the reporter involved.

The Dream Team and Comms ultimately agreed that legendary news anchor Bruce Frederickson was the best choice. His must-watch interviews ranged from sit-downs with Hollywood royalty to world leaders to heroic individuals from various walks of life. The newsman possessed the clout that Elemynt needed to give the conversation with Troy a stamp of journalistic integrity.

Before an agreement was finalized, the Comms team delivered a list of no-gos to the producers. Trade secrets and Troy's personal life were off-limits. In exchange, the company would offer access to areas of the Elemynt campus never before seen on camera. If the producers dared to surprise Troy with accusatory questions, it would be the last interview they ever got from the CEO or anyone else remotely connected to Elemynt.

The night of the airing, Kelsey set up a makeshift screening room in one of the more comfy conference spaces at HQ. Kelsey could watch the interview in solitude while she cleared away the remaining yellow flag emails in her inbox. Her companions for the evening were a bowl of wasabi peas and a vegan cookie from the micro-kitchen.

The start of the TV segment announced itself from the big screen affixed to the wall. A succession of stately images of Troy was shown in an inspiring montage.

"Troy McCray is a man of vision," the voiceover began. "The Elemynt chief keeps one eye on the company and the other on the future of social communication."

The sit-down interview was intercut with footage of Bruce and Troy walking leisurely through the most picturesque areas of campus. The stroll cast Troy as the laid-back everyman rather than a captive subject being interrogated in the hot seat.

"We've built the digital equivalent of the town square," Troy said with gravitas. "It's our number one priority that people feel safe when they interact with their friends and the people they've connected with. We're investing more in security than we ever have before."

The veteran interviewer lobbed a series of softball questions at his guest which provided Troy with a multitude of opportunities to deliver his prepared talking points. To viewers, he was the benevolent genius who was truly humbled by an unfortunate experience. He only wanted to make the world a better place.

There was no direct mention of the privacy issue. No controversial exchanges and no outright apologies. But Troy did radiate love in each of his responses. The message was overwhelmingly clear: Elemynt hears you and we're doing our best.

Bruce concluded the segment with a congenial handshake. "Troy McCray, thank you for your time and best of luck."

Kelsey turned off the television and closed her laptop. Troy did well enough, invoking the charm of his onstage addresses at all-hands. She could go home happy. A turbulent period was put to rest.

The morning after, Bruce posted an adorable selfie with Troy to his Elemynt account. It was the subtlest of signals to the anchor's followers that Troy was a chill guy who happened to be the CEO of a Silicon Valley powerhouse. Troy followed the photo with a post of his own thanking the interviewer and offering a sunny vision of Elemynt's next steps.

"I believe we must continue to be ambitious," Troy wrote. "As the world evolves, so will we."

* * *

Tourists flocked in droves to Union Square, an elegant outdoor plaza in the heart of San Francisco. Enchanted visitors snapped photos of the iconic red and gold cable cars rolling steadily up the steep hills of Powell Street. The hub was populated by afternoon shoppers admiring the luxury shopping destinations, multi-level department stores, and designer boutiques. Children scampered about with their parents in tow. Teens snapped selfies to commemorate the moment with friends.

Kelsey and Daniela soaked in the cheery activity from their perch on a bench under the swaying palm trees. They waited for Jade who was set to emerge soon from a meeting at the Westin St. Francis hotel across the street.

The excursion to the city was a breath of relief after the privacy scandal. Stepping away from campus was an ideal way to reset and take in the area outside the walls of Elemynt headquarters. Daniela was in exceptionally good spirits.

"Ro took me to an art show in Berkeley as a treat," Daniela shared with a smile. "We haven't been spending as much time together because of work so she wanted to do something she knew I loved. The art was spectacular, of course. But there wasn't a work or person in there as beautiful as my girl."

"Aww! She was probably thinking the same about you!" Kelsey said, clapping in admiration.

"I'm sure!" Daniela said. "You know Ro's the quiet masculine type. Under that, I swear she's a teddy bear, which is what I love about her. She's also my rock when I need her to be."

"Lucky ladies!" Kelsey said.

"I'm thinking I want to take her out for a nice date this weekend to say thank you."

"Maybe get her something cute from one of the stores over here?" Kelsey said, pointing in the direction of the Tiffany jewelry boutique across from their post.

"Jewelry?" Daniela doubled over laughing. "If I gave Ro a gift with diamonds, she would think I was breaking up with her. The way to my girl's heart is a pair of new Jordans. Her love language is size 10 basketball shoes."

Work slowed for Kelsey following the past week's media blitz, while Daniela's had ramped up. Her friend was busy preparing for the upcoming Pride parade in San Francisco in which hundreds of Myntors would march in a contingent. Her biggest priority of all was Elemynt's upcoming diversity report that was set to be released to the public in a few days.

There was a large weight on Daniela's shoulders to execute it properly. Diversity reports stemmed from a public outcry in recent years about the lack of diversity at tech companies. In an effort to be transparent, larger companies issued reports outlining the demographic breakdown of their employees. Gender, race, age, and more were tallied as well as those in technical versus non-technical roles and the diversity of employees in managerial positions. Weak numbers were usually offset with descriptions of initiatives the company launched to increase diversity within their workforces.

No company in Silicon Valley could claim impressive numbers, including Elemynt which was comparatively on the lower end of the scale. However, it was better to share the data than not. Foregoing a report was seen as having something to hide.

"We may not be the best, but the Diversity team is trying," Daniela said with reserved optimism. "We don't want public perception to define us."

"Sounds like a fun time," Kelsey said.

"It's a real party," Daniela sighed. "Lucky for us, counting people of color at Elemynt doesn't take long."

The women shared a laugh at the uncomfortable truth. The diversity numbers were what they were.

Kelsey spotted Jade, mistress of all things celebrity, tiptoeing across Powell Street looking like a star herself. She waved her Swarovski crystal-studded clutch bag at the ladies to alert them to her coming presence. Tourists snapped pictures of the well-dressed figure passing them thinking she may be someone famous. In many ways, they were right.

"Hollywood loves Elemynt again!" Jade cheered as she approached her colleagues.

"Congrats!" Kelsey and Daniela returned in unison.

Jade positioned herself on the bench between them. "Things were looking shaky there for a minute, girls. Getting the big-name celebrity partners on the platform has been rough since this privacy commotion. But guess who's bouncing back!"

The girls again congratulated Jade on the achievement with whistles of support. In the wake of the breach, they needed far more positive energy in their lives than negative. Jade was a champion of pulling through for her partners.

"I have an idea for how we can keep the momentum going," Kelsey said.

Jade smiled broadly. "Okay, whatcha got?"

"Back in Boston, I put together a women's speaker series where we brought these strong female voices in to talk to women who worked in the area. How cool would it be to have something like that at Elemynt? We bring in people like celebrities or authors or CEOs to come speak just to the female Myntors. It would be a total inspiration for them! And we get the speakers to go live on their accounts like we did for Lili Skye."

"Loving it!" Jade exclaimed. "A formal event with a girl-power twist."

"Our 'A' student comes through again!" Daniela agreed. "Great idea, Kelsey. People are going to be so into it."

Kelsey was overjoyed that her colleagues were receptive to her idea. With their support, she could turn it into an amazing ongoing event that the women would love. Kelsey again found herself needing Jade to make the asks to her celebrity partners. Luckily, her run of successes netted a more ready "yes" than before. She was on an incomparable hot streak.

"Here's what I want you to do, love," Jade said. "Make a list of the potential influencers you want to go after, and I'll have my team start making calls. And do your best to be realistic, if you can. We're probably not getting like a Hillary Clinton level person to come to Elemynt for free."

"We don't pay our speakers?" Kelsey asked.

"Sometimes?" Jade said with a rise in her voice. "Okay, rarely. Remember what I told Lili in the green room? That I wasn't kidding about. Most people just want to come see the Elemynt campus and go live to their account and say they were here. We are so selective about who we bring in, it's almost an honor to come."

"Gotcha," Kelsey said. "Powerful women who love Elemynt."

"You should make sure you have women of color on your list too," Daniela said. "I'll suggest a few names if that's okay."

"Yes, let's do all of that," Jade said. "Also, make sure you work with Tai on internal promotion. Get her to post it on Commynt, put announcements on the campus TV screens... make it a big deal."

"I was kinda hoping for a headache-free experience," Kelsey said. "Tai is so..."

"Testy?" Daniela smirked.

"Yes, let's go with that," Kelsey laughed.

"Working with that glorious woman is a necessary evil," Jade waved dramatically before catching herself. "I'm not calling her like *literally* evil. She does always have the problems of the company on her back."

Daniela nodded in agreement. "Tai doesn't have to solve crises herself which she wants us to think. Her job is to shape how they're presented to employees. She has to spin bad issues into good news."

"We all have hard jobs, but you don't see me moping and stomping around campus," Kelsey said.

"If I wore cargo shorts and Doc Marten boots every day, I'd probably do the same thing," Jade laughed. "Seriously though, her buy-in is what's going to make your speaker series idea a hit. Internal promotion is what gets the people to show up. If we have full rooms and can show impact, we'll get more support from the Dream Team to keep it going."

"And if it goes wrong for whatever reason — boom — there goes a positive review on your next evaluation and that's a fact," Daniela laughed. "No pressure."

Kelsey was more invigorated to perfect the proposed idea. "One woman is not going to come between me and getting this done right."

"You tell 'em, girl," Jade smiled. "Okay enough about that...who do you want to speak first?"

Kelsey knew exactly who. Grace Oliver. She was an Emmy-winning actress turned executive producer and an award-winning author. Grace was also a huge personality on Elemynt and an icon for women around the world.

There were plenty of celebs on the app who posted cute selfies or behind the scenes photos. Grace did the same while also using her platform to support the causes she believed in. The star was a vocal advocate of women's rights who used her Elemynt account to share inspirational messages for her female followers. The comments on her posts were always filled with sincere messages of gratitude. Kelsey couldn't wait to bring her uplifting presence to Elemynt HQ.

SEVEN

Kelsey stood to the side while a flurry of production assistants and technical crews rushed to set up for the Q&A with Grace.

The on-campus production room that Jade specifically selected for the event was smaller in size than the auditorium for Lili Skye. To heighten the intimacy of the conversation, rows of chairs were lined up in front of a compact stage nestled close to the audience. Video cameras were at the ready for kickoff.

It was Kelsey's first time at the helm of an event of its kind at her actual workplace. She was determined to make its execution flawless. Jade pitched in to arrange the logistics of making it a reality. Daniela offered to assist with setup to make the room picture-perfect. Kelsey in her role as host would pose the questions to Grace onstage. A daunting feat she was happy not to have to tackle alone.

The Q&A was the first in what Kelsey hoped were many events in a speaker series for the Women+ group. It had to go off without a hitch. The company already handed Kelsey her dreams on a platter. She wanted to give something back in return. The opportunity for female employees to meet with icons of various industries would be an impactful come together moment for the women in attendance.

Kelsey's primary concern in the moments leading up to the start was putting aside the fears of what could go wrong. It was very possible that she would forget the questions she was going to ask. She might bore the audience. She might accidentally fall off her stool and *really* entertain them. Kelsey was nervous about being nervous. And for good reason. Her name was on the event. If she failed, it might be the first and last Q&A she ever did.

Jade directed the crew to get the studio lighting just right for Grace. The stage was accented with beams of blue that matched the cover of Grace's book which appeared on the screens around the room. As part of the deal to get her to do the talk for free, Elemynt purchased 200 books that would be distributed to employees. Grace would sign as many as she could in the fifteen minutes she had before she needed to head to the airport.

Daniela and Jade sidled up to Kelsey to check that the space was to the organizer's liking. There were mere moments before employees packed into the room for the hour.

"People are going to love this, I swear!" Kelsey said. "Jade, you are a magical woman."

"Anything for you two," Jade smiled. "I'll be adding fairy godmother to my resume. Now let's get these last-minute touches together, shall we?"

"By the way, Kelsey..." Daniela nudged. "Did you get my suggestions of names to invite for future events?"

"Yep and I promise I'll add them to the list," Kelsey affirmed.

The scramble of workers parted to reveal Grace Oliver entering the room crafted especially for her. Grace's innate star power radiated throughout the rapidly quieting space. She was the kind of celebrity that magazines called "approachable" or the "girl next door." Whether she was sporting an evening gown or business casual as she was that day, Grace's friendly personality always shone through.

The spectating Myntors pointed and chattered in close whispers at the entrance of their guest. Grace was followed by a campus security guard and a young female assistant carrying their Elemynt lanyards.

Grace approached Kelsey with open arms. Kelsey returned it with a friendly embrace of their acclaimed speaker.

"We're so glad you could come today!" Kelsey said. "Employees have been sending us messages for a week now saying how excited they are to see you."

"Are you kidding? The pleasure's all mine!" she said glowingly. "I get to see behind the scenes at Elemynt? I've been using your app for years!"

"We're so glad you are!" Kelsey gushed.

Kelsey introduced Grace to Daniela and Jade who paused their tasks to officially welcome their guest. Jade greeted Grace with an air kiss and a bottled water.

"You two head to the green room for me," Jade said. "You can talk a bit before we get started. Daniela and I will come fetch you when we're ready to get started."

As the pair exited the space, they heard Grace's assistant query Jade.

"I wanted to ask what do I have to do to get verified?" she asked to Jade's amusement.

Grace and Kelsey ventured to the green room around the corner, a compact area outfitted with comfy couches, vanity mirrors, and perfect lighting for picture-taking. The neon green Elemynt logo that centered the room served as the background for VIP selfies. Free swag and sweet treats were available within arm's reach wherever the guest stood.

"Thanks again for taking the time to speak to our staff!" Kelsey said.

"An invitation to come to Elemynt? No way I would miss out on that."

Grace sat on the couch across from Kelsey. Her face was suddenly riddled with concern. The shift caught Kelsey off-guard.

"While I'm here I have a question for you," Grace said quietly. "I'm having a problem with trolls in the comments on my posts. You follow me...you know I speak up for women and the stuff we go through. Apparently, that's ticked off men who are saying ugly things on the regular. I get messages every day from these guys harassing me. It's getting worse too."

Kelsey's heart sunk. She desperately hoped that Grace wouldn't bring up a negative issue in their onstage interview. The goal was to keep the conversation on the inspirational side of things. A narrative about harassers would not only dampen the spirit in the room, it would be front-page news by the time reporters got wind of it.

"Getting harassed constantly is wearing me out," Grace confessed. "I don't want to not interact in my comments. The talks I have with women there are important to me and to them too. Seeing these messages calling me a 'bitch' or telling me I should kill myself...it's just getting stressful."

Kelsey cringed at the thought of having to deal with horrifying treatment on the app on an ongoing basis. She felt genuinely terrible for Grace and the pain she was clearly going through. No human should have to endure that. Elemynt did have built-in settings that could help mitigate the problem she faced.

"Have you used the tools in the app that let you block or report accounts?" Kelsey asked.

"I'm doing all of that, I swear," Grace sighed. "I keep getting responses that the comments don't violate your terms of service? Is there anything Elemynt can do about that?"

The issue of trolls on the app wasn't one that Kelsey could handle personally. She was a communicator for the company. Kelsey anticipated she could get the problem in front of Jade though. The Head of Media Partnerships could possibly fast track the issue to the Trust and Safety team since Grace was a high-profile user. If Kelsey remembered correctly, the team had the ability to put her at the front of the queue for moderation or flag her account for special monitoring.

Grace seemed to be more disturbed by the ordeal than she let on. A forced smile couldn't hide that speaking about the harassment to another person made its negative impact on her life more real. Still, Kelsey admired her resolve to fight through it.

In the meantime, there was nothing Kelsey could do to immediately rectify the issue. A crowd of Myntors in the next room over were awaiting Grace's presence. The confidence she exuded through her Elemynt posts meant a great deal to Kelsey and the women in attendance. Seeing the star's pain played out in front of an audience seeking her motivating words would be hurtful.

* * *

Kelsey ascended to the stage of the event with Grace waiting in the wings.

"Ladies and gentlemen," Kelsey said, nodding to the few men in the room. "Welcome to our Women+ event! We're so glad to have our special guest here. She's a television star and author of the new book 'Lights, Camera...Taking Action.' Please welcome actress, producer, and entrepreneur...Grace Oliver!"

The effervescent audience infused the room with applause as Grace made her way to the stage. The audible appreciation was punctuated by whoops and the invigorated yelling of Grace's name. The superstar was sitting right in front of the Myntors for a private conversation with them. The attendees were riled up for an exceptional experience only their employer could bring.

The woman of the hour joined Kelsey onstage thankful for the generous welcome she received. There was no trace of the sadness they discussed minutes prior. Her incredible smile shone under the flawless stage lighting as they took to the stools provided for them. Kelsey fell right into the interview mode she prepared for.

"Grace, you're an actress, you've become a producer with your own shows and your book just came out. How do you juggle all of that?"

"I think women are natural multitaskers and nurturers," Grace said thoughtfully. "I wanted to have more of a say about how I expressed the creativity inside me. When you're an actress, you pretty much say the lines you're given, then it's a wrap.

So, I made the decision for myself to move from in front of the camera to behind it. Now you see I'm creating content that I know other people can relate to. It's not the same stuff that's out there right now that we've seen forever."

The audience clapped in agreement. Jade and Daniela gave Kelsey a thumbs up signaling that their friend was off to a great start.

"You're one of the most in-demand women in Hollywood so I'm sure you have a lot of opportunities people offer you," Kelsey said. "How do you decide which ones to go after and what to pass up?"

"There's as much success in saying no as there is in saying yes," Grace said confidently. "Knowing what you want your life to look like is magic."

"We love that!" Kelsey said to the audience.

"You also have to think about how far you're willing to push yourself to reach your goals," Grace said. "It's so real...saying no to other people can be the hardest thing. But sometimes it starts with learning how to say no to ourselves."

The audience murmured to each other with nods of understanding. Many of the women were faced with the same decision at some point in their personal and professional lives.

A choice stared Kelsey in the face. She hesitated to ask Grace about how she used Elemynt to connect with other people. She didn't want to open the door to bringing up Grace's topmost concern. Talking about harassment would put Elemynt in a poor light and upend what was so far a poignant conversation.

On the other hand, it was the question every high-profile guest was asked in their on-campus Q&As. The main reason they were invited to headquarters was to remind employees that their work had deeper meaning and infinite social impact. The goal was for them to walk away motivated to continue to excel.

"Oh my gosh, is there anything you can't do?" Kelsey asked instead. An innocent question.

"Well, I don't sing," Grace joked. The audience laughed along politely.

Kelsey could see Jade in the back of the room motioning for her to ask the damn question.

Kelsey inhaled and engaged Grace. "How do you use Elemynt in your daily life? What keeps you coming back?"

Please keep it positive, Kelsey pleaded wordlessly. Don't mention the trolls. The hardships Grace shared in the green room were undoubtedly important. Mentioning them in front of a room full of employees would undo Kelsey's great work and that of her colleagues. Even worse, word of the admonition might get back to Troy who would put a stop to having guest speakers for the foreseeable future. That would be the end of the series before it had a chance to ramp up. Grace nodded reassuringly.

"I share a lot of glam moments with my followers which everybody, of course, loves," Grace said. "I also feel like it's my responsibility to speak up about these important issues like women's rights and gender equality. I have this platform. I want to use it to start a dialogue and for women to support each other."

Kelsey was riddled with guilt knowing the true hurt behind the answer. Only the two of them were aware of Grace's omission of her increasingly difficult challenge with the platform. Grace bared her heart in the green room. In front of the audience, she kept the anguish inside.

"I want to change the world for the better," Grace added. "For me, that starts with using social media for good."

Kelsey breathed a sigh of relief that Grace's answer would end there. The interview would go on without controversy.

The pair continued the onstage conversation amicably with Kelsey laughing along and Grace answering the series of questions with humor and sincerity. The audience lapped up the words of wisdom that arose from the exchange. Daniela and Jade watched Kelsey's performance with delight. The event turned out exactly how the group hoped.

"Any last advice for the people?" Kelsey asked.

Grace shifted to face the audience directly.

"You all work at Elemynt," she said. "You are shaping the technology that's changing how people communicate. You gotta own that responsibility and be inspired to be your very best selves."

A burst of applause expressed gratitude to Grace for her presence and kindness. Grace bowed humbly and blew kisses to the adoring audience. The women in the room could leave proud that they were part of something bigger than themselves. Their ambitions had no limit.

As expected, most of the Myntors rushed to get to their next meeting at the conclusion of the Q&A. Because schedules at Elemynt were regimented into 30-minute increments, it left no time for them to get their books signed. Daniela wisely made sure to add buffer time in her calendar so could she walk away with an autographed copy for herself. She was joined by a restless queue of about 40 of their colleagues waiting to meet Grace at the front of the room.

Kelsey and Jade looked at each other in worry. There were far too many

Myntors and not enough time for Grace to sign every book. Her assistant was doubly worried.

"Grace has to get to the airport," she said nervously.

The assistant's attempt to rush things along was met with a look from Grace that insisted that she calm down. Jade and Kelsey joined Grace at her side.

"Aren't you going to miss your flight?" Jade asked.

"No way, we always add extra time in between meetings just in case," Grace said while continuing to sign books. "This is my thank you for the awesome work you're doing. The airport can wait."

True to her word, Grace stayed to sign the books for every Myntor in line, each with a personal message. She also posed for a selfie with everyone who asked. The effort was above and beyond what she was expected to do during her visit. The employees thanked Grace profusely for her time and presence.

After Grace was done and the room was finally clear, she approached Kelsey to offer thanks for extending the invitation. "You have fantastic people working here," Grace said. "It feels awesome to get that kind of love."

"I promise we'll do our best to get rid of that troll situation," Kelsey said wholeheartedly.

"Anything you can do would be so appreciated."

"Take down my number," Kelsey said. "Feel free to call if a problem pops up."

* * *

Jon slammed his phone on his desk, jolting Kelsey and Sarah out of their daily email routine. He gripped the miraculously unshattered device with anger that Kelsey never saw before from him. His deep breaths and flaring nostrils indicated that something was very, very wrong.

"Washington Chronicle website," Jon said to his team members. "Read it now."

Sarah and Kelsey dutifully clicked over to the news website where they were confronted with a shocking headline. "ELEMYNT BREACH MORE WIDESPREAD THAN REPORTED."

The breaking news story dealt a swift and crushing blow to Elemynt. It accused the company of misrepresenting the number of users whose information was exposed in the breach. The true number was in the millions, not the 40,000 Elemynt told the public.

"Executives sought to hide the true reach to minimize the damage a privacy scandal would cause," the story read.

Many paragraphs followed with quotes from anonymous employees and those "familiar with the source." Kelsey's rising aggravation was not far from Jon's. A smoking gun was revealed and they had no idea who was holding it. Just as their work-life had cleared up for the better, they were back in unanticipated hot water.

Jon paced near his desk with clenched teeth. "One small breach that we moved past. Now someone wants to drag us back into it? For what! What are they hoping to gain from this?"

"We can send a response to the Chronicle and make them update their story…" Kelsey suggested.

"There's also the blog if we want to do a longer statement," Sarah added.

Sarah and Kelsey floated several suggestions to Jon. He waved them away. "We're meeting with the exec team in exactly 28 minutes," Jon said. "Troy will tell us—"

Sarah interrupted Jon's momentum with an appalled gasp. Her eyes were fixed on the nearby TV screens.

"You have got to be kidding me," she said.

Jon hastily reached for the remote to turn the volume up on the TV. The voice of Senator Deniece Layne, the Congresswoman from California, traveled across the open office. A live televised press conference was underway. The Senator stood resolutely behind a podium at the Capitol building. She was in the presence of a packed room of reporters and clicking cameras. The assembly in the room waited eagerly to hear what she would say.

"It is common knowledge that Elemynt is a social media platform that is a part of the lives of many Americans," Senator Layne began. "These recent revelations that the number of this country's citizens whose private information was exposed totaled in the millions comes as a shock."

Jon crossed his arms and glared at the TV. "You read a news story. Congratulations. Is there a point to this?"

"It is important that we uncover the truth directly from the source," she continued. "As chairwoman of the Senate Commerce Committee, I am announcing a Congressional hearing during which we will demand transparency from Elemynt executives about their mishandling of personal information. Elemynt needs to be held accountable through regulation and whatever sanctions Congress determines are necessary."

The Comms team watched the announcement in astonishment, unable to believe the scene unfolding in front of them. Why the United States government needed to be involved in a small data breach was beyond comprehension. A hearing would unearth an issue the company already put behind them and turn it into a ridiculous media frenzy.

With every word the Congresswoman spoke, Kelsey envisioned the negative press coverage, speculation, and out-and-out distrust from the public that would emerge from the hearing. What made the situation more unbelievable was that a longtime friend of Catherine called for and would lead the proceeding.

Jon, who was on the edge of plowing his fist through the middle of the TV screen, composed himself with the decorum required of an open office setting. Myntors at the workspaces around them traded shocked reactions with each other regarding the news. Commynt was undoubtedly on fire with internal discussions centered on the coming hearing.

Minutes after the announcement, all three of the Comms team members' phones were ringing with news alerts and a succession of internal emails.

An indignant Sarah shook her head in defiance. "She doesn't have anything better to do with her time? There's criminals running around the country and she's worried about us."

Kelsey showed her phone to her colleagues. "She's broadcasting the press conference live to her Elemynt account too."

"The irony," Sarah scoffed.

The video was overlaid with a stream of comments from her followers lauding her stance. A few dissenters who stood in support of the company interjected their opinions. They were unfortunately greatly outnumbered.

Kelsey could not shake the feeling that she was responsible for the appalling turn of events. The woman who she convinced to increase her engagement on the Elemynt app was plotting the downfall of the company. Kelsey's hero betrayed her in the worst possible way. The Senator who she was so excited to meet in person was unraveling her world with her misguided announcement.

"This is the United States...we have a right to privacy," Senator Layne said to the cameras. "The abuse of personal information is a violation of that right."

Taking on someone whom she admired would be an unprecedented feat for Kelsey. However, in her mind, she was already formulating PR strategies to counter the attack. There was a myriad of ways to combat the unreasonable framing of Elemynt. They just had to decide which route to take.

"We can put out a statement that shuts down everything she's saying," Kelsey said to the reeling team. "We can add facts and figures. Highlight the people internally who work to secure the platform."

"Fantastic ideas but we're doing none of that," Jon said as he typed away at his phone. "We're not playing defense here. If she wants a war, we'll deliver it to her doorstep."

Jon had regrouped from his infuriated state. He doled out marching orders in a fiery stream of consciousness.

"Sarah, I want you to create a shared doc of the Senator's talking points so we can run interference for Troy."

"Got it," she said.

"Kelsey, you have your corporate card?"

She nodded in the affirmative. It remained sealed in the envelope on her desk.

"Both of you, go to the internal travel site and look up flights out of SFO. We're headed to D.C."

Sarah opened her mouth to voice additional suggestions, but Jon halted any further conversation. "The way you can help is by doing exactly what I say and doing it now."

* * *

Troy sat at his rightful place at the head of the conference room table surrounded by reps from Legal, Security, and Comms along with various executives from the Dream Team. The group watched tensely as the CEO mockingly read aloud the letter from the Senate committee. The missive outlined that Elemynt was to send a representative to face a panel of Congresspeople and, in doing so, be grilled under the watchful eye of the American public. Troy was unamused. Kelsey was petrified.

"Do we have to go?" Troy scoffed. "Are they going to throw us in jail or something if we don't show up?"

"Worse," Wyatt said as he looked over his copy of the letter: "They can create legislation that would change how Elemynt operates. The committee's jurisdiction gives it regulatory power over internet companies, including us."

Jon nodded in agreement. "If we back out of this, it looks like Elemynt has something to hide."

Troy rose sharply out of his ergonomic seat and shoved it into the table.

"Okay, first, everybody loved us. Now that we're a big deal, people are running around with rocks in their hands trying to take us down! It's not like we're the first company ever to have a privacy breach. People are used to them by now but we're the ones who have Senators chasing after us?"

Jon was empathetic to his concerns. "Tech is bigger than it's ever been. Congress wants to look like they're on the ball. We know that they know nothing about what's going on in the industry. Elemynt just happened to become the moving target they decided to go after."

"They're trying to bully us," Wyatt affirmed.

Troy continued his tirade, strutting around the room angrily, consumed by frustration, and talking to no one in particular. "We didn't go around squeezing peoples' arm and telling them they have to put details about their lives on Elemynt. Our platform is free! Anything they share on the app is voluntary. We're building a better platform that has ads people want to see. They don't call hearings on TV or radio stations for trying to do that. Am I wrong?"

The room of stakeholders outwardly agreed but with a hint of shared skepticism. No one could be completely sure of Troy's assessment of the situation except for Wyatt, their legal strongman. Elemynt's general counsel nodded vigorously in agreement with his buddy.

"People need to quit whining about the little stuff," Troy said. "If they don't like how we're running things here, they can delete their account anytime they want."

Catherine didn't hesitate to cut through Troy's interminable rant. "What I'm hearing you say is you do not mind if we have a platform with no users."

"That's not what I said at all."

"It practically is," Catherine said bitingly. "We have no time to be dismissive. We have every necessary department represented in this room so that we can arrive at a solution. We should be focusing less on why this hearing is happening and more on what we're going to do about it."

"Why didn't you stop your friend from calling a hearing in the first place?" Troy shot back.

"Deniece Layne may be someone I know personally but she's also a United States Senator," Catherine said unfazed.

"And Congresspeople make laws," Wyatt jumped in. "The kind that could be our worst nightmare."

A daze fell over the room as Wyatt detailed the many ways Congress could decimate Elemynt's existing business model.

"You think a breach is bad?" he said. "The government could get access to all our security systems. They could require us to make the account and information of every user open to inspection. They can put limits on the data-based advertising that makes us the best in the biz. Any move we make to innovate, they would block."

"None of that will happen if we prepare for the hearing properly," Catherine said firmly. "I first need to know how many people have we lost since the breach?"

"Not that many at all," Gary responded. "There was a dip in engagement right after but most people came back. Less than 10,000 deleted their account."

"That's several thousand users who could be viewing ads right now," Catherine said through clenched teeth. "What are our plans for preventing more losses?"

Gary proudly shared the results of his teams' action. "After the breach, we put a prompt in Elemynt feeds giving people a heads up to check out their privacy settings. Six percent of the people clicked to read the terms of service. Less than one percent of them scrolled to the end. We're talking roughly 600,000 people out of the billion accounts on Elemynt."

"See what I'm talking about!" Troy perked up. "People say they care about their data, but they don't! They're not thinking about user agreements or previous settings. We should make that point to those Senators."

"That is what we are *not* doing," Catherine said. "The less they know about our business practices, the better."

Kelsey sat intently watching the back and forth until she was distracted by what might be considered a controversial frame of thought. A congressional hearing was possibly an unparalleled opportunity for the company to reassert its position in the mind of the public. They could use the testimony as a platform to underscore that Elemynt had the country's citizens' best interests at heart. How to communicate that vision successfully to the hundreds of millions of people watching would be no small feat.

"Troy, I'll have your E.A.s clear your schedule," Catherine said. "We have two weeks to be ready for this hearing. The letter says we'll need to prepare a written statement for Congress' official records and a shorter version to read from for opening remarks."

"We've got a plan, let's smash it," Troy said in better spirits. "Cath, you're gonna be great up there."

"What on earth are you talking about?" Catherine raised one eyebrow.

"The hearing? Congress? You're going to testify for Elemynt."

"You must be joking."

Up until that point, the leads around the table assumed Troy would be in the witness chair speaking on behalf of the company. He was the CEO of Elemynt. The Congresswoman called him out by name in her press conference. His deferment of the task was odd and, for Catherine, unacceptable.

"This is your company," Catherine said. "You will be the one in that room defending it."

Troy was taken aback. "You know the business side of Elemynt better than anybody here and you're used to talking in front of cameras. I can't do it better than you would."

"That's why Jon and Wyatt are going to help you prep so that you will be ready for your moment."

Wyatt, who Kelsey expected to stand in Troy's defense, sided with Catherine. "You're the headliner, man. People believe in Elemynt because they believe in you. The people look up to you."

"If we're going to beat this, we need you in that room winning over the people," Jon added. "Wyatt and I will do the heavy lifting. We'll have your talking points ready for you. A few days of prep and you'll be fine."

The pressure coming from his peers and the lack of dissent from the attendees the meeting meant Troy would be seen as soft if he were to not step up to the plate. Seeing his reputation as a leader at stake, Troy agreed as if it was his idea in the first place.

"Thanks, boys," he said satisfactorily. "I'll be ready to take them down. Right now, I need everybody else to get back to business. We'll worry about Congress later."

The meeting's attendees gathered their laptops and phones to leave, except for Leon. He remained planted in his seat with worry written across his face.

"Before we go…" Leon announced. "We have another problem."

Those preparing to leave stopped in their tracks. Troy blocked the exit door. "Bigger than a Senate hearing?"

"We also need to talk about this situation going on with right-wing posts on the app," Leon said. "We're seeing abnormal spikes in this type of content from outside the U.S."

"Let me stop you right there, pal," Troy held up his hand. "We have a Congressional hearing we have to get ready for. We're gonna be speaking in front of the whole nation. Other distractions… we don't need 'em right now."

"This may come up in the hearing," Leon pleaded. "I'm telling you this is important stuff."

"If the Senator didn't mention it in her press conference, we put a pin in it. Got it, brother?"

"Troy, you need to listen up right now!"

The population of the meeting room was stunned by Leon's uncharacteristic outburst. The vice president of security had just raised his voice to the head of the company. Whatever it was that worried Leon had to be serious enough for him to violate the decorum of hierarchy.

Troy sat back down in his chair. The rest of the group quickly followed suit.

"I have to insist," Leon said apologetically. "Look..."

He blasted a series of Elemynt posts on the screen occupying the center wall of the room. The headlines they contained commanded the attention of the skeptical observers.

"Vietnam Memorial being replaced with Muslim Museum!"

"Congress enacts law making Spanish official language of the United States"

"SHOCKER: Military bans women from breastfeeding on frontlines"

"75,000 People Murdered By Undocumented Immigrants Since 9/11"

"Cops stage school shooting, spray fake blood on themselves!!"

Posts from Elemynt accounts with names like "Defend America" and "Patriot Daily Times" slathered their followers with bombastic pronouncements in images and captions. Each post included a link to what looked to be a news website. The jarring mistruths laid out side by side was troubling to view.

"They're putting up these headlines that sound like they could be true even though they're pretty much fake as hell," Leon explained. "The posts are being faved and shared hundreds of thousands, sometimes millions of times each."

"Elemynt is a platform for all voices," Troy said warily.

"Except these voices are being manufactured specifically to go viral in America to get more people to click on the links. My team found out about the problem when we saw a spike in content being shared in the U.S. that wasn't originating in the country. This one here... 'Illegal Mexicans Take White House Hostage'... was posted from an account in Georgia."

"Isn't that here in America?" Troy said with a drop of sarcasm.

"No, the *Republic* of Georgia," Leon said as he pulled up a map on the screen. "Macedonia, Bulgaria, Kosovo... most of the accounts we flagged are coming from an area in southeast Europe called the Balkans."

Leon detailed how Elemynt accounts originating in the Balkans were pumping out misleading images and over-the-top headlines that weren't far from the stories published by ultra-right-wing American news sites. The foreign actors capitalized on racial tension and anti-immigrant sentiment in the U.S. to make money from the discord. Each time people clicked on the websites in the viral post, the spammers pocketed revenue via the adjacent advertising on the page. It was an ongoing cycle of online deception by predatory accounts amassing hordes of unsuspecting followers.

Kelsey was astounded by the breadth of content that, to some degree, she had no idea was a thing on Elemynt. The highly charged political posts were far from the vacation photos and pics of fabulous meals she was used to faving. Kelsey thought through whether her friends and family were deceived by the scammers. A few of the headlines sounded suspiciously like the posts her father occasionally sent Kelsey and her mother.

"Most times, people aren't clicking on the story at all and still share it, which is crazy," Leon said. "The way the accounts are set up look like they're from real conservatives, so people believe the stories are true without verifying them. They read the headline and send it straight to their followers."

"Wait one second," Catherine halted the explanation. "You keep saying 'conservative' and 'right-wing'. When did we start determining political affiliation?"

"Hello? We're a data company," Troy said proudly.

"It's easier than you think," Gary chimed in. "One way we do it is from the hashtags they're using. For example, #patriot, #america, or #christian. We can also pair their keywords and language with voting district data from previous elections to get better accuracy."

"And that's all we need?" Catherine asked.

"There are other markers too," Gary said. "My product research team found that conservatives used American flags in their captions somewhere around 200 percent more than people who self-identified as liberals."

"Which brings it back to these accounts," Leon said. "One of the stories created by our Balkan friends said that a new emoji with a burning American flag hanging upside down was going to be released on Android and iPhone."

"And people believed that?" Catherine asked incredulously.

"They definitely shared it," Leon shrugged. "A thousand posts on Elemynt with that link in them. Last count, there were 2.3 million total actions on the original post."

The population of the conference room was disturbed by the news of the revelations. The group of execs and stakeholders shared in Kelsey's disbelief that the problem was as widespread as Leon suggested it was.

Catherine was determined to take a practical approach to the issue.

"Is this violating our terms of service?" she asked. "Can we shut them down?"

"Some of it promotes violence against racial and religious minorities, especially Mexicans and immigrants," Leon said. "The moderators are suspending those accounts. Most of the other stuff is just fake headlines. We don't have policies against that in our TOS."

"I can't believe we're talking about this right now!" Troy said in aggravation. "Mexico isn't even in the top 20 countries that use Elemynt. A few posts from a couple of slackers on the other side of the Earth are *not* priority."

"We should be concerned with the optics around this," Jon said.

"And a portion of the revenue of the business," Catherine added. "There are 60 million Latinos in the United States alone. That demo is very valuable to our advertisers. Elemynt is, of course, the best way to reach them. We don't want to alienate that group."

"Again, what does this have to do with a Congressional hearing?" Troy said gruffly.

Leon threw his arms in the air in defeat. "I'm just saying if it came up, I wanted you to know about it first."

Jon moved to bridge the widening rift in the room. "I'll work the issue into the media prep. We should not bring it up unless absolutely necessary."

Catherine agreed. "The update is appreciated, Leon, but we need to move on."

"Hey, by the way, Catherine, there is one thing I need from you," Troy said. "I want you to talk to your friend, the Congresswoman. Let's see if we can get her to cancel the damn thing. You can tell her why her hearing is stupid and unnecessary."

"Deniece...Senator Layne is my friend. Not my employee."

"So convince your friend to change her mind."

Catherine conceded to his request. "I'll see what I can do."

* * *

Every word uttered in the scheduled meeting between Catherine and Senator

Layne would be considered off the record.

Jon smartly suggested that someone from External Comms be in the room with the two during the Congresswoman's visit to campus, despite it being designated a private conversation. If the Congresswoman's inquiries required an official PR response, Catherine would be able to deflect to a Comms representative. Jon assigned Kelsey to the task, taking into consideration her familiarity with the Senator. His time would be spent on the all-important media prep with Sarah helping him along. Kelsey reluctantly accepted the responsibility.

It pained Kelsey to meet the Congresswoman again, this time under the most strenuous of circumstances. She had not detailed to her co-workers the extent of their discussion at the gala. Catherine had graciously ushered Kelsey to meet Senator Layne at the event. The Elemynt executive was now tasked with undoing the result of that conversation. Kelsey was anxious to see how Catherine could talk a prominent legislator down from a Congressional hearing. No matter how much of a boss Catherine was, it would not be a walk in the park.

Rather than meet in Catherine's actual office, the COO arranged for the gathering to be held in one of the plush rooms specially designed for meetings with VIPs. The space was what people imagined the office of an executive at a tech company would look like.

The top floor room sported panoramic views of the San Francisco Bay from its wall-to-wall windows. The office was outfitted with modern seating, a glass and brushed steel desk, and a matching coffee table topped with a neat stack of the latest issues of Forbes and American Vogue magazines. Abstract art hung on the walls to contemporize the space. It was intentionally bland enough to not be a distraction. Additionally, the chair in which Catherine sat was imperceptibly higher than the one in which she seated guests, putting them at an unconscious disadvantage.

Catherine welcomed the Congresswoman with open arms at her entry. A lingering hug was followed by a warm gesture of clasped hands between the two.

"Thank you for coming, Deniece," Catherine said. "I'm hoping we can find common ground."

"That remains to be seen," the senator said politely.

The duo sat in chairs opposite each other while Kelsey stood in the background as not to be intrusive. There was no acknowledgment of her presence.

"I've been told you won't be testifying on behalf of Elemynt," the Congresswoman said.

"That would be Troy's role," Catherine smiled to herself. "He is the leader of this company."

"Then the assumptions that the woman who runs the business would speak on its behalf aren't true."

"Is there something I've done wrong?" Catherine said. "Is there a reason you want me at the witness table?"

"I didn't say that I did. You are the Boss Lady. It's just a thought."

"If it's not me you have a problem with, why have you become so fascinated with the way Elemynt runs its business?"

The moment Kelsey dreaded arrived sooner than she anticipated. She held tightly to a nearby cabinet as Senator Layne outlined the results of her thirty-day trial run on the app.

"At the suggestion of someone in your company," she said without looking at Kelsey. "I posted videos to my Elemynt account of women and families affected by the wage gap. My team and I were expecting comments of support, not the hideous and sexist remarks underneath each post. Apparently, women are whores and sluts for wanting equal pay. An interesting discussion on a platform with a woman at the helm."

The Congresswoman was gunning for Catherine in a way that made Kelsey feel increasingly at ease. Catherine, however, was unmoved. She had faced a string of adversaries in her career. None of them walked away able to tell a story of how they got under her skin. Senator Layne would not be the first.

"You had a bad experience on the app and for that, I apologize," Catherine said unflinchingly. "What has me curious is why you've decided that this requires a Congressional hearing at the expense of taxpayers."

"This isn't about my personal opinions of Elemynt if that's what you're thinking," Senator Layne said. "I strongly support the need to regulate tech as do many of my constituents. The tech industry has no government oversight. You've seen to that."

"And yet people continue to love the platform," Catherine smirked. "If I recall correctly, it was the Los Angeles Times who said our app was the reason you were elected."

The popularity of the Congresswoman's election messaging on Elemynt was no secret. Catherine stopped short of mentioning the hundreds of thousands of dollars in campaign donations made by Elemynt to Senator Layne's re-election bid. The company also contributed handsomely to the election campaigns of several of her fellow committee members and to a multitude of Congresspeople representing the various corners of the country.

Senator Layne also skipped over an important factor — the millions of dollars Elemynt used to fund an army of assertive D.C. lobbyists. Their tireless work sought to influence congressional lawmaking in ways that benefitted Elemynt. Both of the closed-door issues created a stalemate that neither Catherine nor Senator Layne wanted to advance.

"You may not be using the app anymore but your voters certainly are," Catherine said instead. "How many followers do you have now?"

"1.3 million," Senator Layne said without skipping a beat.

"That's an impressive number."

"Good things can also be used in terrible ways, Catherine. But you were aware of that already according to what news reports are saying about your platform."

"You can't trust everything you read," Catherine replied.

Two women who Kelsey admired greatly were engaged in a Wild West showdown masked in gentility, neither conceding their position.

She was sure her presence was not needed for the discussion between friends. An interfering utterance on her part could throw off the balance of decency. Catherine didn't need Kelsey's help. She knew exactly what to say and what not to say to a congresswoman who would soon put the company on center stage.

"You do know we're committed to safety for everyone," Catherine said.

"Obviously not," Senator Layne said. "Your teams took several steps to cover up your actions following the breach. Your users should have been your first priority."

"One billion people trust us and that has not changed," Catherine said diplomatically.

"It's funny, really," Senator Layne said. "Sometimes people don't want to admit that the product they love is bad for them. Take a candy bar for instance. Loads of sugar. It's listed right there on the label."

"I don't follow."

"People continue to eat them knowing that sugar can be detrimental to their health."

"What is your point, Deniece?"

"Even candy bars have regulations," she said smugly. "And to my understanding, a Snickers bar can't give out your phone number and home address to criminals on the internet."

Catherine laughed off the dig. "True as that may be and as much as I'm sure you enjoy your snacks, it seems wrong to punish the company for being successful."

"A company that has made billions of dollars from other people's information and yet is private about its own. Americans want answers. I'm sure you don't have a problem with that."

Catherine did. A dissection of their business that left it open to public scrutiny was unacceptable.

"What exactly are you hoping to get out of this, Deniece?" Catherine asked.

"Again, this isn't personal," the Senator said calmly. "It's my role to balance the wills of Silicon Valley companies like yours with those of the millions of residents of the state of California."

"People love us," Catherine snapped. "And signing up for Elemynt is completely voluntary."

"As is this meeting."

Senator Layne stood up from her chair, leaving Catherine in place. "I hope you'll find time to watch the hearing. It will be very interesting. Oh, and tell Troy to wear a comfortable suit. He'll be sitting for a while."

EIGHT

The ballroom space on the lowest floor of the Marriott Marquis, a towering hotel in the heart of San Francisco, was completely locked down by Elemynt security. An officer was posted at the foot of each escalator, stair, elevator, and door. Multiple sweeps occurred every half hour of the hotel's public area for reporters who by the slimmest chance received word of the company's secret endeavor.

Behind the airtight closed doors away from the whispers of campus, Troy and a team of communication specialists were prepping for the media storm to come. This was the story of the century. Troy would be under fire from the Senate Committee for a range of issues related to the platform. Of the utmost concern to Wyatt and Jon wasn't the information contained in his answers, it was how the leader of the company presented it.

The two worked to perfect Troy's delivery so it was commanding but not defensive. His body language had to project confidence without appearing smug. He needed to deliver precise answers but not sound rehearsed. Troy's personality had to be molded into camera-ready perfection. It was crucial that the head of Elemynt nailed the range of talking points and dodge takedowns that threatened his perch as an idol of the tech industry.

The stakeholders in attendance sat behind Troy out of his line of vision. They took copious notes as he ran through drill after drill. After each mock session, members of the Dream Team huddled to discuss adjustments and failures. No one was to talk to Troy directly during the process. Feedback was funneled exclusively through Jon and Wyatt.

Sarah and Kelsey sat quietly on the sidelines watching the proceedings unfold. Next to them were the young executive assistants ready to act on orders hurled their way. The crop of lower-level attendees was warned by Leon that they were under an especially watchful eye. Their emails and phones were under constant scrutiny throughout the undertaking to prevent leaks. No one could breathe a word of the operation.

Catherine stepped out from time to time solely for her most important calls. She kept them as brief as possible before returning to observe the crucial preparations.

The Comms team did not have the luxury of any such distractions. Their last few days were spent crafting the opening statement that Troy would read to the panel of Senators. They also toiled for days on end to perfect the written statement that would be posted online one day prior.

Other concerns they usually dealt with were put on hold, including the aggravating slew of inquiries from reporters hellbent on getting a comment from Elemynt. A single utterance from the Comms team could turn a run of the mill news article into a viral must-read.

Kelsey sat in the ballroom reassessing in her mind the language the Comms team contributed to the pivotal written statement. The document would be picked apart by the media and online talkers with an opinion on Elemynt, Troy, or the tech industry in general.

Near the beginning of the statement's creation, Leon sent Jon a report detailing the hack and an accompanying timeline to incorporate in their writing. They used virtually none of it. The team obscured Leon's numbers and focused instead on Elemynt's promise to make sure nothing like the error happened again.

After a working draft was approved by Jon, it was delivered to Wyatt's team of lawyers. The sharp legal eyes dutifully redlined wording that could potentially incriminate the company. The written statement volleyed back to Comms to rid the text of complicated legalese, then it was off to Catherine's desk.

Catherine communicated several demands: make it shorter, more focused on the future, do not include numbers the press could spin. It was an unceasing cycle of edits, reviews, notes, comments, and more edits until the statement was finally presented to Troy for his approval. The result was an optimistic proclamation scant on details and free of admission of guilt.

At the appointed time, the communiqué was posted to the company blog where the kettle of journalists hovering over their keyboards could dig their claws into it. Elemynt had no control over the avalanche of stories that would follow. Their only course of action was to ensure the media had plenty of pull-quotes direct from Elemynt to choose from.

The press went as wild as the team expected. They picked up on the most minute bits and pieces of the statement. They spun a few sentences from it into 500-word thinkpieces. Opinion pieces framed Troy as the smug tech bro who didn't care about users, just profit and continued growth. Analyses pointed out that a lack of faith in Elemynt could potentially roll the company back under the one billion user milestone it recently accomplished.

When Kelsey signed up for Elemynt she never imagined that she would be preparing for a congressional hearing as part of her work. The task was so far out of the realm of possibility that she wasn't sure she possessed the skills to pull it off. The situation was the ultimate test of PR mettle. Though Kelsey was nervous her boss would soon be interrogated by powerful lawmakers at the highest level, there was something deeply thrilling about the situation. The adrenaline drove her to bring every skillset and communications approach she learned in the span of her career to the table.

The one letdown for Kelsey was that she was not contributing to the in-person media prep. Wyatt and Jon were in charge of shaping Troy into a press-ready, soundbite machine. So far, he hadn't made much progress.

Troy sat at the front of the dim ballroom casually flipping through a binder prepared for him. The playbook created by Kelsey and Sarah organized potential issues that may arise in the hearing into digestible categories. Suggested talking points were outlined in bulleted paragraphs.

Jon and Wyatt were determined to not let Troy's potentially weak performance as ambassador for the company be its undoing. They took turns bombarding Troy with questions, the answers to which were printed in the binder.

"Mr. McCray, when did you become aware of the security breach?" Jon asked, invoking a Senator's line of questioning.

"There's a lot of things going on at Elemynt all the time," Troy responded sharply. "I can't keep up with every emergency as soon as it happens."

The murmur from concerned observers in the room was nearly drowned out by Wyatt's exasperated sigh.

"Dude, you're serious?" Wyatt said. "You answer harder questions at Q&A. Try it again."

"Remember to project confidence and be likable," Jon added.

"You think I'm not likable?" Troy grumbled.

"We don't want Congress to come to that conclusion. Let's go again."

The suited pair of advisers circled Troy. They peppered him with questions about his knowledge of the breach. He responded. They corrected him. He tried again. They gave him more notes.

After several rounds of questions in which Troy's replies did not meet expectations, he simply stopped talking. Troy reached in his pocket for his phone. He forgot that it had been taken away from him hours before. He opted to sulk in silence. Jon and Wyatt rolled their eyes. They would not let him quit so early in the prep.

"We're not here to beat you up," Jon insisted.

"You sure?" Troy asked flippantly. "You guys are wearing me out."

"These people are gunning for us hard, man," Wyatt said. "One slip up and before you know it, we're under federal legislation by a government that doesn't know squat about tech."

Kelsey understood Wyatt's declaration to also be a reminder to the room of the heat they were under. The elder statesmen of Washington would never have the smarts to understand the always evolving, forward-thinking technological development coming from the company.

"We can't be regulated by people who don't know what they're regulating," Wyatt said.

In addition to fracturing the way Elemynt did business, legislation enacted on the company would lead to greater scrutiny from the media. The color in Kelsey's face drained when she thought of the terror increased press coverage would heap onto the Comms team. News media would be relentless, gathering every nugget of information they could to prove Elemynt's downfall. Regulation would be the beginning of the end for Elemynt.

It wasn't just Congress Troy needed to convince of his virtue, it was the millions of people affected by the breach. Putting on the positive face possible and extinguish his internal fury was imperative. So far, the company's leader was failing the task at hand.

The message Troy had to drive home was simple: Elemynt cares about privacy and its efforts were in the best interest of all people. The mantra was clouded by Troy's internal dialogue — Elemynt was his product and he could do with it whatever he wanted. Kelsey silently willed him to alter his take on the situation.

Wyatt continued in hopes of improvement from Troy. "Here's another one: How much data are you collecting?"

"Five thousand points across a spectrum of—"

The groans that emanated from the back of the room would have been audible in the neighboring ballrooms had they not been sufficiently locked down by security. Their CEO was being honest in the worst possible way.

"Troy, come on bro," Wyatt said. "Don't open the door for them to ask more questions about issues they're not even thinking about."

"I should be in my office running my damn company," Troy steamed. "Not in a hotel basement setting myself up to get ripped apart like a piñata."

"You can't take this personally," Jon said. "The minute you do is when you're going to fall apart."

"And you gotta stop coming off like you're being defensive," Wyatt grumbled.

"Let's do this..." Jon said, putting one hand on each of Troy's shoulders. "If you get stuck, say 'I'll ask my team.'"

"You want me to plead the 5th," Troy rolled his eyes.

"There's a reason why it's a top ten amendment," Wyatt said. "It's gonna be your out."

Wyatt and Jon bore into Troy with a continuation of probing questions. More tips on how to answer them were thrust upon him. Speak clearly. Don't hunch. Pause before you respond.

The chief executive grew increasingly agitated.

Make eye contact. Don't overpromise. Don't ramble.

Troy flew out of his chair in anger, sending it crashing to the ground and frightening the onlookers in the room.

"You guys cut the shit!" Troy screeched. "You don't like the way I talk? You think that I can't take on a room full of old farts that will never have the mental capacity to do a fraction of what I've done?!"

The Myntors gathered to help Troy on his journey sat wordlessly. Kelsey and the group were afraid to make the slightest move.

"I built Elemynt from the ground up before any of you assholes were ever in the picture!" Troy shouted angrily.

"We know that, buddy," Jon said calmly. "We just want you to communicate that properly."

"You want me to be a cookie-cutter, Mickey Mouse CEO who treats Senators like goddamn babies and reads them bedtime stories about how the world works! Fuck that! I have a billion-dollar company to run."

Catherine boiled with internal rage at the outburst. "Cut the crap, Troy! The binder with the answers you're supposed to be giving is right in front of you. This is by no means difficult."

"Then you do it!" he bellowed.

"Is that what you really want, Troy?" Catherine circled him. "To show the world that you were so weak that you needed your COO to stand in for you?"

Catherine spoke aloud what lingered in the observers' minds. The second-in-command could do an infinitely better job at the hearing than Troy. The Boss Lady was more entrenched in the business proceedings of the company and had far more experience speaking publicly. A series of what were essentially interview questions would be a cakewalk, if not a delight, for her. However, the wheels were long set in motion for Troy to take the witness stand. The team had come too far to swap out the two executives.

Troy slammed the binder to the floor and stormed out of the ballroom doors. Bullet-pointed pages scattered in the air. His E.A.s leaped to their feet wondering whether to follow him or not.

"Let him go," Catherine shook her head. "Take a break, everyone. There's food in the rear of the room."

The beleaguered Myntors shuffled toward the table of snacktime delicacies laid out for them. Kelsey peered over the selection of artisan sandwiches and cold pastas. Her appetite was non-existent. The tension that lingered in the air following the interruption sapped her desire to eat. She opted for a steaming hot cup of coffee from one of the brass urns.

Wyatt drifted behind Kelsey while she poured non-dairy creamer.

"You don't want to eat food?" he said. "You look hungry."

"I don't know what you mean by that but shouldn't you be focusing on Troy right now?" Kelsey said tersely. "There's room for improvement there."

"I've worked in D.C. for almost a decade," Wyatt retorted. "I don't need advice from someone sitting on the sidelines."

"From what I'm seeing, I think you do," Kelsey said. "Have you thought about changing up how you're approaching this? Maybe instead of having two people blasting him with corrections constantly, you have one person talking and making the prep a conversation. That person can give a few notes at a time between breaks. Troy has to relax if he's going to be able to pull this off."

Wyatt bristled at Kelsey's suggestion. "I know what I'm doing," he said between gritted teeth.

"I'm sure you do but the results right now are pretty tragic."

The comment was enough to put Wyatt over the top. "If we need advice from a pretty girl who's lucky to be in this room, you'll be the first to know."

Kelsey watched as Wyatt spouted at her in angry whispers the reasons why his career on Capitol Hill outweighed her experience in Comms. Kelsey was entertained by the bombastic display. How a lawyer thought he knew more than a person whose role it was to communicate was beyond what she cared to understand. It was literally in her job title.

Kelsey was unfazed as Wyatt shifted his weight toward her in an assertion of dominance. She knew she was right and no act of machismo would make her think differently.

"You know you're prettier when you smile," Kelsey smirked.

"I have a CEO to prepare for a Congressional hearing," Wyatt said with derision. "Enjoy your coffee, lady."

When Troy returned to the ballroom, all talking ceased. Plates were discarded. People sat upright in their seats keeping their nerves at bay.

Troy was outwardly calm. It was obvious that aggravation still rumbled inside him following the nonstop attack from Jon and Wyatt.

"I have an idea," Wyatt announced to the room. "Instead of having two people giving you critiques at the same time, one of us does the prep and we give you notes during breaks. I think it will be better that way."

Kelsey's jaw almost dropped to the floor. Wyatt outright stole her idea and did so with no intention of giving her credit for it. It took everything within Kelsey not to throttle his neck on the spot. She couldn't speak up because it would further inflame an already fraying situation. Wyatt would frame her as a bitter woman or an opportunist. Kelsey dug her fingernails into her skin to stop herself from putting her foot in his chest.

"So, who's going to lead?" Troy asked.

The question set off an argument between Jon and Wyatt that was strange to witness. Neither man wanted to stand to the side for such an important moment. The two strutting peacocks were unwilling to put their pride away and compromise for the greater good.

The exchange led Catherine to turn her back to the situation so she wouldn't curse at both of them for delaying the monumental task.

Kelsey felt compelled to stand up. The discussion with Jon and Wyatt had reached an impasse, she had been studying the Congresswoman for the longest time and was in the room with Catherine to understand the lawmaker's intentions. Most of all, the idea to limit the prep to one person was hers in the first place.

That plus a winning streak of PR campaigns and shifting the public's mind about Elemynt on several occasions was more than enough reason to step up.

Kelsey could sit in her seat like everyone else watching the impasse or do something about it. By the time she thought through the reasons she should take the lead, Kelsey was making her way out of her seat.

"I'll do it," she said confidently.

For Kelsey, her move wasn't a means of simply reclaiming her idea. She knew well how to arm Troy with the communication skills to address the nation. The dueling pair could argue amongst themselves later. She strode to the front of the room past a shocked Jon and Wyatt and planted a chair in front of Troy.

"Excuse me, what the hell do you think you're doing?" Wyatt huffed. "I don't think this is the time for a junior employee to be giving advice to a CEO."

Jon was equally perturbed. "Kelsey, we appreciate your wanting to help but this is a serious matter."

Kelsey did not budge from the chair. The Myntors looked to Troy for the verdict.

"Let her do the prep," Catherine said adamantly from her side of the room. "Kelsey knows the Congresswoman better than anyone. Whatever you call this.... charade... isn't working."

"This isn't pre-school!" Wyatt howled. "We don't have time to—"

"Kelsey, continue please," Catherine said unwaveringly.

Before Jon and Wyatt could further protest, Kelsey locked eyes with Troy. She called his attention to her and only her.

"Focus on me," Kelsey insisted.

"Sure. Whatever," Troy said.

Kelsey was emboldened to make him execute the mission at hand to the best of his ability.

"Why do you care about Elemynt?" Kelsey asked Troy directly.

"It's the number one platform for bringing people together and—"

"Hold on for a sec, let me stop you there. I asked *why* do you care. This hearing isn't about the breach and it's not about the app either. It's about you and why the committee should trust you as the person leading the company."

"But those psychos in Congress…"

"Do you usually call people psychos when they ask you about Elemynt?"

"They need to understand that we're building a damn good product."

"Okay, let's start there," Kelsey said. "Pretend I'm someone who doesn't understand technology. Like your grandma. Explain to me how Elemynt works."

"My grandmother died when I was 7."

Jon and Wyatt both groaned audibly while the rest of the onlookers attempted to stifle their muttered concerns. Catherine put one hand up, effectively silencing the room.

Kelsey was unshaken. "Okay, someone else's grandmother. Tell me...why do you care about Elemynt?"

Over the next hour, Kelsey coached Troy through answers that were relatable and informative without compromising his authority. She took her time. He spoke with less anger. She encouraged him to speak from the heart. He communicated more fluently. Kelsey gradually elevated the toughness of the questions she swung his way. Troy maintained a cool, even tone, loosening his perpetually clenched jaw.

Out of the corner of her eye, Kelsey spotted Wyatt quietly seething. Catherine looked on proudly. Once Troy relaxed, he delivered knowledgeable answers to the simulated attacks. His cooperation came as a surprise to the dubious spectators in the room.

After her time with Troy, there was no denying that Kelsey did an excellent job. Jon and Wyatt were both still peeved from being ousted from their posts. However, they calmed themselves to congratulate her on a job well done.

"Excellent work, rookie," Jon said.

Sarah rushed to hand Kelsey a bottled water to refresh her overworked vocal cords. "You were a pro out there! I'm seriously speechless."

"Thanks," Kelsey said. "We'll see at the hearing if it worked."

No one knew for sure if Troy would be able to temper his defensiveness while in a room of aggressive Senators gunning for him. It wouldn't go over well if Troy resorted to another tantrum. Headlines like "Elemynt CEO Goes Rogue" and "Is This the End of Elemynt?" would be written before he could finish. Facsimiles of his reddened face would be plastered across televisions and internet sites. The vicious press would be impossible to recover from.

Kelsey's primary concern was that the teams could do all the prep in the world but they still didn't know exactly what questions Congress would ask Troy. Kelsey hoped with every fiber of her being that the undertaking in the ballroom would be enough.

* * *

The fateful time had come. It was the day the media was salivating over, Congresspeople touted as a battle for morality, and Elemynt spent day and night preparing for. Troy would finally make his appearance on Capitol Hill in front of the Senate Committee on Commerce, Science, and Transportation, the menace threatening the well-being of the beloved social media company. The hours-long interrogation was slated to be featured on television networks and news sites across the globe.

The venerable Senate hearing room was jammed to capacity with members of the press and eager observers who managed to score a coveted seat. The chamber itself was the site of decades worth of historic Senate investigations and Supreme Court confirmation hearings. Following in their footsteps was the legislative spectacle of the year with Troy at the dead center. The television cameras tucked around the room would offer uninterrupted coverage of the proceedings. Each one of the rigid chairs in the gallery was claimed within seconds of the doors' opening.

The compact space was dominated by an elevated oaken dais at the front of the room where the members of the committee would tower over Troy. The Great Seal of the United States was boldly displayed on the marble wall behind them.

Troy's place for the coming hours would be the black leather chair with nailhead trim in front of an excessively wide witness table. A thin microphone would broadcast his words to the world. In front of the seat was a lone glass and a frigid pitcher of ice water available for his consumption.

Myntors at Elemynt's various global offices gathered at unofficial watch parties to witness the historic event together. Their fearless leader was advocating on behalf of their company in front of the legislative body and millions more watching and judging.

The three members of the External Comms team were seated in solidarity directly behind where Troy would testify. To Jon's left, Wyatt sat upright in the finest suit in his wardrobe. Together, they projected maximum confidence for the cameras. That was all they could do. The rest was up to Troy.

The restlessness in the room was amplified by the roaming photographers perched in the space between the dais and the witness table. They trained their cameras on the empty chair in preparation for the big moment. The aisleway was kept clear for Troy's entrance.

The buzz of anticipation around Kelsey hushed to a whisper as the members of the committee filed in. The Senators took their designated places in the high-back chairs on the tiered dais. Their young staffers sat behind them ready to answer whispered questions or supply new information at a moment's notice. At the center of the dais was the committee chairwoman, Senator Deniece Layne. The friend turned foe who presided over the hearing maintained a rigid expression. Kelsey badly wished to know what was going through the Congresswoman's head in the minutes leading up to the hearing's start.

Kelsey was caught up in a daze of thoughts to the point that she hadn't noticed the stream of incoming text notifications on her phone. Nearly everyone she knew reached out to find out how she was feeling about the hearing. Kelsey roundly ignored them. Nothing was more important at that moment than what was happening in the hearing room.

After what seemed like an eternity, Troy entered the chamber to face his combatants. He was welcomed by a horde of photographers who snapped away at the man under fire. Troy forewent his usual T-shirt and athletic shoes for a jet-black Armani suit and polished Oxford dress shoes. He was talked down the day before from wearing a green necktie which he insisted would be a nod to his company's trademark color. In its place, he wore a camera-ready, solid blue tie. Blue meant confident. Trustworthy.

Something as simple as a green tie or the juvenile patterned dress socks he initially favored would be unnecessary distractions. The goal was, as Jon reiterated often, to make it through the hearing generating as little press as possible. The idea was ultimately wishful thinking. The media were set to pounce the minute Troy opened his mouth.

The Elemynt CEO settled into the witness chair in the face of hundreds of simultaneous shutter clicks. The paparazzi jostled for the best possible photo... the iconic image that would be seared into the minds of the public. Troy did his best to maintain a friendly, but not too friendly disposition. The committee members, on the other hand, glowered at him intently from the dais.

Senator Layne rapped her gavel forcefully on a wooden block to open the proceedings. The photographers dutifully cleared away. The anticipatory chatter from the gallery slowly quieted.

"The committee will come to order," she struck the gavel again.

The room fell silent within a second.

Senator Layne, speaking firmly, read from her stack of papers the purpose of the day's events. "This hearing will examine the privacy and security standards of the social media company Elemynt. Committee members will discuss possible resolutions to recent crises with the chief executive officer who is here in attendance, Mr. Troy McCray."

The senator continued with a statement that equated to a compendium of damning facts and figures about the company culled from news reports. Kelsey was annoyed that none of the "evidence" came directly from Elemynt itself. Her manifesto was an over-dramatized attempt to bury Troy before he had the chance to defend himself.

"The outsized reach of Elemynt demands that we encourage transparency into how this technology is managed," Senator Layne said. "Proper oversight will be essential moving forward."

Her droning statement was followed by that of the committee's ranking member, Senator Scoffield. The Republican Congressman from Tennessee doubled down with another pre-written speech announcing how un-American Elemynt and the developments surrounding it were.

"Mr. McCray, you may begin with your prepared statement," Senator Layne said glibly.

Troy's time to shine was at hand. His prepared statement was posted more than 24 hours prior. However, hearing the words directly from the mouth of the esteemed CEO was the highly-anticipated moment the room was waiting for.

Troy took a sip of water. He began with greetings.

"Chairwoman Layne, Ranking Member Scoffield and members of the committee..." he read from his notes. "Thank you for the opportunity to testify today."

Every sentence, word, and punctuation mark of Troy's statement was meticulously crafted, reviewed, edited, and lawyered to nail Elemynt's signature talking points. The company's leader spoke of its global reach, the happiness of the people who used it, and the unique human stories made possible by their platform.

"Our focus at Elemynt is helping people connect in ways that are unique to them," Troy said to the rapt chamber. "The greatest strength of our platform is the people who use it every day. Our growth is rooted in their feedback. We look forward to continuing this dialogue now and onward into the future."

Troy's voice was free from emotional rises or a petulant attitude that the press could latch on to. Arriving at the ideal tone for his recitation required days' worth of coaching.

"Thank you for that," Senator Layne said flatly. "We're moving on to the next part of our hearing."

After the formalities were through, the line of questioning was set to begin. Each of the lawmakers would have five minutes to ask questions of the witness. The cycle would continue as long as the committee desired. The Senators peered at Troy from the lofty dais, waiting for their turn to attack.

Kelsey shifted in her increasingly uncomfortable seat. Whatever Troy said next would change the fate of the company and their lives forever.

An uneasy silence fell over the chamber as Senator Layne scribbled notes to herself. The gallery waited anxiously for what would emerge from her pursed lips. Finally, she spoke.

"Mr. McCray, how much revenue did Elemynt earn last year?" she asked.

"I don't have those exact figures in front of me," Troy said. "I can check with my team…"

"Our records show Elemynt earned $42 billion last year," she interrupted. "Would you say that's accurate?"

"Congresswoman, I'll have to check with my team."

"Is that figure in the ballpark to your understanding, or no?"

"I'll check with my team," Troy repeated.

"Let's say for the sake of argument the figure is correct," she soldiered on. "That would mean not only is your company completely invading the privacy of hundreds of millions of people, you are also making a significant amount of money from that continued violation. Billions of dollars, in fact. Does that sound right?"

The spectators gasped at the pointed attack. The tense showdown with Catherine at headquarters was a sliver of a preview of the Congresswoman's determination. Outside of a nearly unnoticeable smirk, Troy kept his cool.

"Congresswoman…" he paused, giving himself time to think about his response. "The data we use to match people with advertisers has been volunteered by each individual. We do not solicit or sell private information."

The statement wasn't 100 percent true, however, it was the simplest way of explaining Elemynt's revenue streams. No need to volunteer any more than that.

"Would Elemynt be willing to make changes to the volume of data it collects if it meant a decrease in your revenue?" she asked.

The question was a setup. If Troy said yes, the legislators and the public would hold him accountable for making good on his declaration. He would be required to amend the fundamental business practices of the company. Slashing the information available to advertisers would give them fewer reasons to bring their business to the platform. The downward spiral for Elemynt would begin the instant the changes were made.

If Troy said no to altering the way Elemynt collected data, his inflexibility would make him look like a money-hungry tech bro who sacrificed defenseless people on the app to make a quick buck.

Kelsey hoped with all her might that he would deploy one of several vague responses in his arsenal.

"We are exploring every option to address the issue and meet the expectations of the people who trust us," Troy said.

A perfect answer. A twinge of happiness shot through Kelsey.

Sensing that she would get no more from him than a corporate platitude, Senator Layne shifted her approach.

The Congresswoman used her allotted time to pepper Troy with a litany of potential data privacy regulations, several of them on par with the warnings Wyatt imparted. Congress had many options for unraveling the company. The Senator intended to inform him of each one.

"We cannot let Elemynt's irresponsible attitude toward data privacy be reflected in our government," Senator Layne said crossly. "This committee must carry out our duty to protect the safety and security of Americans everywhere."

Whispers of agreement emanated from both the gallery and the collection of senators staring down at Troy. It was evident that they would take satisfaction in seeing him destroyed.

"My time is up so I will yield to the gentleman from Tennessee, Mr. Scoffield," Senator Layne concluded.

The attention in the chamber shifted toward the Congressman to the right of the committee chair. The pile-on was set to continue. Senator Scoffield rolled back the sleeves on his baggy suit jacket and adjusted the mic to his liking. He was ready for his moment.

"Quite frankly, I don't care for Elemynt personally," the Senator said with an Appalachian lilt. "From my view, Elemynt has made the world more anxious about one's social status with these faves and shares. It's divided relationships and made people more worried about documenting their lives instead of enjoying them. Can you explain to me, sir, what are the advantages for someone to use Elemynt?"

Troy grinned at the opportunity to land Elemynt's central talking point: "The ability to connect with friends, family, and loved ones whether they are next door or halfway around the world. Experiencing life through other people's eyes by way of the images they post. The free exchange of ideas in what we call the 'global town square.'"

"How many people do you have working for you at your company?" the Senator asked curiously.

"We have more than 20,000 employees working together to develop the platform."

"And you pay all these people?"

Troy paused to consider the seriousness of the question. "We do. That's why we make money, sir," he smiled.

A small ripple of laughter echoed through the Senate chamber at Troy's simple but humorous response. Jon and Wyatt stifled tiny laughs. Anyone who had the slightest knowledge of the tech industry was aware it wasn't a string of penniless volunteer organizations. Kelsey herself was equally amused.

The chuffed Senator ignored the commotion to continue his line of questioning. "And these businesses are paying you for what?"

The spectators in the room reset their composure while Troy educated the befuddled Senator.

"Congressman, we have an ad-supported model that allows everyone who joins to connect with the world and not have an admission fee be the barrier to entry. Through our unique system, advertisers can reach specific groups of people on the app and those people are able to receive promotions that are relevant to their interests."

Had the hearing not been a solemn affair, Troy would have received a round of applause from the audience behind him. He touted the company's core values in a way that observers could respect. A billion people were given a free service to express themselves and communicate with those they cared about. Elemynt was a tool built on goodwill. It just happened to make a profit.

The next up to bat was the newly-elected Senator from Massachusetts. She let the audience return to a composed state before beginning her five-minute inquisition.

"We've heard from Madam Chairwoman about the extent of the privacy breach and the results thereof," she said. "What were the hackers able to see when they accessed the accounts?"

Troy spoke of photos and incidental contact information, the staples of pretty much all social media platforms. He refrained from mentioning the hundreds of data points for each person that allowed advertisers to target accounts with granular detail. There was no reference to facial recognition technology, location tracking, or the private information that wasn't explicitly volunteered by each person on Elemynt. The response was a skewed version of the truth. Lies by omission. The Senator let Troy go on without interruption.

"We encourage people to read our terms of service which outlines exactly how their information is used to make our platform better," Troy said.

The Senator sat back in her chair, satisfied with the sanitized version of the impact. "Thank you, Mr. McCray."

Senator Neil Adkins, the ever-popular Democrat from Texas, promptly commenced his turn at the mic.

"Now, I've read your terms of service," he folded his fingers on the desk. "I love a good book, Mr. McCray. In fact, I was reading 'Don Quixote' last summer and that's a long 900 pages. However, there are dictionaries shorter than your terms of service. The language gets so confusing my law students would struggle with it and they're a very smart bunch. My question for you is why are Elemynt's terms of service so long and complicated?"

Troy thought over an answer he could contain to a few tight sentences. "We want the people who use Elemynt to have a complete understanding of our platform. It answers every question they could possibly have."

"And each person who signs up has to click 'yes' to join your platform?"

"They do, sir."

The Senator remained unconvinced. "You expect people to read through this long privacy policy on the small screens on their phone," he said with suspicion. "That seems unrealistic, Mr. McCray."

"We do our best to keep people on Elemynt informed about the app," Troy said. "We recently added a prompt in feeds to encourage people to check out their account settings. Our teams found that it was well-received."

Troy declined to mention how many clicked through the prompt or that virtually no one was making changes to their settings. The less information Troy provided, the better.

While the Senator pondered the impressiveness of the app's proactive outreach, Troy leaped on the moment to expand his explanation. "It's important to us that the average person on our platform is able to understand our terms of service. That's why I'm happy to announce Elemynt will be launching an in-app educational campaign. The goal is to help users better understand what data Elemynt shares with advertising partners. This will be a huge opportunity for people to understand better how Elemynt creates the product they love."

Kelsey was taken aback by the proclamation. This was her first time hearing about such a campaign. From the curious looks on the faces of her colleagues seated next to her, it was theirs as well. Product marketing could have been working on the project under Troy's direction. If that was the case, Kelsey wondered why he hadn't told his team about it. They spent an infinite amount of time on prep and the impactful tool never came up once.

The enraptured Senators and journalists in the chamber listened as Troy proudly explained his exciting new project.

"Our plan is to create explainer videos that will be inserted into people's Elemynt feeds to give them information on important privacy topics like how to manage what information Elemynt uses to show ads."

The Senators and the audience whispered to each other about the astounding new development. The novel idea was in line with Elemynt's bold commitment to right past wrongs. Troy's announcement undermined solutions the lawmakers may have pitched with an impressive solution of his own.

"We've invested a lot of resources in this area," Troy said confidently amidst the commotion behind him. "I promise you this will be an ongoing area of effort for us. The people who use the app are our partners in growth."

Senator Layne struck her gavel to bring the commentary in the gallery to an end. Reporters were deep in their phones shooting off messages of the unexpected pronouncement to their newsrooms. Readers and viewers needed to be informed of Troy's latest offering ASAP.

After the audience settled long enough for the hearing to continue, the Chairwoman called on Charles Blumenthal, the professorial Senator from New Hampshire.

"I think people who know me are aware I am a fan of your platform, Mr. McCray," he said. "I get to see what my grandkids are up to while I'm here in D.C. I also keep up with my fellow Senators and what they're posting. That said, I do have an important question for you..."

Kelsey braced herself for what was undoubtedly a response to Troy's daring program.

"Sometimes after I upload a picture, I see there's a misspelled word or two in my caption that I need to change. To do that, I either have to delete the post and start over or leave it up. Can Elemynt add an edit button so I can make those corrections without the hassle?"

It was a sincere but remarkably specific question for which a Congressional hearing was perhaps not the proper venue. Watchers in the gallery sharing space with Kelsey chuckled at the ask. Many of them had the same question for their own account.

"Probably no edit button anytime soon," Troy said. "It's to protect the integrity of posts. Let's say, for example, a photo on Elemynt is shared by a whole bunch of people. Then the poster goes back and changes the caption on the original post using that feature, they may completely change the meaning and why people shared it in the first place. It's kinda like making edits to the Constitution after it was put into the law."

"That's why we have amendments," the Senator protested.

"But the original document is still there for everyone to read. There are no eraser marks on the Constitution."

The hearing room roared with laughter, including hearty guffaws from Congresspeople on the dais. Kelsey couldn't help but chuckle to herself too. Troy was being his best self. Clever, honest, and endearingly personal.

"Is that one of our lines?" Sarah whispered to Jon.

"No, he came up with that on his own," their manager said contentedly.

The fit of restrained laughter from the gallery would not be the last. What followed in the hearing was much of the same. The exchange set off a series of similar exchanges in which committee members sought to get a better understanding of how the app and its features worked.

"How do I know who is 'faving' my photos?"

"Can advertisers read my private messages?"

Senator after Senator followed with inane questions that a few keystrokes in a search engine could have revealed. Kelsey was increasingly bewildered that one of the most influential founders on the planet was being asked how to reset passwords, what happened to pictures after they took them, and how the Senators could get more followers.

Troy was the young, hip son home from Spring Break helping his elderly relatives fix their internet. The Congressional hearing turned into an IT help desk. Troy was visibly amused by the line of questioning as was Jon, who took the opportunity to idly check messages on his phone.

To say the Elemynt teams overprepared for the fateful day was an understatement. The exchange between Senator and CEO was not the doomsday scenario the Myntors were expecting. The hearing was a farce almost to the point of being comical. Troy seized the opportunity to spread his message of care and commitment to the journalists in the room and the people watching at home. He draped the room with charisma, powering through trivial questions that posed no threat to the company.

Even when he was asked more difficult questions — concerns about digital piracy and online surveillance did arise — Troy made use of his time with Kelsey to mature his response. He spoke in plain terms with no air of resentment. He was evasive where he needed to be, expressing claims he was not aware of details and promised to have his team look into it. He talked in broad strokes about the platform's undertakings without revealing incriminating information. Angry Troy was nowhere to be found. The Comms team would have stood up and given him a rousing round of applause if they hadn't been sitting in view of millions of Americans.

Troy continued to field questions about the company well into the afternoon. Three hours into the hearing and he hadn't shared anything revelatory about Elemynt or its data collection practices. Reporters seated behind the team grumbled in disappointment. They weren't going to get the hot scoop they came for.

Most of the Senators' chairs were empty. Photographers packed up their gear and skedaddled. The remaining journalists chewed on granola bars and peered around the cramped seats to see who would be the first to leave. There was no news here. They resigned to return to their offices and to file whatever stories they did have.

Jon, who was infinitely pleased, whispered to Sarah just out of earshot of the cameras. "I want you to have language for Troy ready to post to his account. Thank the Senators. Keep it brief and uplifting."

The last Senator to speak was Franklin Astor, the Republican from Indiana. The Capitol Hill veteran had spoken favorably about Elemynt in the past. He used his time with Troy to highlight the best of Elemynt rather than its faults. He glowed about online communities that arose through the app and the elevation of global discourse. He cheered the improvement of the lives of people everywhere through one digital tool.

"Mr. McCray, I admire you as an innovator and an entrepreneur," he said. "You are what some would consider a manifestation of the American dream."

"Thank you for the kind words," Troy said with a winning smile.

"You've created well-paying American jobs for your company and helped scores of business owners who use your platform do the same."

"One of the reasons we're proud to have built this platform," Troy bowed.

The Senator was not alone in his admiration for the CEO. Troy may not have been an elected official, but a billion people used his product and many more heralded his place in Silicon Valley history. He was more influential than most politicians could ever hope to be.

With the remaining minute in the hearing, Troy made one last pitch for his company. "Technology can change humanity for the better. I believe with all my heart that a bright future for Elemynt means a better future for everyone in America and throughout this beautiful world. We are doing the work because global harmony is our number one priority."

After almost four hours of testimony, the hearing came to an uneventful end. Troy's time in front of the Congressional committee would be an insignificant blip in history. A faded memory of wasted time and nothing more. It was the best possible outcome Kelsey and the team could ask for and a terrific notch in her belt. Another outstanding win for TC, the champion of the people.

Whatever flaws Elemynt had were overshadowed by the ineptitude of Congress. They couldn't regulate a product if they didn't know the fundamentals of how it worked. There would be no legislation that day.

Troy stood up to shake hands with the lingering committee members, including Senator Layne. She was noticeably agitated that the hearing was not the dramatic blowout that she anticipated. Kelsey was satisfied knowing the Congresswoman's ideal scenario of further sullying the name of Elemynt would never be realized.

The employee discussion in Commynt was a collective celebration of victory. Kelsey read the messages of Myntors in offices worldwide praising their leader's phenomenal performance in front of the legislative body. Troy took on the country's top lawmakers and walked away from it unscathed. Messages of appreciation filled the various internal threads.

"Congrats to the best boss ever!"

"Totally inspiring!

"Thank you to Troy for creating a company we love."

There was hardly a post in Commynt that didn't relate to the hearing. Memes with photos of befuddled Senators were traded back and forth. GIFs of Troy's

"We make money, sir" moment received hundreds of faves and shares. Employees called out the committee members' moronic questions, likening Troy to a nimble David slaying a feeble-minded Goliath.

Troy successfully championed the best aspects of Elemynt that Myntors held dear to their heart. The jubilation would keep employees motivated in their work for months to come.

* * *

At a stately home just outside of D.C. owned by an unnamed friend of Troy, a lavish private affair was underway. The daunting hurdle overcome by the CEO earlier that day was deserving of a fantastic celebration.

The opulent great room was filled with those to whom the hearing owed its success — members of the Dream Team, the company's legal eagles, an enthusiastic group of E.A.s, and the powerhouse Comms team. Echoes of laughter rang through the high ceilings and across the polished marble floors. Steaming trays of luscious dishes were set out next to the open bars patronized by the unwinding guests. They could relax knowing that the press would hear no word of their jubilation.

Elemynt's Security team commandeered the electronic devices of the catering staff before they entered the property. Guards roamed the halls to ensure no interlopers made their way in and no photos were taken by the strict list of attendees, including Myntors. The company would take no chances with having their post-hearing conversations on front pages the following day.

The partygoers excitedly recounted to each other their favorite parts of the hearing. They discussed the juvenile questions with the hilarity afforded by hindsight. Each person called out the moment they knew their CEO won the showdown. Jon, Sarah, and Kelsey were the most relieved of the guests. Their arduous task had come to a close.

Kelsey watched from across the room as Catherine escorted Troy into a nook away from the center of the party.

"This privacy explainer you promised to Congress..." she heard Catherine inquire. "The undertaking no one in the company has ever heard of and is no way in the works? Where did that come from?"

"I didn't say *when* it would launch or what it would look like," Troy spoke with his head held high. "Only thing I said was that we were working on it."

"Does this product exist is what I'm asking," Catherine prodded.

"It will when we create it," he said with a wink. "We can worry about it later."

The conversation was interrupted by the ceremonious pop of a champagne cork. The party guests gravitated toward Wyatt who stood proudly with a raised glass. Kelsey was not a fan of his, but thankfully his hyper-masculine shenanigans during prep were behind them.

"A toast!" Wyatt said triumphantly. "To one of the smartest, most creative, and, might I say, studliest CEOs in the world."

Troy nodded in appreciation to his general counsel and friend. Catherine smilingly applauded the efforts of the teams assembled in the room.

"To the future of Elemynt!" Wyatt crowed.

"Cheers!" the room roared as glasses clattered all around.

Jon, Sarah, and Kelsey clinked their flutes together echoing the sentiment with a small tribute to the Comms team. While the champagne flowed, Kelsey happily sipped her sparkling water. She maintained a personal rule that she did not drink at work or related events. She would always present herself as professional though the night's festivities had her considering whether she should make an exception.

Jon had a toast of his own for his group. "You all make me proud. Times like this show how strong Comms can be when we push as a team."

Sarah and Kelsey nodded their heads in agreement. The success of the hearing was a collaborative effort. There was no mention of Kelsey's individual contribution but reading between the lines she could tell she was being acknowledged.

"I want us to double down on this," Jon said. "Push Elemynt as the steward of innovation in tech. Pitch stories about Troy as a man on top of the industry clearing the path for others."

Catherine approached the group right as they were commencing a round of brainstorming. "Our diligent Comms team, always hard at work. I love to see it."

The Boss Lady joined their circle to congratulate the trio most responsible for Troy's success that day. Catherine's focus was on Kelsey in particular.

"Cheers to you, Kelsey," she said. "If you hadn't steered Troy in the right direction, we'd be drowning our sorrows in whiskey instead of champagne."

"It was my pleasure. Hopefully, there's no round two of this," Kelsey joked.

"We've done the work so that won't be necessary," Catherine said. "Jon, make sure Kelsey receives a stellar review."

"Maybe she deserves a raise too?" Sarah hinted.

"I'm sure Jon is taking great care of her," Catherine smiled.

The matriarch of Elemynt floated away as swiftly as she came to speak with other staffers in the room. Jon trailed behind her, leaving Sarah and Kelsey alone to chat. Kelsey overflowed with gratitude for Catherine's commendation. To be acknowledged by the executive she admired greatly made the trying experience of prepping for the hearing worth it. Kelsey hoped she could continue to wow Catherine with her work.

"Look at you making impact!" Sarah patted Kelsey on the back.

"All in a day's work," she replied coolly.

"It was more like a week and a half. But who's counting?"

They both shared a laugh at the long way they had come to arrive at a point of relief and contentment.

Attendees in the great room continued to mix and mingle with more drinks being enjoyed in tribute to the company's achievement. The louder the music spun up, the more animated the revelry became. Soon, the ritzy affair was a full-blown party on the dance floor. Sarah gestured for Kelsey to follow her into one of the home's ornate hallways.

"Kelsey, I have something I need to tell you," Sarah said. "I'm going to be away from Elemynt for about a month."

"Oh no, is everything okay?" Kelsey asked in a panic. "Is it a family thing? Medical? You don't have to tell me if you don't want to."

"It's nothing like that," she laughed. "I'm going on 'recharge.' The cool thing at Elemynt is when you've been at the company for more than four years, they give you paid time away for five weeks. It's so you have some time to get your life together, reset a little, and come back feeling like a new person. The wedding's coming up soon and my fiancé and I decided to take a nice, long honeymoon."

Kelsey was struck by a rare sting of insecurity. Sarah being away meant that she and Jon would be responsible for the entirety of the External Comms team's duties. It was true the team was on a roll. However, the reality was Kelsey was still fairly new to the company. She had so much yet to learn and the job did not come with an instruction manual.

"You can do this, Kelsey!" Sarah said with encouragement. "Trust me, I wouldn't leave if I didn't think you could pull this off with no problem. A few stories here, a few reporter calls there. It's nothing you can't handle!"

"I guess but Jon's always traveling with—"

"I know that you know what you're capable of," Sarah said. "Did I ever tell you we had 500 applications for your job? And you beat out everyone! You are the very best there is! So, don't ever doubt that you belong here."

Kelsey studied the walls of the magnificent home for a sign of how to move forward with the news. Kelsey reminded herself that she was a strong woman. She never backed down from a challenge. Sarah's absence might actually be less a problem and more of an opportunity for her to excel. She could take on more projects, be ambitious with additional tutelage from Jon.

"Also, you kinda don't have a choice...plane tickets are non-refundable," Sarah ribbed. "You sure you don't want some champagne?"

NINE

The bright, sunny day in Palo Alto was optimal weather for the campus volleyball tournament underway in front of Kelsey. Her athletic co-workers in tank tops and Elemynt T-shirts volleyed and spiked their way to victory. Sand flew in spectacular fashion on the court constructed especially for their enjoyment.

Thought it was quite a sight, the campus volleyball court was an odd place for a meeting with her manager. In his calendar invite, Jon instructed Kelsey to meet him under the covered patio overlooking the area with no additional details. Kelsey hoped he wasn't looking to play a quick match. Sand and stilettos did not pair well together.

Jon suavely approached the seating area outfitted in slacks and Sperry Docksider loafers. It was thankfully not the attire of a man prepping for a pickup game of volleyball. However, Kelsey would have been more relieved if she knew what the purpose of the meeting was.

"I prefer to have these conversations in a more relaxed environment," Jon said as he sat beside her in a patio chair.

Kelsey's mind raced with what she could have possibly done wrong that required an ominous conversation. She was nothing short of excellent in her first few months at the company. In the weeks following Sarah's departure, Kelsey hit the gas on her communication efforts for the team. Well-placed TV interviews. More magazine covers. Trend stories and spotlight articles galore lauding Elemynt as the go-to destination for connecting with friends, new friends, and family near and far. Kelsey arranged for members of the Dream Team to headline conferences, address gatherings of world leaders, and be the media darlings celebrated the world over. She was on a PR winning streak.

"It's time for your PRA... your performance review assessment," Jon said in his even tone. "Us managers document your performance and keep an ongoing record of how good or bad you're doing."

Kelsey was familiar with the term. Every six months, Myntors were individually evaluated on their performance in the last two quarters. If the employee excelled, they received bonus stock, raises, or sometimes promotions shortly after. The review process also determined if it was time for a Myntor to move on to another company. A part of Kelsey thought she was doing pretty well. But without Rachel by her side and Jon on his work trips, she couldn't say for sure. Working in a bubble of independence meant it was hard to gauge how well she was doing in the eyes of her manager.

Kelsey heard in passing that the review cycle was coming up. However, she was still new to the company. Kelsey didn't believe she had been at Elemynt for long enough to participate.

"I didn't prepare anything," Kelsey fumbled. "If you want, I can draft a list of my accomplishments. Or I—"

"Relax," Jon chuckled. "None of that is necessary right now. This isn't what you'd call a formal evaluation."

Kelsey loosened up, but only slightly.

"I want to congratulate you on meeting your KPIs so far," Jon said. "You've landed stories in 22 of the top 50 most popular news websites. That's excellent. The favorability index of Elemynt on major tech blogs is up ten points. Another outstanding achievement."

"Thank you!" Kelsey brightened. "There's more on the way! I have stories lined up with eight more journalists this week."

"And that's why we're lucky to have you," Jon smiled. "To show our appreciation for your hard work, I'm going to add a bonus to your next paycheck. Additional stock units too."

"Jon, that's incredible! Thank you! But don't I have to be here a full six months before I'm eligible for bonuses?"

"When you make the type of impact you have, anything's possible," he smiled.

Kelsey was overcome with such good feelings that she wanted to go spike a few volleyballs herself. She imagined that the occasional cheers coming from the sandy matches nearby were for her.

"Sarah is on Recharge which means we'll be working closer together," Jon said. "Keep achieving these impressive results and you'll have nothing to worry about."

"The next half is going to be even more amazing," Kelsey promised.

"Good to hear!" Jon said. "You're a strong asset to this company. I know I'm not here in person often, but I can see that you are a team player with creative ideas."

Kelsey continued to thank Jon effusively for his generosity. She was also hugely appreciative to Elemynt for motivating its employees with incentives, financial or otherwise. They made her feel close to the company. She couldn't put a price on the happiness she felt welling inside her.

"How can I support you going forward?" Jon asked. "I want to make sure I'm giving you what you need as your manager."

"Your emails and check-ins are super helpful," she said. "I'm still ramping up, so I appreciate any advice you have along the way."

"I got you covered," Jon affirmed. "Things can get shaky around here sometimes but that's all a part of the job."

"I'm here to roll with it!" Kelsey said. "I'm seriously looking forward to taking on more projects."

"Then our next big meeting should be a perfect way for you to start. It's very top secret. Only the Dream Team has been briefed so far."

Kelsey bristled with excitement. "What is it?"

"You'll find out soon," Jon smiled.

* * *

The leather and metal ergonomic chairs that encircled the polished oak table in the executive conference room were filled with members of the Dream Team. Other stakeholders packed into the seating on the perimeter of the space. The mood in the room was electric for reasons unknown to Kelsey. High-level Myntors brimmed with optimistic chatter. Unlike most other meetings she attended, no one was buried in their laptops or phones. Troy sat proudly at the head of the table overlooking the operation that was once the idea of a solitary university student. There was one noticeably empty seat by his side.

The good cheer reached a high when the apparent man of the hour entered the doorway. Ravi Mahajan, the Chief Financial Officer of the company, was a big brain packed in a slender body. He circled the room handing out stacks of documents enclosed in plain folders.

"These do not leave this room," he said with stern politeness. "Do not copy or share them electronically without my or Troy's authorization."

Whatever was in the folder was a serious matter. Kelsey opened to the first page. On it, the words "Initial Public Offering" were emblazoned in bold letters. Kelsey couldn't believe the momentous step for the company that was a topic of discussion for years had finally arrived. The ladies estimated on the yacht that the IPO would happen soon. She didn't realize it was right around the corner. Kelsey was bowled over that she would be a part of the pivotal launch.

"Ladies and gentlemen, today is the beginning of a new era at Elemynt," Ravi said with a well-earned smile.

A vibrant round of applause echoed throughout the supercharged room. Elemynt was on the precipice of the most epic chapter in its storied history.

A successful IPO was a badge of prestige for any company who made it a reality. Being publicly traded on the stock market required a strong profitable outlook and the diligence to undergo a grueling process. Elemynt would be rewarded handsomely for its efforts. The hefty financial capital early investors put into the company would be returned and then some. The influx of many billions of dollars from new investors as a result of the offering would drive Elemynt's next generation of big innovations.

Troy had come a long way since his days at Stanford University. When Elemynt began to show success in its early years, the founder received more offers to purchase the company than he could keep up with. His answer was always the same: No. Troy was confident that Elemynt would be more valuable than the high-dollar cashouts dangled being in front of him.

Ravi opened his copy of the folder with hands that spent many nights and days poring over financial documents. The CFO was hired for his deep connections to Wall Street and strong understanding of the requirements to transition to a public company. His priority was ensuring Elemynt had the proper financial infrastructure in place to take the leap. The number of meetings that led to the one they found themselves in must have been huge.

"I want to remind you all that this will be a long and very difficult process," Ravi said. "The end result is going to be worth it."

"Yes, it will be," Troy said with power in his eyes.

Ravi outlined to the energized group the changes the company was required to implement on its journey to the IPO. He spoke of the need for new automated accounting systems, restrictive budget planning, financial compliance mandates, and detailed reporting requirements from the U.S. Securities and Exchange Commission.

Kelsey's knowledge of the concepts he mentioned was limited. Financial concepts weren't her side of the business. However, she did understand that the increased scrutiny from the media surrounding an IPO required a concerted promotional campaign to go along with it. Investors put their dollars into companies the public had a high opinion of. Just when she thought she'd conquered the biggest challenge of her career, a financial makeover of Elemynt pushed her further along.

Troy radiated confidence in front of the Dream Team. The IPO was a landmark step in the further growth of the company he helmed. Kelsey did notice the hint of ambivalence seeping through the cracks of his posturing.

Troy held onto worries that the new era of accountability to outside forces would restrict the distance of the leaps Elemynt could make toward innovation.

"We're gonna want to keep the investors who believe in us happy," Troy said. "My goal is to make sure we're not losing our independence in this process."

"We can be both profitable and independent," Catherine replied empathetically.

"Right on," Troy said. "We're planning early so we can make this as smooth as possible. Jon, you and your team will take a break on this one. We're bringing in a public relations company that specializes in IPOs to do comms. Your team can send press and whatever other questions you get from the media to those guys."

Kelsey felt pangs of dejection at the news that External Comms wouldn't be taking the lead on promo around the IPO. It was the biggest news in the company's history and she would have no role in developing its public relations strategy. Her disappointment was numbed somewhat when Troy emphasized that the separation was also due to legal requirements. Her spirit received another boost when Troy threw his arms open wide like the feathers of the proudest peacock.

"Which brings us, ladies and gentlemen, to this year's E-Con...who's ready??" he shouted.

The answer from the huddle of elated Myntors was a thrilled and thunderous affirmative. E-Con — short for "Elemynt conference" — was the highlight of the year for the popular company. The annual gathering where Elemynt announced new features and technology was the closest thing to Christmas for tech enthusiasts. Thousands of influencers, marketers, and creators traveled from all over the world to witness in person the exclusive one-day event. Millions watched live from home as Troy and a slate of higher-ups shared news of ventures that would change the face of social media technology. In addition to ticketed guests, journalists and television crews representing the most influential media outlets traveled to the Bay Area to cover the event live.

E-Con was a major event that the company spared no expense for. The best venue, the best giveaways...the various components down to the smallest details was designed to leave an outstanding impression on those lucky enough to attend.

Receiving one of the coveted badges to see E-Con and Troy in person was like winning a medal at the Olympics or coming in first place at NASCAR. Right off the bat, a considerable number were set aside for tech and media VIPs. The remaining attendees were selected through a lottery system from hundreds of thousands of eager online applications.

The centerpiece of E-Con was Troy's keynote address in which he outlined his vision for the company's next year and beyond. Troy was always backed by a sleek presentation and videos interspersed throughout that illustrated with visual flourish the impact of Elemynt. His many fans hung on to his prescient words. Whether it was viewed online, on television, or in person, watching the company's long-awaited announcements in real-time was to participate in a global cultural moment.

"I promise this year's E-Con is gonna be bigger and better and more awesome than anything people have seen from us," Troy said proudly.

Because of the coming IPO, Kelsey had no doubts that was true. The tentpole event would double as an advertisement to potential investors of the future profitability of Elemynt.

Troy gave a brief overview of the expected run of show. Elemynt's head product guru Gary would announce the latest in virtual reality technology. That would be the headliner of the day. Other speakers who were not yet selected would announce other features like interactive messaging, 3-D integrations, and easier ways to connect in the app. The event would conclude with the fan-favorite keynote from Troy.

"E-Con is in February, so for the IPO we're aiming for a date in early spring," Catherine said.

Jon was jazzed for the External Comms team's time to shine. A successful marketing push of the event and the products announced was considered the ultimate win for him. Together, the team would create a swirl of official blog posts, media placement, executive interviews, and more.

"Lucky for us, reporters love E-Con," Jon said to the table. "They'll make our jobs easy. But as you all know, we don't settle for just easy."

"Big thinking..." Troy said. "That's what I'm looking forward to from you."

"In the meantime, no one here talks about the IPO outside of this room," Ravi admonished the group. "Not to the press or to other Myntors either. You can potentially unravel our plans if you do."

Neither Ravi nor Troy needed to worry about a peep escaping their lips. No one wanted to be the person to whom a leak was traced. One word and they'd be unceremoniously bounced out of the company with no recourse. Billions of dollars were on the line. Drastic measures would be taken.

"One last thing before we break..." Troy said. "Can someone tell the People team to come in?"

Kelsey always felt a spark of delight when Melissa, the Head of People, bounded into the room. Hearing about the next cool thing Elemynt was doing for staff was always a treat. Her spritely demeanor upon her entrance communicated without words that more good news was on the horizon.

"Jingle, jingle!" she exclaimed. "Who's ready for a holiday party?"

Jubilant applause encircled the already enlivened table in anticipation of the epic internal event. The tech industry was known for its lavish, larger than life holiday parties that were a physical testament to the company's great work throughout the year. For Elemynt, one of the biggest tech firms in Silicon Valley, the holiday party would be an all-out bash.

"We want employees feeling good going into the IPO," Troy said. "Happy people are productive people and we need everybody at 100 percent."

"We don't have to worry about that at all," Tai said. "People find out we bought one sprig of holly and the whole campus is geeked."

Melissa continued her announcement by projecting a series of festively adorned charts on the room's largest television screen. She clicked through the highlights of the plans as they currently stood.

"The Events team secured a venue at a cost of $150,000 and we're looking at $100 per person on food and drink."

"And this doesn't include contract employees, right?" Troy asked.

"Yep, same as every year," Melissa said.

"Contractors aren't allowed to go?" Kelsey found herself asking aloud.

Tai scrunched her nose at Kelsey. "They can come if they're the plus one of a full-time employee. There's a bunch of benefits they don't have access to. This is one of them."

"Because of the additional expense," Melissa added.

"They can ask Myntors in Commynt if anyone has an extra ticket," Tai said.

It didn't resonate as fair to Kelsey that a large segment of the employee population of Elemynt would not be allowed to come to the company party. Asking around for an FTE charitable enough to extend an unneeded invitation was a bizarre position to put a contract employee in. Elemynt spent a sizable amount of cash to throw the annual party. It couldn't hurt to pay a little more so everyone at the company, full-time or contractor, could attend. All Myntors should have the opportunity to take part in the fun.

The rest of the people in the room were content with Tai's answer. The split in benefits between contractors and FTEs was evidently nothing to lose sleep over. Kelsey decided she wouldn't either.

"Getting started on planning Comms for this now," Tai said. "We make official internal announcements about the date two months out. Messaging is only for employees. No press."

External Comms may not have been in the loop for the holiday party itself, but Kelsey sensed an opportunity to make the all-important impact in another way. If she saw a chance to make it happen, she would take it. Also, the room was on her side following the hearing and the success of "Friends' Day."

"Question," Kelsey piped up again. "Are we thinking about how to bring the holiday spirit into the app?"

"Usually we add seasonal graphics on the logo," Gary acknowledged her. "Snow and holly... make it fun."

"I have an idea that would grow engagement and get us good press."

Jon perked up. "What's up, rockstar?"

"More people are posting photos around the holidays with their friends and family, right? How about we have a personalized holiday graphic in each feed that includes a photo of who the person takes the most pics with during the holidays? The memories would be like a reminder to them of why they love Elemynt. They could share it with their followers... it would be fun for everybody!"

Kelsey's suggestion sparked an idea in Gary. "I like where you're going with that! We can also use our location algorithm to see where the person takes the most pictures in November and December. If they travel during that period, it's probably where they spend time with family. I would love to see my kids at grandma's house last year in my feed."

"Pics of grandmothers get great engagement!" Troy exclaimed. "What about using facial recognition to identify people that appear in those photos we pick up? We can match the faces with active Elemynt accounts and tag both people."

"Looks like we can start a new holiday tradition here..." Gary said.

"Another way to have people feel more warm and fuzzy ahead of the IPO," Troy mused. "Alright, Gary get on it, let's make holiday magic. Kelsey, you're a genius."

The meeting attendees were equally enchanted with the awesomeness of the idea. Kelsey pitched a killer PR campaign to the CEO and again landed it flawlessly. The impact she would garner through the collaboration with Product would be praiseworthy and also a lot of fun to execute. Tai rolled her eyes at the praise heaped on Kelsey. However, her co-worker's perpetually sour attitude wouldn't bring down Kelsey's high spirits. She was a rising superstar living out her dreams.

There was a wide range of events on the horizon to be excited about. The IPO, E-Con, the holiday party...the possibilities for greatness were endless. On top of that, the company's participation in the annual pride parade was the following week. Kelsey couldn't wait to put on her most fun outfit and celebrate Daniela's hard work that pulled it together. The favorable stories resulting from the ladies' efforts left other Silicon Valley companies weeping in the dust.

* * *

Kelsey waded through a sea of rainbows in search of the assembled group of her Elemynt colleagues. Attending the pride parade in San Francisco was a first for Kelsey and surpassed her wildest expectations. Thousands of people were lined up on Market Street, the main thoroughfare of the city, ready to march in the parade. A million more filled the adjacent sidewalks waiting for the start of the jubilant procession.

Dozens of floats touting participants that ranged from community organizations to department stores to gay dating apps stretched from the iconic Ferry Building of The Embarcadero to the Civic Center miles down the road. Rainbow flags draped proudly from the doorways and windows along the route of Downtown San Francisco.

Among the parade marchers were drag queens in head-to-toe sequins and guys with unreal, rock-hard abs dancing in their underwear to the pounding beat of pop music. Cheerleaders and flag twirlers organized themselves on the street alongside the roaring bikes of lesbian motorcycle clubs. Fuzzy men with bare chests and what looked like leather straps on their upper torsos greeted each other happily. Marching bands tuned their brass instruments while local politicians and celebrities prepared for their rides in sleek convertible cars. Kelsey was instantly enamored at the sight of people celebrating at the sensational event. Representatives from non-profits, area businesses, city agencies, corporate participants, and religious groups prepped for the long-awaited send-off.

Witnessing the parade festivities in person was a completely new experience for Kelsey. As a woman who absolutely liked guys, she had never been to a pride parade though she did see plenty of photos on Elemynt. She didn't want people getting the idea that she was a lesbian. Not that it was important. Some of her friends who were also straight attended the party before. She recalled faving their fun selfies and live videos of the dazzling activities. Elemynt and also supporting Daniela gave Kelsey an excuse to finally see it for herself.

Sensing that she was lost, one of the parade organizers a drag queen with sky-high hair helpfully escorted Kelsey in the direction of the Elemynt group. After a gushing thank you, Kelsey joined the hundreds of Elemynt employees lined up for the send-off. They sported tees in vivid primary hues that together made up the colors of the rainbow. Each shirt was emblazoned with the company logo. At the head of the contingent, a select few Myntors hoisted the Elemynt banner triumphantly.

Kelsey spotted Ro near the front of the pack wearing an Oakland A's baseball cap over her braids and a purple T-shirt that read "Butch Please." She stood by proudly watching her girlfriend Daniela give last-minute directions to her fellow Myntors. The co-leader of Elemynt's presence at Pride enthusiastically carried out her duties.

"She's always the hard worker," Kelsey said to Ro.

"More than y'all know," Ro said. "This Pride thing? She wants all the employee groups at Elemynt to get the same love too."

"If anyone can pull it off, it's our girl, Daniela," Kelsey said. "She'll make it happen."

"You're right about that," Ro smiled. "My girl gets things done come hell or high water. It's like very day, she gives me more and more reasons to love her."

"It's not hard with Daniela working all the time?" Kelsey asked.

"We both are," Ro said. "What's really key is we both come home to each other. We know we have support when we get there. That's what keeps what we have strong, you know what I mean?"

Kelsey nodded in agreement. That wasn't her exact experience, but she understood where she was coming from. For a second, her thoughts went to Brad, the man who continued to show her support from wherever he was in the world. Kelsey hoped Daniela and Ro could pull through in the same way.

The conversing pair were joined by Jade and her two daughters who frolicked their way through the confetti-covered street. The cuties were mini versions of their mom — pint-sized fashionistas in matching rainbow tutus and flashes of glitter streaked through their hair.

"Sophie and Stella, say hi to Kelsey and Ro!" Jade said.

"Hi, Kelsey! Hi Ro!" they said in near unison.

The girls looked as adorable as they did in their pics on the Elemynt app. The photogenic pair's popular account that mommy added photos to for them. They were the same bubbly duo on and offline.

"Are our future Myntors marching in the parade too?" Kelsey smiled.

"They'd love it for about five minutes," Jade laughed. "A few miles is too much for their little feet. The plan is to meet up with Todd in a bit. We couldn't come without saying hello to other favorite girls!"

"Mommy, can we take the picture now?" Sophie said as she tugged at her mom's pleated skirt.

Jade handed her daughter the phone to the girls' delight. Sophie and Sarah instinctively posed with social media ready smiles in a succession of photos. The cuteness received adoring oohs and from nearby wide-eyed adorers. The two took turns snapping wonderful photos of each other. They created picture-perfect moments with ease.

Ro offered to take photos with both of them in the frame. They said yes with the joy that only toddlers could exude.

Kelsey didn't realize that when Jade said the day before that she would swing by to say hello, she would be bringing her daughters as well. Kelsey was unsure whether a pride parade was an appropriate venue for children. She gently pulled Jade to the side while Ro was occupied with the little ones.

"You're not worried about the kids being out here?" Kelsey asked.

"Why, should I be?" Jade said while keeping an eye on the girls.

"There's some adult things going on out here, yeah?" Kelsey said.

"There are titillating moments, sure, but that's a small part of what's going on," Jade said. "For me, I love that they get to see that there's different kinds of families out there. We want to teach our girls to be accepting of people who might be different."

Jade pointed to the many families around them. There were surprisingly more straight couples along the avenue than there were same-sex partners. Kelsey was not completely convinced of Jade's point. If she had daughters, there no way she would bring them around the questionable environment.

"Mommy and Daddy are here to answer their questions if they have them," Jade said reassuringly. "Kids these days… they're smarter than people think."

"I'll say," Kelsey said. "Look at those divas with the cell phone!"

"Aren't they naturals?" Jade laughed. "We've been coming for years now and, let me tell you, the girls couldn't wait to get here! They get to run around a place where people are happy and there's color and costumes. Trust me when I say they are thoroughly enjoying themselves."

A miles-long cheer traveled down Market Street as the honk of car horns signaled the start of the parade. Motorcycles revved their engines, marching bands lifted their instruments, and the crowd of spectators went wild with anticipation.

"Showtime, everybody!" Daniela shouted to the frenetic Elemynt group. The hundred or more Myntors responded with cheers of their own.

Jade and the girls waved goodbye to Ro and Kelsey as the two Myntors joined Daniela at the rear of the pack. Kelsey's fellow employees snapped last-minute photos to capture their excitement, then assembled themselves into one unit. Together, they represented LGBTQ+ Myntors, allies, and the company that they loved. The banner with the Elemynt logo prominently displayed led the way for their journey through the exuberant San Francisco street.

The infinite number of spectators that lined the parade route cheered, waved, and smiled at the Myntors as they passed through the street. The sound of groups chanting slogans of support of equality and tolerance blended with booming dance music from the festive floats. Ro and Daniela held hands tightly and gave each other the occasional peck while the trio marched merrily down the path.

Kelsey watched as members and friends of the trans community waved flags with vivid stripes of light blue, pink, and white. Same-sex couples held their children on their shoulders so they could get a better view of the celebration. An elderly woman in a wheelchair proudly held a sign that read "I love my gay son."

"There's no greater love than loving yourself!" a man on a megaphone yelled. "Live life openly!"

People of every age, race, gender, religion, and, to Kelsey's surprise, sexual orientation came together to celebrate in unity. It was a freeing experience for those in attendance and the flock of Myntors, Kelsey included.

The eyes of bystanders lit up at the sight of the Elemynt banner making its way down the avenue. Employees laden with rainbow beads adorned with a medallion of the Elemynt logo tossed them to the crowd. Parade-goers clamored to get a memento from the hottest social network.

A small boy waving a tiny rainbow flag attached to a stick called their attention. "Miss, can I get a T-shirt please?"

Daniela lovingly handed him two. One for the excited kid and another for his grateful mother.

Kelsey noticed that seeing Elemynt employees in person was a revelation for some of the observers. They gasped and pointed out to others the appearance of the crew representing the company. It dawned on Kelsey that they had never associated the app with having a slew of people who worked to build it. For many, it just existed as a product that they used every day.

Kelsey wanted to tell them that, yes, there were hundreds of employees in front of them at the parade, but there were many more around the globe. Elemynt was built for the people by real people. The message Elemynt sent by being at Pride and supporting LGBTQ+ causes was that it cared about all communities. The bystanders could feel the mutual appreciation as the Myntors passed in their direction.

Ro and Daniela looked so cute together as they walked hand in hand through clouds of multicolor confetti. Daniela was more relaxed than Kelsey had seen her since they first met. The light between the pair shined bright in the full view of the festive crowds.

"I totally need to take a picture of you two!" Kelsey exclaimed to the couple.

"No, that's okay," Daniela held her free hand in front of her face.

"Another time," Ro said, waving Kelsey away politely.

Kelsey was struck with confusion. She struggled to understand why a Myntor would not want to take pics amid the burst of color and happiness. At the very least, it was an opportunity for Daniela to memorialize her hard work.

"What's the deal?" Kelsey asked. "Did I do something wrong?"

"It's not you," Daniela said. "It's my family."

"Are you going to send them photos of you two?"

"My parents...they don't know that I'm gay," Daniela said solemnly under the roar of the crowd.

"You're one of the organizers of this whole parade group!" Kelsey said in disbelief. "You have a girlfriend! An amazing one."

"The thing is I'm not out and they don't know about Ro," Daniela said. "My family thinks I'm straight and I've never given them a reason to think otherwise."

Kelsey suddenly realized that in the time that she started following Daniela on the app, her colleague had rarely posted pictures of her with Ro. When they did appear together, it was usually in the company of friends or with space between them not indicative of two long-time lovers.

"I thought Pride was about being yourself?" Kelsey frowned. "Letting the world know you're proud to be who you are. Did I miss something?"

"Hey, it doesn't work the same way for everybody," Ro said gruffly.

Daniela's girlfriend stood in firm support of her partner for new reasons Kelsey could not discern.

"My family is strict Catholic," Daniela explained. "Like first row at mass every Sunday Catholic. And…"

Daniela held back a torrent of emotions that threatened to upend the spirit of fun around them. Ro held her love's hand tenderly.

"My family believes that homosexuality is a sin and that gay people will end up in hell," Daniela sighed. "They would never accept my truth and… I don't want to lose my relationship with them. If I'm in the Bay Area away from my relatives, holding Ro's hand is no big deal. Back home in Florida… I would never. And I don't put up posts that would give them a reason to think I was gay. My parents, my cousins…they all follow me on Elemynt."

Kelsey was crushed with remorse for bringing up the subject. She assumed Daniela was out like every other gay person she knew. It wasn't the 1800s. There was no reason for gay people to have to live in a closet.

"I have a cousin who came out and they cut him out of the family," Daniela said with a heavy heart. I haven't seen him in years. We're friends on Elemynt though."

Daniela managed a weak smile through her pain. "I want to come out and be open and honest with them and with myself but…I'm proud of myself for getting to a space of at least being happy with who I am."

Kelsey wanted to stop walking and pull her friends to the curb. Daniela and Ro were inclined to keep moving with the bustle of Myntors. Stopping would worsen the flow of emotion. Ro moved the three closer to the center of the group of distracted Myntors so they were better shielded from the gaze of spectators.

Daniela tapped a tissue to the crease of her eye to prevent tears from falling.

"Maybe it won't be so bad if you just talked with them," Kelsey said optimistically.

"It's not the words that are hard," Daniela said. "It's what would happen after. My family is my heart and... I don't want them to shut me out because of who I love."

Ro comforted her grief-stricken girlfriend, holding her tightly in her loving arms. From their interaction, Kelsey inferred that the discussion about Daniela's coming out was one the couple had many times before. They didn't stop moving down the crowded street.

"I'm so proud of you babe," Ro hugged her. "You've been through a lot and you're still here. You gotta do what your heart says. Trust yourself, love."

"Ro, does your family know about you?" Kelsey asked sympathetically.

"My family is old school Dominican so, you know, it took a while for them to accept their daughter was different. We don't talk about it period. They don't ever bring up me liking girls. It's kinda like the family secret everybody knows about."

"You're not out either?" Kelsey said with a raised eyebrow.

"Ay, check this out," Ro said sharply. "I don't know if you're understanding this but not all gay people go through the same experiences. We're still dealing with stuff like high HIV rates in our communities. My black and brown trans sisters are getting murdered every day. A lot of places outside these major cities? Pride is still about protest. Yeah, you got people marching here and whatnot but most people are coming to party. That's cool but what happens when they go home? What's messed up is that some folks don't have a place to come home to, especially these kids out living on the street. It's wrong, but it's real."

Kelsey was uncomfortable that Ro would bring up negativity in the middle of a Pride celebration. People were having a good time, as she said. They were smack dab in the most uplifting environment Kelsey experienced in her life. The whole situation was baffling.

Kelsey decided to get them back on track. A parade was their time to enjoy themselves and celebrate their LGBTQ+ colleagues. She did have one last question that she hoped Daniela wouldn't take the wrong way.

"Why be in charge of Pride?" Kelsey asked Daniela. "I'm sure someone else could've taken it off your hands."

"Because if I can't be fully out myself, I can at least help other people find their tribe," Daniela said resolutely. "I'm also doing it for the people who look like me and Ro to see themselves represented. The rainbow is a spectrum of colors and you know Elemynt isn't the most diverse place. Every color in the rainbow should feel included."

Ro hugged her girlfriend tight until Daniela's usual joyful character returned. A kiss planted on Daniela's lips brightened both their spirits.

"Aight, no more crying today," Ro said, wrapping her arm around Daniela. "We're gonna celebrate and get our rainbow on!"

"Yep, let's do it, babe," Daniela smiled.

Kelsey didn't mean to come off as if she was telling Daniela to do something she was uncomfortable with. That wasn't her intention for sure. It was hard not to look around at the spectacle of love around them and not feel like she should be living as openly.

After a few blocks of shaking off the unpleasantries, the three ladies were back in the spirit of the parade. They continued their journey down Market Street with the Myntors soaking in the joyous occasion and glitter-infused fun. Ro showered Daniela with the occasional reassuring peck of love amid the impassioned crowd.

Kelsey was so entrenched in the high-spirited stroll that she almost didn't feel her phone vibrate. She opened it up to find three missed calls — all from Grace Oliver. At the top of her notifications was a pleading text message: "Call me as soon as you can." Whatever it was must have been serious if someone of Grace's stature was calling Kelsey directly.

The raucous parade was far too loud of an environment to have a conversation over the phone. Kelsey's anxiety spiked at the decision she had to make. Step to the side and catch up to the girls later or wait until the end of the parade to return the call. If Grace indeed had an emergency, waiting to respond might be a huge mistake on her part. Kelsey was too nervous to continue the mile-long walk left without returning the pressing calls. She would be too consumed with thoughts of what may be wrong to ignore them.

Kelsey held up her phone to Daniela and Ro. "Hey, I have to go. It's a..."

"A work emergency?" Daniela completed her sentence.

"Would you be mad if I left right now?" Kelsey asked.

Kelsey's social graces made her fearful that the couple would think she was rudely running out on them. She hoped they wouldn't be offended by that. Daniela had to understand. She was a PR professional who was aware of the 24-hour commitment they made to the company.

Ro didn't seem perturbed in the least. Perhaps it was because Kelsey's departure would give Ro more freedom to spend quality time with her girlfriend. Kelsey took the cue and exited gracefully, thanking the ladies for an extraordinary day she would never forget. They waved sincere goodbyes and in a few steps were gone.

Kelsey moved hastily away from the revelry of Pride events. She waited until she was several blocks away from the noise of the parade to return Grace's call. When she answered, Kelsey could hear the Hollywood ingenue sobbing hysterically.

"It's so bad right now!" Grace cried. "I seriously can't deal with this!"

"With what?" Kelsey said aghast at the star's frantic state.

In a tearful reply, Grace explained that a speech she gave the previous day at the United Nations in support of women's rights unexpectedly went viral. The praise she received from the women she championed for was overshadowed by legions of men on the internet unleashing vicious words at her.

Grace's posts on Elemynt were inundated with hundreds of comments telling her to kill herself or threatening her with violent sexual assault. The sick replies ranged from "get back in the kitchen" to promises to "rape her filthy cunt" until her body was a corpse. When Grace altered her settings in the app to turn off comments on her posts, new Elemynt accounts popped up that were specifically created to attack her.

"They put up fake pictures of me being set on fire or stabbed to death with blood spilling out," she cried. "This stuff is horrible! All I said was women should be treated as equals by society and now this trash is being sent my way!"

"It's trolls trying to get under your skin," Kelsey said consolingly. "They see the good work you're doing and they want to throw you off."

"I get it and I keep reporting these people in the app," Grace sighed heavily. "I don't know how your team works but I'm not hearing anything back. These guys won't let up! It's like the more accounts I report, the more they're creating."

"Can your assistant report the accounts for you so you don't have to look at them?" Kelsey asked.

"That's not her job," Grace said defensively. "Why do we have to click on each account to make them go away? Don't you have some system you can use to get rid of these guys all at once?"

Kelsey tried to reassure Grace that the situation could be resolved while simultaneously battling her own rising fear. She had no idea how Elemynt's tools for reporting spam and threats on the app worked behind the scenes. They were handled by a completely different department at headquarters and in the global offices. She had no direct line to them. The situation was light years beyond the realm of Comms.

For Grace to be subjected to an onslaught of hate-filled replies made Kelsey feel like she had let her down in a huge way. Grace gave them the gift of her presence at the Q&A. In return, the star was inundated with distasteful comments that were not representative of the Elemynt experience. Kelsey instinctively felt protective of Grace. She did not want her to fall victim to numbskull, loner jerks on the internet.

"I can't keep on doing this," Grace said frantically. "I'm scared to go online or log in to the app because of what I might see. I think I'm going to delete my account."

"Please don't," Kelsey pleaded. "You inspire tons of women out there to be the best version of themselves. I'm one of them."

"I have to think about myself and how I feel for once."

"What about for now you stay off Elemynt for a while?" Kelsey suggested. "Let this stuff die down? I'll do whatever I can to get these idiots off the platform for you."

"If you could make it go away, I'd appreciate it with all my heart," Grace relented. "I don't want to leave my online community behind. You know that. But with this going on, I will if I have to."

The moment the phone call ended, Kelsey dialed Jade in a ferocious panic. If there was anyone who knew how to possibly mitigate the issue, it was her. Grace's account was verified and she was considered one of Jade's celebrity partners. From Kelsey's understanding, Jade and the Media Partnerships team had the resources to resolve situations promptly for top talent.

Kelsey could hear on the other side of the call that Jade was still at the parade festivities. Her daughters and Todd were in the background laughing and having a good time. Kelsey hurriedly explained Grace's mounting plight to her colleague.

"Don't worry. We handle these things all the time," Jade said calmly. "I'll have one of the partner managers take a look at the account as soon as they can. It's a Sunday so it might take a while."

"You're the best," Kelsey exhaled.

Kelsey hung up the phone satisfied that Grace's predicament would be rectified. Before she began her journey home, Kelsey sent a message to Jon to keep him abreast of the situation. Jon responded with a video call to her work phone, his preferred method of communication. Behind him in his hotel room was a view of the sculpted shapes of the Sydney Opera House in Australia.

Jon listened carefully while Kelsey explained the events of the last thirty minutes. She made sure to sound calm while conveying the gravity of the issue.

"Sorry to hear that happened," Jon replied. "I'm glad it's being worked on."

"I'll keep you updated," Kelsey promised.

"Good," Jon said. "In the meantime, the Diversity team is meeting with Catherine tomorrow. I want you to be there. Elemynt has a lot of initiatives for women in the works. I want you to be knowledgeable about them in case we get a press inquiry about this. Or similar issues in the future."

Kelsey agreed that the more background information she received on the company's efforts to support women, the better.

"Remember, this isn't our domain," Jon said. "It's Daniela and Scott and the Diversity team's. No need to take the lead here. You'll know what to do."

TEN

The meeting could have been about any number of things. User experience, quarterly reports, the finer points of scrum versus agile…it didn't matter. Kelsey was thrilled to be in Catherine's personal conference room, seated across from the beloved executive. Kelsey accepted that it wouldn't be just the two of them speaking that day. Kelsey was seated alongside Daniela, her manager Scott, and Melissa, the Head of People. Their laptops were powered up and ready for the discussion of the yearly diversity report.

Like all U.S.-based companies with more than 100 employees, Elemynt was required by the government to submit a report each year that outlined the demographics of its employees. The EEO-1 form required counts by race, gender, and job category, among other data points. Because of this, every year employees were asked to report their self-identified biographical info to be tallied by the company. The reports were kept confidential by the government and Elemynt was under no legal obligation to release theirs.

However, since the public outcry in the years prior regarding the lack of diversity in the tech industry, it was common for Silicon Valley institutions to release an annual report themselves. A self-published diversity report allowed the company who authored it the opportunity to add context to their yearly demographic data. The company could set the narrative around their progress rather than have the media manufacture one for them. The strategy was a key public relations move.

The reports proudly touted in glowing language current diversity initiatives and highlighted those on the horizon. The company's goals for growth in various categories were outlined to overshadow less than stellar numbers that may arise. Spinning the report into a positive outlook was the smartest option. To not issue *same as on page 121* (handwritten)

a diversity report at all was seen as having something to hide.

Kelsey was never required to steer the publication of a diversity report when she led Comms at UltraTalk. The Boston company consisted of far fewer employees than Elemynt and didn't meet the federal threshold. An undertaking of that nature would have been voluntary and mostly unnecessary. Kelsey wouldn't be at the helm of Elemynt's report either. As Jon said, it was Daniela's communication strategy to lead.

"Alright, let's hear it," Catherine said to the gathered Myntors. "Should we start with the growth of our female employees?"

"Sure thing," Scott said as he projected the latest data on a screen. "I'm happy to say the number of women at Elemynt is up three percent over last year, which puts us at 36 percent. We're doing better with women in senior leadership positions too. There was an increase from 19 percent to 26 percent, which is excellent."

"Beautiful work, everyone," Catherine said with smiling satisfaction.

"Since we first started publishing reports, the number of women in technical roles at Elemynt has more than tripled," he added.

"Even better!" Catherine exclaimed. "I love hearing good news first thing in the morning."

Hearing about the increase of women at Elemynt brought Kelsey's thoughts back to Grace and her ordeal. Hopefully, Jade was able to resolve the issue for her expeditiously. Kelsey imagined that having more women on staff would result in more female voices thinking through ways to resolve some of the harassment issues on the app. A rise could also lead to them being a higher priority among the relevant teams.

Scott laid out for the group the various efforts the Diversity team undertook to increase the population of female Myntors. They partnered with university computer science departments with high numbers of women graduates. Together, they created curricula that prepared students for the rigorous interview process at Elemynt. Many fruitful partnerships with "women in tech" organizations were forged in the past year. There was also the creation of "Elemynt University," an in-house program in which women of a wide spectrum of ages enrolled to learn firsthand what it took to have a successful career at the tech giant. The venture received high praise from the media and participants.

A hearty round of applause in the conference room lauded the Diversity team's extraordinary work. Daniela clapped graciously. Her face, however, told a different story.

"I have to mention Elemynt still has a way to go with hiring black women and Latinas," Daniela said. "Both of the groups are at less than one percent of the total employee population."

Scott attempted to hush Daniela to keep the positive vibes in the room going. Daniela was happy for the overall growth, but she would not let her point be glossed over.

"The number of women of color in management positions could use some improvement too," Daniela said. "We have about ten Latinas in senior manager or executive positions in the U.S. offices. As for black women managers... we only have six."

"Six percent?" Catherine asked.

"No, six. Single digit. In the whole company."

"Well, we'll have to leave that specific number out, won't we?" Catherine said. "We're doing fantastic with our women and I'm sure the black and Hispanic numbers will grow as well."

Daniela did not seem to be surprised by the rebuff of her concerns. She likely had similar discussions many times before to encourage more representation of people who looked like her. Her demeanor suggested it wouldn't be the last time she would bring it up.

"Daniela, I do want to congratulate you on organizing our Pride efforts," Catherine said. "Job well done. I assume we've seen an uptick in our LGBT employee numbers?"

"We're up another two percent," Scott offered. "Thanks for your financial support on that front. We also have more veterans and employees with disabilities than we have in the history of the company."

"We're not going to overwhelm people with percentages in this report are we?" Catherine asked.

"It'll be more fleshed out than that," Daniela said. "We have the design team working on custom graphics for this year's report. The Marketing team has their photographers out to get pics of diverse Myntors for us to include, so we'll see those soon. But I do have one more concern."

"What's that, Daniela?" Catherine said, fixing her gaze at her.

"Elemynt is still overwhelmingly white and Asian. Almost 90 percent of our employees self-identify in either one of those categories. The rest is a mix of black, Latinx, Native American, and 'other'."

"But we are working to bring more of them in," Scott said with urgent optimism. Daniela was detracting from the positive steps forward made by his team.

"I bring it up because that's the number the press is going to latch onto," Daniela said.

"We are making improvements year over year so that's something," Melissa piped up.

"I'm worried it's not going to be enough for the public. Moving the minority categories up a single percentage point is going to be more of a story than the rest of our numbers."

Scott leaped into full damage control against his own head of communications. Daniela was countering his narrative that the demographic makeup of Elemynt was on a dramatic upswing. Any progress on diversity was good, he emphasized. The messaging would be commended by those interested in diversity at Elemynt.

Catherine was somewhat wary of his take on the outcome. "I can't help but think that with the resources we've allotted your team that we should have made more progress by now?"

Scott was visibly shaken by the accusation. "We've stepped up our recruiting efforts," he powered on. "Right now, we're running into two issues. First is retention. Our exit interviews are showing that employees of color don't feel comfortable here. They feel like being the only one from their background on their teams had negative effects on their work. That sentiment is twice as high for our engineers of color."

Catherine tsked at the assessment. "And what's the second issue?"

"We're recruiting talented people of color," Daniela jumped in. "But they're disproportionately not making it through to the end of the interview process. Statistically, we're finding that managers are hiring people who look like them. White men are hiring white men, et cetera. It's an ongoing thing."

"I believe your team created a diversity training program for managers to counteract behavior along those lines," Catherine said. "What was the progress exactly?"

"We used to have mandatory sessions," Scott said. "But we're finding that the trainings are causing more problems than they're solving. We're getting feedback from managers that they hate being 'forced' to make diversity happen. They want to focus on the 'best' candidates."

"They said 'hate'?" Catherine balked.

"No, not specifically but that's pretty much how they're feeling. Maybe 'resentment' is a better word."

Scott further explained that the Recruiting team notified him that women and minority applicants were consistently receiving lower scores from their hiring panel after their interviews. This was the case even when the person had similar qualifications as other candidates.

The recruiters also received feedback from Black, Hispanic, and female candidates that hiring managers were being hostile toward them or not paying attention while the candidate was talking. Because they felt like they were being discriminated against, a large portion of the minority applicants who were ultimately offered jobs ended up turning them down. They indicated that they preferred not to work in what they anticipated to be a hostile work environment.

"We're doing what we can to balance out the inequality," Scott said. "Our internal referral system that lets employees recommend candidates has been a huge asset for finding amazing talent."

"But the problem we're running into is that most Myntors are not recommending diverse candidates," Daniela interjected again. "The way the recruiting system works, referrals are getting priority callbacks. That puts applicants from underrepresented backgrounds who don't have an internal connection at a disadvantage."

"Aren't most of the engineering candidates white men?" Melissa said. "We can't not hire them. That's illegal."

"That's true but it's possible to stop handing them advantages in the process," Daniela said. "We're seeing the same hiring trends in other departments too. About half of the positions at Elemynt are non-engineering roles. With your blessing, Catherine, if we add extra resources for recruiting in teams like marketing or sales or design, we would see a big increase in diversity numbers."

"Your suggestion is noted, Daniela," Catherine replied. "Thank you."

Daniela slunk back in her chair for the tiniest fraction of a second before sitting more upright than before. However crushed she felt, Daniela was compelled to remain an engaged power player at the table.

The discussion regarding hiring reminded Kelsey that she was grateful to Jon for bringing her onto the team. Like he had mentioned to her before, Kelsey beat out lots of talented candidates for her role, including what she assumed was a fair share of men. If more managers thought like Jon, the company would move further with diversity.

"What if we counted contractors as part of the report?" Melissa asked sunnily.

"There's a lot of people from diverse backgrounds in those positions."

Daniela shook her head. "I wouldn't recommend it. We usually do separate charts for the diversity percentages of technical roles and executive positions, which is what the people who read these always look out for. I worry that if we sort by contractors too, it'll show we have a disproportionate number of people of color in contract positions."

"It was just a suggestion," Melissa winced.

"Daniela, I acknowledge your concerns," Catherine said. "In the meantime, in this report, we will give the news their headline. I want you to focus on our gains with women and LGBT employees. When we mention minority groups in the report, I want that followed by news of what we've done so far."

"We're working more closely with historically black and Hispanic colleges," Scott perked up. "We have our external community partnerships with African-American groups too."

"Put that in the report," Catherine said. "Any and all you're doing, put in the report."

"We can also do profiles on some of our Myntors of color," Melissa said. "Put them on the blog and the company website? How's that sound?"

"That's great," Daniela said. "I just worry that people are going to focus on those low percentages of Black and Latinx employees."

"We can't do anything about that now," Catherine said. "It won't change that we need to deliver the report before people come sniffing around for it. Scott, what is the schedule for publishing?"

"Posting Monday after the all-hands so Myntors see it first," he said. "Then a blog post Tuesday morning linking to the report."

"And your team will keep working to make our numbers better for next year," Catherine said sternly. "Make the most out of those resources we give you or we'll have to reorganize our staffing."

Chills permeated the room from what Catherine's statement could suggest. Scott silently pleaded with his eyes for Daniela to not say more. Daniela's bottom lip lightened. Her unaddressed concerns would remain so. Kelsey sat back watching the tennis match peter out.

At the meeting's conclusion, Catherine was whisked out of the room by her aides with Melissa filing out after her. What was supposed to be an encouraging moment ahead of a solid diversity report turned into a contentious spat between boss, manager, and employee.

Daniela pulled Scott to the side. "You know this report is going to bury us. There's a whole lot more that we could be doing and nothing is going to change unless managers are held accountable for diversity."

"Daniela, we're doing what we can."

"We're fighting a house fire with a pail of water."

"Catherine has been our ally," Scott said exasperatedly. She's given us the resources to make improvements."

Daniela was unconvinced. "She's done enough so we look good on a diversity report and we're still failing at that. We need Myntors to understand that diversity is a benefit for everyone. The different perspectives we get out of it make this company a better workplace."

"No one knows that more than me, Daniela," Scott said. "I need you on my side on this one. You know Catherine has the best intentions. We need to follow her lead."

* * *

Daniela didn't say much as she and Kelsey made their way out of the building. Her mood soured significantly since their exit from the meeting.

"Congrats on all your hard work," Kelsey said encouragingly.

"That's what it is...work," Daniela sighed. "I never thought doing more than the bare minimum would be so controversial. I know Scott means well, but I don't understand why people are so happy about changes that barely move the needle. A little bit more effort in diversity would go a long way."

Daniela and Kelsey emerged into the bustling hub of campus where employees milled about between meetings. A crowd of chatting Myntors sipped bubble tea from a food truck stationed in the plaza for the day. Kelsey ruminated on Daniela's observations about diversity at Elemynt. There were mostly Asian and White faces around them. However, a speckle of people from other backgrounds was there too.

"How do we know these numbers for sure?" Kelsey asked. "Maybe there's more diversity than you think?"

"We send out an online form to employees and people check boxes," Daniela said. "When they don't identify their race and gender, we have to go through their ID pictures and guess by looking at them or checking out their name. Next year, we're going to start using the facial recognition technology we have internally to do a lot of the heavy lifting for us."

"That'll free you up to work on your projects."

"I wish time was the issue," Daniela said exhaustedly. "I'd have more stories to pitch the media if people here stopped blaming 'the pipeline' for the company's lack of diversity. They love to say there aren't enough black and brown people in engineering. What's funny is half of the jobs at Elemynt aren't even technical like that. I keep asking where are the salespeople of color, the designers, the partner managers... No one ever has an answer other than 'we're working on it.'"

"We have more women on staff now..." Kelsey replied. "That's a good thing."

"But not women of color."

"You don't think this is a win for all women?"

"All white women," Daniela said emphatically. "There are more than 6,000 white women at Elemynt. You know how many Latinas there are? 54. In a company of 20,000 employees, there are only 54 Latina full-time employees. What gets me is the number of Black and Latinx people who work here is out of sync with the demographics of our users. And the diversity initiatives we're doing only seem to boost the number of white women. Which means those of us that are here feel like we have to represent our whole race in our performance to convince managers it's okay to hire more people of color."

"I may not be a minority but being a woman in this industry is not easy either, okay?" Kelsey grumbled.

"Sure, but white women are still way more likely to be hired here than a woman of color. Also, you usually get offered higher salaries than we do for the same job. Catch what I'm saying?"

Why Daniela was bullying her, Kelsey had no idea. She wanted to root for her friend but not if she acted so aggressively. If Daniela were nicer about what she was trying to accomplish maybe she would get somewhere.

"I can't change that I'm white just like I can't change that I'm a woman," Kelsey said defensively.

"I'm not denying that you have pain," Daniela said. "What I'm saying is what white women face is nothing compared to what black and brown employees have to go through."

"Seriously, Daniela? It can't be that much worse."

"Okay, has another Myntor ever asked you to take out their trash because they assumed you were part of the cleaning crew? Has security ever double-checked your badge because they thought someone who looks like you couldn't possibly work here? Have you ever had someone not bother to pronounce your name correctly or started speaking to you in first-grade Spanish because they thought you couldn't speak English?"

"I would never do that. I don't see co—"

"Don't you dare say it."

"You have no idea what I was about to say!" Kelsey protested.

Kelsey was increasingly feeling attacked by her friend. And this time it was for a sentence she didn't let her complete.

"You were going to say 'I don't see color,'" Daniela said. "Well, I do. Every day I walk through this campus, I only see a handful of people who look like me. I can go in buildings and not see a single Latinx employee. I feel the eyes on me when I'm walking the hallways because I don't look like the Myntors they're used to seeing."

Kelsey reeled from Daniela's continued attack on her. Daniela was trying to guilt her for a part of who she was that she couldn't control which was beyond unfair. Kelsey was increasingly frustrated that Daniela saw how upset she was making her and yet she kept on talking as if her words weren't hurtful. Kelsey collected herself so she could go on about her day without the negativity. Daniela was frustrated about her job and Kelsey would forgive her for that.

"I'm sorry that you're feeling that way," Kelsey said.

"Thank you for the apology," Daniela said. "But I want you to know that hurt you're feeling right now is how I feel almost every day of my life working here. I took this role because I don't want other people, regardless of what their background is, to feel like they're being treated differently because of who they are."

Kelsey breathed deeply and changed the subject.

* * *

Kelsey stood petulantly in the wings of the auditorium waiting for the week's all-hands meeting to begin. After her unpleasant encounter with Daniela, she needed the well-timed palate cleanser to clear her mind. The trademark upbeat music echoing throughout was already putting her in a more congenial mood.

Kelsey looked out at the crowd of laptop-toting Myntors filling the many rows of seats. There were African-American and Hispanic people there. Not a ton, but they were there. Elemynt was doing its best and that she could be sure of.

A mass of applause from employees welcomed Gary to the all-hands stage. Kelsey clapped along as well while halfway ignoring Tai who sidled next to her in their usual spot.

"Are you ready for the next evolution in online advertising?" Gary said to the energized room.

A boisterous cheer akin to a game-day sports arena rang in the space. It was a known fact that whenever the VP of Product spoke at all-hands, a new product or feature would be debuted. Whatever it was must have been good based on her colleagues' elevated response. Tai, who was usually tight with concern about whether all-hands was on track the way she planned, was unsarcastically enthused.

"One of the things you all should know about me is that I love Taco Bell," Gary said as he paced the stage. "My wife...you could say she's not a fan."

The room was tickled with laughter at the thought of the executive having a back and forth with his wife about tacos and 7-Layer burritos.

"What she *does* love is a good discount when she's shopping," he said. "How many of you guys are the same way?"

Hands shot up around the auditorium in the affirmative.

"Well, I'm here to tell you that Elemynt is going to be putting discounts directly on your phone. I'm proud to announce the next generation of location-based ads on the app!"

The towering screen behind him flashed with examples of the new feature depicted in colorful images and video clips. The audience cheered mightily at the debut of Elemynt's next landmark innovation. Kelsey too was excited to hear more about the brand-new technology.

"Based on GPS signals built into the app, we know when your phone is near a neighborhood business that you love or may be your next new favorite," Gary said. "Elemynt will now send you a push alert for a coupon for that business so you'll get not just an ad, but a discount for that store too. Now, when I pass my local Taco Bell, I can get a coupon and eat more tacos for less money! What do you think about that?"

The resounding congratulations from the gathered Myntors layered the room with an exuberant spirit of camaraderie. An offer system built directly into the app was an outstanding and obvious next step for Elemynt's current targeted advertising framework.

Gary talked enthusiastically of people potentially receiving gift cards to test drive new cars when they were near a neighborhood dealer. They could snag free donuts with a purchase from their local coffee shop, last-minute flight deals when they visited an airport, or discounts on memberships to a gym in their area. The possibilities were limited only by the imagination of advertisers.

Kelsey whispered to Tai above the sustained applause. "Is this public? We don't want the press to get the hold of this yet, do we?"

Tai rolled her eyes. "I told you Myntors always hear about major announcements direct from us first. That's part of our open culture, remember? They trust in Elemynt because we trust them. And anyway, Marketing Comms has an announcement post ready to go first thing in the morning."

"Why don't we do it today?" Kelsey asked. "Monday...first day of the week?"

"Game time for us is Tuesdays," Tai huffed. "Best time for the company to announce anything. It's not Monday when reporters are still going through their emails and it's not later in the week which gives us less time for their stories to go viral. You're still learning, it's cool."

"Tuesday, got it," Kelsey repeated.

Kelsey sighed and let the exchange go. She didn't feel like picking a fight with yet another unnecessary adversary. As luck would have it, Daniela joined Kelsey in the back of the auditorium to have a prime view of the next presentation.

"Here goes nothing," Daniela said to no one in particular. She lifted her head high.

Next up to the all-hands stage was Scott to represent the latest efforts of the Diversity team. The response from the audience to his entrance was more muted than Gary's, but pleasant nonetheless. The game-changer announced by the VP of Product was a hard act to follow. Scott turned up the volume on his typically perky aura.

"Hey, everybody!" he waved to the room. "Many of you know Elemynt's annual diversity report is coming out soon. I'm here to give you a sneak peek."

The screen behind him brightened with the image of a rainbow of smiling faces holding phones and laughing joyfully.

"I'm proud to announce that the number of women at Elemynt has increased to an amazing 36 percent!" he smiled. "We also have more LGBTQ+ and veterans on staff than in the history of Elemynt! Our diversity is growing more every day."

Scott made use of a handheld clicker to flash the impressive stats on the screen. They were met with a brief round of handclaps.

"We're keeping to our goal of increasing the number of Latino, Black, and

Native American Myntors," Scott continued. "Right now, each group makes up about one to two percent of our workforce. Our recruiting team is working to improve those numbers. Diversity is an important part of the culture at Elemynt and makes us a better company."

"I wrote those lines for him," Daniela sighed. "We go back and forth sometimes but I will always make sure he sounds fantastic when he gets in front of a crowd."

Kelsey appreciated Daniela for being the best at her job no matter what. She remembered that the Head of Diversity Comms role wasn't without its particular challenges.

Scott continued with optimistic declarations about the strength of Elemynt's diversity measures. The uneven demographics in the report that Daniela had reservations about weren't referenced much beyond his initial statement. He also made no mention of female minorities like Daniela suggested.

"It will get better next year, for sure," Kelsey said.

"I guess any progress is good," Daniela brightened somewhat. "We just have to keep moving forward on this."

Daniela's words in their earlier conversation were for sure abrasive. However, Kelsey would always support her friend. They were in it together. Tai made a motion for the all-hands production crew to move the program along.

Following Scott's presentation was the Q&A portion of all-hands. After the requisite questions from the online poll, employees organized themselves in a queue behind the mic for their turn to query Elemynt's top execs.

The first person in line was a slender blonde who approached her turn with hesitancy. "Hi, I'm Lucy from Small Business Sales. First of all, congrats on diversity. It's so needed. What I want to ask is what are we doing about the treatment of women on our platform? There's been some issues with that lately?"

A hush of importance fell over the room and, oddly, a few snickers.

"Women are dealing with a lot of harassment," she said in defense of her question.

Lucy looked around in hopes of support from others around her as Troy made his way toward center stage with a mic in hand.

"It's an issue we have to think about more," Troy said assuredly. "We know that we need to do better and we will."

Troy's answer sparked a tiny bit of concern in Kelsey. Sarah shared with her previously that if a Myntor received a response similar to the one Troy just delivered, it was not likely that action would be taken on the problem soon. Not that it wasn't important, it was just probably not high on the list of priorities. Sarah may have overgeneralized though. Kelsey was sure that there was a concerted effort somewhere in the company to address the issue. The existence of the moderators was proof that Elemynt cared about resolving the issues of harassment. Kelsey wished Sarah would return soon from her honeymoon to confirm.

Lucy was followed by a guy rocking tousled hair and the ever-popular hoodie and khaki shorts.

"Hey, I'm Vince. I work in Platform Engineering," he said. "Yeah, it was mentioned earlier that Elemynt was going to be changing recruiting? The question I have is what we're doing to make sure we're not lowering the bar with our hiring? I just wanna make sure we're thinking about having the same level of talent we always had."

Scott signaled to Troy that he would take the question. The CEO dutifully handed him the mic.

Scott considered his words before offering his response. "Here's the thing, bud. When I hear someone say 'lowering the bar', it's usually in a conversation about diversity or hiring more Black and Latino employees. When people use that phrase, a lot of times they've assumed that people of color are less qualified than everyone else. That's a biased stereotype that we don't condone here."

The auditorium deadened with stunned silence. The head of Diversity had taken down the questioner with a heavily critical response. The brusqueness was uncharacteristic of an all-hands gathering.

"Just say we're working on it!" Tai growled through her teeth. "Daniela, W.T.F.?"

"I didn't write that for him," Daniela said, scrunching her face. "He's going off-script..."

And he wasn't done. Scott's pacing across the stage became more purposeful. As if he was gaining momentum.

"There are lots of qualified candidates out there who don't get a second look because people are making assumptions based on their race or gender," he said. "When we talk about bringing more diversity, we're saying to hiring managers if they have two candidates that are equally qualified, they should consider bringing in someone with a different perspective than people already on the team. That doesn't mean hire less qualified people. We don't lower our standards like you're maybe suggesting."

The candidness of Scott's answer shocked the watchers in the auditorium, most of all Daniela. She had encouraged him after the meeting to be bolder in his stand for diversity at Elemynt. She never expected that he would shoot down what was supposedly a common opinion in such a frank way. Scott was intent on not letting employees disassociate Elemynt's commitment to workplace diversity from the company's core value of connecting communities of all kinds.

Vince didn't leave the mic after receiving his answer like questioners usually did at the weekly meeting.

"I think companies should hire the best candidate for the job," he retorted. "And they should fit in with the culture here too. It's not for everyone."

The sulking employee didn't give Scott a chance to respond. Vince stormed away from the mic stand, likely embarrassed that he had been shredded in front of his peers.

Tai's blood boiled watching the scene unravel. The reason they stuck to a script when it came to all-hands was to avoid tense moments like the one the entire company just witnessed. All-hands were supposed to imbue employees with optimism, not leave them feeling upset. Scott's response did the latter and more.

"Come back a sec," Scott called to Vince.

The Comms ladies cringed in anticipation of what the diversity head may say next. There was nothing they could do to stop Scott. Rushing to the stage and tackling him before he could comment again was not an option.

"When people say 'I want the best person for the job,' a lot of the time they're subconsciously assuming that a white person would be the most qualified for a role. That won't always be the case. People can come from a diverse background and also be the smartest person in the room."

Vince didn't seem to be satisfied with the follow-up response. His screwed expression revealed that he was ready to dig in his heels on the topic. There was no doubt in the mind of those watching that doing so was a bad idea.

Troy returned to the stage, interrupting the crackling tension. Kelsey hoped his words would calm the growing unease that swamped the auditorium. Scott bowed out to make way for the CEO.

"Diversity is important to our success as a company," Troy said into the mic. "I'm proud of the progress we've made with increasing the number of Myntors from underrepresented groups who work at Elemynt."

Tai mouthed along with Troy's words. He was communicating one of a few pre-written responses he kept on hand for questions about diversity. The words may have been crafted in advance but Troy voiced them with the deepest sincerity. All parties watching could walk away knowing that Troy was committed to the issue while still valuing the varying perspectives of his troops.

The all-hands meeting closed out with the "Community Spotlight" video that Myntors looked forward to each week. Melissa, always effervescent in her role as Head of People, took her turn on the stage.

"We think you're going to enjoy this one," she said cheerily. "Take a look."

The video screen filled with images of the cutest puppies rollicking with one another and having the absolute best time in the company of their adoring owners. The cuteness onscreen charmed the hearts of the hundreds of employees.

Owners of a St. Louis-based animal shelter told in the video of how they used their Elemynt account to post images of each of the pups. They also frequently went live on the app so people could watch their daily playtime. The shelter received an overwhelming response to their efforts and the number of adoptions skyrocketed. Their Elemynt posts drew so much attention that the shelter started sharing photos of adorable pets from other nearby shelters to find them to new homes as well.

A smiling animal lover in a shirt embroidered with the shelter logo bounced a pup in her hands. She waved its fuzzy little paw at the camera. "The doggos say thank you!"

The entire auditorium swooned with affection. The shelter's use of Elemynt to share photos of adorable pets in need of a home was a perfect example of how the app was doing good in the world. Like Sarah said, these were the stories people loved to hear about.

The bouncy music of all-hands closed out the presentation while the inspired crowd of Myntors to return to their respective workspaces on campus. Everyone was content with the week's event... except for Tai.

Tai accosted Daniela with venom in her eyes. "Dude, say thank you to your boss for me for ruining my afternoon. Troy is going to be so pissed."

"He's my manager," Daniela shot back. "I'm not his."

"But you *are* on his team. And you help put together his messaging for the report."

"What's your point, Tai?"

"He doesn't want to stick to the script... I have to hear about it from Troy. Let me go talk to him so you and your boss don't get fired. Wouldn't be a problem if you did your job right."

"How about you have a blessed day," Daniela said.

Their counterpart stalked off with the grace of a rhinoceros leaving Daniela and Kelsey in the emptying auditorium. Tai worked with Troy for years on end. Surely she could come up with a way of appeasing him.

"She needs to get a hobby," Daniela said with folded arms.

"No one's getting fired, Daniela," Kelsey said reassuringly. "It's not your fault Scott said that."

"Oh, I know," she said resolutely. "I'd love to see them try and fire the diversity team before the diversity report is released. That would be quite a news story, don't you think?"

ELEVEN

Kelsey held a premade sandwich from the micro-kitchen more tightly than necessary. Tomatoes and spinach leaves fell flat on her desk. After the tense showdown at all-hands the previous day, Kelsey couldn't fathom what the conversation would be like when Scott published his summary of the upcoming report to Commynt. The post was a lightning rod in the making.

At 10 a.m. exactly, Scott's synopsis went up on the internal site. The language was decidedly positive. The number of women was growing at a rapid rate. Awesome. Significant advancement in the number of LGBT employees was made. Super great. People of color at the company were still hovering at single percentage points.

"We're working diligently to increase our numbers," he reiterated.

Near the bottom of the post was a brief acknowledgment of the challenges of recruiting African American and Hispanic employees in technical roles.

"Our aim is to fix the pipeline so we can ensure the future of a generation of engineers of color," he wrote.

Scott followed the declaration with announcements of the company's continued investment in the education of youth in STEM — science, technology, engineering, and mathematics. Additional programs, community initiatives, and external partnerships would roll out over the next quarter. The writing was mostly harmless and overall pretty inspirational. Comments began to trickle in on the post. The number of faves ticked upwards. Scott's message was met with heaps of praise from Myntors about the company's efforts.

"Thank you for what you're doing!"

"Congrats to Troy and Catherine for thinking about diversity."

Kelsey let out a sigh of relief. The shakeup at all-hands was thankfully resolved by Troy's closing message. Diversity at Elemynt was a priority and the man at the head of the company affirmed it. Going against Troy would be silly.

Kelsey absentmindedly watched as more comments appear on the post while she checked her email.

Reporter request. Message from Jon.

Suddenly, the number of comments on the diversity post escalated at an alarming rate. The thread was filling up faster than Kelsey could read. The forty or so responses ballooned into hundreds. Kelsey frantically scrolled to identify the origin of the firestorm. Unfortunately, she found it.

"We've been hearing the same promises about diversity for years now," a Myntor wrote. "Why are we satisfied with incremental change?"

Oh no, Kelsey winced.

"I've been the only person of color on my team since I got here," another employee said.

"I'm the only POC in my entire building," read another.

A chorus of "same" and "me too" followed the outlandish comment. The unexpected wave of contention was enough to send the thread into a tailspin. Myntors fired off their takes on the issue, creating a battle between die-hard Elemynt loyalists and dissenters aiming to air out their grievances about diversity at the company.

"I don't think it's fair to bring in unqualified people just because they fit a minority."

"This company is 90 percent white and Asian. Why does a small percentage of people of color bother you all so much?"

"Do we want diversity at Elemynt or do we want to bring in the best?"

"Our focus on diversity means more qualified people are being passed over for women and minorities. We talk about equality but these diversity quotas are discrimination."

"You know how painful it is to have outstanding qualifications and output, and still be called a 'diversity hire'?"

"Calling all people of color inferior and saying hiring them is a token gesture is racist. It's very hurtful knowing so many of my colleagues think this way."

"This is a great company. You should be thankful you work here."

"We have diversity of thought."

"It should be the work that's important, not what you look like."

"Troy doesn't have to do any of this. Go work somewhere else if you know so much better than him."

Myntors brazenly shot off their opinions knowing full well their comments were linked to their internal profiles. Disciplinary action against employees on either side of the argument was not likely because no one crossed the line in their commenting. There were no racial slurs and no epithets. However, the politically charged discussion was teetering precariously on the edge of decency.

The back and forth under the original post carried over into threads in smaller groups on Commynt. The women's group. Black. Latinos. The take on the issue skewed differently depending on the group, but the confrontations followed along the same lines. Employees arguing down Elemynt's claim of progress on diversity faced off against Myntors demanding more evidence that diversity was beneficial to the company.

Kelsey messaged Daniela on eChat in a panic. The Diversity team had to be doing something in response to the heated debate. Kelsey needed to know for herself exactly what that was. It was only a matter of time before the threads blew up into a nightmare for External Comms.

"Are you seeing this?" Kelsey typed in a chat window.

"On it," Daniela replied.

A beat of silence.

"Have you seen the convos on Mask?" Daniela asked.

After their conversation on the yacht, Kelsey hadn't felt the need to download an external app for anonymous discussions about the company. She fumbled through her phone's app store and signed into Mask with her Elemynt email address. An even more horrific discussion was underway in the various threads.

"These social justice warriors play the race card because it's the only way they'll get a job."

"Elemynt loves hiring people because of their skin color or because they have a vagina. How hard is it to judge people based on their resume?"

"All of a sudden we care about having more Blacks on campus. Now white men have to suffer."

"SJWs are ruining Elemynt. I'm sick of it. Fave if you agree."

Endless vitriolic comments were pushed through that, from what Kelsey could tell, came mostly from white men. Mask was completely independent of Elemynt but the animosity needed to be contained before the public caught wind of it. Kelsey went into strategy mode, devising plans to shift the tone in conversation. Striking the right chord took the kind of PR thinking she was known to excel at.

She stopped.

Jon told her before. The report and its consequences were Daniela and the Diversity team's issues to solve.

Kelsey and Jade texted their friend words of support in their group chat. They encouraged her to be strong and think strategically. If she needed help talking through solutions, her colleagues would be there for her.

A short time later, a sharp alert came through Kelsey's phone. Elemynt's official diversity report was posted on the company blog. The beautifully designed page presented a glowing review of their efforts so far and the uptick in numbers across the board. The existing partnerships with diverse community groups were touted. Future initiatives were proclaimed. Sunny photos of Myntors from various backgrounds were interspersed between the text. A quote from Scott rounded out a series of colorful charts and graphs.

"Diversity is more than just a word at Elemynt," he wrote. "Inclusivity and celebrating multiple points of view is what drives our company forward."

The Diversity team also arranged for Scott to participate in an exclusive interview with one of the largest news media outlets in the country. The story's publication was timed to the release of the report. In the news story, Scott acknowledged that while there was more work Elemynt needed to do regarding diversity, the company was committed to the task of creating lasting internal change.

The public statement from Scott highlighted a glaring omission in the raging threads on Elemynt. There was no response from an Elemynt executive to be found. An inspiring message of peace from Troy would have completely changed the direction of the conversations. Tai had to be working on a statement that would be delivered to all employees. Time was ticking. Kelsey reminded herself again that this was not her fight. There was nothing the member of External Comms could do other than sit and wait.

Kelsey clicked away to the main page of Commynt. There had to be other non-diversity discussions she could read to distract herself. Her coworkers were good people. Kelsey needed reassurance that there were positive vibes in the air elsewhere at the company. A marriage proposal, a big promotion for someone... any good news would be welcome.

Scott's post remained at the top of the day's "Trending Posts" listed in the sidebar. Number two was a post entitled "Reverse racism at Elemynt." Kelsey clicked on it with dual feelings of curiosity and dread.

"There is an issue at this company that needs to be talked about," the post read. "This is something I've been thinking about for a while. It's my duty as a Myntor to call it out."

Kelsey rolled her eyes. She was in no mood for more drama. She kept reading.

"The mural in Building 20 is amazingly racist. It erases the contributions of white men at this company."

Kelsey recoiled at the flagrant statement. She was appalled that a random guy thought that the best way to follow up the diversity report was with a post calling a piece of art on campus racist. The utter gall of it was reprehensible.

The mural was far from deserving of negative criticism. She happened to pass by it once in its location near the building's lobby. The central image of the art was a tree with sprawling roots planted in the ground. Leaves sprouted from the trunk to form a raised first. Surrounding the tree were abstract figures of people of various colors — yellows, oranges, browns, and deep reds. There was no white specifically, however it wasn't the glaring omission the guy was making it out to be.

On top of that, Kelsey was familiar with the artist who created it. Mimi Andrade was famous worldwide for her color-filled, large-scale murals that always depicted faith in humanity and uplifting different voices. If the mural's worst offense was portraying men, women, and people of other races on equal footing, that said more about her colleague's biases than it did those of the company.

"I hear a lot of people at Elemynt talking about diversity," the post went on. "The real racism is against straight, white men. This company is encouraging managers to hire more ethnic people which means white male employees are not getting jobs because of it. I didn't choose to be born white or a man so I don't understand why it's okay to be discriminated against because of it."

Kelsey controlled herself from doubling over in laughter. The notion that Elemynt was discriminating against white men was terribly hilarious. The diversity report they just published very clearly said that the company was made up of mostly white men. Most of the engineering positions were held by white men. Senior leadership was also overwhelmingly white and male. If it weren't for Catherine it would be even more so.

Kelsey stopped reading and scrolled back to the top of the post. She needed to know who the guy was. The author was listed as "Luke Schultz." The accompanying photo showed a white guy who clearly cut his hair himself and the complexion of someone who spent most of his time indoors. His profile listed him as a mobile software engineer.

Kelsey wondered if there was a person on Luke's team who wasn't a white or Asian man. According to the stats in the diversity report, it couldn't have been more than one or two, if there were any at all.

The note continued with increasingly audacious statements. "Elemynt is censoring conservatives on the app by filtering out their content from people's feeds. It's taking away their freedom of speech. And we have a mural in the building that celebrates that."

From what Kelsey understood of the content moderation process, it was only the egregious content — attacking groups of people or violent content — that was being taken down. It was hard to believe that there was an anti-conservative agenda going on behind the scenes. If anything, Troy erred toward letting people say whatever they wanted on the app in the name of open discussion. The terms of service were in place to ensure it wasn't a free for all. Posts from people on both the right and left of the political spectrum were being filtered through moderation at similar rates.

"I want my fellow colleagues to know that it's okay to be white," Luke doubled down. "Excluding us because of diversity is not the way to go."

How Kelsey felt about her whiteness wasn't important. She was more concerned that this guy was going to be a major headache for the Comms teams if they didn't get in front of it soon.

The post received a staggering number of comments that increased by the minute. Most of the responses were from Myntors incensed that one of their own would say such hurtful things about their coworkers. Employees did not hesitate to come down hard on Luke in response.

"It's thinking like this that makes it harder for women and people of color when they do get in these roles. Who wants to be treated like this in their workplace? Nobody."

"Racism must be so exhausting."

"Have fun talking to HR!"

"If I was a mediocre white man I'd be upset too. More qualified people who don't look like you taking your job."

"You've been told your whole lives that you are special. Now that other people are given opportunities and resources, you've found that they're your equals or better than you. And that chaps your ass."

The African-American and Hispanic employees in the threads were curiously unsurprised by Luke's train of thought. What was disturbing to them was that a white employee would voice the prejudiced thinking out loud. The minorities indicated that they often heard similar comments behind their backs and sometimes, in less direct language, to their face. There were many more white people who felt the same way, they said.

And indeed, they were correct. Luke's memo opened the door for other white employees disgruntled by the company's diversity policies to air what came off as long-held grievances.

"When people say 'diversity' here they mean we should have everybody except white men."

"People who aren't even alive who had my same skin color did stupid things and now it's being held against us. This is reverse racism and because we're white it's okay."

Kelsey was floored that a significant number of Myntors held the same beliefs. Also, voicing the negative attitudes so strongly in internal forums would be unheard of in any other workplace. The open culture of Elemynt cleared the path for employees to make statements that would get them fired elsewhere. The circumstances surrounding the exchanges were deeply unsettling.

Scott finally posted in the comments under Luke's memo after what felt like forever. His response was a basic, two-line note that indicated the company did not allow for discrimination. Kelsey scoffed at the trite offering. The situation had already escalated beyond what a message from a higher-up could heal.

Kelsey's apprehension soared thinking about what to do next. It wouldn't be long before Luke's post became fodder for the media.

A cursory check of several news websites revealed that Kelsey was correct in her assessment. Her fingers trembled above her laptop's keyboard. Copies of the leaked memo were at the top of the majority of online tech publications. Coverage of the internal flame war seeped its way onto major news sites. Cable news channels were steps ahead of their cohorts with Elemynt blasted prominently in the lower third of the screens. "RACIALLY CHARGED MEMO," "CONSERVATIVE BACKLASH," and "FIGHT AT ELEMYNT" titillated viewers with the controversy.

If journalists were on top of the issue, Kelsey was certain Tim Westbrook was as well. The vulture did not disappoint. A freshly-posted story on the Washington Chronicle site detailed the history of the controversial sentiment among Elemynt's ranks. The lengthy article included quotes from anonymous employees sharing personal examples of discrimination they faced at the hands of white, male Myntors. When paired with Elemynt's dismal track record at diversity, Tim's screed painted a picture of a company failing its workers.

Kelsey screamed internally at the near-instant proliferation of thinkpieces from bloggers across the internet. A range of current and former tech employees posted their takes on diversity in the industry. The consensus was the same. The road to diversity in tech was blocked by powerful majority demographics resistant to change. The coverage of the memo was more than a press fire. The entire building was burning down and the ashes were scattered around her.

Kelsey didn't know where to start. Her mind tumbled trying to think of who to reach out to first to create a PR plan of action. The unsettled Myntor shot off emails to the major internal stakeholder she could think of. Jon. Tai. Daniela. Scott. The Dream Team. Something needed to be done immediately. They desperately needed to come together to figure out what.

Daniela was the first to respond.

"Get to the 'Lombard Street' conference room in Building 4 ASAP."

* * *

Kelsey navigated through winding corridors past engineers working on Elemynt's next great products. Kelsey wondered how many of the mostly Asian and white men that filled the desks secretly felt the same as Luke did. Who among them contributed to the hellfire tracking across the Elemynt campus.

The atmosphere in the executive conference room was a frantic mess. Representatives at the intersection of Comms and diversity rumbled about the disruption of internal harmony and subsequent media frenzy caused by one random mural. Kelsey took a seat between a solemn Daniela and an enraged Tai.

Leon was buried in his laptop at the head of the table next to Troy. He read through updates without taking his gaze away from his screen.

"Someone wrote 'it's okay to be white' in permanent marker on the wall of one of the bathrooms," Leon said.

A room full of gasps brought other conversations to a dead halt.

"Who was it?" Troy screeched. "I want them fired!"

"Unfortunately, we don't know as of this moment," Leon said. "We don't put cameras on the bathrooms."

"There are cameras in every single corner of this campus and parking lot and the streets outside the parking lots but we don't have a camera on the bathrooms?"

"We could get sued for that," Leon said. "My team is getting a log of the employees who badged into that building between the time of the memo and when the incident was reported. They'll find out."

Scott hung his head in guilt that the situation following the diversity report was spiraling out of control under his watch. He had high hopes that his series of public statements were positive steps forward. Daniela remained silent. The reaction to the report was what she predicted and more. She didn't want to fan the flames by uttering a justified "I told you so."

"If we wanna stop a civil war from going down..." Tai jumped in. "We need to land the right communication with employees."

"Let's start with this mural," Jon said. "Do we think it's too political?"

"No way," Melissa replied. "We specifically don't pick controversial artists or topics."

In addition to her role overseeing employee relations, Melissa was also in charge of the Operations team responsible for the design of Elemynt's various offices. Her culpability in the fiasco had not gone unnoticed.

"It's not like we put Satan on the wall," she added. "Should we cover it up or something?"

"It's my company and I'll have whatever I want on the walls," Troy said emphatically. "If employees don't like the art, they can pack their bags and leave. The mural stays."

Removing the mural was an act of concession that Troy would avoid at all costs. As much as he had faith in his workforce, Troy had no plans to let one note allow them to cross the line of disrespect. More importantly, he would not stand for distraction from business as usual.

"Excuse me, can I say something?" Daniela said, not waiting for a reply. "We know this isn't about the mural. It's an attack against people from underrepresented backgrounds that are working hard every day to make this company the best out there."

"And we appreciate all of our employees," Melissa said sweetly. "We also have to allow Myntors a place to express their opinions."

"People are out here attacking our co-workers of color and hiding behind 'opinions'," Daniela said. "It's not just Luke either. Employees are in the comments agreeing with him knowing nothing's going to happen to them."

Scott was in reluctant agreement. "What he wrote is the center of attention now. Not the work the Diversity team has done to make this behavior go away."

"I'm going to say something that we might not want to hear," Daniela stated boldly. "Our target audience for diversity workshops on campus is white, cisgender men who we're trying to make comfortable with having co-workers who don't look like them. When we do have workshops for people of color, they end up focusing on how to get better positions and convince their managers of their worth. Whether we want to admit it or not, Elemynt treats groups differently and that's why they're responding the way they are. They're tired."

"I have to agree with Daniela on this one," Melissa said. "The anti-diversity feeling isn't unusual."

"Well then fix it!" Troy yelled adamantly. "This is what I pay you all for!"

Kelsey was frustrated that Daniela presented more problems by focusing on minorities and not the wider issue at hand. It wasn't that no one cared about her concerns. It was just that their time in the meeting would be better used problem-solving.

On the other hand, Kelsey did feel bad for her to some degree. Daniela's role was to pitch stories to the media that were the output of the Diversity team's work. If they weren't doing a good job of satisfying all employees, it made her job harder. Unfortunately, the epic fail had become the responsibility of other departments to clean up as well.

Kelsey wondered where Catherine was and what she'd think about the debate. Her absence was felt. She was likely in another meeting with important figures.

Tai was keen to rebut Daniela's landmine of a statement. "You're worried about your department right now and that's cool. The rest of us... we're thinking big picture."

"Daniela, we understand where you're coming from," Jon added. "Let's concentrate on what we can do now. We can handle the rest later."

Daniela's pleas for the company to address what she saw as the root of the issue were put on the backburner. Restoring harmony to the Elemynt population started with shutting down the negative media attention. They would work backward from there. Pressing the issue may have further problems for Daniela.

"Here's what we're going to do," Jon said. "No statements to the press. The less we feed them, the faster this goes away. Let them rely on the diversity report for quotes from us. They'll link to it in their articles. People can read our official position there."

Jon's direction was the ideal PR strategy. "Elemynt could not be reached for comment" would have to do.

"Cool, what about internal comms?" Troy asked.

"I'm thinking it's not a good idea to discipline Myntors for what they said about the memo," Tai said. "That'll make things worse. I don't think a statement from you is gonna cut it either. That's more for people to comment on."

"We can also talk to the artist to make sure she doesn't make any public statements," Kelsey offered.

"And Leon can put cameras on the mural to make sure no one's sending pictures to reporters," Tai said.

Attendees of the meeting went around the room voicing their individual contributions to dissolving the internal unrest and its repercussions. Daniela, a consummate professional, outlined a series of clever ideas for promoting Elemynt's core values internally minus mentions of diversity. Scott would follow Jon's lead and cease media interviews. Upon seeing the game plan rolled out by his team. Troy sat back in his chair satisfied.

"Let's move fast and get back to what we came here to do," Troy said.

* * *

As much as Kelsey and the execs at Elemynt would have loved for the controversy around the diversity report to cease immediately, Luke Schultz made sure that wouldn't be the case.

Kelsey flipped the channel to Fox News to find the now ex-Myntor sitting smugly across from Jack Frazier, a regular presence on the popular network. Luke spun tales of his woeful time as an Elemynt employee. The eyes of the television host glinted with obsession at the pronouncements of his victimized guest.

The two were a match made in heaven. Luke was one in a long line of media sensations standing in defense of majority culture to be featured on the show. Jack was known for making newsmakers martyrs by rallying his right-leaning viewers to action.

"Elemynt doesn't value the conservative voices," Luke said with robust self-confidence. "People are in there attacking me because I'm a white guy speaking the truth. Elemynt doesn't want people to know what's really going on."

"Incredible," Jack said with affected shock. "The way you've been treated is shameful. We need more people like you standing up against this politically correct nonsense."

Jack turned to face the camera directly. "I want all my viewers to use the voices that Elemynt wants to silence. Show them what happens when a red wave crashes their platform."

Soon after his television appearance, an influx of photos of a heroic Luke Schultz and screenshots of his internal diatribe swamped Elemynt feeds. The hashtags #SupportFreeSpeech and #WhiteIsRight were posted hundreds of times per minute. Reporters were likely hounding the former employee for quotes at the same rate they were piling into Kelsey's inbox.

Conservative talking heads spun Luke's termination as proof of what they preached to their viewers — tech companies were run by a liberal workforce located in the hotbed of radical California values. Kelsey estimated it wouldn't be long before Luke was gifted a book deal and became a bigger headache than they started with.

While Luke was being hailed as a free-speech hero by conservatives, left-leaning pundits were lambasting the very idea of his existence. Kelsey watched as figures on the TV labeled him as emblematic of the racist and problematic views tied to the far-right. In their view, it was an abomination that Luke was hired by Elemynt, a company that touted itself as a platform for all. Civil rights leaders appearing on-air decried his denigration of the contributions of women and people of color. They questioned how Elemynt could give a bigot the space to make poisonous remarks.

The agreement among higher-ups to stand idly by was not working. Rather than allow the issue to fester, the Comms team released a very brief statement in which Scott outlined Elemynt's internal speech policy.

"We believe that open discourse is important to fostering diverse points of view, even for sensitive topics," it read.

Scott noted that the memo did raise important questions about Elemynt's potential biases. The company was "taking the feedback very seriously," he said.

Scott's internal-only note to all employees was less succinct. "We support Myntors' ability to express themselves and engage in healthy debate," it said. "However, this does not mean anything goes. Several parts of the post are in violation of our employee code of conduct. We are here to help each other, not to offend our colleagues or make sweeping statements regarding specific groups. If we find that you are clouding our culture in this manner, your employment may be placed under review."

The explicit message, a product of collaboration between several teams, was enough to stall further internal discussions on Commynt. Myntors may have had strong opinions, but no one wanted to be seen as an outlier worthy of termination.

Another series of news alerts came through Kelsey's phone. An online campaign to raise money for Luke generated more than $50,000 and climbing. Luke told the media stories of the outpouring of support in private messages from his former co-workers. He shared news of being lavished with job offers from fellow conservatives. He boasted of receiving backdoor offers from other tech companies.

Reading about the successes of the renegade employee only served to frustrate Kelsey more. Her job at the moment was to do nothing and wait for the storm to pass. However, she couldn't be alone with her thoughts. Kelsey flipped through the TV channels in hopes of finding programming that would give her the uplift she needed.

"Breaking news of events unfolding live on the social media app Elemynt," a TV anchor said urgently. "This may contain shocking images."

Kelsey nearly dropped the remote control at the further mention of her employer. Another story was brewing that had nothing to do with Luke.

The news cut to shaky cell phone footage of a violent confrontation. A crowd outside of a school surrounded two men, beating them into a bloody mess. The participants shouted anti-Mexican epithets and called the brutally wounded pair "invaders." The rioting was punctuated by flashes of fists and an older white woman with a megaphone yelling "we have to protect our kids!"

The attack was the result of a series of viral posts on Elemynt, the anchor detailed. Posts that originated from an anonymous account warned that child kidnappers were invading the U.S. They described in alarming language how kids in states bordering Mexico were found dead with their internal organs removed.

News had circulated among neighbors in a small Texas town that two Mexican men were drunk outside of a school and intent on kidnapping students. A mob of mostly white residents stormed their location in search of justice.

The television showed video of the men being savagely beaten as they tried to run away. Because of the sheer volume of the crowd, police could not navigate to the center of the commotion.

The elderly woman with the megaphone egged the mob on. "They're drunk criminals! They're stealing kids!"

The feverish crowd roared in response. Their demand for justice wouldn't be satiated until the men were no longer breathing.

"A local police spokesman said there was no evidence the men committed any crime," the anchor read from his TelePrompTer. "It is unclear who is behind the anonymous account sharing news about kidnappings that law enforcement is saying is unfounded. The Elemynt account has more than 100,000 followers and has posted racially charged hate speech for at least a year."

Kelsey turned off the television. The last thing she needed at the end of a hellacious day was gratuitous displays of violence. A situation like that would have happened whether Elemynt existed or not, she told herself.

Kelsey resolved to cut down her time spent with the office television. She had to remain focused. Elemynt needed her.

* * *

A group of Myntors toting open laptops formed outside the glass door of the small meeting room. Kelsey ignored them. She was waiting for a video call to begin. The execs were late. The meeting was supposed to start 25 minutes prior.

With each ticking minute, the crew of six scheduled to have the room next grew more impatient. At one minute past the hour, one of them knocked on the glass. Kelsey waved them away.

Another three minutes passed.

A rail-thin, geeky type opened the door and poked his head inside. "Hi, we have this room?"

"Can you give me a few minutes, please?" Kelsey said.

"But we booked it..."

"I'm sorry but this is a very important call!" Kelsey said without flinching. "There are other rooms available."

Kelsey closed the door on the heels of the startled Myntor. She didn't mean to raise her voice. Under other circumstances, she would have politely relinquished the room. However, the meeting with members of the Dream Team was too important to miss. Her tolerance for interruptions was razor-thin.

The always wonderful Tim followed his Chronicle report about diversity at Elemynt with another critical take on the company. In quotes and text, he described the proliferation of the radical right on social media and Elemynt's lack of moderation of accounts that targeted Latinos with racist language. It was a flimsy story, but one that Kelsey knew to be much more severe of a problem than the reporter probably realized.

There were thankfully no internal leaks to confirm his suspicions. However, the writing did conjecture that many of the offending Elemynt accounts were not created by Americans. The websites they linked to were populated by articles written in shoddy English. Tim's theories were unfortunately on track with Leon's initial warnings regarding the issue. Which meant another meeting. Another go-round of Troy possibly being upset. It would be fantastic if Leon used the time to announce his team had put an end to the problem. Close the case and move on.

Kelsey hoped Sarah was off somewhere enjoying her extended honeymoon, far from televisions and newspapers. It turned out to be a grand time to take a break from the company. Through the turmoil, Kelsey remained optimistic. If the temporary shake-ups worked out the way Jon assured her, they would be resolved by the time Sarah returned.

The VP of Security finally signed into the video call with Troy and Gary seated in the room with him. Jon dialed in shortly after from a location unknown to Kelsey. Catherine was again absent. Kelsey wondered what other critical matters the CEO could have been working on to prevent her attendance.

Troy rushed to air out his frustration. "First Luke Schultz and his stupid crusade and now we're dealing with a whole race of people being offended. And we're doing what?"

"Keeping a critical eye on it," Leon responded.

After more suspicious activity from the Balkans was detected on the platform, Leon directed his team to examine the extent of the foreign activity on Elemynt. The numbers that came back were a grave cause for concern. Accounts originating in the Eastern European countries were working ruthlessly to attract clicks from conservatives by shilling half-truths and outright lies.

Posts with declarations like "Mexican Leaders Force Devout Christians into Death Camps," "Billionaires Create Emergency Fund to Send Blacks Back to Africa," and "Muslims Burn American Flags, Set Nearby Children on Fire" were increasing in number.

The continuing series of incendiary posts received astronomical numbers of faves, shares, and comments on Elemynt. The dodgy "news" sites they linked to spoofed the accounts of real news organizations. The more engagement the accounts generated, the more money they earned at Elemynt's expense.

"These headlines are stupid!" Troy said. "You'd have to be an idiot to believe them!"

"If I can interrupt for a moment," Gary raised his hand. "We shouldn't be framing conservatives as not smart people. The culture is changing in America.

doesn't understand intricacies

They're sensitive to there being more danger around them. People are sharing these posts because they reflect their view of the world. That doesn't make them dumb, just alert."

Gary was prickly in his response. Almost defensive. It dawned on Kelsey that he likely self-identified as a conservative. She assumed that because they were in the Bay Area, a place known for its liberal views, that everyone at Elemynt identified as such. It was understandable why the characterization of conservatives as uneducated or easily duped would spur him to be upset.

"My teams are working overtime to come up with a solution," Gary said. "We're dealing with guys creating posts faster than the moderators can review them."

"Why can't we shut down the accounts and be done with it?" Troy asked.

"People on the outside might think Elemynt suspending 'conservative' accounts is obstructing free speech," Jon responded.

"This isn't a drop in the bucket either," Leon said. "We're talking 120 million people served content from Balkan accounts in the past day. Elemynt's algorithms think the content is popular so it's pushing it to the top of people's feeds."

Troy was resolute in his annoyance. "A couple of teenagers in wacko countries are posting memes and you want us to restructure our entire algorithm around it?"

"It's not the ideal approach but doing nothing is not going to make this go away," Gary said.

"We do have one thing, right Gary?" Leon said. "One of the teams at the last Hack Week developed a prototype that shadowbans the kind of inflammatory language we're trying to get rid of."

Curse words were easy for the app's algorithms to spot, Leon explained to the group. Harassment and violent threats that didn't include pre-determined keywords were much harder to detect. The system created by the crew of engineers analyzed contextual language in posts and captions to automatically flag offending accounts. The individual would then be "shadowbanned" — able to post but it wouldn't appear in other users' feed except theirs.

"The team won first place for it," Leon said optimistically.

"And there's a reason it wasn't deployed," Troy said. "We're not gonna call attention to bad behavior on Elemynt. That's stupid. We go live with that feature and everybody will be saying how Elemynt has a problem that was so bad we had to develop a tool around it. These posts… it's just people talking."

"You know what…I wish that was true," Leon protested. "There's actually been an uptick of racist language and harassment in comments on the platform. The anti-immigrant language we've been tracking is up 300 percent over the last half. The Trust and Safety team doesn't have a lot of moderators to begin with. Which posts they're taking down and deciding to leave up is random as hell. Black people and Latinos are pissed. The users that are sharing this stuff are pissed too because they think we're censoring them."

"Those posts can't be more than a fraction of a percentage of the content on Elemynt," Troy said defensively. "We're not risking our engagement numbers to stop a few losers. Keep doing what you need to do to get it under control but I don't want this taking up all your time. There's too much else for us to be focusing on."

***

Kelsey slumped her weakened body against the closed door of her apartment. Another late evening of feeling disheveled both inside and out after a long day of work. She summoned her remaining strength to keep herself from collapsing onto the floor.

Kelsey clutched a take-out box filled with food she slapped together at the last minute at one of Elemynt's dining halls. Cooking fresh meals after draining days had become a Herculean effort. She barely possessed the brainpower to make it to the couch. The strain that lingered when she left campus was not the work-life balance she imagined for herself.

The privacy breach and the issues that followed were a test of her wills. Then there was the congressional hearing and she barely made it through that. Now, on top of the residual conversation about diversity, the looming shadow of a PR crisis because of Leon's reports was at her back. Kelsey knew she was a strong woman. She just wasn't sure how strong.

Kelsey fished two slices of cheese pizza out of the random assortment of foods in the container. The time for making healthy decisions was not that day. There was nothing at that moment that a salad could do for her. She needed fat…sugar. A distraction. She needed pizza.

Kelsey's anxiety from the day dissipated somewhat with each bite. She made it through the previous tough times and lived to tell the tale. She was a tough cookie. Kelsey reached for a stack of Oreo Thins, flipped on the TV, and settled in for what she hoped would be a relaxing evening.

A piercing ring interrupted the welcome solace. Her phone. She should have turned off but…it was too late. Her anxiety was rising back to its pre-pizza levels.

Kelsey held the phone in her hand watching her father's name flash across the screen. She didn't want to answer it. She had to answer it. She didn't feel like talking. Her father was always her comfort. There was more comfort in solitude.

The loving daughter accepted the call.

She barely said hello before her father launched into a barrage of questions. "How's it going at Elemynt? Have you seen these stories about what's going on in Mexico? Is Elemynt doing something to figure out what's real or not? How are you?"

His daughter was an employee of Elemynt. Somehow that translated to her having the key to cracking the code to the veracity of the news stories that populated his feed.

Every sensational story he saw the app, whether true or not, commanded his attention. Her father constantly reposted political content to his account. When he wasn't doing that, he was sending them to Kelsey and her mother via text message. It was becoming an obsession.

Kelsey couldn't be the one to tell him to ease off the platform that she worked for. She hoped someone would. She eyed the pizza sitting inches away from her.

"Dad, it's been a long day. Can I call you tomorrow?"

"No problem," he said with cheer. "Your mom says hi!"

Kelsey uttered a soft goodbye to her father. After a second, she instinctively called Brad. She needed a comforting voice who understood the stress she was under.

Brad's handsome face appeared on the video chat. Behind him were swaying palm trees dancing in a nighttime wind. While her love sat shirtless on a hotel patio, she recounted the week's events. Words spilled out in one continuous, uncontrollable sentence.

"It's like a new scandal every other day," Kelsey sighed. I don't know if I can take it."

"How does it feel being responsible for tearing apart the fabric of society?" Brad joked.

"Was that supposed to be funny?" she balked.

"Kinda. But there's a reason you're in the news all the time."

"You seriously think we're in a room somewhere plotting the downfall of society?"

"Hey, hey. I didn't mean it like that," he smiled. "Your man is always here for you, babe."

"Brad, you're in Guatemala."

"But who loves you?" he winked at her. "You don't have to be so sensitive about it."

"That's easy for you to say. You haven't seen the inside of an office for more than a year."

Kelsey tried to give Brad the benefit of the doubt. The ocean air and high-altitude trips had likely gone to his brain. Still, he was frying her nerves.

"Your job is stressing you out. I get it," Brad shrugged. "Bad things are happening at the company and you found out Elemynt isn't as great as it says it is."

"Are we talking about the same app?" she retorted. "The one you use 365 days out of the year?"

"Yeah, but I don't work there."

"Each time you post, it's paying our salaries. If it's that bad why don't you log off?"

Kelsey's patience with Brad was wearing thin. She wanted to hang up and make him leave her alone, but she also wanted a real answer.

"People are following me because I inspire them," he said coolly. "I'm posting positivity. We need more of that in this world."

"Brad, there's more to life than thirst trap pics in exotic locations."

Kelsey checked the time on her phone. She truly didn't care what it said, she was done with the conversation. "Seriously, I have to go."

"Wait a sec," he said. "Have you thought about getting a job at another company? If it's stressing you out like that..."

"This is my dream job," Kelsey said impatiently. "I'm not leaving."

"Sounds like a nightmare to me."

That was it. Kelsey had enough of Brad's antics for the night. She was furious when she should have been happy talking with him.

"Why can't you actually support me for once?" she yelled at the phone. "Tell me that I'm strong or I can get through this. Why do you feel like you have to tear me down more when things are already bad?"

"I didn't mean it like that," Brad said dismissively.

"I know because you only care about yourself," Kelsey said, unleashing her inner frustrations. "You're out there traveling the world and running away from your problems and somehow you think you're better than me. Having a bunch of followers does not make you a good person, Brad."

Kelsey hit end on the call with an angry press of her finger. She flung the phone toward a far corner of the couch and threw her head into the pillow. Kelsey boiled from the exchange with the man who supposedly cared about her. Brad acted as if he was out saving orphan children while he blamed her for problems she had no part in creating. This was a man that she "loved" and he was being worse to her than anyone else in her life. She picked up the phone again, this time to block his number.

Kelsey refused to go to bed angry. Brad was not the only person in her life. She had many more people that she could reach out to other than the inconsiderate jerk.

Kelsey pulled up her group chat with Jade and Daniela. She pounded out on her phone's keyboard a brief version of her infuriating exchange. "Can you believe??" she added.

"Don't let one guy get you down," Daniela replied with a series of heart emojis.

Jade followed with a smiley face emoji. "Sweetie come hang with me. Girl time. Can you fly down to L.A. in the morning?"

Kelsey wanted to leave the planet. Somewhere very far away.

"Do I need to bring anything?" she texted back.

"Just get here as early as you can. Sending you the address."

TWELVE

Kelsey didn't have to lift a finger. The moment her chauffeured SUV pulled into the driveway of the chic Ritz-Carlton Marina Del Rey hotel, her every need was attended to. A uniform-clad bellhop cordially assisted her with the small carry-on bags she hastily cobbled together. She was offered spa water by the receptionist and greeted with gusto by the property's manager. She was treated like royalty. After little sleep and what seemed like an eternity on a flight to the Los Angeles airport, she felt far from a glamour queen.

Kelsey navigated through the ornate hallways of an upper floor to the room where Jade was supposed to be waiting for her. A chicly dressed gentleman in shiny leather pants answered her rap on the door.

"She's here!" he proclaimed to the room.

The door opened to reveal a gorgeous suite outfitted with gold and sky-blue decor that blended seamlessly with the azure harbor just outside the windows. Hairdressers and stylists bustled about, organizing bountiful racks of gowns and cocktail attire. The dance-pop music that circulated through the breezy space upped the energy to nightclub levels.

In the center of the commotion was Jade, draped in a fluffy white bathrobe and being attended to by a makeup artist. Ring lights positioned on either side of her highlighted the beautiful brushstrokes applied to her gorgeous face.

"Look who made it!" Jade leaped to greet her. "Hey, loves. This is Kelsey, our guest of honor!"

The workers around the room offered spritely hellos before returning to their beautification duties. Jade air-kissed Kelsey and escorted her to one of the two makeup chairs.

"Jade...what's going on?" Kelsey asked.

"We're heading to the Emmys tonight."

"Excuse me, what?" Kelsey exclaimed.

She couldn't have heard Jade correctly.

"You and I will be on the red carpet at the Primetime Emmys. Your tickets are on the table over there."

"You didn't tell me you were going to an award show!"

"*We*, darling," Jade emphasized. "And I've seen so many red carpets over the years, it's almost a part of my life at this point. I know that's not something normal people say..."

"Totally get it! You're one of the most respected people in the entertainment industry."

"Allegedly," Jade laughed.

"Okay, but seriously what am I supposed to wear to a nationally televised event?"

"You didn't think these racks of clothes were for me only, did you?" Jade grinned. "The one on the left is for you and they're all your size. Pick one and then the glam squad will get you ready for our lovely night out."

Before she could comprehend what was happening, one of the stylists whisked Kelsey away toward her hand-selected wardrobe. An array of options to choose from were presented. Elaborately embroidered evening gowns, slinky body-con dresses, creations made from silk charmeuse and organza, and even a mirror-spangled jumpsuit should she feel daring that evening. A rainbow of twinkling jewelry called to Kelsey from velvet-lined cases. Rows of complimentary heels in varying heights were ready for selection.

"This thing with Brad, we're putting it all behind us, yes?" Jade said from her chair. "Nothing like a little high fashion to take your mind off things."

Kelsey would follow Jade's lead. She didn't let on to how deeply frustrated she was by the events of the past few days. Jade arranged the excursion to L.A. as a distraction and she was determined to accept it as such.

Kelsey held one of the more sparkly numbers up to her figure. "I have a personal question for you, Jade. Actually, it's a professional one."

"Ask away," Jade said lovingly. "I'm an open book."

"How do red carpets become a part of your life? Do you get invited to because you lead entertainment partnerships at Elemynt or because you were a big deal at the Creative Talent Agency when you were there?"

"I think it's both," Jade said as she reviewed the array of jewelry. "People see me as some kind of symbol of a modern era. I'm the bridge between a traditional industry that's been around for a hundred years and the digital technology of today."

"You're the best of both worlds," Kelsey smiled.

"Darling, these are no longer two separate worlds we're talking about. Think about tonight. This is an awards show that's been on television since before you and I were a twinkle in our mothers' eyes, now completely transformed by Elemynt. People are sharing their thoughts on the app with hundreds or sometimes millions of people at the same time the broadcast is going. And they don't have to wait for a TV camera to follow what their favorite celebrity is doing today because they follow them on Elemynt. Some people aren't watching the show at all and are still commenting on it live. That last part was what used to blow my mind."

"It's the digital town square like Troy says," Kelsey gushed.

"More than that. We're creating *moments*, honey. History happens on Elemynt live and in living color."

"How many times have you told partners that?"

"You want me to guess?" Jade said with a tickled laugh.

Jade shared that since her family relocated from L.A. to the Bay Area to start at Elemynt, she found herself in the city often. Most of the accounts on the app with the largest followings were big-name celebrities, the majority of whom lived in the Southern California area. As such, the Elemynt office in L.A. was a major hub for the work of the Entertainment Partnerships team.

Jade described how a constant rotation of stars visited the office for private ideation meetings or to go live in the in-house production studios. They snapped selfies in the colorful photo installations or spoke in front of Myntors to promote their various projects. Like Elemynt HQ, a visit to the satellite office was an exclusive rite of passage for the industry's most popular talent.

"I keep thinking about how hard this Congressional hearing must've been on all your partnerships," Kelsey sighed.

"You'd think it would be a series of tragedies, but it hasn't been," Jade said. "First off, celebrities aren't sitting around watching CSPAN all day."

"They have movies and TV shows to make," Kelsey said.

"Yes, that and there's no better avenue than social media to connect with fans and promote new projects. A viral post on Elemynt can be serious money in the bank. Literally, one awesome photo with tons of faves and shares can have more impact than a major studio marketing budget. That's why people come to my team. We help them unlock those million-dollar ideas."

"Or help them verify their dogs."

"I swear if anyone asks me for a checkmark tonight, I'm running out of the building," Jade cracked up.

Jade instructed Kelsey to head to a private bathroom area in the suite to shake off the dust of Silicon Valley. They had a short time to get freshened up and in the car to head to the venue. Kelsey floated through her personal beauty regimen, ecstatic about the night ahead. When she returned, she found Jade slipping a dazzling collection of multicolor Lynn Ban rings on her fingers.

The activity in the suite was a production in and of itself. The makeup and hair team went to work beautifying Kelsey while Jade twirled in the mirror in her black and silver sequined Balmain gown. The more glammed up Kelsey became, the more the worries of her life became a distant memory. The sunny yellow Valentino gown Kelsey selected was the final touch that took her day from bright to brilliant.

The ladies wouldn't dream of leaving the hotel without first snapping their fair share of pre-evening selfies. Kelsey and Jade took a succession of photos in their fabulous dresses. Mid twirl. Full length. Looking in the mirror. Close-ups of their makeup. Long shots of their gowns.

Kelsey gleefully sent the photos to her parents and friends back home before posting the best images to her Elemynt account. Sharing the experience of the exciting night ahead of them with her followers felt incredibly rewarding. The job certainly had its share of fantastic perks.

Jade and Kelsey took a final selfie together to send to Daniela.

Their elated friend responded with a video message. "Have a great time, glamour girls!"

* * *

At L.A. Live, the sprawling entertainment complex in the heart of the city, a red carpet served as the golden walkway for the hundreds of celebrities attending the annual Primetime Emmy Awards. The stars in designer gowns and crisp tuxes graced the carpet surrounded by oversized Emmy statuettes that gleamed in the California sunlight. Hundreds of fans and paparazzi screamed the name of their favorite television personalities as they approached. The stars flashed smiles and posed for the bevy of cameras capturing their ravishing beauty. Security guards clad in tuxedo black and coiled earpieces stood watch over the merry scene.

Kelsey still could not believe she was at the star-studded event. Attending the Emmys was a dream come true for the girl who fantasized about one day walking down a Hollywood red carpet. She was deeply thankful to Jade for making what was once a farfetched ambition a reality.

Kelsey hadn't realized from years of watching the pre-show telecast that there were two red carpets divided by a long stretch of velvet rope. The celebrities populated the larger side while the adjacent carpet was the queue for the non-famous industry movers and shakers. Kelsey and Jade were flanked by producers, writers, and other people who appeared behind the scenes to create the entertainment people enjoyed the whole world over.

The separation between the two carpets was only a few feet. Kelsey was within speaking distance of the heavenly faces that appeared on television and glossy magazine covers.

As the duo inched up the carpet with the other ticketed guests, Kelsey watched as the celebrities posed and waved to exhilarated fans. The stars were followed by handlers in headsets who directed them to the specific news media personalities with whom they would interview.

Microphones and cameras hovered inches from the flawless faces. The famous attendees spoke of their excitement for the evening in brief, witty remarks before they floated a few steps to the next interviewer.

Kelsey spotted Grace to her left making her way down the prestigious red carpet. The sparkle of her light blue, iridescent gown was accompanied by a megawatt smile, to the delight of the crowds around her. Kelsey wanted to say hello but yelling at Grace from her vantage point would be uncomfortably gauche.

Grace stepped up to one of the several major network TV hosts waiting to interview her for their live, on-air segments. Kelsey moved closer to the velvet rope so she could hear the exchange.

"Here we have Grace Oliver, television superstar and producer!" the tuxedoed gabber said to the camera. "Congrats on all your success!"

"Thank you so much," Grace said humbly. "I'm excited to bring my next series of projects to life."

"That's wonderful!" the interviewer cheesed. "We have a question from our fans watching from home. They love your Elemynt account! You're a big user of the app…what inspires you to speak up about women's issues the way you do?"

Grace shook her head in thinly-veiled despair. "My answer to that is different than what it used to be, unfortunately. The abuse I've had to put up with on Elemynt has been...very overwhelming. I think I bring positivity to the world and people give that back to me most of the time. But it's incredible the amount of hate there is on the platform. The violent words... the threats... I'm dealing with it more and more every day."

Kelsey gasped audibly watching the words depart Grace's lips. She could not believe that the star was sharing her troubles live on camera in front of millions of people.

"Because the harassment won't stop regardless of what I do, I decided to deactivate my account," Grace said with brewing confidence. "Elemynt is — and I hate to say this — a toxic platform that doesn't operate with people's best interests in mind, especially women. I think the company should be building better tools to protect people from this really terrible behavior. We have to hold Elemynt accountable."

"Are you saying that women should rethink using Elemynt?" the startled interviewer asked.

"I'm saying that nothing's going to change if people let themselves suffer quietly and not act," Grace said. "If other women closed their accounts on their app like I did, it might be a wake-up call for them. I'm on the optimistic side of things. I think the company can change, you know? But for me personally, I can't keep putting myself through hell every time I open the app."

The red carpet suddenly moved in slow motion around Kelsey. She was dizzy. Sick. The public betrayal of trust sliced her heart in two. The guilt of knowing that she let Grace down destroyed her ability to think straight. Kelsey did what she could to help the star when she called. Elemynt was there for her. There was no way the situation had become worse. Grace would've reached out. Kelsey assumed that it was handled but... the Myntor steadied herself as she reeled from Grace's televised attack against her employer.

Jade turned around to find that her friend was not behind her. "This way, Kelsey. Isn't this place fabulous?"

"Did you hear that, Jade? Grace... she just slammed us on live television."

Jade's pursed lips and prolonged wince were evidence that she had not.

"I'm sure it wasn't that bad," Jade said. "These interviews are fluff. A treat for the fans at home."

The exchange was far from a light declaration. This was the Emmys. The most prominent media outlet in the world packed the risers. Grace's announcement that she quit one of the most popular platforms in the world would be front-page news. It was probably already going viral while Kelsey stood around doing nothing.

"I have to go!" Kelsey said, searching frantically for the exit. "I have to go now!"

Kelsey's sudden manic behavior startled the industry types idling their way into the theater. They distanced themselves from the madwoman interrupting their enjoyment of the gilded occasion.

"Kelsey, wait a minute, hun," Jade held her hand. "It's a Saturday night in Hollywood. I thought we were going to let this take your mind off things?"

Jade earnestly attempted to convince her friend to continue toward the enchanted experience ahead of them.

Kelsey knew that even if she stayed, sitting still for the duration of the show would be impossible. The news unfolding outside the walls of the theater would wreck her ability to appreciate the good fortune of being there. Furthermore, it wouldn't be long before her phone started ringing off the hook. Kelsey briefly considered jumping on calls at the hotel suite. However, it was highly likely that the stylists were still there packing up the remaining garb. No meetings in front of outsiders. The L.A. Elemynt office was far from the venue. Kelsey needed to get there as soon as possible.

A brawny security guard hustled her along. "You can't stop on the carpet," he warned them sternly.

Jade led Kelsey by her trembling hand. "If you want out, you have to keep moving forward. This way."

The women managed their way into the crowded lobby of the venue. The decked-out Microsoft Theater was packed with celebrities and industry superstars hustling toward one of the biggest nights of the year. Kelsey was fixated on one thing — finding the exit.

Kelsey jostled past the packs of Hollywood bigwigs too entranced by the night's opulence to notice her full-blown anxiety. A nuclear bomb had been dropped on the red carpet and she was still middling about in her evening gown.

Jade comforted her shuddering friend. "We'll get you out of here, but you have to relax. Trust me."

The two Myntors were also in the vicinity of a number of reporters. An Elemynt flak freaking out at a nationally televised event would be a cover story by night's end.

"Over there," Jade pointed to a production assistant armed with an earpiece and tablet. "There's your ticket out of here."

"Thank you for everything," Kelsey sighed. "I wish I didn't have to leave but—"

"Don't worry about it, darling," Jade said soothingly. "This isn't the last awards show in the world."

Jade understandably could not join Kelsey in her journey to the L.A. office. The face of Elemynt disappearing from the festivities would raise eyebrows among partners. Also, Jade needed to be there to do damage control if necessary.

The overburdened P.A. pointed Kelsey in the direction of a black curtained corridor. Kelsey hiked up the bottom of her dress and moved as quickly as her Saint Laurent heels would allow.

"Ma'am the show is this way," another suit-clad security guard bristled.

Kelsey ignored him, gunning for the cordoned parking garage just ahead of her. She maneuvered her way through a crowd of uncredentialed onlookers while her phone buzzed insistently. She had no doubts about who was calling.

"While I'm assuming you've seen this Emmys nonsense," Jon said as soon as she answered.

"Heading to the office now," Kelsey said, doing her best to mask her heavy breathing.

"Get to a computer fast," he insisted. "We'll figure this out."

Kelsey's rideshare car sped her toward the L.A. headquarters where she could problem-solve without distraction. In between replaying Grace's interview in her head, Kelsey mourned the evening that wasn't meant to be. She was missing the ceremony for one of the biggest nights in entertainment and the glitzy after-parties that would follow. Kelsey reminded herself for the length of the seemingly interminable ride that her decision was for the best. Had she stayed for the revelry, the likelihood Kelsey would have a job to return to the next day was an indisputable zero.

* * *

Kelsey powered into the Elemynt building in her rustling evening gown, barely acknowledging the bewildered security officer at the front desk. She blazed past the office's elaborate photo opps where countless celebs snapped the coolest pics for their accounts. The office's synthetic beach complete with surfboards and plastic trees had no chance of competing for her attention. A recreation of the Hollywood sign in the atrium was of no importance to her. She tore through the gauntlet of decadence without pause.

Kelsey snatched an Elemynt hoodie from a nearby box of swag to cover up her glaring red carpet attire during the urgent video call. She settled into the largest conference room in the furthest portion of the office where she wouldn't be listened in on by weekend visitors who may happen to show. Kelsey dabbed at her brow with a tissue before punching in the code to join the emergency meeting.

Jon's annoyed face filled the screen. Her manager was the sole person on the call so far. He tilted his head at the sight of Kelsey.

"You're in L.A.?" he asked leerily.

Jon's many travels included trips to the office where she was taking shelter. The conference room she occupied — "Prius vs. Them" — was not in HQ. She had not given him a heads up that she was not in the Bay Area.

"Yeah, I was there at the Emmys," Kelsey said solemnly. "I saw everything."

Before she could explain why she was in attendance, a series of Elemynt execs logged into the call one after the other. In less than a minute, Catherine, Troy, and several members of the Dream Team joined Kelsey and Jon for the reconnaissance meeting.

The emotions in the grid of faces ranged from bewildered to furious. Jon read with restrained frustration several Elemynt posts from celebrities voicing their support for Grace. They too were victims of ongoing harassment on the app, they shared. The debacle was snowballing beyond one interview. Critics and spokespeople for women's organizations piled on to cast Elemynt in the most negative light. Alerts for news stories covering Grace's statement blitzed Kelsey's phone in a non-stop plea for attention.

"I can't tell you how much I *hate* this," Troy said petulantly. "The plan is to make this go away, right?"

"This issue cannot be swept under the rug," Catherine said. "We need to give the press something. We announce that Elemynt is hiring more moderators to review harmful posts and take them down if necessary."

"You want to add more staff?" Troy asked incredulously. "We're supposed to be keeping our costs down before the IPO. We don't want investors thinking we have a problem."

"I'd much rather spend the money on a few hundred staffers than to sink our reputation completely," Catherine said.

Leon spoke up from his corner of the screen. "I know I brought this up before but... the tool from Hack Week I mentioned? Can we move forward with that? It would save us from having to train more new moderators."

"What are you talking about, Leon?" Catherine asked.

The second-in-command's absence from the meeting about racially charged speech left her out of an important bullet point of the discussion. Leon filled Catherine in on the existence of a system to programmatically identify harassment and hate speech. He insinuated it would greatly reduce the likelihood that Grace and other women would continue being exposed to the offending comments and posts she called out in her interview.

"And why didn't this go live?" Catherine fumed.

"Because it would kill engagement," Troy said steadfastly. "We need every fave and share we can get if we're going to keep our investors happy. We reduce activity in the app, we dig our own grave. We're not deploying. Next solution. Let me hear 'em."

Kelsey was astounded that senior leadership wouldn't activate a solution that would enable people to have a better experience on the platform. Troy was focused exclusively on being seen as if they were addressing the issue, rather than solving the actual problem. The assembled Myntors would follow his lead.

The strategy left Catherine in the worst position out of the Elemynt executives. News stories in the wake of Grace's proclamation criticized the "Boss Lady" and her supposed lack of attention to issues regarding women. Female leaders who once lauded Catherine's prescribed paths to success denounced the inaction in her company. Questions circulated about how much Catherine knew of Elemynt's historically poor approach toward curbing harassment.

Kelsey conjured ways to protect her hero from a potential onslaught of further press. She couldn't let Catherine and the pro-female ideas she stood for be dragged through the dirt. They needed to convince the world that Catherine Rowe was the champion of women the public knew her to be.

"Catherine, you're our greatest asset," Kelsey said. "We don't have to give out the specifics around what we're doing if we remind people one of the most prominent advocates for women is looking out for the women on Elemynt. That should be enough to get us through this while we're figuring out which way to go."

Catherine thought momentarily about Kelsey's proposal. It was a risk to push her further into the limelight. However, the team needed to take risks to move past a situation that would otherwise linger in media discussions for weeks or possibly months.

"Let's put a pin in it and we can follow up offline," Catherine said.

"There's another thing I want us to do," Troy jumped into the exchange. "Call up the product research team. I want them to do a survey of women who use Elemynt. I need to know if this harassment thing is actually affecting how they use the app."

"Now why exactly do you think that is necessary?" Catherine sneered.

"I want to know what they're thinking," he said. "They can't hate Elemynt as much as these celebrities say they do. No way."

"This isn't the time for a sideshow," Catherine insisted. "We need to focus on immediate solutions to pull us out of this mess."

"That wasn't a suggestion," Troy said. "They have problems, let's hear it from the women themselves. No one outside of the team working on the study has to know about it. Put them under extra NDAs if you have to. I want it done quickly and quietly and I want the results in my inbox as soon as they're done."

The group no other choice than to acquiesce to Troy's request.

"Fine," Catherine said. "In the meantime, what are we doing about showing the public we care?"

The query was undoubtedly Kelsey's area of expertise. She had a series of PR campaign wins under her belt. She fixed her mouth to speak but was interrupted by Tai of all people.

"Here's an idea," Tai said. "It's almost October, yeah? That's Breast Cancer Awareness month. We do a campaign that says we donate a dollar for every person who includes a special hashtag in their caption. Up to a million bucks?"

Kelsey was taken aback by the daring proposal. "We have a million dollars for something like this?"

"Of course, we do," Catherine said. "Tai, I want a draft from you by B.O.D. tomorrow."

For a person who was always peeved at other people for encroaching on her so-called "territory," Tai didn't hesitate for a second to waltz her way right into Kelsey and Jon's. External Comms was their domain. Kelsey wouldn't even think about suggesting campaigns for Internal Comms. It was too late to say as much. Catherine put her official stamp of approval on it. And to top it off, she put Tai in charge. Kelsey restrained herself from rolling her eyes. Her workplace camaraderie had its limits.

There was an intrusive click on the video call. A solid black square appeared on the screen. The participants instinctively silenced the conversation.

"Hi, who just joined?" Catherine asked.

Wyatt appeared in the frame looking comparatively more disheveled than his usual self. The top of his collared shirt was damp. His tie hung loosely around his neck. The general counsel ran his fingers through his unkempt hair to straighten up in front of his audience.

"We have a problem," he said.

"Everyone is aware of what happened at the Emmys," Catherine hissed.

"No, something bigger," Wyatt huffed. "Congress wants us back in D.C."

Catherine nearly choked with surprise. "You've got to be kidding."

Wyatt received early notification from a prominent friend that Congress planned to drag Elemynt back to the witness stand once again. This time, they planned to question the company on its complicity in the spread of misinformation coordinated by Balkan operatives. Tim's story on the issue had made its way to the halls of Capitol Hill. Senator Layne and the Committee on Commerce, Science, and Transportation were drafting a formal letter as they spoke.

Kelsey's heart sunk to the conference room floor. Another ridiculous hearing to contend with. The last one was an enormous mental hurdle to conquer and that was with the understanding that it was a once in a lifetime moment. To have to go through it again…Kelsey's soul was shredded to pieces. She never should have left the hotel suite. The best day of her life, the one where she would hobnob with celebrities holding golden statuettes, was descending into the ninth circle of hell.

"When have they decided this hearing is supposed to take place?" Catherine asked indignantly.

"Not one hearing. Two," Wyatt said. "The Senate hearing is the Friday after next. The House plans to hold a similar proceeding the Monday after that."

Wyatt read through details that he was able to procure with the measured calm of a veteran legal professional. Dread engulfed the video call participants as he spoke. Kelsey's muscles were rigid with tension. Congress was doing their absolute best to wear Elemynt down. It was working. The nerves of the steeliest people on the call were unraveling.

Catherine, the most resolute among them, listened critically to Wyatt's rundown. "We will not have another media circus and Troy will not be in that chair again," she said. "Wyatt, I want you to testify on behalf of the company. Give them what they want without dragging our CEO down in the process. Can we count on you?"

An overly confident Wyatt swelled with pride. "Without a doubt."

Catherine's decision, one that was curiously made without Troy's input, was the best route for the company to take. The committee was likely feeling sore after the buffoonery they displayed during their encounter with Troy. The renowned leader of Elemynt had shown that he was competent and, most of all, cared about the people his app served. Catherine would not let them stage their retribution at the company's expense. Troy had no objections.

"This is a rough period that we will pull through," Catherine said. "I want all hands on deck to make sure this does not escalate past its current level."

The sound that emanated from the conference room screen was swapped out with keyboards clicking and emails being fired off from phones. The troops would not rest until all plans to squash the external criticism were executed to a tee. Jon cut through the noise with a suggestion of his own.

"We can address these problems in one shot," Jon said confidently. "I have a solution that will work."

Jon's idea was indeed brilliant. He suggested that Elemynt hold a private round table with select women's groups and civil rights organizations that focused on minorities. The opportunity for them to have rare face time with the company would be seen as a step toward taking in continued conversations with the people. The gathering would also serve to debrief the representatives on Elemynt's work around diversity.

"We invite the groups most likely to be vocal against us in the media," Jon said. "If we get them in our corner fast, we can slow the press cycle."

Jon's penchant for proactive communication was at play. His idea was one that Catherine could get behind.

"Kelsey, I want you and Daniela to meet with these civil rights groups before the hearing," she said. "Exactly as Jon says."

"Don't you think I should be the one to lead it?" Jon asked in surprise. "My role here *is* vice president of communications."

"Which we understand," Catherine said. "But in order for this to be effective the way we want it to be, we need a woman speaking in front of that group. Do we need to call in Sarah to run point?"

"She's on Refresh," Jon said firmly. "Kelsey can handle it."

Kelsey knew that she would play a role in restoring the peace between the app and its detractors. What she did not expect was to be responsible for a powwow with a room of potentially harsh critics leaping at a chance to vocalize their grievances. As a public relations professional, Kelsey was committed to championing the values of Elemynt. However, there was a big difference between writing a blog post and standing on the front lines of a brewing war.

"How soon do we want to this?" Kelsey asked tentatively. "Will people show up?"

"They'll be there," Jon said. "We hold the meeting in the NYC office. Most of the larger groups are headquartered in the city. Have Daniela and the marketing team start organizing immediately. The invites go out ASAP."

Kelsey's task was set for her. She again did not have much of a say in the matter. Her task was set for her. She had been exemplary in her work so far. If Kelsey messed this up, her winning streak would be obliterated."

The group launched into a flurry of instructions and pre-planning for the various components of the brand rebuilding. Most of the prep for the two impending hearings would fall on Wyatt and the Legal team.

Kelsey was barely listening. She was consumed with thoughts of a last-minute meeting of civic organizations in New York. She and Daniela were directly responsible for pacifying the people most likely to give them hell in advance of Congressional hearings that would be viewed nationwide. As if it wasn't stressful enough, had less than two weeks to accomplish the nearly impossible feat. One that Daniela didn't know was coming.

* * *

The morning rush of New Yorkers breezed past Kelsey and Daniela as the two strolled down the busy artery of Fifth Avenue. The window displays of the luxury stores were a lovely distraction before their off-the-record meeting set for that afternoon. They extended an invitation to about 50 representatives of women and minority civil rights groups. Every single person accepted. As the head of Diversity Comms, Daniela would lead the presentation with Kelsey standing by to help answer questions.

The dreaded meeting was a firestorm waiting to happen. The organizations represented people who were directly maligned by the adverse effects of the company's harassment policies. Rebuilding relationships with these influential groups would not come easy. However, to get the public back on its side, Elemynt needed their buy-in. The hearings were two days away.

Kelsey couldn't ignore her creeping doubt.

"Do we think this is the best way to go?" Kelsey asked Daniela. "A face to face meeting?"

"The directive came from the exec team," Daniela said. "I wish I could say there was another option."

"If this goes wrong, it's our heads on the chopping block," Kelsey sighed.

Their friend Jade stood to lose as well. Many of her celebrity partners had ties to the causes represented in the room. If the event didn't create a peaceful resolution, the relationships she worked overtime to build would be instantly frayed.

Jade was not one to sit idly by despite remaining in California. She went into overdrive helping Kelsey and Daniela as much as possible with the crucial aspects of the event. She solicited her partner manager dedicated to civic influencers to outline talking points for them. She directed the Events team to outfit the meeting space with exceptionally welcoming decor. Jade put one of Daniela's standard diversity presentations in the hands of the Marketing team to beautify it with photos and graphics that sold warmth and the story of Elemynt. The rest was in Daniela and Kelsey's hands. Time would tell if the gathering would be a successful aversion of a PR fright-fest or an acceleration of the company's contentious issues.

Daniela shook her head glumly as they meandered down the sidewalk. "Ro had an art show this weekend and I'm missing it for a melanin apology tour."

"A what now?" Kelsey squinted.

"Getting up in front of a room full of people of color and telling them that Elemynt loves them. That we're doing everything possible to support them when you and I know that's not the truth. We haven't given them a reason to earn their trust."

"They're coming today so maybe they don't hate us completely."

"They'll be there so they can throw daggers at us."

"Okay, then should we add bomb-sniffing dogs to the event checklist?" Kelsey joked.

Daniela cracked the tiniest smile.

"You know what we need?" Kelsey said. "A shopping trip. We can have a little fun before our big moment."

"If we're going to stand in front of a firing squad, we might as well look good doing it," Daniela replied. "Do they sell bulletproof vests at Bergdorf?"

"No, but they do have an excellent selection of LBDs."

* * *

The ladies walked the polished linoleum floors of the famed department store, making their way through the racks of covetable clothes from high-end designers. Work never stopped so they did double duty. The pair talked through the run of show for the meeting while browsing through their options for attire.

"We can ask Jade to verify the orgs in the room," Daniela suggested. "That would be a good give."

"Shouldn't they be verified already?" Kelsey said as she thumbed through the women's suit jackets. "If not, should we be inviting them? We're expecting a certain level of prominence, right?"

"It's kind of a crazy situation," Daniela said. "A lot of larger non-profits like the Red Cross are verified but if I were to guess I'd say half of those who focus on people of color specifically are not, even though they should be. At least in my opinion. They may not be household names for everyone in America, but they are for households of color. They're at the same high risk for impersonation as the other ones are, they just don't have a contact at the company to get the checkmark."

"Hmm, okay," Kelsey thought it over. "That should be an easy fix."

The two Myntors stepped into adjoining dressing rooms to sort through their haul. Kelsey slipped into a figure-hugging jewel-tone dress. It was a size 4. Her size. But it wasn't fitting. Kelsey tried to zip it up. The zipper threatened to pop away from her.

Kelsey swallowed a lump in her throat. She hadn't seen the inside of a gym for weeks and the growing flab around her waist was readily apparent. Her diet was also derailed by an ongoing series of indulgent trips to the Elemynt dining halls. Stress plus being around endless heaps of delicious food was a deadly combination. She vowed to herself to visit the hotel gym or at least go for a run around the city while she was there.

"You know you can put a dress on your corporate card, right?" Daniela said from the neighboring dressing room. "It's a work-related expense if we're wearing them today."

"Well that's fun," Kelsey said while rifling through roomier options. "But also, I'm drowning in receipts that I'm supposed to be adding to expense reports."

"Oh, that's easy," Daniela said. "Take pics of your receipts and upload them to the company app. It's connected to your corporate card."

Strips of white paper were the furthest thing from Kelsey's mind. However, her smallest problems were collectively snowballing into larger issues. The mental exertion required of her lately was taking its toll on her ability to work at her best.

Kelsey suspected that Daniela was being worn down too but, like her, was too proud to admit it. Kelsey understood that Myntors in Comms roles were under high pressure to carry out their duties, no matter how exhausting. The physical taxation of putting on a dress that should have been a perfect fit was not helping her sanity.

* * *

Kelsey, Daniela, and their haul of oversized shopping bags climbed into the first yellow taxi they could flag. The sooner they arrived at the office, the more time they would have to rehearse.

Other than sharing their destination with the driver — Elemynt's New York headquarters in the Tribeca neighborhood — Daniela was uncharacteristically quiet. Kelsey watched as her c-worker scrolled through her phone somberly. A cloud of sadness grew stronger with each flick of her index finger. Daniela threw her head back in frustration. Her share of bags clattered to the floor.

"Everything okay?" Kelsey asked with concern.

"This crap is non-stop!" Daniela said exasperatedly. "It's like every day, I'm seeing more and more of these horrible posts saying the worst thing about my people. Mexicans are wetbacks invading this country...stealing jobs... killing white babies. We're roaming in caravans and stabbing anyone who tries to stop us."

"None of that's true though," Kelsey said.

"I'm aware," Daniela said. "Have you noticed I stopped using Elemynt as much as I used to? I had to get away from constantly coming across these toxic posts. I don't need that negative energy in my life. But I can't escape it. My family texts them to me all the freaking time. My mom, especially. My friends too. They want me to somehow stop people from posting them."

"Because you're on the Diversity team at Elemynt."

"Yes, and one of the most visible people of color at the company. You'd think the exec team and these product managers would want to listen when their colleague is telling them how bad it's getting for a community of people on the app, but no. They either tell me it's not a problem or say they'll work on it then put the issue on the back burner so I'll leave them alone."

"Come on, you're a boss lady!" Kelsey perked up. "Catherine's our COO! She's shown us how to make our voices heard at our jobs. We just have to not back down and keep being vocal about what we want."

"Hate to break it to you, Kelsey, but that doesn't work for everybody," Daniela said.

"You're kidding, right? Women are seriously more empowered to speak our minds than we ever were before."

"White women are," Daniela stewed. "Not women of color. White women. My Latina and Black sisters...when we speak up we're called 'aggressive' or 'angry'. We constantly get shut down when we share our opinions and then end up with reviews about not being a 'team player.' We figure out pretty quickly that sometimes it's just better to sit back and say nothing and not rock the boat. Otherwise, we're risking ruining the opportunities we do have. It's enough of a struggle for women of color to get in the door in the first place. So yes, as much as I want to claim to be a 'boss lady', in the real world that mentality works for people who look like Catherine. The kind of women who have the social capital or resources to fall back on if taking a stand backfires on them."

"Wait, okay this is sounding a bit dramatic," Kelsey said skeptically. "It's not like you have *no one* in the company to help you out."

"You sure about that?" Daniela said. "Black and brown people have been dealing with abuse on the Elemynt app since it was first created. Yet, we just so happen to be doing this reconciliation meeting now that it's a famous white woman being attacked. I've been doing everything I can for the execs to take any kind of serious action on this since I got here and so have many more people before me. You think that's not being vocal? White women get praised for standing up in the workplace and then get best-selling books out of it while we're left chasing after scraps."

"This isn't a contest of who's had the biggest struggle," Kelsey sulked.

"You're a part of the problem," Daniela said flatly.

"Me? What did I do?" Kelsey sat up in her seat.

"Your speaker series? How many women who aren't white and straight have you invited to come to campus?"

"Excuse me!" Kelsey said incredulously. "Why is that an issue if the advice they're giving is useful to all Myntors?"

"Not everyone comes from the same background or shares the same experiences. You haven't brought in any queer women or trans women and definitely no Latinas. Have you looked at your audience for these things? It's mostly white women at each one. You'd have a much more diverse room if you took the time to diversify your speakers."

Kelsey was offended that Daniela would suggest that she didn't care about all her colleagues equally. She put way too much emphasis on race when it wasn't necessary and it was becoming very annoying.

"You've said it yourself there aren't a lot of Hispanic women or African-Americans at Elemynt," Kelsey snapped back

"Yes, you're right," Daniela said. "We are a small number compared to the rest of the workforce. But the fact is we do exist. Just because there are fewer of us doesn't mean we don't deserve to have representation too. A lot of black and brown employees... we go to events like yours and time after time, we don't see people who look like us so it makes us less likely to come. Whether you mean to or not, what you're doing is sending a message of exclusion."

Kelsey reeled from her coworker's accusation that she was only working to help white women. It was distasteful and wrong and a complete fabrication. Furthermore, to say that someone could not benefit from programs like hers because of the color of their skin was ludicrous.

"We're *all* women and we have to deal with the *same* ugliness," Kelsey said tersely. "For instance, we make less pay than men. It's wild that they see us as not being as smart as they are."

"I may have had similar experiences as you because we're both women..." Daniela said. "You, however, have no idea what it's like to be Latina. How many times has someone called you aggressive for speaking up in a meeting?"

"Never, but I—"

"Has anyone at work touched your hair without asking?"

"That's not a thing."

"Hmm. How about the fun stuff outside of work? When's the last time you watched a telenovela with your tías?"

Kelsey stared blankly. It was some kind of trick question that she didn't have the answer to.

"Let me make it really easy for you," Daniela pressed. "Tell me...what's the difference between a chancla and a chuleta?"

Kelsey didn't know how to respond to Daniela's series of very aggressive questions. Her insane antics were an abhorrent way to talk to her friend.

"Here's one you should be able to answer. When's the last time you had a conversation with a Latina who wasn't me?"

Daniela's overwhelming beratement of Kelsey was more than she could bear. Kelsey was being attacked for being White as if she signed up for it because she couldn't stand to be another race. The accusations Daniela levied at her brought streams of tears to her eyes. She cried knowing that her friend would come for her in a terribly offensive way.

Daniela was steadfast despite Kelsey's welling emotion. "Listen, if you want to uplift women, you have to uplift all women. Not just the ones who look like you."

Kelsey looked to Daniela for a glimmer of sympathy. What she received in return was a stony expression that refused to acknowledge how hurt Kelsey was feeling by the attack. Her tears flowed harder than before. Kelsey never imagined that she'd be discriminated against so unfairly.

Daniela was unmoved by her colleague's sadness. It became apparent that Daniela was waiting for Kelsey to finish her bout of crying. Kelsey dabbed her eyes to not further destroy whatever makeup remained on her reddened face.

"You think I want to be the person who keeps bringing up women of color at Elemynt?" Daniela said. "I don't. I'm tired. But if I don't do it, who else will?"

Kelsey composed herself. She saw an opportunity to prove Daniela wrong.

"You say I don't support people of color. How about you let me lead the presentation for you?"

Daniela shook her head wearily. "I don't think that's a good idea, Kelsey. Really."

"You said it yourself. You don't want to be seen as the token Latino."

"That's true, but it would be much better for people of color to hear from someone who understands where they're coming from."

"I work in Comms," Kelsey said brightly. "We can talk to anyone!"

Daniela stared at her friend in amazement. She was holding herself back from saying something that Kelsey could not pinpoint. Daniela was evidently too tired to express whatever was on her mind.

"You're stressed enough," Kelsey said. "Let me do this for you."

"No, no...how can I explain this to you?" Daniela stared out the window.

"It'll be fine, I promise."

"You know what, girl?" Daniela sighed in exasperation. "Go for it."

THIRTEEN

The common space in the Elemynt building that on most days served as a lunchroom for the Myntors of New York was transformed into a stylish mini-theater. A wood-paneled backdrop adorned with an embossed Elemynt logo graced the largest wall of the space. Fifty soft-backed chairs arranged in a semi-circle faced the front of the room. Forgoing the normal row seating would make the presentation feel like a conversation and put people at ease, Jade said. Together with the live palms and leafy plants, the atmosphere evoked an air of serenity.

At Daniela's suggestion, the organizers also skipped the customary raised platform and podium for the event. They would instead use a handheld mic that allowed the speaker to be closer to the audience. Doing their part to decrease the tension in the room was priority number one.

Elemynt's Events team arranged for guests to be greeted with a stunning buffet of breakfast treats as soon as they entered. Luscious pastries of varying flavors and textures were artfully arranged under frosted cloches. Alongside them were fresh whipped butters and fruit jellies in ceramic ramekins. Roasted Peruvian potatoes, an assortment of cured meats, and a table's worth of other delicacies were included in the spread. Brass urns filled to the brim with fair-trade coffees and artisanal juices awaited the guests' arrival. Stylish crates of exotic teas were ready to be steeped and sipped.

The rest of the sprawling workspace of the New York office would be completely inaccessible to the meeting's guests. Every area except the direct route to the bathroom and the lobby exit were cordoned off with ropes and metal stanchions. Uniformed security guards roamed the pathways to prevent renegade attendees from snooping around.

The Elemynt Marketing and Sales teams that populated the building worked with the most influential institutions in the world. The secrets contained at their workstations could not be compromised.

In an unoccupied corner of the soon to be full space, Daniela did one final check-in.

"Are you sure you've got this?" Daniela asked Kelsey.

Kelsey for the life of her could not understand why Daniela didn't trust her to lead the presentation. They both worked in Comms. They were both capable. Daniela let her closeness to diversity as a minority cloud her judgment. Kelsey would wow the gathered representatives with the charm that was a key tool in her PR arsenal.

"Let's get this show on the road," Kelsey said.

Daniela took her position in the back of the room to watch over the activity of the esteemed guests. They represented Hispanic groups, African-American coalitions, women's rights leagues, and other notable civic organizations. Most of them entered the room in wary of what Elemynt might convey to them during the time. To say they were defensive from the start would be an understatement.

Kelsey greeted the suspicious faces seated before her with an enthusiastic hello. "Thank you for coming today to hear about our latest innovation in diversity!" she said into the mic. "My colleagues and I are so happy to share with you what we're doing to build out Elemynt's vision of the future."

Kelsey paused briefly for applause. She was met with raised eyebrows and crossed arms. The clearing of a hacked cough was the sole audible response.

"First, I want to start by showing you a brief presentation," Kelsey continued. "Then we can open up the floor for questions. How's that sound?"

Again, nothing in return. Perhaps the gathered representatives did indeed come to listen. A bulletproof vest was less necessary for Kelsey to protect herself from the firing squad than she previously thought.

A large TV screen at Kelsey's side lit up with the start of a glossy video presentation. A succession of clips of people from various backgrounds with splashes of natural sunlight across their faces played over inspirational music. They glowingly held their phones while interacting with the Elemynt app. Voiceovers of how the people found happiness, love, and personal satisfaction through Elemynt were intertwined with impressive numbers touting the app's growth over the years. The cheery clips were followed by inspirational images of the programs Elemynt created in minority communities, followed by smiling faces representing the company's diverse staff. The golden outlook that emanated from the presentation would soften the most hardened soul.

Kelsey smiled broadly following the end of the video. "As you can see, Elemynt enables people all over the world to connect in ways that weren't possible before. A lot of you in the room know this firsthand because your accounts have hundreds of thousands of followers who enjoy your posts every day. The messages of community and togetherness that you share are what Elemynt fully supports."

Kelsey inferred from their watchful stares that they were embracing her message of goodwill. Elemynt truly did care about people. She took satisfaction in being the one to spread that message to the people before her.

"I want to thank my colleague Daniela there in the back for launching Elemynt's new campaign highlighting the great work our diverse employees are doing at the company."

The guests in the room spun around in their seats to see who Kelsey was referring to. Daniela offered a polite wave. Other than a few nods of acknowledgment here and there, the attendees were laser-focused on Kelsey.

There was one noticeably disaffected person seated in the front row. The Hispanic man in the navy-blue suit and tie spent the entirety of Kelsey's presentation looking down at his phone and huffing occasionally. Kelsey was determined to win over every person in the room. She turned up her charm to its highest level.

Kelsey launched into the story of Susie, the seven-year-old with a lemonade stand who, through Elemynt, was able to bring together her community to eradicate child hunger.

"And this wonderful little girl—"

The sharply raised hand of the man in the first row interrupted Kelsey's recitation.

"Hi, we'll have time for questions at the end," Kelsey said.

"I have a question now," he responded.

"Okay..." Kelsey stumbled. "Let's hear it. Can you say your name and what organization you're from?"

"I am Tomás from La Bandera," he said to the room in a strong Spanish accent. "We are an organization that represents the interests of Latinx people in America. Our focus is on human rights and the well-being of our people."

"Thanks for being here," she said.

"Sure, okay. Thank you for this presentation, however, all of us here are very interested to know what it is you are doing to remove the hate and harassment on your platform?"

Kelsey readied herself to deliver the answer to one of the main questions she anticipated she would receive.

"Elemynt is going above and beyond to protect minority communities from bad actors," Kelsey said proudly. "We use a combination of algorithms and human moderators to detect language that violates our terms of service."

Tomás was not impressed. "And still this is doing nothing to stop the atrocious behavior and the lies that our people face on your platform."

"I was about to say... bad behavior is a small fraction of the content on Elemynt," Kelsey said congenially.

Kelsey's expertly crafted response was interrupted by several more hands shooting in the air. Sensing that she would not be able to continue her presentation until she addressed them, Kelsey opted to answer a question or two. She would get back on track once she got those out of the way.

Daniela gave her an encouraging "okay" sign from the rear of the room.

"Yes, in the front," Kelsey pointed to a woman who identified herself as Silvia Rios, vice president of the Hispanic Opportunity Coalition.

"Do you think Elemynt's male and white privilege allows you to ignore the hate because it isn't directed at your majority demographic?"

Kelsey wasn't quite sure what to say. The question was one she hadn't anticipated. She shuffled through a bunch of prepared responses in her mind. Nothing seemed to be the right fit. Kelsey searched Daniela's face for an appropriate reply. Her co-worker returned nothing other than a wary grimace. Daniela was as curious as the rest of the attendees in the room about what Kelsey would say in response.

"We've received reports that black and Hispanic employees have left the company at higher rates than their white counterparts," Silvia followed up. "Is it because you're not listening to them?"

"Diversity is a core priority for us," Kelsey said sweetly. "We're not where we want to be, but I promise that we are making progress."

The woman was less than satisfied with Kelsey's explanation. "Maybe instead of running to us when things go bad, you could lean on their insight."

Kelsey brightened in the face of adversity. "Some of our best employees are African American and Hispanic," she said.

The commotion of people shaking their heads and sucking their teeth

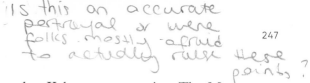
Is this an accurate portrayal or were folks mostly afraid to actually raise these points?

following her comment was not what Kelsey was expecting. The Myntor was determined to get them to understand her point. She mentioned the names of women in managerial positions at the company. She also name-dropped one of her favorite executives — the inimitable Catherine Rowe.

Someone piped up from the back. "Having one white woman in the middle of a bunch of dudes is barely diversity."

"She's your crutch," another voice said.

A cross-looking woman grabbed for the mic. "You throw money at so-called partnerships and say nice things, but your true colors are showing in your actions."

"Is that a question?" Kelsey responded.

"An FYI. You've got the brightest minds in the world working at your company and yet you can't seem to fix the diversity issue."

The accusation was followed by a round of inquiries from the audience that came at Kelsey in rapid-fire succession. The representatives leaped at the chance to lob a question at their target at the front of the room. Daniela's verbal assault before their arrival at the venue turned out to be a primer for the intensity hurled Kelsey's way. A production assistant zigzagged around the semi-circle to hand questioners the mic. Some didn't bother to wait. They raised their voices before the microphone made it into their hands.

"Why do you continue profiting from minority communities but won't move to eradicate hate speech against them?"

"How much are you making off ads on these racist posts?"

"Can you tell us more than 'we're working on it'?"

Kelsey crumbled in the spotlight as the groups savagely eviscerated her. Her dreams of the presentation being a fruitful event that would turn the tide in favor of Elemynt were dashed. The attendees offered nothing but problems and no solutions, which was upsetting. Kelsey was only trying to help. It was as if they didn't want to listen to a word she said.

The PR-friendly answers Kelsey delivered were challenged left and right. Her emphasis that Elemynt was a company that cared was met with derision and sharper questions. The minority groups got their chance to confer with Elemynt reps and they didn't hesitate to vent their various problems to the crumbling representative. Kelsey stood before the group on the verge of a mental breakdown.

Daniela finally had enough of the weak performance of her colleague. The uneven back and forth had gone on too long. Daniela made her way to the front of the room to stand at Kelsey's side. It took all the power in Kelsey for her not to shove the mic into Daniela's chest and run out of the room.

"Thank you to my colleague," Daniela said graciously. "I'm happy to take more questions if you have them."

"I didn't know Elemynt had Latinas on staff," someone quipped.

"Estamos aquí," Daniela replied with a knowing wink.

Kelsey took the exchange as her chance to make a swift exit from the stage. Daniela gently held her in place so she could not move. Kelsey could not fight her grasp in front of a hundred watching eyes.

Daniela listened empathetically to each question before she responded. She nodded with understanding and answered in the most open way possible. She shirked company platitudes in favor of honest answers that showed she understood the guests' frustrations. The mood became considerably calmer with each one of her responses.

Tomás from La Bandera again had a question. Kelsey was frightened at what he might say.

"¿Porque deberíamos creer en cualquiera de las promesas que Elemynt nos hizo?" he said in Spanish.

Daniela didn't skip a beat. "Nos preocupamos por todos en esta sala. Como alguien que ha sido víctima de acoso en línea, al igual que mi familia, entiendo sus preocupaciones. La verdad es que debido a que tenemos recursos limitados, no podemos movernos tan rápido como deberíamos. Pero prometo que siempre estamos trabajando diligentemente para apoyar y servir mejor a las comunidades que representan. El cambio comienza con conversaciones como esta."

Appreciative applause and "gracias" were heaped in Daniela's direction. It was clear that only half the room spoke Spanish and understood what she said. What wasn't lost in translation was that Daniela showed a level of empathy that Kelsey could not by literally being able to speak the language. Whatever she said dampened the harsh energy in the space.

Daniela answered the remaining questions with words of compassion. The way she was able to connect to the individuals gathered around her left Kelsey speechless by her side.

"Gracias a todos," Daniela concluded. "A huge thank you to everyone for coming out today. We know you have many places to be. If you want to stick around for a bit, my colleague and I will be in the back if you'd like to talk more."

Kelsey had an overwhelming urge to run out of the room to a remote corner of the office where she could compose herself. Daniela would not let her escape her fate. She firmly grabbed Kelsey's hand and escorted her through the crowd to engage with the people as she promised they would.

The roundtable was far from the amicable outcome they expected and the blame was squarely on Kelsey. Her go-to comms tactics failed her. Her best was not good enough. And there was no guarantee that Daniela's assurances would sway the groups' stinging opinions of Elemynt. Kelsey doubted they could roll back the catastrophic damage she caused.

"You saved me," Kelsey sighed. "Thank you."

"No 'thank yous' necessary," Daniela said while keeping one eye on the queueing attendees.

"But those people out there... I tried to give them the info they needed..."

"Try not to take it personal," Daniela said. "They haven't had opportunities like these to talk to us. This was their chance to ask the questions that are top of mind for them right now. Sometimes it's better to listen than to talk."

"But this was supposed to be their time to hear from us."

"Even if that was how it was supposed to go down, you walked in here presuming that you understood their concerns because you're a woman. You didn't care to relate to them."

"That's not fair. I've dealt with oppression too."

"Sexism and racism are not the same and I need you to understand that. They both have their own challenges, but they manifest in different ways. Being a woman does not mean you automatically understand what those differences are."

"Why didn't you say something then?"

"If I remember correctly, you didn't want to listen when I said the presentation would be better coming from a person of color. You saw an opportunity to speak onstage and you took it. I'm not saying you can't do this because you're white but if your plan was to walk in the room and talk over people...you set *yourself* up for failure. You barely hear me out when I explain these things to you."

While Kelsey and Daniela were sidelined by their conversation, a growing line of attendees formed in the rear of the room to speak to them. Those that did not plan to stay helped themselves to the remaining food and took selfies in front of the decorative Elemynt logo. When the guests exited, members of the People team handed each person an Elemynt swag bag filled with branded a T-shirt, water bottles, stickers, and other goodies.

One person did not intend to wait for the ladies to move toward the assembly of lingering guests. Tomás from La Bandera walked forcefully in their direction.

"Thank you for the croissants," he said. "But Latinos are still being murdered because of your platform."

"We're doing our best to correct the situation," Kelsey offered meekly.

"Try harder," he snapped. "I don't want to see more of my people tormented because of your company's ignorance."

Tomás stalked away, ignoring the bright-colored swag bags and curated food, and closing the exit door behind him.

Kelsey was aghast at his cutting admonishment. Daniela shook her head in empathy.

"We need some kind of Band-Aid like now," Kelsey said in a panic.

"I'll ask the Diversity Team if we can deliver a donation to La Bandera," Daniela said. "We have a budget set aside for non-profits that we can pull from. Anything more than $50,000 has to be approved by Catherine."

"You see how ticked off he was? I don't think 50K is going to cut it," Kelsey said.

"We can go up to one hundred thousand then. I'm sure Catherine won't have no problem with it."

A fat check might appease Tomás, but all the money in the world wouldn't take away the anguish that plagued Kelsey. Her awful performance nearly cost the company the reputation they were supposed to be defending.

Kelsey wanted to tell Daniela that she was indeed a good person. She cared very much about people. Kelsey didn't mean to come off as insensitive or that she wasn't listening. She defaulted to what she was trained to do in the span of her career: deliver the message and do it in the most succinct way possible. No one could ever understand how deeply heartbroken Kelsey felt. No one from Elemynt at least.

Kelsey excused herself from the room. In a distant corner of the office, she picked up her phone to call Brad. She needed to hear a familiar voice to calm the crushing stress making her brain go haywire.

Brad picked up the phone on the first ring. "You alright, babe? What can I do?"

"Brad, I need you," Kelsey's voice quivered. "How soon can you meet me in D.C.?"

"I'm in Basque Country right now. Can you—"

Kelsey sniffles of distress caught Brad off guard. He sensed Kelsey's welling tears through the phone. His girl needed him at that moment. If he didn't support her then he might lose her forever.

"I'm on the first flight there," he said.

* * *

Kelsey slowly wandered the marble-floored hallways of the Smithsonian National Portrait Gallery in anticipation of Brad's arrival. The landmark building in the heart of Washington, D.C. served as her refuge from the terrible events of New York. It was a familiar space. Her family visited many times when she was a child admiring the stately works of art. Memories of the good times brought her additional comfort.

While she waited for Brad, Kelsey milled about admiring the portraits of notable American women displayed on the cream-colored walls. A striking image of Supreme Court Justice Sandra Day O'Connor hung next to one of pioneering feminist Bella Abzug. A portrait of television icon Diane Sawyer was flanked by a smoky black and white photograph of the actress Marlene Dietrich. The inspiring figures blazed trails for Kelsey and many other women to attain goals they were told were faraway dreams for their gender. Kelsey imagined herself as a trailblazer of sorts too. A future executive at a top-tier company. She could one day be on the walls too.

Kelsey dismissed the thought. She had a few hills to climb at Elemynt first, chief among them the upcoming set of hearings.

She reached for her phone and took photos of the works like the other museum visitors around her. She would post the pictures to her Elemynt account later if she felt up to it.

When Kelsey finished viewing the portraits in the hall adjacent to the lobby, she found herself scrolling through her Elemynt feed. She needed a distraction from her thoughts of the unfortunate results of the summit. The audience trashed her. They didn't want to listen to her remarks. Kelsey wanted to give the advocates in the audience credit for fighting for what they believed in. However, she did not appreciate was that it was at her expense.

As Kelsey admired more of the art in the adjacent galleries, she felt the presence of someone admiring her.

"I don't know what's more beautiful, you or that painting," she heard Brad say.

"Well…it's about a hundred years old and can't tell you how much it misses you."

Brad leaned in for the hug that Kelsey was desperately in need of. She wanted to be held in the embrace of someone who loved and cared for her. She needed reassurance that everything would be alright with the world. For that moment in Brad's arms, it was.

"Sorry to pull you off your trip," Kelsey said.

"It's cool, babe," Brad said soothingly. "I was dicking around Europe anyway. Did I tell you I was following around this band out of Oslo? Cool stuff. You gotta hear their music."

"Is it in English?"

"It's like Björk meets Aerosmith. Want me to play it for you?"

"Not right now," Kelsey said quietly. "I just want to hang if that's okay. Me and you."

The pair navigated the museum halls toward the Kogod Courtyard, an airy atrium with a wavy glass-and-steel roof that rained natural light on the patrons. The sprawling area was populated with locals and visitors of all ages reading, chatting, and working on laptops in the iconic public space.

The pair navigated to an uninhabited corner where gleaming tables and chairs sat amidst plantings in white marble containers.

"How did it go at your workshop?" Brad asked.

"It could've been better," Kelsey sighed. "Let's leave it at that, okay?"

"What about the privacy stuff? What's the latest with that?"

The breach was not what Kelsey intended to talk about when she invited Brad to the gallery. The meetup was supposed to be a time for her to clear her head. Kelsey gave Brad the official company line on privacy.

"Things change very quickly at Elemynt," she said. "They're working to address the issue as soon as possible."

"Is that what they've trained you to say?" he laughed.

"I am not a dog!" Kelsey said testily. "Don't be a jerk."

"Oh, come on! Elemynt is making money off of selling people's lives. They're scanning our messages and sharing them with these ad guys. And now this harassment thing? Ho boy. I don't know why more people don't just delete the app."

"Says the man who still has an active account."

"Hey, I'm traveling around the world bringing beauty into people's lives."

"No, you're a random hot guy with a six-pack and a smartphone running away from his problems instead of trying to fix them."

"Why are you always so sensitive to everything?" Brad laughed. "I know you're upset about this hearing..."

Kelsey would have strangled Brad had they not been in the center of a legendary American cultural institution. Brad was insulting Kelsey to her face. It was true that the hearing was weighing on her but that was no excuse for Brad to be coming down on her the way he was.

"Not everyone wants to pack up and leave and their problems behind like you did," Kelsey said curtly. "Poor you. You got your feelings hurt because you lost your job. I'm supposed to stop my life too?"

"You chose your career over your friends. How about that?"

"I didn't leave you," Kelsey seethed. "You left me. I'm not a quitter, Brad. If you were my friend, you would support me and my career and not make me feel bad about it."

Nearby museum visitors began to stare at the bickering couple. Kelsey felt the scrutinizing eyes on her back. She wanted nothing more than to shrink away into oblivion. Brad was making Kelsey feel horrible about performing her duties and at the same time embarrassing her in front of strangers.

Kelsey moved to calm herself. "Can we take this convo somewhere that's not in front of a hundred people?"

The pair strolled in silence until they eventually made their way to the cavernous third floor. The historic space with its grand vaulted ceilings and galleries of outsized works of modern art had a sparse weekday crowd. The floor was mostly unoccupied save for an elderly couple walking in arms and a few solo travelers admiring the art.

Kelsey found herself drawn to an immense multimedia interpretation of the U.S. map with the 50 states outlined in multicolored neon tubing. The grouping of televisions nestled in each one flickered with images and audio clips that mirrored what the states were best known for. The videos played over one other in discordant harmony.

Inside the outline of Idaho, the multiple screens panned across a giant pile of potatoes. California flashed with zeros and ones representing strings of binary code. In Kansas, clips from Judy Garland's adventures in "The Wizard of Oz" played on a loop. Kelsey wanted a tornado to sweep her up and take her away from Brad's side. The flashing lights illuminated her frustrated face.

Brad struggled to put his words together.

"Kelsey, I'm sorry," he finally said. "After they fired me, I kinda resented that you got to stay. You had your great position and you weren't there for me."

"It's not my job to always be constantly by your side propping you up," Kelsey squinted. "You are your own man. If you loved me you wouldn't make me feel bad for the career choices I've made. You're supposed to make my life happier, not harder."

"That's not how I want you feeling," Brad said. "How do I make you believe that I love you always?"

"I need to know that I'm more than just a 3 a.m. call to you," Kelsey said, jabbing her finger into his chest. "I'm not just some girl you video chat with when you're lonely or because you're bored."

"I swear you mean more to me than that," he said. "I call 'cause I care about the person on the other end of the video. Truth is, I've traveled around the world and there's no girl out there like you. You're smart, you're strong, and I gotta say...sexy as hell."

"Actions speak louder than words," Kelsey said softly.

"I promise I'll be a better man for you and I'll start proving it," he said, caressing her face. "I don't wanna see tears on these beautiful cheeks of yours. Just kisses from me."

Under the multicolored lights of modern art, Kelsey and Brad exchanged the proposed kiss. Then another. She allowed him to hold her in his arms, perhaps not because he was her former lover but because Kelsey missed a reassuring embrace. Her worries melted away as he drew her in closer to him. For a moment, there was no Elemynt. No hearing. Only him, her, and the warmth between them.

FOURTEEN

Kelsey gazed at the panoramic views of the Washington D.C. skyline from a balcony several floors up. Elemynt rented out the presidential suite of the five-star Mandarin Oriental Hotel not far from Capitol Hill where the Senate hearing would take place. The main area of the luxurious space was transformed into a war room. The elegant seating was rearranged to face the extra televisions brought in from the D.C. office. The fifteen or so staff members wouldn't miss a moment of the proceedings.

Representatives from the Legal team were ardently buried in their laptops and phones. Executive assistants hustled to and fro attending to urgent needs. Kelsey and the present staff members were ushered through the hotel's rear entrances earlier so they wouldn't be spotted. To the outside world, they were in just another hotel room. Nothing to see.

The adjacent study and den were cordoned off for private phone and video calls. Catherine, their commander in chief, took ownership of one of the rooms to discuss outstanding security issues with Leon.

Troy, who was more than satisfied with his past performance, opted to stay at headquarters to continue business as usual. The weekly all-hands was moved from its normal time on the coming Monday to that afternoon. Troy was intent on delivering his weekly message in person following the day's Congressional proceedings.

The hearings would be a continuation of Troy's stellar performance in front of the Senate committee a few weeks prior. This time, Wyatt would take his place in the witness chair.

The company's general counsel was more than qualified to assume the duties. After years as a Washington mover and shaker, Wyatt could anticipate the

Senators' lines of questioning and be ready with the right response. Sending in the head lawyer instead of the CEO would also create less of a spectacle for the press to feed on.

The media frenzy that Congress hoped to generate by calling the hearing turned out to be a dull roar compared to previous events. The issue with Balkan operatives spreading untruths on the app was less about the company's role and more about the behavior of bad actors on the platform.

Wyatt would handle both the first hearing slated to begin in fifteen minutes and the similar hearing from the House Committee on Energy and Commerce set for Monday. Myntors at the various Elemynt offices again organized watch parties but with less zeal than before. The hearings wouldn't be as much of a thrill as the first showdown with Troy, their fierce leader. Elemynt was subjected to the overreach of Congress before and had won the battle squarely.

Wyatt himself dismissed media prep because as a veteran of the D.C. legal system, he maintained that he didn't need it. No one argued otherwise. His role in helping Troy successfully prepare for the first hearing was universally praised. Barely anyone in the days following acknowledged that it was Kelsey who played the largest role in honing Troy's performance. Nevertheless, what Wyatt lacked in media spotlight polish he more than made up for in Washington experience and legal prowess.

Jon would sit behind Wyatt in the hearing chamber to serve as his silent wingman. The plan was for Jon to stay in constant contact with Kelsey, messaging her if communications issues needed to be addressed during his physical absence from the war room.

Kelsey was in an improved state of mind. Her night with Brad was a wonderful reprieve from the serious business at hand. He was already off to his next destination — Italy's Amalfi Coast — where he would rest before his next adventure. Her beau sent her a series of messages of encouragement that morning. They were kind and welcome. However, Kelsey couldn't let thoughts of Brad distract her from the task ahead.

Kelsey ignored the stream of emails from reporters that crowded her inbox. Since the Comms team had already shared the written opening statement on the company blog and another post would go up after, there was no need to respond. Elemynt officially said its peace. She would mostly do what the staff in the war room and the audience in attendance at the hearing was doing: sitting, watching, and waiting.

"It's time," one of the aides said.

The attention in the suite turned to the TVs where CSPAN played at a high volume. Kelsey found a seat in one of the plush hotel chairs. Her phone was held firmly in her hand.

"He's got this," Leon confirmed to Catherine.

She nodded in agreement. "He's the best we have."

Wyatt strode into the storied hearing room prepared to defend the billion-dollar company on everyone's lips. An American flag pin shone on the lapel of his tailored black suit. His deep blue tie was crisp.

The general counsel moved with ease through the gauntlet of press and spectators. Photographers dutifully took photos of the Elemynt representative. There wasn't quite the swarm as there was for Troy. That was to be expected.

Wyatt was unfazed as he took his place at the witness table in front of the rows of gawking Senators. He placed a legal notepad next to the name placard at the edge of the table in front of him. A pitcher of water and glass were stationed by its side.

A strike of Senator Layne's gavel opened the Senate hearing. Her firm voice brought the remaining chatter in the chamber to a halt.

"We have reason to believe that Elemynt continues to ignore repeated threats that endanger the lives of Americans," she read boldly from her notes. "Elemynt has become a machine for spreading false information, empowering white supremacist movements, and amplifying societal division. Individuals in countries like Macedonia, Georgia, and Bulgaria are creating social media campaigns to turn Americans against each other. They are undermining our ability to trust our neighbors."

The team bristled at the rush of quiet commentary visible behind their onscreen general counsel. The Congresswoman was articulating what the attendees and the world were thinking. The notion that Elemynt was a morally compromised company tearing at the fabric of American values had unfairly crept into the mind of the public.

"The decisions made by Elemynt's executive team are in direct contrast with the interests of the extraordinary number of people being victimized," Senator Layne continued. "Our concerns mirror those of Americans across the country."

Wyatt sat motionless during the droning opening statements by the Congresswoman and the committee co-chair. The two Senators each took a turn enumerating Elemynt's stats and supposed unpunished sins.

"Mr. Schumacher, we appreciate your presence. Though we did anticipate Elemynt would send an actual executive," Senator Layne remarked condescendingly.

Catherine laughed to herself. "They're lucky we showed at all. Next time, we'll send an intern if they want to make those kinds of comments."

Wyatt was unperturbed by the chair's dig. "I'm more than prepared to speak on behalf of Elemynt on the topics at hand."

In his opening statement, Wyatt spoke eloquently of Elemynt's innovation and successes. With impassioned words, he shared how the app was able to bring the world together. Hundreds of millions of Americans and people around the world were avid users. Save for the actions of a few poor intentioned users, Elemynt was a place of harmony that brought out the best in the people who used it.

Wyatt's proclamation pleased the crew in the hotel suite, including Catherine and Leon. Kelsey exhaled. The hearing was off to a good start. For once, she was proud of Wyatt for his performance.

"Thank you for your statement, sir," Senator Layne said, shuffling her papers. "I will begin with my five minutes of questioning. I have before me a large number of examples of violent or dehumanizing speech on the app that appears to violate Elemynt's standards. How is Elemynt deciding which photos and comments to take down?"

The Congresswoman delivered a perfect opportunity for Wyatt to deliver the company line.

"Elemynt has several steps in place to curb hate speech and harassment," Wyatt said. "We rely on a combination of artificial intelligence, user reporting, and thousands of content moderators on staff trained to enforce the rules of the app. We suspend accounts that violate those rules."

"Thank you for that. However, according to these examples..." she said, waving a page. "I can go on your platform and post an image untruthfully saying Mexicans are killing small children in the streets and not have my post taken down."

"We moderate the platform," Wyatt said. "We also allow room for free speech."

"I see. Under your policy of free speech, I could also post in the comments saying women are quote 'sluts' and 'whores' with no repercussions. Is that correct?"

"I'm not sure that language would be covered. I'm more than happy to forward you our terms of service."

"Thank you, sir, I have a copy," Senator Layne said coarsely. "I'm also aware that currently, the responsibility is on victims to report this content to Elemynt."

"There's an easy system built into the platform for people to contact us with those kinds of issues," Wyatt said assuredly.

"How many reports would you say Elemynt receives a day?"

Wyatt shook his head due to both not knowing the answer and working through the legal ramification of sharing that specific information.

"How many reports, Mr. Schumacher?" the Senator repeated. "Hundreds? Thousands?"

Backs straightened in the gallery. The room anxiously awaited his answer as did the Myntors in the suite.

"Madam Congresswoman, I'll have my team get back to you with that information," Wyatt said.

"So you don't know?"

"I'll have my team to get back to you after the hearing."

"We'll hold you to that."

Wyatt breathed a nearly imperceptible sigh of relief that he was able to shirk the question. The suite was equally satisfied. So far so good. The Congresswoman, however, was not done.

"What are the demographics of Elemynt's content moderation staff?" Senator Layne asked. "Where are they based?"

"I believe the majority of our moderators are based in Texas and Dublin."

"Ireland. I see," she paused for effect. What you're telling us is people who are not from America are making decisions regarding American communities."

"Only if the artificial intelligence isn't able to make a decision on its own," Wyatt said.

"Yes, and who is programming the artificial intelligence?"

Wyatt stared blankly. He needed to find a way out of the answer. The Senator stepped on the moment, not bothering to wait for his response.

"Considering your company employs mostly white men, would it be safe to say white men are making the rules?" she asked.

"I don't think that's an accurate characterization."

"According to your diversity report, it is. It's not surprising then that your company has problems with the attacks on Mexican-Americans when you barely have any Hispanic people on your staff."

The cheap snickers in the hearing room were more juvenile than what was becoming of a legal proceeding. Kelsey could not deny that the senator inarguably landed her point.

"This is a farce!" Catherine laughed it off. "Our report says two percent. A toddler could fact check that."

No one enjoyed the cutting exchange more than the observers in the chamber. They were giddy watching the kind of takedown they had come for. The opposite reaction hung in the air of the hotel suite. Her colleagues were worried about Wyatt's ability to recover from the shakeup.

On the screen, Jon sat behind Wyatt trying his best not to be visibly agitated in front of the cameras. Kelsey worked with him long enough to know that the continued shifting of his weight from side to side was a surefire sign that things were not off to a good start.

Wyatt propped himself up to make a comeback, but the committee members were not planning to give him the chance. The next senator intended to double down on her colleague's line of questioning.

Senator Fiona Osmeyer, armed with a stack of notes and a cross demeanor, stared down at Wyatt.

"Mr. Schumacher, let's assume that about half the people on your platform are women," she said. "That aligns with the population of women in America. There are a billion users on Elemynt, right?"

"Yes, according to our latest data."

"Great. So that would make half a billion women who are potentially targets of harassment because of their gender. How many women do you have working on this issue? How many female decision-makers?"

"It depends on how you define 'decision-maker,'" Wyatt said.

"Let me ask another way. How many women do you have in executive-level roles? Other than your COO Catherine Rowe."

Catherine fumed at the unexpected mention of her name. The hearing was about Elemynt, not her. The watchers in the suite kept their eyes focused on the television so as not to inflame the moment.

Wyatt kept his cool. "Madam Congresswoman, we are a platform for everyone regardless of gender or race or—"

"I admire your dedication to diversity, Mr. Schumacher," the Senator cut him off. "But according to your report you released, less than 20 percent of employees in management positions at Elemynt are women. Would you say your staff reflects the demographics of your users?"

The obvious answer was no.

The media in the gallery salivated seeing the general counsel quiver under the watchful eye of the Senator. Wyatt poured a cup of water from the nearby pitcher. He took a swallow.

Kelsey had to again remind herself to breathe. Everything would be fine, she told herself. Her colleagues seated next to her didn't seem as sure. The shared confidence was slowly morphing into trepidation.

Senator Leland Sanford, a favorite among conservatives in the country, followed the inquisition with queries of his own.

"Mr. Wyatt, I've talked to many of my constituents back in Mississippi and they're finding that you are in fact taking down conservative content from your app," he said in a thick Southern drawl.

"Congressman, that's not factually correct," Wyatt quickly responded.

"I also have a copy of a blog post here from one of your former employees, a Mr. Schultz, that has called you all out for being biased toward liberal views. And come to find out, when I watch the news, they're sayin' that this is a big problem at your company. How do you respond to that?"

Other than a memo from one employee with questionable ethics, the Senator shared no evidence of bias at Elemynt. They were stuck in a ridiculous cycle that frustrated Kelsey to no end. The media accused Elemynt of censoring conservatives. Senators, in turn, cited the news reports. The news then reported on Senators' complaints of censorship. On and on the cycle continued. It was playing out again in front of a room stacked with TV cameras angling for their next viral clip.

Wyatt repeatedly denied bias in how the company enforced its terms of service. "We employ a diverse workforce, including our content moderation teams."

"I believe you said just a second ago that you're taking down certain accounts," the Senator glared.

"Mr. Congressman, we are not discriminating against anyone," Wyatt said testily. "We are following the terms of service outlined in our app. If you want a copy, I can have my team forward one to you."

The process was wearing on Wyatt and not because he wasn't knowledgeable. He was the senior-most legal adviser at one of the country's top tech companies. It was being in the spotlight that was chipping away at his confidence. A crowd of journalists hungry for a scoop breathed down his neck while the line of Senator fired shots at him. He could not hide from the heat of the chamber lights. The water line on the pitcher before him lowered faster and faster.

It was evident to Catherine, Kelsey, and perhaps the Myntors in the suite that Wyatt was in hindsight in dire need of the media prep that he dished out to Troy. Though his ego-driven self-assessment would tell him otherwise, Wyatt was not a PR professional or a courtroom lawyer or evidently a person capable of speaking in public on behalf of an institution. However, he needed to summon all three if they were to escape the showdown without incurring regulatory action. The fate he was so adamant about them escaping.

Wilson Dewitt, the bespectacled senator from Utah straightened his mic to properly lay into Wyatt.

"As we've heard from my fellow Senators, Elemynt has allowed itself to become a tool for foreign interests to weaken our democracy through propaganda and vicious lies. They aren't seeking political gain or influence. These operatives are generating income off the back of hostility because of your platform, Mr. Schumacher."

Wyatt sat in the chair with no words in response to the declaration. What the Senator said wasn't a question. Kelsey willed her colleague to remain silent in response.

Senator Dewitt dramatically slammed a stack of papers the size of a book on the dais, rattling the spectators in the suite.

"This is a collection of the hundreds of divisive stories I found to be shared on your platform. Horrible titles like, for example, 'Illegal immigrants throwing Americans in mass graves,' 'Congress mandates that schools show students gay sex', 'FBI funding Mexican mercenaries.' One here says the Pope was found guilty of rape and murder. And this was just what we collected."

Wyatt sat stone-faced, his hands fidgeting under the desk. Kelsey could see him running through options in his head. There was no response he could give that would make him or the company look good in light of the accusations.

"How many people do you estimate have seen these kinds of posts?" the Congressman asked.

"I can't say for sure but…"

"I can have the team get back to you," Catherine filled in the blank.

"If you had to guess how many would you say?" the lawman pressed.

Kelsey pleaded in whispers for Wyatt not to return anything resembling a guess. Leon, who knew the exact number, was more prayerful than the rest of the gawking Myntors in the room.

Senator Dewitt removed his glasses and scowled with intensity at Wyatt. "Mr.

Schumacher, is lying a habit at Elemynt?"

"Excuse me, Senator?"

"We happened to discover after the first committee hearing that 30 million people were affected by your breach. Not the 40,000 your company stated. Why did your boss lie in front of this committee?"

"I can't say that I agree with that characterization," Wyatt said weakly.

"Then tell us how many people have seen these posts?"

The fatigue from the hearing reddened Wyatt's eyes. His professional reputation as a man of his word was on the line as was his job at Elemynt.

"Hundreds. Thousands," he mumbled to himself.

"Which is it, sir?"

Wyatt was shaken to his core. "Congressman—"

"Mr. Schumacher, if you had to guess what would you say?"

Wyatt sighed and took a sip of water. "Hundreds of millions."

The collective gasps that emanated from the hearing room and hotel could be heard throughout the District of Columbia. Elemynt's general counsel just admitted publicly the extensive scale of the Balkan plot and turned Congress' suspicion into a confirmed fact.

And why? Kelsey thought. Because someone threatened to call him a liar?

Wyatt's selfishness opened the floodgates for undue harm that the company would never recover from. He tossed out internal numbers that even the least skilled Elemynt employee would take to the grave. There was no hope for self-preservation in his honesty. He allowed himself to be put in a situation where he would be ruined either way. The subsequent chorus of murmuring in the Senate chamber echoed in the hotel suite.

Catherine was thoroughly livid. She had entrusted Wyatt with an important task that he failed at spectacularly on a national stage. She stormed out of the main room, nearly knocking over a lamp and several chairs in the process. Leon chased after the executive leaving a trail of expletives in her wake.

"That man had one job!" she yelled. "Sit there and say a few soundbites. It is not that difficult!"

"Maybe it won't be that bad," Leon said. "He has the rest of the hearing to make up for it."

"Can we pull him out of there?" Catherine asked.

Kelsey ran after the pair to halt the rash decision-making in progress. "We can't do that unless we want to make the problem worse. Look...the reporters are all over this already."

The crowd of journalists visible in the gallery drilled into their phones the headline story that Wyatt generously produced for them. They leaned forward in their seats to catch additional internal-only knowledge the loquacious general counsel wanted to volunteer.

Catherine completed her furious exit out of the great room with a slam of the door of her makeshift office.

"He can pull through," Kelsey heard Leon say on the other side of the door. "I know he can."

Congressman Dewitt smiled with self-assurance after the made-for-TV exchange. The committee members did their homework. They were determined to not recreate the follies of their time with Troy.

Wyatt deflated with the slow death of a balloon deprived of air. The ramifications of his confession circled through his mind. His commitment to not lying in front of the D.C. establishment that reared him brought many more people to shame. It was a crack under pressure no one could have anticipated.

The hearing quickly gained steam. The senators sensed their chance to tear into Wyatt and produce their viral moment in front of the cameras. They burrowed past Wyatt's surface-level answers. They postured themselves as fearless inquisitors for their constituents watching back home.

The senators' game plan was clear. Spend their five minutes railing against the company, barely letting Wyatt speak and only to support their claims. They hurled questions at him like heavy stones in a showy attempt to bury him.

What was supposed to be a breeze for Wyatt turned into a battle of wits. His smarmy nature wasn't helping and neither were his non-answers. Every "I'll check with my team" only shortened the senators' patience more.

The onslaught was almost terrifying to watch. The hearing would not be the carefree cause for celebration that Myntors back at headquarters and elsewhere enjoyed after the first hearing.

Catherine emerged from the study to join the room for the questioning from the last remaining senator. Ruth Brenwick, the congresswoman from New Jersey, looked to be more level-headed than her combative counterparts. At least Kelsey hoped that she was.

"Mr. McCray, your CEO, told us in the last hearing that your company is currently valued at one billion dollars? Is that right?"

"According to external estimates, yes," Wyatt sat up.

"And one of the main metrics used to make that assessment is 'daily active people,' meaning the number of users who have engaged in the last 30 days. Am I right?

"Yes, that's correct."

"You also use these numbers to bring advertisers to your platform," the senator said stoutly. "Mr. Schumacher, you've said in your testimony that you use algorithms and artificial intelligence to respond to reported cases of harassment. Elemynt also uses algorithms to determine what content to put in people's feeds based on what they've engaged with before. Then you feed them similar posts which keeps them using the app and available to see ads. Am I getting this all correct?"

"That's an oversimplification," Wyatt said.

"Okay, stick with me here," Senator Brenwick twiddled her pen. "Hate speech generates engagement on your platform and a lot of it from what you've told us already. People are sharing those posts, which tells your algorithms that type of content is worth promoting to more people. If I interact with posts that are horrible to women or people of color, isn't it likely that I will be receiving more of that content? And then through advertising, you make money off that engagement?"

"I wouldn't characterize it that way. The algorithms are complex..."

"I understand that," the Senator interrupted. "But it's safe to say that taking down violent posts would cause a drop in those important numbers you're being valued by. You would be jeopardizing your business model."

"Madam Congresswoman..."

"In other words, hate is good for business."

Wyatt's face turned a sickly crimson. He could not restrain himself from gritting his teeth.

"You've decided profit is worth the destruction of American lives," she doubled down.

Again. Wyatt was failing again in the most astonishing way possible.

"Mr. Schumacher, what does Elemynt do successfully other than make money?" the senator asked curiously.

Wyatt, flustered by the line of questioning, stammered and stumbled.

"I don't know...I—"

"You don't know?"

The Myntors in the suite gasped in horror at his lack of response. Wyatt could have said a range of answers: Elemynt brings people closer together. The app connects them with family and friends. What should have been a lightning-fast reply was nothing but crippling dead air.

"That idiot!" Catherine clenched her fists. "I'm going to kill him!"

Catherine unleashed her boiling anger and was justified to do so. The scores of journalists seated behind Wyatt were astounded that he made their job so easy. Wyatt Schumacher, general counsel of Elemynt, gave the media a litany of damaging quotes to choose from in their quest to tear the company apart. Kelsey's hope for a flawless hearing shattered into a million pieces.

Video of the damning silence in which Wyatt couldn't defend his company would appear on every news website on the planet. Cable news networks would blast the clip on a loop for days on end. Water coolers around the country would soon be dominated by the discussion of the exchange. Wyatt single-handedly incriminated the company he was supposed to protect.

The senators glanced at each other with satisfied smirks while the observers in the gallery burst into dozens of chattering conversations. The raucous murmuring in the hearing room overshadowed Wyatt's attempts to clean up his testimony.

Senator Layne, committee chairman and victor, banged her gavel. "This chamber will come to order!"

* * *

The intense yelling coming from Catherine's command post ricocheted through the rest of the suite. From the one-sided phone conversation, it was obvious Catherine was intent on having Wyatt fired. Troy, who was supposed to be prepping for his all-hands message, was adamant that Wyatt would not be terminated for the infraction. He was Troy's long-time buddy. That trumped the punitive suggestions Catherine levied.

"Congress is drafting legislation as we speak!" Catherine bellowed. "I want him out of here!"

Wyatt and Jon entered the room at the worst possible moment. The disgraced counsel was a marked man. One of Catherine's assistants whispered to Jon. She pulled him into the study with the enraged executive.

Wyatt slumped into one of the empty seats near a window. He said nothing. The staffers around him avoided his humiliated gaze.

"Troy, it's you who should've been up there!" Catherine yelled from the adjoining room. "You are the one who insisted to me that you never wanted to be put in a situation like that again. Well, thanks to you that brick-headed leech failed and now we're suffering the consequences."

The scuffling over the phone between Catherine and Troy grew uncomfortably heated as the conversation went on. The Myntors standing by had no choice but to listen as the livid second-in-command tore into her superior.

"He's not doing the next hearing and neither are you!" she roared.

Kelsey was bewildered by what Catherine's verbal threats could mean. There was one more hearing to do that Monday. Backing out after Wyatt's performance would be admitting defeat. Elemynt needed to defend itself in whatever way possible against the barrage of criticism from the media and the legislators. A poor reputation in the eyes of the public was a fast track to the downfall of the company.

Catherine exploded back into the main room, startling the unnerved staff.

"Pack it up!" she said commandingly. "I want everyone at the D.C. office in one hour! Move it!"

The staff in the suite hurriedly grabbed their belongings and rushed toward the door. The executive assistants especially understood that hesitating one moment meant their badges would be deactivated before they reached the office.

Catherine confronted a pitifully despondent Wyatt. "Call all of the counselors on your team and tell them I want them there *before* I arrive. Can you handle that or should I have someone else do it?"

"It'll take a minute to get a hold of them," he said wearily.

"Wyatt, the only two words I want to leave your lips are 'Yes, Catherine.' Am I clear or should I draw up your termination papers now?"

FIFTEEN

The Washington D.C. office was a buttoned-up version of Elemynt headquarters festooned with visual displays of patriotism.

Along the largest wall was a stunning American flag made of dime-sized red, white, and blue Elemynt logos. A bronze sculpture of a bald eagle framed the view of K Street three stories below.

Nearly every Myntor in the building — whether at their desk, in meeting rooms, or on their phone — was glued to a screen awaiting the start of all-hands. Troy's response to the day's disaster was a moment not to be missed. The staff was desperately in need of his leadership. They craved the verbal reassurance that the fraught situation would be alright.

The cadre of staffers imported from the hotel war room dutifully filed directly into "Star Spangled Banter," the largest conference room in the D.C. office. Catherine yanked the opaque glass door closed behind them.

The COO plucked the remote out of the hand of one of her aides setting up the video conference system. She turned on the all-hands livestream without assistance. Catherine, more than anyone, wanted to hear what Troy would say to the legions of employees in his company. Wyatt's bungled performance in front of Congress was an unignorable strain on morale. If there was ever a time to pull through for Elemynt, this was it.

No one was more aware of the weight of the moment than Wyatt, who sat silently in a corner. The fluorescent lighting shone on his sickly face. Pride had clouded his judgment and he paid the ultimate price.

The jolly music that announced the start of each all-hands pierced the tension of the sterile conference room. On the screen were hundreds of Myntors gathered in the auditorium waiting for Troy to take his place at the front of the stage.

Troy walked out from behind the curtain beaming with the sunny smile of an unbroken leader. He began his remarks not with regrets, but with a vibrant shout out to the hard-working Myntors throughout the company.

"I want to thank everybody for continuing to make Elemynt the success that it is," he said to perfunctory applause. "Our daily and monthly active people metrics are on a steady climb thanks to you. With the new features and platform improvements being rolled out over the next few months, we're going to take that even further."

More polite applause.

"Now some of you may have seen what happened in front of Congress..." Troy said, downplaying that nearly the entire workforce watched the hearing in real-time. "We fully support our staff, including our general counsel, who bravely represented us today. We're never as bad as people say we are and we're never as good as we think we are. Our goal is to keep rolling and remember we're doing this for the people who use and love Elemynt."

Jon nodded along with the sentiment. "Inspiring," he said under his breath.

Catherine didn't utter a word. Her eyes stayed locked on the screen. The troubled staff in the room followed suit. No movement, no talking.

Troy paced the stage, gesturing toward the rapt assembly. "When you go home to your family and friends this weekend, they're going to ask you about this hearing. They may ask about the Balkan issue. When they do, I want you to share with them all the inspiring connections Elemynt has made possible. Tell them about how Elemynt helped find a missing girl and reunited her with her parents. Tell them how a charity for the disabled was able to raise millions of dollars in one week. Tell them the story of why you came to Elemynt and why we love where we work."

The audience of Myntors murmured to each other about their personal reasons for turning out their best work for Elemynt.

"These may be challenging times," Troy continued. "But coal under pressure is what makes diamonds. I want each of you to continue to shine your brightest."

The auditorium burst into a round of inspired applause fueled by a collective sense of pride. Troy did what Kelsey thought was nearly impossible. He found the words to get the people who made up the company back on track. The renewed confidence in Elemynt they shared would extend far beyond that day's all-hands gathering.

There was one problem. They had one more hearing to go. Monday. Three days away.

The attendees at headquarters may have had renewed confidence but the group in the conference room lacked the same motivation. The pariah that threatened to bring the company down a second time was sitting across from them.

Catherine muted the screen.

"Call the committee chair's office," she said forcefully. "Let them know I will be filling in for our general counsel at the hearing. I want every mention of Wyatt scrubbed from our official documentation."

The room scrambled to carry out her directives. Laptops were flung open and emails were dictated at an incredible speed. Catherine was taking control.

Jon cleared his throat above the commotion. "Congress is going to announce the change immediately. When they hear you're going to testify…"

"Let the press report what they want," Catherine said steadfastly. "We, however, are not speaking a word of it until the second I am in front of that committee. I want a media blackout. No one talking to reporters for any reason. We will not allow ourselves to be defined by disaster."

At Catherine's instruction, the Washington D.C. office was closed for the weekend to staffers not working on the hearing. Extra security guards were stationed outside the conference room door and at every conceivable entrance to the building. Badge readers were reprogrammed to limit others except the select few from gaining access. They would take no chances.

Inside the room, the crew labored away to prepare for Catherine's appearance. Rather than spending time with media coaching as they did with Troy, the woman in charge wanted detailed backgrounds on each of the Representatives on the House committee. They dug up their public statements on Elemynt, causes they supported, legislation they championed, who donated to their campaign and how much, who they were married to, how many children they had, how they spent their time outside of Capitol Hill.

Together, the group watched a run of interviews given by each committee member. The back and forth of past hearings were analyzed with obsessive scrutiny. The team used the information to create individual psychological profiles of the Representatives who would sit on the dais. They collated details of their speech patterns, topics of interest, questions they would likely ask, and how they would ask them, down to the possible phrasing.

Wyatt's Legal team rallied to bring their collective best to the table. Their leader's contribution was a series of nods and whispers of additional information and a concerted dedication to staying out of Catherine's way. In his stead were two of Catherine's lifelong friends, each a high-powered lawyer ready with advice for how to sidestep questions regarding Congressional regulation.

The collective armed Catherine with refutations of the wide range of accusations Congress could levy. They fired questions at her, she fired back. The Boss Lady dedicated her every waking minute to honing her responses. She was hellbent on not replicating the same fatal flaws Wyatt did.

Not a single Myntor in the group left the office the entire weekend. Like her embattled colleagues, Kelsey slept in nap rooms or on couches scattered around the office. She used the company showers. Her meals came from the micro-kitchen. She possessed neither the will nor the desire to leave. If saving the company meant a few hours of lost sleep, Kelsey was all for it. Catherine deserved her best.

Late Sunday night, Catherine finally excused herself back to her untouched hotel room. Her sole reason for leaving — she didn't want to appear tired on camera. A crew of on-call hair and makeup artists would make doubly sure of it.

Kelsey and the team did their best. Whether it would be enough to conquer the hearing was the million-dollar question. What happened next was out of Kelsey's hands.

* * *

Catherine's turn to testify in front of the legislative body was a few short minutes away. The self-satisfied members of the House Committee on Energy and Commerce sitting high above the chamber awaited her arrival as did the speculating observers who managed to cram into the gallery.

The standing-room-only area behind the witness chair was packed with reporters, photographers, camera operators, and riled up members of the public, all squirming in anticipation of the third chapter of the Elemynt saga.

Jon and Kelsey shuffled past the restless onlookers toward the seats saved for them by Catherine's executive assistants. A third familiar figure sat adjacent to the two placeholders. Sarah, who was supposed to be away on a foreign island drinking out of coconuts somewhere, smirked indignantly at her colleagues.

"Aren't you supposed to be on leave?" Jon frowned as they exchanged seats with the E.A.s.

"Looks like you needed my help," Sarah said flippantly. "It's amazing how I leave the country to enjoy my honeymoon and what do I see on the TV? Two more Congressional hearings were called. That's just insane to me. Laying on the beach worrying about whether my career is in danger is not how I wanted to spend my time away."

"We prepped a lot for this one," Kelsey said in protest.

"Like you guys did with Wyatt? I hope this one goes differently or else I'd hate to see us out on the street."

Jon was visibly agitated by Sarah's unannounced presence. She had the right to be there. Permission was not required to attend a public hearing. However, she hadn't told him or the team that she was back in the States, let alone in Washington D.C. After a weekend of preparing for surprises, the unexpected appearance of their teammate did not set the proper tone for the day.

Neither Jon nor Kelsey had the energy to defend themselves against her unnecessary sarcasm or to fill Sarah in on the events of the last few weeks. Kelsey believed in her heart of hearts that Catherine could pull it off. On the other hand, Wyatt's undoing left Kelsey unsure of what was to come. The legislators and their sharpened claws were ready to cut down attempts by Catherine to redeem her tarnished company.

A swell of commotion rattled the historic chamber. Catherine strutted through the hearing room doors without an ounce of fear. The horde of photographers documented her steps to the witness chair while onlookers trafficked in spiteful theories of what the next few hours had in store.

Catherine was unmoved by the bedlam swirling around her. The clicks of the cameras and the cold stares from the panel of Representatives would not shake her determination. She was in the midst of adversaries who would gleefully watch Elemynt crumble if it meant boosting their political clout in front of the millions watching at home. The committee members wouldn't be easily persuaded but Catherine would do her damndest to try.

The herd of eager photographers dispersed with the rap of the chairman's gavel. The chatter in the hearing room dulled to an eerie quiet. In a resonant bass, Rep. Lewis Meade called the hearing to order.

The demeanor of the House committee chair differed slightly from that of Senator Layne. Where the Congresswoman spoke grandly to match the showiness of a highly publicized proceeding, the seasoned politician was laser-focused on Catherine, the central figure of the hearing.

"Ms. Rowe, we thank you for joining us today and also for not sending a subordinate," he said with folded arms. "Though we hope you'll be equally as open to answering our questions."

The audience in the chamber stifled laughter at his shrewd jab. Catherine did not flinch. There was nothing funny to her or the team seated behind her about the chairman's greeting. It was a painful reminder of Wyatt's poor performance in the previous hearing.

Rep. Meade launched into his opening statement. Kelsey braced herself for a lengthy defamation of the company.

"The evidence showing that Elemynt has prioritized profits over ethical behavior is mounting with each passing day," he said, reading from the papers before him. "The app has been used to perpetuate harassment and ignite hate, in many cases with deadly consequences. Additionally, Elemynt is allowing itself to become a tool for Balkan operatives to seed false content on the platform. This is a betrayal of the American people. Our intent today is to remedy this issue expeditiously."

The audience mumbled to themselves in agreement. They arrived at a shared conclusion that Elemynt was a nefarious company buffered by greed and ambition. Kelsey strongly hoped that Catherine would prove them wrong.

The executive scribbled notes on her legal pad while the chairman and co-chair read through their accusatory decrees.

It was no secret what Catherine would say. Her written opening statement was made available to the public the day prior, per Congressional rules. How she delivered it to the cameras was far more important than the words alone. Her character, demeanor, phrasing, and body language would be judged and dissected by millions.

Catherine launched into her remarks without hesitation.

"Chairman Meade, members of the Committee... Elemynt is a reflection of the wide variety of people who engage with it. Around the world, people with different backgrounds, languages, religions, and political beliefs contribute to the billions of posts uploaded to the app so far. We are doing and will continue to do everything we can to make sure Elemynt is the safest platform for all who use it. I thank you for the opportunity to speak today. I'm happy to answer your questions."

The committee chair dutifully acknowledged Catherine's statement to the hearing room.

The introductory formalities were over. His five minutes of questions began. Kelsey dug her fingers into her seat.

"You and representatives from your company have told us Elemynt was built with the promise of connecting the world," Congressman Meade said snidely.

"What we are witnessing instead is that Elemynt has become a tool that has made it easier to discriminate and attack others. My first question for you, Ms. Rowe... why doesn't Elemynt require people who post to use their real names or submit identification when they join? Doing so would cut down on anonymous abuse and the false stories on your app."

A question Catherine prepared for.

"That would have several unintended consequences," she said into her mic. "Vulnerable people like LGBT individuals or those who are posting from countries where freedom of speech is limited risk real danger if their identities were to be publicly tied to their accounts. As you alluded to earlier, we believe that sharing on Elemynt should be open to everyone. We will always prioritize the safety of the people on our platform."

"Except Elemynt does not have the best track record when it comes to maintaining users' privacy," the Senator scoffed.

"As an active user of Elemynt yourself and someone who's visited our campus multiple times, Congressman, you've seen firsthand the diligent work that we do," Catherine said firmly. "In fact, your wife and I were speaking just a few weeks ago and she told me of the funds she was able to raise for her charity using the app. As a people-first company, we strongly support missions like hers."

A chill fell over the room. Sarah and the spectators in the chamber reeled from the specifics of the response. Congressman Meade stumbled over his words, grasping for his next question.

Catherine sat patiently. She waited supportively for him to prepare a challenge that would actually land.

Next up to bat was Representative Neal Holmes, the Republican congressman from Arizona. He was determined not to fall victim to the same pitfalls as his bruised colleague.

"Ms. Rowe, over a billion people around the world are using your platform," he said. "But your company somehow keeps finding ways to dodge government regulation. Do you think Elemynt is above the law?"

"Elemynt currently operates under a strict set of guidelines that are well within federal laws," Catherine responded.

"That's because my colleagues in Congress have relied on tech companies to regulate themselves. We see how that's turned out. I'm asking you now....is Elemynt open to regulation?"

"Very much so," Catherine said with unwavering confidence. "We're happy to discuss it as soon as legislation is drafted by Congress."

Another collective gasp in the room dismantled whatever momentum the Congressman thought he accrued.

Catherine laid down an unexpected challenge to the committee members. Enact legislation and the company would adhere to it. Except despite their long line of questions, the lawmakers did not understand enough about Elemynt to know what they were regulating or how to go about it. It was a tech company, that much they knew. How a tech company functioned exceeded their limited understanding of the industry.

Catherine's proactive commitment made whatever the Congressman said next look like he was grasping at straws. He couldn't create rules on the spot. Catherine could, but she had no plans to aid the committee to do so.

"Thank you," Chairman Meade said. "The Representative's time is up."

The journalists in the room typed a million words per second as Catherine demolished the dreams the legislative body had of tearing her down.

Her responses were a reflection of the diligent preparation the staff did in the days prior. Questions derived from a casual read of recent news stories would not be enough to shake her. To their credit, the committee members whom she studied exhaustively tried their best.

Representative Carla Lopez. 45. Two kids. Largest campaign donors were the NRA and gas companies.

"Why is Elemynt so secretive? How is it that you know how many times I've taken a photo of my kids and yet we never get to know anything about your company?"

"Elemynt doesn't know more about you than what you post to the platform," Catherine said.

Representative Mavis Johnson-Hope from Missouri. Proponent of universal health care. Husband was a civil engineer.

"Could Elemynt make its code open to review by lawmakers or technology experts to find potential vulnerabilities?"

"Thank you for the question. Our code is proprietary information," Catherine said. "It would be equivalent to giving our business away."

Paul Sheridan. The Republican Congressman from Kansas. Loved God, country, and tax loopholes.

"Would you be open to an external audit of the company to determine whether there is any political bias in your operations?"

"Elemynt welcomes all voices," Catherine said. "As for the audit, we welcome your suggestions on how to best carry that out in a manner that meets your criteria."

Leroy Otis. The second-longest-serving Democrat on the committee. Member of the Congressional Black Caucus.

"Will Elemynt commit to diversifying your team of moderators?"

"We plan to partner with civil rights organizations to flag content to our moderators in an escalated queue," Catherine said, alluding to a system that did not exist.

"So, these groups are doing your work for you, then?"

"We see it was a partnership in which we can both learn from each other."

Catherine curbed the lawmakers' inquisition at every turn. She produced a news-ready soundbite for each issue they brought up. Question after question was met with the leadership one would expect from the highly-regarded industry executive. Catherine was infallible.

"Would you like to take a break?" the committee chair said, looking at the advancing clock. Two hours of non-stop testimony had flown by.

"I'm happy to continue," Catherine said.

"Let's do a few more then," the chair sighed.

Catherine wooed hostile lawmakers and turned skeptics into supporters. The Representatives listened while Catherine invoked the polish that Troy and Wyatt lacked. The Comms team sat proudly behind her. Sarah, who entered the hearing doubtful of its success, could not deny that they did the impossible. However, it was still too early for Kelsey to relax.

Another hour down. The committee chair piped up again.

"How about that break?" he asked exhaustedly.

"I'm fine, thank you," Catherine said.

"Well, I need one," he said. "We readjourn in thirty minutes."

Catherine didn't leave her seat. Her only movement was to accept words of early adulation from Jon and the team. The media in the gallery used the time to notify their newsrooms of Catherine's incredible performance in front of the committee.

The hum of activity in the chamber ceased at the return of chairman Meade. The hearing continued.

After several more hours of testimony, the hearing arrived at the final questioner of the day — Representative Kay Hurst of Pennsylvania. She thumbed through the notes she penned throughout the proceedings.

"Ms. Rowe, we know Elemynt has had some issues in the past. We also know that Elemynt is leading the charge in the innovation that makes this country exceptional."

Catherine nodded in agreement. The Congresswoman was expressing what Catherine would have stated herself.

"We don't want to stop Elemynt from building its business. However, we do want you to act responsibly and in the best interests of the American people."

Catherine smiled wordlessly. No need to add more to the final statement. She accomplished what she set out to do.

With a solid bang of the gavel, the committee chairman brought the hearing to a close.

"Thank you for your attendance, Ms. Rowe," he said. "We will circle back with your team with further questions we may have."

After a five-hour whirlwind of inquiry, the hearing was over. Catherine had done it. The disaster of Wyatt's performance and the horrid press cycle that haunted them were no longer a threat. The company came out of the interrogation looking better than it did before.

Catherine confidently gathered her notes, strode past the clamoring reporters, and returned to her duties as chief operating officer of one of the greatest companies in the world.

* * *

Civil rights leaders who once called for boycotts praised Catherine's commitment to evolving the platform. Celebrities who decried the actions of the company were enamored with the promises she made. Even some of the attendees at the NYC event appeared on television news to speak in favor of Elemynt. They crowed of their involvement in the resolutions Catherine proposed.

Catherine was the eloquent leader that defended the company in ways that Wyatt failed to accomplish. Furthermore, her grace under pressure was a prime example of the bold feminism in the workplace she stood for. Her excellence was a win for women everywhere.

Catherine followed up the success of the hearing with a pre-written op-ed published on The New York Times website. It served as her proclamation to the world.

"Elemynt has embraced the feedback of the people who trust us," she wrote. "We will take crucial steps to rectify issues that prevent people on the app from having the best experience possible. Our teams are already working diligently to make adjustments and set policies that we believe will increase the safety of our platform."

The evening of the hearing, Elemynt would move forward on its pre-planned party in the Dupont Circle area of D.C. Scores of government officials and noted lawmakers, including Representatives who questioned Catherine earlier in the day, would gather for open bars and petite hors d'oeuvres under extravagant displays of the Elemynt logo.

Kelsey planned to skip out on the festivities. After successfully making it through a twin set of hearings, she needed rest. She didn't have it in her to schmooze.

Kelsey was also relieved that Myntors at headquarters and Elemynt offices around the world were invigorated by the turn of events. Their once shaky morale was renewed by the words and actions of Elemynt leadership. The negative public perception was a fleeting moment that would be lost to time.

Tai's job of building internal loyalty would be infinitely easier. Her company-wide communication only needed to reiterate the shared sentiment of optimism for the future. She had Kelsey and External Comms to thank for it.

* * *

Kelsey took a moment for decompression in the way that came most natural to her. A brisk walk was in order. She wandered the green space outside the U.S. Capitol near the exit of the hearing room building.

Kelsey accepted the congratulatory texts from Jade and Daniela with sincere thank yous. Brad sent his love in the most earnest language he knew. He underscored his love and support for her from afar. Kelsey had a support system that came through for her in a big way.

To Kelsey's surprise, Jon came running up behind her on the pathway. He was brimming with pride in her and the actions of his team.

"Going for a victory lap?" he smiled.

"Taking a few breaths of fresh air," Kelsey said. "I was holding it the whole time I was in there."

"Yet again, Kelsey saves the day," he said appreciatively. "You're a real rockstar, you know that?"

"Just doing my job, I guess."

"Smart and humble. You don't see a lot of that these days."

Kelsey and Jon strolled side by side along the tree-lined National Mall. The miles-long grassy expanse was surrounded by white marble structures, large museums, and memorials to brave men and women. The landmark area was host to a myriad of renowned political protests and speeches. The inauguration of presidents, Martin Luther King Jr.'s "I Have a Dream" speech, and now just a few feet away, Catherine's historic address to Congress.

"What's next?" Kelsey asked her manager. "Should I set up media interviews for Catherine? I can also prepare a statement."

"I want you to come to Tokyo with me," Jon said.

"You want me to do what where?" Kelsey stopped in her tracks.

"I'm flying to our office in Tokyo soon. We're doing a knowledge share about Comms strategies. The goal is to use Elemynt's success in Japan as a case study for the company's expansion. I want you to be there."

"Okay, but I don't know anything about Japan. Sarah is back too so..."

"Yes, she is. However, Sarah wasn't in that room helping Catherine get on track or setting Troy up for success in the hearing. Sarah didn't steer the ship. You did."

Moving up the ladder from private conferences in Washington, D.C. to strategy meetings in Tokyo was quite a leap. Kelsey was unsure that she did so well in her efforts that an overseas trip was a fitting reward. Jon's face showed no hint of reservation.

Kelsey recognized the offer as an unparalleled chance to grow in her career. If she wanted to achieve her dreams of being head of a Fortune 500 company, she could not say no when grand opportunities presented themselves. If this was her moment to learn about the company's varied strategies for success. Kelsey would absorb invaluable lessons that she could apply to her current work and her future.

"You're our shining star," Jon reiterated. "Are you game?"

Before Kelsey knew it, the "yes" Jon sought escaped her lips. It was bookended by the broadest, most radiant smile.

"Thank you, Jon!" she said enthusiastically. "You won't regret it."

"I believe that 100 percent," he said. "We leave in two weeks. In the meantime, let's milk the positive press from this hearing for everything it's worth."

SIXTEEN

Kelsey was in awe of how easy her international travels were. Elemynt took care of the whole trip, including a first-class ticket from San Francisco to Tokyo and a three-day stay at a five-star hotel. Kelsey's suitcase was stored safely in a coat closet as soon as she entered the Tokyo office thanks to the friendly receptionist. Her laptop and personal items were by her side as was a small gift of specialty regional teas gifted to her at the front desk. The hardest decision she had to make that day was which tea to try first.

Kelsey was intent on impressing Jon with her contributions during their meetings in the city. She had much more to offer than writing blog posts and landing stories in the media. Her time at Elemynt inspired her to craft broader ideas that required interoffice collaboration. Making impact globally took elevated thinking and Kelsey was up for the challenge.

The two Americans sat side by side at the sleek conference room table across from seats that would soon be occupied by their Japanese colleagues. Kelsey took a moment to soak in the view of the impressive Tokyo Tower outside the windows. The landmark reminiscent of Paris' Eiffel Tower shot up into the cloudless afternoon sky. Surrounding the grand structure was one of the most tech-savvy cities in the world with its mile-high buildings and bustling population. Kelsey greatly looked forward to the knowledge share between the two cultures.

"I want you to use this opportunity to bring your ideas to the table," Jon said to her. "You're coming in as someone who is fairly new. We're in need of fresh perspectives."

"I'm thinking we can start with the strategies that they think would translate the best for us in the U.S.," Kelsey said. "Then we can work through together how to maximize those ideas."

"You're also looking to expand the types of media partners we work with. Make sure you ask about their game plan regarding that."

"Of course!" Kelsey smiled. "Ready when you are."

Kelsey leaped to greet her fellow Myntors when they entered the room. The smartly dressed man and woman introduced themselves as Toshiro Higa, director of communications for Elemynt Japan, and Aimi Watanabe, head of entertainment partnerships. Toshiro was the former general manager of a national television station and joined Elemynt in a role similar to Jon's focused exclusively on Japan. Aimi was an ideal fit for a Media team role. In her previous position at a high-powered PR firm based in Kyoto, she worked directly with the country's top celebrities and influencers.

"Tokyo e youkoso!" Toshiro greeted them both. "Welcome to Tokyo."

"Arigatou gozaimasu!" Kelsey replied confidently.

"Woah ho!" Jon exclaimed. "Speaking Japanese, are we?"

"A little bit," Kelsey smiled graciously.

The ease of the trip gave Kelsey a short time to learn basic Japanese phrases. She planned to drop a few here and there to bridge the cultural exchange.

Toshiro and Aimi smiled in appreciation of her interest in their culture. As soon the gathering of Myntors was comfortably seated, Jon delved into the purpose of their meeting.

"We are one of the fastest-growing countries on Elemynt," Toshiro said in response to Jon's inquiries. "Fifty million daily active people in Japan. The app is a big success in the country. This is with us having less staff and engineers than you do in HQ."

"That's why we're here," Jon replied. "We want to bring some of those strategies back to the States. Tell us. How are you doing it?"

"Japanese prefer to be anonymous on the internet," Toshiro explained. "This is due to mostly following friends instead of people they do not know. Accounts in Japan, in general, have smaller follower numbers, but spend more time on the app."

"You're seeing more growth because people have fewer followers?" Jon asked skeptically.

"Americans focus more on celebrity culture," Toshiro said.

"People in Japan prefer to show off their hobbies and interests," Aimi added. "Posting meals is very popular as is sharing photos of the city around them wherever they are."

"Yes, it is the personal touch that makes their followers most engaged," Toshiro said.

Kelsey was fascinated listening to details of the stark differences between Japanese and American users. People in the U.S. tended to aim for a high number of followers. Aspiring to become influencers or online celebrities like the people they followed was pretty common. Not allowing strangers to follow their accounts was the preference of a small portion of the stateside users but certainly not the majority.

"We launched a successful program last year that encourages people to share what they love personally," Aimi said. "We partnered with popular individuals to go on walking tours of their cities to take photos and share them on the app. The series inspired other people to do the same."

"You show users that there are communities with similar interests on the platform," Jon cut her off.

"We're doing that too, yes," she said.

Kelsey jumped into the fast-paced conversation. "Aimi, how do you see us duplicating these programs in America?"

Jon did not give his colleague a chance to respond. "Japan may be the fastest-growing country on the app, but America has more people using it than you all do."

Toshiro cut Jon off in turn. "Yes, but your teams put more resources into attracting celebrities to the platform or so I'm told."

"You heard that correctly. We find it's a winning strategy for us."

The conversation took a weird turn. It seemed to Kelsey as if Jon was working overtime to prove that he was more knowledgeable about Elemynt's history of public outreach than Toshiro or Aimi. Toshiro drew from his perspective as one of the rising managers within the company to cut down Jon's staunch assertions. The battle of one-upmanship between the two men in the room left Aimi and Kelsey with no entry point into the conversation.

Aimi remained pert in her chair waiting for her opportunity to speak. More time passed and she barely got a word in. Neither of her male colleagues allowed her the space to vocalize her thoughts.

As the conversation went on without her, Kelsey found herself staring out the window at the Japanese skyline. She tried to keep from being distracted. However, not being acknowledged made her mind wander. Jade sent her a list of cool places she could visit while in Tokyo. Kelsey would travel around the city in her downtime to check them out for herself.

"You have problems in America with your growth currently," Toshiro said with a heightened tone. "That *is* why you're here?"

"With our current needs, our time would be better spent further targeting high profile influencers," Jon insisted. "We'll take your thoughts into consideration."

The meeting continued with much of the same. Jon and Toshiro going back and forth while giving Aimi and Kelsey little time to speak.

The hour-long exchange surprisingly ended in robust, agreeable handshakes between the two men. It was as if the head to head create mutual respect between them. They congratulated each other with hearty smiles on their individual triumphs in their markets. The congeniality was a 180-degree turn that left Kelsey bewildered.

Kelsey and Jon were thankfully scheduled for more meetings over the next few days in the Tokyo office. Her first — the one that should have been her first foray into global brand-building — was less about useful strategies for growth and more an hour-long lesson on cross-country diplomacy.

Toshiro genially insisted the group conclude the day's events by journeying to a bar. A "kyabakura" he called it.

"I know the best one," Toshiro said. "Everyone will enjoy."

"We'll toast to our time in Japan," Jon smiled.

Aimi hurriedly excused herself from the plans for the evening. "I have work in the office I need to complete by the end of the day," she said.

"No worries, I'll be there," Kelsey said.

Kelsey would certainly join the team for the outside of the office gathering, though she didn't plan to drink. She would uphold her personal rule about not consuming alcohol during work-related events. However, she wouldn't miss the opportunity for a bonding moment with her colleagues. If she wanted to break through to international markets as Jon did, she needed to be a part of the conversation.

* * *

As dusk turned to night, the Myntors, including a few additional colleagues, arrived by car at the lively Kabukicho district in Tokyo. The area dazzled visitors with flashing neon signs and brightly-lit billboards advertising clubs, restaurants, and a variety of enticing businesses. The multi-colored, amusement park-like neighborhood rivaled the showiness of Las Vegas back in the States. The wide roads were filled with energized night owls deciding where to end their night with a bang. Kelsey could not begin to translate the many, many glowing Japanese characters splashed across the signs.

The further the crew ventured deeper into the wall-to-wall light show, the nature of the streets they cruised began to shift. Posters of clusters of women with doe eyes and teased auburn hair lined the buildings' walls. Oversized displays of Japanese women in bathing suits or lingerie showcased their ample talents. Kelsey struggled to comprehend their proximity to rows of massage parlors and multi-story sex shops.

Unable to digest what was happening, Kelsey's confusion was overshadowed by a desire to get to their destination as soon as possible. Kelsey looked around at the small group of her Elemynt colleagues. She was the only woman.

Toshiro pointed excitedly to their destination — what looked to be a regular bar with thankfully no trace of the adult-themed visuals they encountered along the way. The small crew shuffled through a narrow hallway lined with plum-colored velvet wallpaper. A spiky-haired man in a loose-fitting suit welcomed them into the club with warm greetings in lightning-fast Japanese. From what Kelsey could tell, the man who she assumed was the club manager had met Toshiro and his fellow office workers several times before.

"My friends Jon and Kelsey," Toshiro said, gesturing toward his American guests.

The unidentified man pointed at Kelsey, chattering in more words that she didn't understand. Her co-workers smiled and shook their heads in amusement. He belly laughed in response.

"Thank you for visiting," he said to her. "We hope you enjoy your evening."

Kelsey hoped so as well.

The huge club was dominated by a spread of candle-lit leather booths occupied by Japanese businessmen, boisterous Americans, and a slew of tittering women in garish evening wear. Above the crowds were chandeliers that glinted under a decadent purple and blue lighting system. Bouts of laughter emerged from the various corners of the room, punctuated by the giggling of female attendees.

Kelsey gasped involuntarily at a suddenly apparent fact. She was the only woman in the club who was not employed there.

They sat in their booth. A hostess clad in a figure-hugging dress dotted with one too many rhinestones handed the Myntors a menu. Instead of food, there were photos of doll-like women, each with a number beside it. Jon, Toshiro, and crew laughed amongst themselves pointing and selecting from the line-up provided for them.

Kelsey may have been nervous before but now her heart in her throat. She tried to control herself from freaking out. She told herself she had to be confused. She was misunderstanding the culture. This was a perfectly normal, after-work bar.

After a time, he young women that corresponded with the photos chosen by her colleagues swayed toward the group. They settled into the seats next to their patrons and, for a few, directly into their laps. Kelsey noticed that the startling behavior was not unique to their area of the room. Most of the roaring businessmen in neighboring booths appeared to be veterans of the club entertaining clients in their first experience at a kyabakura. To her surprise, it was evidently not Jon's.

Jon handed the petite woman he selected his Elemynt corporate card. It was swiftly replaced by cocktails prepared by their new female friends.

Kelsey was overcome with abrupt panic. This was by no means a regular bar. From the seediness of the activity around her, she wasn't sure it was even a bar at all. The laughter of corporate men downing expensive whiskeys in the company of busty young women made Kelsey's skin crawl. The team was supposed to be having after-work drinks...not whatever this was.

The purpose of the club became frighteningly clear to Kelsey. The male patrons paid significant amounts of money for the women to talk and drink with them. In exchange, the eager hostesses made their male clients feel special all night long. It didn't take much work. Young, cute girls who offered their devoted attention, laughed at every joke...the men were in liquor-fueled ecstasy.

"This is an important occasion!" Jon announced to the booth. "A landmark moment for Elemynt's continued expansion."

He motioned for the hostess to fetch a bottle of high-end sake. The female companions gladly filled each man's glass while pouring tiny sips for themselves. Kelsey passed on the offer of alcohol. Not in this lifetime and definitely not in this place.

"A toast to a new era of Elemynt," Jon crowed.

"Kanpai!" everyone except Kelsey exclaimed.

Jon finished his glass. The hostess quickly refilled it. Jon ordered the crew to take shots. The girls clapped and laughed in merriment.

Kelsey had no doubts that Jon had been to the kyabakura before. He knew everything about what a visit to the den of lust entailed and yet he invited Kelsey to come along. For the life of her, Kelsey could not understand why he would such a thing. First of all, she didn't want attention from other women. This was far from a professional environment. Her male counterparts talked jovially about their marital affairs and previous escapades in nearby massage parlors. They traded comments about how Elemynt could save money by having the female Myntors fulfill similarly entertaining roles at the office. The display of machismo was revolting.

Jon was so wrapped up in the chauvinistic spectacle that he didn't notice that Kelsey was sitting motionless by his side. She summoned enough nerve to slowly shift away from him in the booth. He sensed her movement. Jon's red-knuckled hand pushed a glass of dark liquor in her face.

"It's a team outing," Jon said over the increasingly rowdy conversation. "Drinks are on the company."

Kelsey refused the generous offering. "Can't we go to a regular bar? Does it have to be…" she gestured at the women giggling in the laps of their suitors. "… this?"

"It's how they do business here," Jon said matter-of-factly.

"Is that right?" she retorted.

Exactly what kind of business required a night of lascivious, hedonistic debauchery, Kelsey did not know. Why the outing was being funded by Elemynt also escaped Kelsey's understanding. The reason Kelsey and her boss were in the country was for a series of work conversations. Ones that in hindsight could have been conducted over video conference.

Kelsey needed to get out of there fast. She came along for a networking opportunity. The only people being networked were the obnoxiously attentive girls. She urgently searched for a way to slip out of the booth in a manner that wouldn't offend her co-workers. The men would be too distracted by their sexy playthings to notice her anyway.

"Stick around for a minute," Jon grinned as he raised his glass. "Are you a team player or not?"

Kelsey checked the time on her work phone. 10 p.m. 5 a.m. in California. She fought against her instincts and resolved to give the club another fifteen minutes. That would be enough for Jon and more than enough for her. She could say she stayed and didn't cause a fuss and they could go about their meetings in the morning.

Kelsey sipped room temperature water fighting back her burning desire to leave. She watched with disdain as the cavalcade of hostesses sang American karaoke hits with their drunken patrons. Time ticked away excruciatingly slowly.

Kelsey felt Jon inching his way across the booth in her direction. He moved uncomfortably closer. Before she knew it, he was practically on top of her.

That was it. It was time to leave.

Jon put his arms around his subordinate, essentially blocking her exit. He pulled her back towards him. The repugnant smell of whiskey on his breath stung Kelsey's nostrils.

"You know since I met you…" he slurred. "I sensed there was a real connection between us. You feel it too?"

"No!" she sputtered in a frightened whisper. "Jon, please stop!"

"This is a company built on trust," he breathed in her ear. "Can I trust you?"

Jon slowly moved one arm toward her bare leg. The other arm draped over her left shoulder, strikingly close to her breast.

"Jon, I really have to go," she attempted to brush him away.

"I gave you everything you wanted," Jon said. "What do I get in return?"

Kelsey shivered from the assault of Jon's revolting touch. She didn't cry out for fear of causing a scene. However, her manager's hands were in places they had no business being. Kelsey's heart rate skyrocketed as she struggled to move out of his reach. She had done nothing to welcome his advances. His judgment was clouded by rounds of alcohol. The manhandling of her body persisted the more she angled to get away.

"You look so sexy," Jon said as he leaned in to kiss her.

"I said stop!" she yelled loud enough for everyone in the booth to hear.

"Fuck you, cunt," he said as he forcefully yanked her closer. "What are you on your period or something?"

Kelsey bolted out of her seat in front of an appalled audience of hostesses and Myntors. She grabbed for her oversized purse which remained in the cursed booth. Jon's last-ditch effort to yank her arm was foiled by a hurried spin toward the exit door. Kelsey walked backward down the velvet front hallway to ensure that Jon or his other drunk teammates weren't following her. The last image she saw of her manager was him polishing off the remaining whiskey in his possession. It was quickly refilled.

Kelsey ran panicked into the streets, further assaulted by the blinding lights of the district. She felt violated. Unclean. Enraged that a man she valued as a colleague saw her as an object of his lustful desire. The combined onslaught of frustration, horror, and outright shock led her to an urgent desire to flee her surroundings. She needed to get out of the city. Out of Japan. She needed to leave the horror show as soon as possible, meetings be damned.

Kelsey waved down the first taxi she saw and tumbled into the backseat.

"Haneda Airport, please!" she said, slamming the car door shut.

As the car sped off, Kelsey attempted to rationalize Jon's lewd behavior. She couldn't as much as she tried. Alcohol or not, the vile act was irredeemable. He assaulted his employee. He violated her trust. Jon was a pig and she refused to be subjected to his unconscionable behavior.

The blur of foreign writing whizzing past the windows reinforced to Kelsey that she needed to get out of the area. She would pay for the cost of the first flight back to California herself. She had her purse with her passport. That's all she needed to make her escape from Jon's grasp. There was nothing in her suitcase in the coat closet at the office that couldn't be replaced. Whatever it took to get her away from the horrible nightmare she found herself embroiled in.

* * *

Every interaction with Jon reminded Kelsey of the atrocious night in Tokyo. Being in the same space as him — either physically or digitally — caused her to replay in her mind the assault that devastated their working relationship and her sanity. She couldn't help but feel his vulgar touch each time she was in his presence. Despite her best efforts, self-pep talks and locking herself away in the solitude of her apartment, Kelsey was unable to force away the painful memories she grappled with constantly.

What troubled Kelsey greatly was that in the time following the incident, Jon hadn't said a word to her about his action. She received no apology or sign of regret or even an acknowledgment of its occurrence. No communication in person or in an email or eChat, which, of course, would have incriminated him. Her manager carried on as if nothing happened. Tokyo was just another work trip for him. The horror that tore apart her focus wasn't worth a second thought to him.

For weeks, Kelsey trained herself on how to avoid Jon. If he was in a room with her, she would focus on her laptop or pretend to write detailed notes in a notebook. If he dialed into a video call and Kelsey was made to watch him on the screen, she trained her eyeline just above or below the TV so she wouldn't have to stare directly into the eyes of the man who violated her trust.

Jon was the boss and Kelsey was his employee. An inescapable fact. However, she would not let Jon's actions drive her out of the company she loved.

Kelsey didn't intend for one night to have such a drastic impact on her life, but the sad reality was that it did. She felt herself slipping away. She didn't speak to others unless they initiated the conversation first. Kelsey posted to Elemynt less frequently and rarely left her apartment outside of required work hours. Family, friends, and colleagues alike assumed the reduced communication was because she was busy with her duties for Elemynt. This was mostly true. Kelsey filled every second of her life with work to keep the turmoil from invading her headspace. If she sat still for too long, the run of traumatic events she endured since moving to Silicon Valley — from the night in Tokyo to the hearings to the onslaught of press surrounding the breach — would suffocate her with anxiety.

* * *

Another day, another endless string of meetings, just like Kelsey preferred it. After the close of one, she hustled to the next, giving only the bare minimum head nod or weak smile to the fellow Myntors she encountered along the way.

"Kelsey! Hold on, wait!" she heard Jade exclaim.

Her friend was practically chasing her down the pathway with Daniela following closely behind her.

Kelsey wanted to run in the other direction. The inquisition heading her way could be avoided with a swift close of a conference room door. Instead, she froze. A conversation with Jade and Daniela after weeks of shunning their communication was inevitable.

"How'd you know where I was?" Kelsey sighed.

"We checked your calendar," Daniela locked eyes with her. "It was the only meeting not marked as private."

Kelsey inadvertently missed adding the tag to hide her location. She silently cursed to herself.

Daniela and Jade pulled their sullen colleague into a vacant meeting room. They shut the door firmly behind them. It was one of the rare conference spaces on campus with partially opaque glass walls. They were insulated from the watchful eyes of nearby coworkers. Tiny wins.

"Kelsey, you look like hell," Daniela sat on the table.

"Thanks?" Kelsey said, lowering her head. "I appreciate the compliment."

"It's an observation," Daniela said tenderly. "I'm telling you this because we're worried about you."

"What she's trying to say is you're not looking like your usual self," Jade chimed in. "We haven't seen you in forever. If something's wrong, you can tell us."

"It's nothing!" Kelsey yelled before regaining her composure. "Sorry. It's nothing."

Jade and Daniela looked at each other stunned that their mild-mannered friend would raise her voice at them. Kelsey appreciated that they didn't take the unplanned burst of emotion personally. The two recognized that she wasn't ready to share details of her current state of mind. Daniela and Kelsey managed to work through the aftermath of the hearing. However, Tokyo threw a wrench into their time spent reconnecting.

"How about some fresh air?" Daniela said perkily. "Want to take a field trip to the juice bar?"

"Not today," Kelsey said as she meandered aimlessly around the room.

Jade stepped in front of Kelsey to block her unending path. "Let's go all out. How about a spa day? Us three girls getting manicures and massages…"

Kelsey lifted her head long enough to face her friends with tearful eyes. "I appreciate you caring about me. I just need time to myself right now."

Daniela opened her mouth in protest but ultimately held her tongue. She wanted to protect Kelsey from whatever was troubling her. Daniela acknowledged that if it was personal space that she desired, they would give it to her.

Kelsey's duo of friends solemnly made their way toward the glass door. Kelsey shut her eyes and sat in one of the meeting room's deep chairs. There was nothing the two could say to make her want to recount details of the moment that continued to haunt her.

Daniela allowed Jade to step out of the room but hovered just short of her own departure. "Kelsey, I'm going to text you something. Promise you'll read it?"

Kelsey nodded while keeping her head down.

"Okay, girl," Daniela said as she finally exited. "Know that we love you."

Kelsey would not make it to her next meeting. She sat in the empty room, laptop and phone in hand, waiting for her body to guide her to her next move. With nothing else to do but breathe, Kelsey read the text from Daniela.

It was a name. "Dr. Jill Klein."

* * *

Kelsey stood motionless outside the therapist's office. She stared at the gold nameplate on the closed door. It took her weeks to muster up the nerve to make the appointment.

Kelsey never thought of herself as the type of person who needed therapy. She wasn't losing her mind, just drained, she told herself. It was true her anxiety had climbed to astronomical heights. But it wasn't a situation she couldn't pull through on her own. As time went on, Kelsey gave in to the rising feeling that she couldn't mend her fractured life by herself.

Before Kelsey could turn the knob, the door gently opened in front of her.

"I thought that might be you," the therapist said. "I'm Dr. Jill. Come on in."

The soft-spoken woman with gray strands of wisdom streaked through her curly black hair gestured for Kelsey to join her inside. The small office wasn't the padded-walled insane asylum Kelsey imagined it would be. A stream of sunshine poured into the tall windows of the tranquil space. It overlooked an adjacent floral garden. Inside, leafy green plants resided next to bookshelves filled with tomes on psychiatry and self-help.

Degrees from UC Berkeley and Northwestern University were displayed proudly on the wall near Dr. Jill's armchair. The brown leather couch that welcomed Kelsey's presence was somehow both rich in comfort while providing firm support.

Dr. Jill sat across from Kelsey. She was far enough to not be intrusive but close enough to engage with her guest's expressions.

"I understand this is your first time going to therapy?" she said, looking at her notes.

"My friends thought I should come," Kelsey said.

"Your friends care about you." Dr. Jill replied in a soothing voice. "Let's start easy then. How are you?

Kelsey's mouth went dry. A simple, yet loaded question. Kelsey could say that she was under more stress than she ever imagined possible. Routine responsibilities at work were becoming more arduous tasks. She was both terrified by and couldn't tear herself away from her email. She didn't know what terrible threat would arise from each message. She was exhausted. She ate too much. She shut herself out from the world. Kelsey blurted it all out at once in what felt like a confused jumble of words.

"I'm so freaking tired," Kelsey wept softly.

Dr. Jill allowed her the space to cry out her repressed emotion. She spoke again when the flow of Kelsey's tears slowed.

"Sounds like there's some anxiety there," she said softly. "What do you think you need right now to release that stress that has a hold on you?"

Kelsey stared at the ceiling, considering her words. "I want my life to be as perfect as I thought it would be when I first started the job."

"There's no such thing as a perfect life," the doctor said sympathetically. "Why isn't your job meeting your expectations?"

Kelsey recounted the mounting stresses caused by a string of unfortunate events at Elemynt. However, she stopped short of telling Dr. Jill about Tokyo. She did not want to relive that night.

Kelsey sensed the therapist knew she was holding back on sharing a traumatic incident at the center of her anxiety. Thankfully, she didn't force the issue.

"Women are taught to bottle up our pain," Dr. Jill said reassuringly. "Showing emotion is sometimes seen as a sign of weakness. I believe it's our emotional intelligence that makes us exceptional. Kelsey, when's the last time you took a vacation?"

The burdened Myntor struggled to remember.

"Before I started at Elemynt," Kelsey said.

"Have you considered taking time off for a few days? It may help you release some of the built-up negative energy you're experiencing."

Kelsey shifted her weight on the couch. "I don't really have time to do that. They need me at work."

"You're no good to anyone if you're not good to yourself," Dr. Jill said, clasping her hands. "If you ignore the burnout, you are going to leave your job. And it doesn't sound like that's what you want to do."

"Not at all," Kelsey sniffled. "It's the kind of position I always wanted. I worked so hard for it."

"Taking care of your mental health requires effort too. A little bit of commitment to your own well-being can go a long way."

Kelsey slumped on the couch at the thought of adding one more task to her plate.

"I'm sorry. I…. just don't have the time right now," she said.

"I understand," Dr. Jill said. "What about hobbies? How did you spend time outside of work before you started at Elemynt?"

"I ran. I trained for marathons. I love spin class."

"That's a great way to go!" the doctor smiled. "Think about how you can do those things more often. Even if it's small breaks now and then, doing the activities you love can restore your sense of peace."

Kelsey wasn't buying it. "By the time I get home, I don't want to do any of that."

"Here's what I'd like you to try," Dr. Jill leaned forward. "Before you step through your front door, I want you to pause. Breathe. Say to yourself 'I'm choosing to leave the problems from work outside.' Separate yourself from that negative energy. Don't bring it into your home with you."

Kelsey spent the rest of the appointment with Dr. Jill learning meditation techniques that would help relieve her anxiety. Together, they arrived at a mantra for Kelsey to employ: "I choose happiness."

After employing the breathing exercises and chanting and whatnot, Kelsey's mind should have been clear. The thoughts of work that ratcheted up her stress levels competed for her attention. Wallowing in the depression was much easier. Fighting it was infinitely harder.

An hour in the room away from the world and her time was up.

"You have the power, Kelsey," Dr. Jill said encouragingly. "Be as patient with yourself as possible. We have to accept that change won't happen overnight. But it will happen."

Kelsey's first time in therapy and her emotions were not resolved. Granted, it was only one session, but Kelsey had the highest hopes that she would emerge with a miracle cure.

What the doctor shared should have been enough to motivate her to soldier on. However, Kelsey was so beaten down by the events of her employment that she didn't feel like the strong woman she once was. Kelsey desperately wanted to be that woman again.

"When you want to set your next appointment, you can call my number anytime," Dr. Jill said.

"I don't know what my work schedule coming up is going to be," Kelsey sighed.

"And that's okay," she offered a smile. "If you need to talk before you come in, feel free to give me a ring."

"Thank you for listening."

"That's what I'm here for," the therapist said. "Remember what we talked about today. We can see how you're feeling next time we meet."

The appointment was over and Kelsey was drained. She was sent back into the world to face it alone.

* * *

Sarah pulled Kelsey into a conference room built for two. An unannounced tête-à-tête between the team members could only mean one thing — Sarah noticed how much her disposition at work had slipped for the worst. She had been away for weeks and noticed the distinct difference between the bubbly Kelsey who she left behind and the drained phantom who she worked alongside.

Kelsey was by no means slacking in her responsibilities. She sent emails and did press calls and landed interviews like she was supposed to. But her downtrodden demeanor reflected that she wasn't fully engaged.

For one, Kelsey was rarely at her desk. She preferred to work in private where she wasn't under the watchful eye of an open office. Isolating herself was the only way she could get her work done. It wasn't meant to be a long-term thing, but neither was her distress.

Sarah regarded Kelsey with the kindness of a longtime friend. "If something's going on, you have to let me know how I can help. I can take a few of the press calls off your plate or fill in for you in meetings. Whatever it is you think you need, let me be here for you."

"It's just…" Kelsey sighed heavily. "This guy at Elemynt… did something inappropriate. He got handsy and I was uncomfortable…"

"You know what you have to do right?" Sarah held her hand. "Go see HR. They can take care of it for you."

"I don't want to make a big deal out of it," Kelsey said nervously.

Kelsey found herself downplaying the severity of Jon's actions. She also had no intention of telling Sarah that Jon was the perpetrator. Disrupting the team with her confession would exacerbate the problem.

"At least let them know," Sarah said reassuringly. "You can file a report anonymously if you want."

"You think I should?"

"If you don't want to keep letting whatever this guy did keep you down, then yeah. Of course. I hate seeing you upset like this. Kelsey, you're a fantastic Myntor who does amazing work. You deserve better."

Sarah offered Kelsey a tissue with which she wiped away her falling tears.

Carrying the burden of Jon's indiscretion weighed down every aspect of Kelsey's life. It was no way to go about her days. Kelsey wanted to do the work. She wanted to be happy again. Keeping the secret inside was hurting her more than it was hurting him. Her next move was obvious. It was time to talk.

* * *

Kelsey ventured across campus toward the human resources office. She walked the least trafficked paths possible so as not to be seen. She intertwined her hands together to keep them from trembling. Her earlier email to HR was met with a swift response from an HRBP — her human resources business partner. The insistence of the friendly liaison that they talk the same day had Kelsey on edge.

Kelsey was frightened that in being honest about the encounter in Tokyo that her motives would be open to dissection. She had no idea what questions they would ask or what the punishment for Jon would be. HR might ask her why she waited so long to notify someone. She was panic-stricken that the lapse of time would make her claim less believable. Kelsey wasn't sure if she'd be seen as a sympathetic cause in need of support or, conversely, an employee with an ax to grind.

She stopped in her tracks. There was still time to turn around. Maybe it wasn't a big enough deal to bring HR into it.

Kelsey surveyed the majesty of the Elemynt campus. The place that brought out the best in its employees. She would not allow herself to be run out of the most incredible job of her life. If Jon was getting in the way of Kelsey's ability to carry out her performance, he should be the one to deal with the consequences. No career was worth jeopardizing because of the actions of one man.

The human resources conference room at Elemynt was the same as the others at HQ with one notable exception. There was no video conferencing system in sight. No TVs and no phone.

Kelsey was alone with her HR business partner, Linda Minotti, a sandy-haired older woman outfitted in an oversized Elemynt sweatshirt. In front of her was a yellow legal pad. Kelsey's name was written at the top in block letters. The rest of the pages looked to be empty. Linda's job was to listen.

Kelsey mustered up the courage to have the conversation she came there for. With labored words, she recounted the details of the ordeal in Tokyo. She described how Jon encouraged her to go to the club and how he touched her without permission. She spoke of her rebuke of his advances and his resulting physical assault.

Kelsey was steadfast as she spoke. She didn't want emotion to distract from the severity of Jon's actions.

Linda listened intently, nodding occasionally. After a while, Kelsey noticed the woman across from her hadn't written anything on her notepad. Kelsey paused. She was expecting some kind of feedback about what she shared.

Linda set the notepad to the side. "Miss Pace, we reached out to your manager after we received your email. Jon says that you were the one cozying up to him at your team outing. When he rejected your advances, you ran out of the room and didn't return."

"That's not what happened!" Kelsey protested. "He grabbed me!"

"Were you drinking that night?" Linda asked in an accusatory tone.

"I don't drink," Kelsey said flatly. "I only had one and that's because Jon was pressuring me to do it."

"So, you do drink."

"Not in work situations, no. I'm telling you it was Jon who was forcing me to have one!"

Linda began to scribble a series of notes on her pad, leaving Kelsey to wonder what she was writing. The response or lack thereof was strange and increasingly uncomfortable.

Linda looked up again, this time with a pointed stare.

"You are aware that relationships between managers and employees are prohibited at Elemynt," she said sharply.

"No, I didn't but I—"

"You should think about cutting back on attending non-work functions with your colleagues."

"I told you Jon touched *me!*" Kelsey yelled out in frustration. "He forced himself on me! Why is that so hard to understand?"

Elemynt's HR representative, who was supposed to be on Kelsey's side, was calling her a liar because Jon said that she was. That was all it took for them to take up his side. There was no recourse for Kelsey. It was her word against his and because he made up this story about it being a work outing and that she was just a drunk slut, he was innocent and she was an employee out to sleep with her boss. The wall she had to put up between herself and her hurt so she could communicate like a reasonable person came crashing down. The will she had to muster to go through with the meeting in the first place was huge and the result was that she was devastated all over again, probably more than before. Kelsey burst into uncontrollable tears.

Linda showed no signs of empathy.

"Kelsey, you're letting your emotions get the best of you," she said. "We value passion at Elemynt. But you can't let that passion overwhelm your decision-making. You're a high performer at the peak of your career. Don't let one indiscretion on your part ruin that."

Kelsey was astonished at Linda's inference. She couldn't tell if the woman was trying to fire her or what, but she was insinuating as much. The HR rep made her intentions abundantly clear. The company was protecting Jon and, in doing so, protecting itself. Kelsey cursed to herself for not foreseeing that might be the case.

In the span of her time at Elemynt, Kelsey's role was to cover up the company's indiscretions. She made problems go away. Now she was the problem. Her accusation was a thorn in the company's side.

"You can understand how I'm trying to help you?" Linda said with faux compassion. "You don't want to be seen as not being a team player, right?"

It was time to leave. HR was not on Kelsey's side and she would not waste another breath on them.

Kelsey reached to slam the glass door behind her as she exited. It was air-cushioned. The door let out a barely audible hiss as it closed softly behind her.

Kelsey walked the building's halls in distress, unsure of where she was headed or why. HR didn't care about her horrifying experience or that her manager, a sicko who should have been fired immediately, might harass other women in the future. They plotted out ways to take her down before she set foot in the room. The more Kelsey opened up, the more ammo she'd give the company to use against her. They would call her a liar no matter what she said.

Lost in thought, Kelsey found herself pacing toward Catherine's office. The second in command at the company had always stuck up for her. She believed in Kelsey from the start. She desperately needed whatever support Catherine could offer. If there was anyone who could convince HR to take Kelsey's claims seriously, it was her.

Catherine's executive assistant Andrew sat guard in a desk near the entry to her office. He smiled when Kelsey approached.

"I need to talk to Catherine," Kelsey said.

"She's busy right now," Andrew replied. "Do you want to leave a message?"

"Is she in a meeting? I can't..." Kelsey stammered. "Please. Tell her it's important."

A few back and forth messages on eChat between boss and assistant and Kelsey was allowed inside. She entered the office to find Catherine methodically poring over her laptop and stacks of financial documents. The coming IPO kept most of the Dream Team busy for weeks on end. There was much more work to do to ensure the success of Elemynt's defining moment.

Kelsey was surprised by the extraordinary amount of physical paperwork gathered in neat stacks around Catherine's office, an odd move for the head of a technology company. In between the collections of memos and reports were several laptops and phones. The COO moved deliberately around the room, seemingly knowing what each item represented, what needed attention when, and the role it played in the progress of her day.

"What is it now?" Catherine asked at the sight of Kelsey. "Tell me it's nothing to do with privacy or Latinos or..."

"Jon assaulted me on a work trip," Kelsey blurted out. "I just reported it to HR and they're treating me like a crazy person."

Kelsey again described his unwanted advances, this time to a woman who she knew would understand her pain. Kelsey desperately wanted it to be the last time she had to relive the details of the fateful evening.

Catherine stood silent. Processing. After a brief moment, her lips parted to speak.

"What I'm hearing is you would no longer like to work on the Comms team?" Catherine said.

Kelsey was taken aback. "That's not what I'm saying. Jon is the one—"

"You want to transfer to another department at Elemynt then."

Kelsey was startled by the suggestion. There was no other team she could move to that wouldn't be a demotion for her. She also had no plans to leave one of the world's most influential companies for reasons that were not her fault. Also, Catherine made no mention of Jon's misdeeds. Kelsey was wracked with confusion at her idol's response. She hoped that she was simply misunderstanding what Catherine was saying.

"If I were you, I'd consider moving past this," Catherine said, steadily walking toward her. "Or...if you go public with your little story you will always be the girl who wrongfully accused one of the most respected men in tech of something that is ultimately insignificant. Do you think you'll get a new job after that? And you can forget about a recommendation."

Kelsey's face ran red with anger. "I'm coming to you as a woman... what happened to supporting each other?"

"I see you're being ungrateful," Catherine said. "We have supported you by keeping you in this role."

"So, I can keep getting trashed by the men around me? I'm supposed to keep going and be a good woman who keeps quiet at the job? Isn't that what you've always fought against?"

"I am standing up for a company that is changing people's lives for the better," Catherine said, slowly approaching Kelsey until she was within breathing distance of her face. "Whether you want to get with the program or not, that's your business. But do not tell me how to run mine."

Catherine grimaced at Kelsey, daring the employee to challenge her. Kelsey, helpless and slightly frightened, made no moves against her aggressor. There was no telling what Catherine would do.

A buzz from Catherine's desk phone sliced through the unsettling encounter.

"Catherine, you have an incoming call from the Securities and Exchange Commission," the voice of her assistant said.

"I have to take this," the executive turned away. "I trust you'll make the right decision."

Catherine commenced her call as if Kelsey was not still in the room pleading for her sympathy. She would receive none.

Kelsey retreated wordlessly into the labyrinth of open desks outside the office door. The hurt she felt inside was manifesting into physical pain. For months, Kelsey fought with every part of her being for the company she adored. She constantly put Elemynt's best interests before her own. In the end, there was nothing to show for it other than a scathing rebuke from Catherine and the idle condemnation from HR. Kelsey cursed herself for not seeing the response coming. Catherine did what she always did best. Stick up for the business at any cost.

It was right there in her book. "Boss Lady" Rule #11: "Protect what's important to you." Or Rule #6: "You don't have to be well-liked to be successful."

Catherine followed through on her guidelines for thriving in the workplace at

Kelsey's expense, leaving her subordinate to fend for herself. She was alone with no one else in power to turn to.

Kelsey's phone rang sharply. The screen displayed an unknown number with a Palo Alto area code. Her first thought was that Catherine was calling back to apologize. She was very wrong. The cold voice of Linda from HR was on the line.

"We'd like to offer you two choices," Linda said. "One: stay and work it out with your manager."

"And what's the second option?" Kelsey grumbled.

"We are willing to offer you severance equal to one month of your base salary. Your health coverage will be extended for that one-month period and we will also waive the relocation fees that you owe because you were at the company for under a year. You'll also forfeit any stock units you've accrued. You have one hour to take the offer, or it will be revoked."

Kelsey mashed the end button on her phone in disgust.

The result of her honesty...stepping up and doing the right thing... was a series of attacks on her livelihood. Elemynt was going out of its way to protect one of their own. She was a fool to ever reach out to Catherine or HR thinking they would aid her in her plight. Kelsey was so enraged that it took everything within her not to let out a fierce scream that would shake the halls of the building.

Kelsey raced to the nearest nap room where she could cry her eyes out without her colleagues watching. Outside of the solitary space was a company that broke her down consistently, over and over again and she let them do it. She made extraordinary sacrifices for her job that had repercussions in every area of her life. And yet the moment she asked for support in return, the alleged tramp was shut out and demonized. Kelsey didn't have the faintest idea of what she should do next. For the time being, she would continue barricading herself behind the door to cry alone.

Kelsey's phone rang again. She sorely regretted not turning it off after the last call. The name on the screen shook Kelsey to her core. Jon.

"We're doing PRAs this afternoon," he said in her ear. "I'm putting time on your calendar. Be there."

The call ended with no chance for her to respond. Seconds later, a calendar alert came through.

* * *

Kelsey sat across from Jon in the obscenely well-lit conference room. A clear glass wall separated them from passersby. The anticipation of what he might say ate away at her. They hadn't been as physically near each other since Tokyo. She had no choice but to look directly at him.

Jon's expression was for the most part blank except for subtle hints of the smugness she'd come to associate with him. They sat quietly for brief seconds that felt like an eternity. Jon's eyes bored into hers. Kelsey did not flinch. She wouldn't give him the satisfaction.

"Thanks for coming," Jon said. "You're familiar with how performance reviews work?"

"I am," Kelsey said curtly.

"How do you think you're doing?"

Weeks ago, in preparation for the process, Jon asked Kelsey to solicit feedback from three colleagues and to write "self-feedback" grading her own work. Kelsey wrote a concise recollection of her accomplishments, the hardships, and the triumphs in the previous six months. What worked and what didn't. Kelsey performed well, all things considered. She landed stories about Elemynt in top national publications and earned media in many more. She received glowing reviews from her peers and praise from Troy himself.

Kelsey was given an excellent review from Jon in the earlier part of the year, as well as an unexpected bonus. Her work in the second half was even stronger. Her co-workers told her that she without a doubt deserved an "exceeds expectations" ranking for the half. Jon didn't have ammo to ding her with. In light of recent events, she expected at the very least to receive a designation of "meets expectations."

"You remember we outlined the goals expected of you this quarter," Jon said. "I'm concerned there've been more negative stories about Elemynt in the press than positive ones."

"How is that my fault?" Kelsey said shakily. "I didn't create the privacy breaches or the hearings in front of Congress."

"I still don't believe you're stepping up to the plate," he bore into her. "You aren't meeting the metrics that were asked of you."

"Are you seriously saying—"

"We also don't feel like you're embracing the Elemynt spirit," Jon interrupted her.

It was an ambush. Jon was gunning for Kelsey with every negative critique in his arsenal despite him never complaining about her work once in her time there. He skipped right over mentions of her successful efforts and listed with impunity of the ways she was failing at her job. The one where she was constantly praised as a "rock star" or a "winner."

Kelsey thought over the many ways she made "impact" since she arrived. The countless conversations with members of the press. The late nights prepping for hearings and launch dates and campaigns. In her mind, Kelsey furiously protested the blatantly inaccurate characterizations Jon made of her to her face. Instead of unleashing her rage on her pig of a manager, she sat silent. Total shock. What he was doing was incredible. It was payback for her rejecting him. There was no other reason.

"You'll be receiving a 'meets some expectations' this half," Jon said nonchalantly.

"A what?" Kelsey exclaimed. "What didn't I meet?"

Kelsey asked him for examples. Goals that were outlined at the beginning of the half that she did not complete or exceed. He said nothing in return. She had never received negative feedback for any job in her entire career. She did everything Jon asked of her. Kelsey was crushed by the realization that she would be deemed a failure in her official record.

With the recent friction and her rejection of his advances, Kelsey subconsciously expected Jon to lower the grade in her assessment, but not flip it to the complete opposite end of the scale. She went from a perfect review last quarter to being characterized as a disappointment of an employee and no explanation of what she needed to improve on. Kelsey was by no means concerned with the bonus compensation that came with a stellar review. It was her tarnished record that concerned her most. The PRA was the linchpin to the future of her career and Jon was trashing it because he possessed the unchecked power to do so.

"I want to share some constructive feedback with you," Jon said to his employee. "You can come across as abrasive sometimes. I know you don't mean to, but you need to pay attention to your tone."

Kelsey sat emotionless. She balled up her fists under the table until they were blood red. Jon wanted her to freak out. He wanted her to run out crying and never come back. She would not let him break her in view of the office.

"If you can't be a team player then maybe you should consider exploring other options for your career," Jon pressed.

"Are you firing me?" she asked.

"No, nothing like that," he smirked. "I want you to take this feedback and put it toward your professional development. That's what this company is about... continued growth."

Kelsey was struck by the sudden understanding of what was really happening. Elemynt couldn't fire her for reporting sexual harassment, but they would do everything they could to push her out. There was no way she would give up just because they wanted her to. She earned her position. She very much intended to keep it. If Kelsey wanted to leave, that would be her decision. Not theirs. Where there once was despair, Kelsey's heart hardened in anger.

Kelsey forced a smile. Internally, she raged at Jon in words she would never say out loud.

"You have time to grow between now and your next PRA," Jon said as he rose from the table. "Remember. This is *your* company."

Jon exited the room leaving Kelsey alone to fight back the tears that dared to fall. Fiery breaths rushed from her lungs into the frigid air of the conference room. Jon upended her life once in Tokyo and now he was taking a sledgehammer to her career.

Kelsey gripped her phone tightly in a feverish attempt to not be consumed by the rage boiling inside her. The anonymous faces that passed by the glass-enclosed room would not see her freak out. Her attempts to regain her composure were interrupted by Sarah's gentle knock on the door. Kelsey's co-worker took a seat next to her. Horrible timing.

"Is everything okay?" Sarah asked with concern. "I didn't mean to interrupt. It's just that I saw you looking upset and I wanted to see if there's anything I could do."

Kelsey didn't want help from a single soul. In an attempt to make her prying colleague go away, Kelsey succinctly explained Jon's assessment of her work in the past half. Backstory was omitted. Jon rated her performance poorly and that was the end of the story.

"It's just PRAs," Sarah said encouragingly. "Okay yes, he's our manager but... it's the feelings of one guy. They're subjective. One bad review isn't going to bring you down."

Sarah was either daft or in denial. There were immediate effects that every employee was made aware of within days of setting foot on campus. Negative performance reviews meant no salary increases or bonuses or stock compensation, all of which were the furthest from Kelsey's mind. What continued to concern her greatly was that a poor comment from her manager damned future advancement opportunities. Kelsey would forever be judged by the black mark on her record as long as she was at the company.

Sarah's misguided pep talk was having the opposite effect of what she likely intended. Kelsey mustered up the last trace of pleasantness she had within her. "Sarah, can I have some time alone please?"

"Okay, well, don't forget…let me know if you need anything," Sarah said as she bowed out of the room.

Kelsey steadied herself on the table. Deep breaths. Don't panic. Jon doesn't control you. You are your own woman. Another deep breath.

Kelsey heard the advice given to her by Dr. Jill. replay in her head. She had to take the vacation her therapist recommended. Soon. Immediately.

Since it was late in the year, Kelsey had planned to use her personal time off to visit her parents for the holidays. Waiting was ridiculous, Kelsey realized. The company offered unlimited PTO. She could take it whenever she wanted. But not right then. She didn't want to be seen as not being a "team player" by running for the hills. But if she lost her mind and chucked a conference room phone through the glass like she wanted to, she really wouldn't be a good Myntor.

Kelsey grappled with a decision that had detrimental consequences either way. She had to get away from campus. She would be no good to her team even if she stayed. She was at her wits' end. There was no better time to make use of the benefit given to her than the verge of a breaking point.

Kelsey took a moment to compose herself before replying to Jon via eChat.

"If it's okay with you, I think I want to take a few days off," she wrote. "Sarah is back and I haven't had a day off since I started here."

He responded to her message minutes later. "That's a good idea. You need to get yourself together and fly right."

Kelsey's thought process on how to carry out her decision to leave was interrupted by an incoming email alert. Jon again. For some reason, she still had not turned off the wretched phone. Attached to the message was a document containing her official review. Her grade was blasted across the top: "meets some expectations." One grade above "fails to meet expectations."

Kelsey dashed back to her apartment to pack her bags for an unknown destination. She didn't care where as long as it was far away from Palo Alto, the

Elemynt campus, and most of all Jon.

Kelsey flung open her laptop and clicked on the first travel website that appeared in her online search. Images of Paris, Greece, and other far-flung destinations she visited before dotted the site. An image with palm trees and waves lapping on a sandy beach caught her eye. Costa Rica. That would do. A relatively short trip meant she could be in the remote location without delay.

Within minutes, Kelsey purchased her ticket and stuffed a suitcase with whatever was in arm's reach. She would leave on the first flight out in the morning.

SEVENTEEN

Every wall of the hotel elevator was covered in floor-to-ceiling mirrors. It had to be a cruel joke.

The horrid funhouse created endless replicas of Kelsey's sickly skin and puffy eyes. Reddened acne populated her once clear complexion. In the garish light, Kelsey saw a woman who aged five years in the months since she started at Elemynt. She looked like a fucking mess.

Kelsey welcomed any and all distractions from her run-down existence. There were scores of amenities at the hotel — three glorious pools, a day spa, a five-star restaurant plus a smaller restaurant with local eats, a bird sanctuary, and an unparalleled view of the Costa Rican coastline. She couldn't see the shore under the cover of the nighttime sky, but it would undoubtedly be a better view than the wreck standing in front of her.

Once in her assigned room, Kelsey exhaustedly dropped her bags to the floor with a dull crash. She walked with labored steps across the terracotta tiles, past the four-post bed, toward the balcony that called to her. She gently opened the doors to take in the environment that would be her sanctuary for the next few days.

It was nearly pitch-black outside. The only light to be seen was the faded gleam of faraway stars and the timid fire of gas lamps that dotted the garden below her. The ocean air swept Kelsey's unkempt hair from her face, clearing the way for a reservoir of tears to be released. It didn't matter that she could barely see through them. Her clouded view wasn't of the Elemynt campus or the Bay Area. Kelsey took comfort in being insulated from the problems that dogged her three thousand miles away. This was her time to relax and to breathe and she intended to do so. The wind carried her tears away.

Kelsey drifted from the balcony toward the comfort of the bed. The battered

Myntor fell into the deepest sleep she experienced in months.

* * *

Kelsey woke up, her eyes uncomfortably locked to the ceiling. It was time to get up. She attempted to move her body. An invisible force kept her glued to the bed. Her muscles did not cooperate. Her heart pounded in her chest. Her breathing was heavy. Unnaturally deep. If she was able to move, Kelsey would have been trembling with panic. It wasn't a heart attack. It wasn't a dream. She was frozen in place. Her body and mind were disconnected. An impending sense of death overwhelmed her.

The harsh daylight streamed into the open windows. It was jarring and intrusive. The unruly Costa Rican breeze teased her with its freedom. She attempted to roll her body to the edge of the bed. Nothing. Her limbs would not cooperate. The more she fought the anxiety, the more it fought back. It tormented her with every weighted breath. Her eyes were locked to the ceiling.

Kelsey tried to reason with herself. You're okay. You're in Costa Rica. You're here to relax. What are you worried about? Get up. Look at the sunshine. Enjoy a nice breakfast. You're okay. It's okay.

The more Kelsey tried to talk herself out of the panic, the more rigid her body became. Everything was not okay. The peace she expected after a night away from the shadow of Elemynt was supplanted by an overwhelming terror.

The root of the problem. Removing herself physically from her environment unconsciously allowed her to take stock of all the problems in her life. The job. The scandals. The disappointment. The cutthroat maneuvering. The night in Tokyo and HR's response. Jon. The lies. A tornado of thoughts in which she was squarely in the center.

Kelsey cried hot tears that she hoped would relieve her of immobility. She willed herself to exit the bed that would not let her escape. Breathe. She conjured the words of Dr. Jill: You are in control of your life. I choose happiness. I choose peace.

An hour passed.

Kelsey unexpectedly managed to lift herself up from her horizontal state. She rested her back against the headboard. She could hear the aggravating laughter of families and couples outside her window. Lapping waves from the nearby beach blended with the splashing of hotel guests in the warm pool. Happy moments were just outside of her reach. That could be her. She could be happy too. Kelsey's brain wouldn't let her focus on anything other than her many, many problems. Too much to think about.

Two hours.

Three hours.

Finally, it happened. Kelsey felt herself swing her legs out of the bed. She moved on autopilot toward the bathroom. The panic attack was subsiding. Her silent phone laid haphazardly on a dresser. It hadn't been switched from airplane mode since she left Palo Alto.

Kelsey scrubbed herself clean of 24 hours' worth of misery. The shower was a small triumph, but her mind was far from stable. She couldn't face the day. Or people. There was no way she could step out of the door. No spa or a sumptuous meal at one of the hotel's restaurants. Room service would be her savior.

It wouldn't be until dark that Kelsey would finally leave the room. She slipped on sandals and a floral sundress. She moved like a lost spirit through the hotel's halls. The area was unnaturally quiet save for a few voices laughing on their balconies.

Kelsey ambled past the glimmering pool, through the dimly-lit tropical garden, and onto the sandy shore of the midnight beach. She was alone. She needed to be. The physical reaction to her troubles left her terribly frightened. Her level of anxiety manifested itself in horrible ways. She had turned her life over to work. She didn't quite understand why. It was a job. No way was she supposed to have committed so much of herself to what was ultimately a paycheck.

Beneath the heavy panic was a strong woman. One that Kelsey lost sight of. She shivered from the night air of the beach. She needed shelter. Sleep. What she had to do to get back to the version of herself that she liked was yet to be seen.

* * *

When Kelsey arose in the morning, she was exceptionally grateful to not be welcomed by paralysis.

Kelsey instinctively turned on the phone that was left untouched since her arrival. The moment she did, regret coursed through her body. A slew of missed call alerts, emails, and text messages rang through the placid hotel room. Her parents, her friends... Jon. Kelsey's despair transformed into fury. She could not understand why on Earth he would be texting her when he knew very well that she was on PTO. No one from work should have been calling her and absolutely nothing was so important that she needed to be contacted while she was away.

Kelsey refused to read the intrusive messages he sent her. She slammed her phone back down on the wood surface of the dresser where she resolved it would stay on silent for the rest of her time in Costa Rica.

Kelsey didn't want to be left alone with her thoughts. She needed distractions to make it through the next two days of her time away. And so, she went for walks on the beach. Dipped her toes in the pool. Half-hearted attempts to mirror the levity of the hotel guests around her were made with disappointing results.

Kelsey filled her belly with local food and beer. She gravitated toward the on-site spa. It was impossible to cry while having a mani-pedi. She. Her nights ended with her watching the sun set on the golden shore.

There would be no photos to remind her of her stay. Social media would not be exposed to her shameful experience. She blocked thoughts of Elemynt whenever she could. It was an exhausting process. Even with her best efforts, they continued to creep through. There was no escaping the trauma. Attempting to do so just made it worse.

Three days in paradise and Kelsey had no choice but to return. She couldn't stay forever.

* * *

The music room was ironically the quietest space on campus. Scattered around the sunken couch on which Kelsey was slumped were guitars, pianos, drum sets, and woodwind instruments available for employee use. Sound-insulated walls prevented riotous jam sessions from bleeding into the hallways. Because morning meetings took precedence, no one came into the room before noon. If her schedule required Kelsey to be on campus, she retreated to one of her newly cherished places for solace between meetings.

Kelsey had for a while worked from home. Spending too much of her time there was having the opposite effect she desired though. Nothing to break up thoughts that led to her initial downward spiral.

Despite the media desert between Thanksgiving and Christmas she found herself in, there was still work to be done. Jon repeatedly implored her to pitch stories to the reporters who continued to write during the stretch of time when most took off for the holidays.

Kelsey considered whether she should just actually meet "some expectations." Going above and beyond in the last six months resulted in her being rebuked by her contemptible manager. If physically distancing herself from the world was what it took to stay sane under his watchful eye, she would continue with that way of working.

On this day, however, her isolation was disrupted by the presence of her friends. She regrettably invited them to her sacred space to talk after their continued petitions to do so. Daniela and Jade, their eyes full of concern, sat across from her in chairs intended for keyboard players and drum soloists. She avoided their inquisitive stares. Kelsey curled herself into a ball like prey cowering from an oncoming attack.

"Radio silence?" Daniela asked with hurt in her voice. "That's what we're doing now?"

Kelsey shook her head defeatedly. She opened her mouth to say she was fine but all that escaped her lips was empty air. She didn't want to relive past hurt or endure another panic attack, especially in front of her friends. She sighed heavily.

"I just need some time to myself, if that's okay."

"Oh no, hun, you need the opposite of that," Jade said. "A good time out with the girls."

"You can't lock yourself away like this," Daniela said. "Whatever it is will be alright. Where's that glowing girl we love?"

Daniela. Always looking out for the people around her as usual.

Kelsey watched her friends' lips move as they spoke what she assumed were encouraging words to her. She wasn't really listening. Too many other thoughts.

Jade took Kelsey by her uncooperative hand. "I don't know what demons you're up against and... I promise we won't ask. But we need our Kelsey back."

Neither of the ladies intended to leave their friend alone. Her silence was evidently a cry for help.

"Here's what we're going to do..." Jade said. "Next week is the big holiday party. You're coming with."

"That's a great idea!" Daniela followed. "It'll make your spirits merry and bright."

Kelsey reluctantly conceded to their point. Sequestering herself in her apartment or the presence of trumpets and oboes were not sustainable ideas. Whether a company-wide holiday party with thousands of coworkers was the best venue for recovery remained to be seen.

* * *

Elemynt employees in their finest cocktail attire jostled their way into the line formed outside the San Francisco Armory. Elemynt's epic holiday bash, the most exclusive event in Silicon Valley and one that had been on everyone's lips for months, had arrived to great fanfare. The Myntors and their guests were bestowed a golden ticket to a wonderland they would never forget.

Kelsey was two seconds away from throwing her invite to the first person who asked. There were still tons of contractors on Commynt clamoring to be given a plus one to the event to which they received no invitation. A dumb company policy that excluded thousands of employees was one of the lesser of Elemynt's recent sins. Kelsey wondered why she should deprive someone of a ticket when she would much rather be anywhere else.

The sole reason Kelsey showed up was that being asked repeatedly why she wasn't there would reignite the pain she had been doing her best to suppress. Stepping away from posting on social media was not a crime. Being away from the app for an extended time was somehow translated as the person having a personal crisis, which she was but that was no one's business but her own. It was time to have a holly jolly Christmas. Jingle all the way.

Nothing could have prepared Kelsey for the grand spectacle on the other side of the Armory doors. Cascades of twinkling icicles encircled a faithful recreation of a snow-capped winter village. Acrobatic performers dressed as angels and sugar plum fairies swept gracefully across the ceiling. Platters filled with the most delicious looking food were sampled by queues of starry-eyed Myntors. Sugary donuts lined the wall of a gingerbread themed sweet shop. Open bars with generous bartenders pouring specialty cocktails dotted the festive expanse. At the center of the room was a towering Elemynt logo ice sculpture in its arctic glory. The party was nothing short of holiday heaven.

Kelsey drifted along the perimeter of the massive dance floor packed with thousands of revelers. A high-energy rapper and his accompanying DJ forced their music through the thundering speakers. Beams of neon laser lights transformed the party space into a jaw-dropping visual display.

The holiday event was specifically designed for partygoers to take the coolest, most jealousy-inducing selfies. Elaborate photo areas constructed along the walls were stuffed with sparkling Christmas trees, lovable snowmen, and giant menorahs.

Catherine was positioned in a charmingly decorated area of the venue with oversized candy canes sprouting in various directions. Her squad of assistants stood several feet away so the crowd of fawning Myntors could take their turn snapping photos with her. A few toted copies of "Boss Lady" for her to sign. They would make cherished holiday gifts. Kelsey avoided the area altogether.

Troy was nowhere to be found though Kelsey was sure he was in the building somewhere. She heard rumors that there was a VIP area reserved exclusively for the Dream Team and other senior execs. Wyatt may or may not have been a part of that group. If the general counsel was in attendance, he was going out of his way not to talk to her or other rank and file Myntors.

Kelsey checked her Elemynt app on a whim. Her feed was packed with posts from her colleagues indulging in the splendor. The guess were bowled over by the extravagant experience created just for them.

"Best party ever!" one caption read.

"Happy f—king holidays!" another exclaimed.

Attendees around Kelsey talked jovially in small clusters while knocking back glasses of their holiday-themed cocktails. Kelsey was in the company of thousands of Myntors and yet she couldn't shake a feeling of isolation. Her team of three people was nowhere near as large as the sales team, for example, or the legions of engineers. Finding Jade and Daniela in the crowds of Myntors packed into the venue would be a laborious undertaking, one that she didn't feel up to doing.

Kelsey resigned herself to becoming a recluse for the evening. By shunning human contact, she could avoid questions like "what team are you on?" and the inevitable slack-jawed gaze when she shared that she was a company spokesperson.

Kelsey reluctantly took a few pics of the merriment of the evening. Her friends would ask her for photographic proof of Elemynt's legendary soirée. She would save herself a headache and just do it.

Kelsey made the rounds, capturing the most visually compelling moments, then returned to her original solo spot. She fought the temptation to hide behind her phone the whole night. She didn't want to leave anyone with the impression that she wasn't a team player.

To her relief, Kelsey spotted Jade and Daniela who quickly pulled her over toward their group of friends. And Tai. Considering the presence of certain people, it wasn't an ideal gathering. However, it was better than continuing to remain alone at an uncomfortably large party.

"I'm moving into that gingerbread house over there, I want you all to know that," Jade quipped. "Me, Todd, and the girls are going to have candy cane furniture and walls of glazed donuts for decor."

"Don't forget the unlimited crab cakes and mini quiches right outside!" Daniela laughed.

The topic of the lively conversation between friends ranged from the lavishness of the annual gathering to their plans for the upcoming quarter. The frivolity of the exchange was in stark contrast to Kelsey's downtrodden spirit. She wrestled with second thoughts about being in attendance. She would be far happier at home in the comfort of her space on her couch snuggled under her blankets. She could bake her own damn holiday treats if she wanted to.

Even Tai, the socially awkward, perpetual curmudgeon was present and engaged. Her Grinch-like attitude was dulled by sugar cookies and chugs of seasonal lager.

"Tai, is this the function you dreamed it would be?" Jade asked with a smile.

"It's what we planned for," Tai said between bites. "Now that I'm here it's like, okay, what's next?"

Kelsey wondered to herself why Tai would show up to a party if she was an unapologetic introvert. For someone who was a stellar communicator in her Internal Comms role, she loved to sulk on the sidelines during real-life events. The ambivalence annoyed Kelsey, especially because she was all in when it came to Elemynt.

An announcement rang through the hall above the pumping music.

"Everybody, get ready for the man who made tonight possible!" the voice boomed.

Tai sped toward the stage area to join the herd of Myntors cheering their idol's coming arrival. Tai's M.O. was clear. Her performance was fueled by her loyalty to the company and to Troy in particular. Like the bubbling Myntors around her, Tai believed so passionately in Elemynt's mission that she pushed past her natural capabilities to give her work everything she had and more.

The spell Elemynt cast over its employees was deep and unrelenting. To be hooked on Elemynt was to be an eternal devotee in sickness and in health. Kelsey could no longer share in their blind optimism. She saw too much to ever be enchanted by the Elemynt mystique again.

A blast of bass-heavy rock music from the stage area signaled the arrival of the man, the myth, the legend Troy McCray. Kelsey drifted in the direction of the hysteria to be witness to the coming theatrics. Troy did not disappoint.

The CEO of Elemynt emerged from a cloud of smoke and lasers to a crowd of adoring fans.

"What a great year for Elemynt!" he yelled into his mic.

The Myntors rallied enthusiastically in response, forgetting that the majority of the year had been a complete shitshow.

"This here…" Troy said, gesturing to the tremendous display of holiday cheer. "You deserve it! This party is for the best squad a guy could ask for!"

"We love you, Troy!" a random Myntor yelled.

"Aww, I love you too!" he chuckled heartily.

"You're the man!" someone else contributed.

"You are the man too, person I can't see!"

A roar of hearty laughter from the crowd patted Troy on the back for the cheeky interaction.

"More good things are on the way if we continue to work hard," Troy said. "We have to focus on our goals. Not what anyone else has to say about us, right?"

A chorus of "hell yeahs" rang out in support of his declaration. The mass of Myntors in the venue was beside themselves with pride, wrapped in Troy's words of appreciation. The excitement in the armory reached a fever pitch.

Kelsey estimated that the employees around her had to be drunk, drunk on excitement, or both. There was no mention of scandals. It was all in the past. Elemynt was about the future. They cheered for every honey-coated word Troy said.

"Alright, you guys have fun!" Troy yelled. "Let's party hardy!"

The DJ cued up a dance track to carry Troy's buoyant energy into the rest of the high-octane evening of fun. Flurries of artificial snow fell from the ceiling onto a sea of awestruck partygoers. Another incredible opportunity for selfies and photos. Elemynt created magic for them. The praise for Elemynt was at an all-time high.

Kelsey's attention snapped elsewhere. She saw him. Jon. Across the way her manager ambling around a sparsely populated area of the venue. Kelsey instinctively recoiled in horror at the sight of her aggressor. Kelsey had done her best over the past weeks to escape Jon only to have him thirty feet away from her. Kelsey almost ran out of the nearest exit until she realized he had his sights on another young woman.

Jon approached the twenty-something Myntor from behind. The vice president drunkenly wrapped his arms around her waist to her startled horror. The woman pulled away from him, aware of his intoxicated state. She didn't want to make a scene in front of thousands of co-workers.

Jon would not let her escape. He wrestled her back into his arms, groping her in the places he touched Kelsey once before. His hands trailed from her breasts down her trembling frame to her rear. When he spun the employee around to plant a kiss on her lips, she returned it with a wild slap to his face, startling the groups of Myntors around them. The bystanders assumed up until then that the gross fondling was consensual. The woman ran crying toward the exit that Kelsey intended to escape out of moments before.

Kelsey choked at the sight of Jon's vile come-on. Her breath rapidly accelerated to the point where she was hyperventilating. She steadied herself in anticipation of a coming panic attack. The shock in the woman's face reflected her own experience at the "work event" in Japan. To see it play out in front of her was the most terrifying sight of her life.

Jon's reddened face showed no hint of remorse. Only alcohol-induced confusion. He made no acknowledgment of the stunned co-workers that surrounded him. He simply stumbled his way out of the area in a shroud of artificial snow.

Kelsey rationalized that what she saw before her had to be a dream. There was no way Jon groped another girl and in full view of fellow partygoers. The holiday carols playing in overhead speakers could not drown out Kelsey's agony at being an unwitting witness to it.

Kelsey was stuck in place, wracked with anguish, shaking with disbelief. She could not fight back the idea that her inability to have Jon held accountable for his actions had possibly empowered him to replicate his behavior, this time with other employees. Kelsey had not considered up until that point that there may have been more women before her that were also subjected to his lustful advances.

Kelsey desperately hoped that one of the party attendees who watched the scene unfold would report him. For some reason, none of them moved from their spots. They whispered to each other but made no urgent movement. It took a minute for Kelsey to realize the problem. No one knew who Jon was. He didn't have his badge on and because he worked behind the scenes at Elemynt they wouldn't have a name to give security. "Guy in a polo" described half the people in the room.

Kelsey had no recourse to notify the authorities in the room either. She called out Jon before and the results were disastrous. She stood no chance against him.

HR wouldn't believe a word she said. Or, more likely, they would look the other way again. She was hopeless in her options.

No more party. Kelsey was done. She wanted nothing to do with the cursed, holly and jolly event. She mournfully dragged herself out of the venue, following in the footsteps of the afflicted woman before her. Someone else would have to take on Jon. She didn't have the strength or the mental fortitude in her to do more than she already had.

* * *

Kelsey coped with her deteriorating mindstate the only way she knew how — packing her days with work and nothing else. A free moment to think was a chance for the memories of Jon's disgusting actions to push their way into her thoughts.

Being rooted in a workplace where she was constantly surrounded by people became too much for Kelsey to handle. The employees around her were always so happy and full of joy about their work while, in the meantime, Kelsey could barely focus on her responsibilities because of the anguish that stalked her. The tiniest reminders made her relive the horrid encounters at the holiday party and in Tokyo down to the last detail.

Putting up a facade in front of her co-workers and pretending everything was okay became a grueling daily chore. Kelsey had to further isolate herself before she made the rash decision to vacate her role.

If Kelsey was to continue working at Elemynt, she would maintain the least human contact possible. No meetups with Jade or Daniela. She deliberately avoided sitting at her desk or in common spaces to do her work. She put fake meetings on her calendar with the names of random publications to ensure she had the rare opaque-walled meeting rooms to herself.

Kelsey went on seeding news stories with publications about the excellence of Elemynt. She answered emails and phone calls promptly. She carried out the responsibilities required of her so there was no reason for higher-ups to complain, least of all Jon. She was more thankful than ever for her manager's packed travel schedule. Jon's flights to the far corners of the world took him away from the office and out of her presence.

Sarah, however, had rarely been away from HQ following her early return from her honeymoon months prior. Kelsey could tell her close colleagues were suspicious of her increased absence from her workspace. Kelsey had no intention of explaining to Sarah her self-imposed solitude or Elemynt's gutting failure to protect her from the man that caused it. Sarah would have to deal.

Each day after work, Kelsey traveled straight home. She ate from the brown takeaway boxes in her fridge obtained from hurried, in and out trips to Elemynt's on-campus restaurants. The woman who was once a vivacious go-getter spent her evenings buried under heavy blankets. Calls from her parents, Brad, and her friends went unanswered. The pain was hers to fight through. They wouldn't understand anyway. Elemynt was supposed to be a golden opportunity that people across the globe would die to have.

EIGHTEEN

Another Monday rolled around and with it came an important meeting Kelsey could not miss. It was one of the last gatherings before E-Con, an event many months in the making and the yearly high point for the company. The highly-anticipated launch of Elemynt's new line of products and features would take place at one of San Francisco's grandest venues.

Kelsey and Sarah spent an enormous amount of time prepping for the media launch. Kelsey threw herself into the work, thankful it was the kind of uplifting PR she came to Elemynt for. There was no video conference in place for the meeting given its top-secret nature. To her chagrin, Kelsey was required to attend in person.

Breathe, she told herself before she walked into the executive conference room. Kelsey repeated her mantra to calm herself down: "I choose happiness. I choose peace."

As usual, the clandestine meeting space was always packed to the brim with higher-ups eager to hear news of the company's latest big moves.

Kelsey took a seat next to Sarah who brimmed with happiness.

"The big day's almost here!" Sarah crowed. "So exciting, right?"

"Yes, it's incredible," Kelsey said with forced cheerfulness.

No matter how hard she tried, Kelsey would never be able to match Sarah's level of enthusiasm. One too many people in the room who made her life a living hell. Catherine, who was chief among them, didn't bother to look in Kelsey's direction which was fine with her. Kelsey's hands were full with planning anyway.

Monica, the vivacious head of the Events team, introduced herself to those in the meeting room whom she had not met. For the last several weeks, she was in and out of the venue organizing the huge number of production staff it took to put on an event of its size.

While the Events team worked diligently to make E-Con a success, Sarah and Kelsey put their all into making sure the messaging for the press was on track as well.

The external hype from the media and fans of Elemynt was through the roof. Major news organizations in the U.S. and beyond were covering the most anticipated features and speculating on what Troy would say in his preeminent keynote.

Select news media would be awarded a coveted spot in the venue where their typing fingers would be at the ready. Tech bloggers to high-profile journalists would watch the livestream to bang out coverage the moment the announcements came. The number of emails in the Comms team's press inbox was staggering.

"First things first," Troy said gleefully. "Let's discuss the hottest ticket in town, shall we? How do we get the right people in and keep the wrong people out?"

"We have seats for about 650 people," Monica said. "That includes VIPs and reserved seating for Myntors. My team is sorting through the public lottery entries now and we should have a final guest list soon."

"How many people entered the ticket lottery?" Catherine asked.

"80,000," Monica said.

The assembly in the conference room gasped in delight at the amazing number of responses. E-Con was indeed more popular than ever. No shake-ups could bring down the people's app. The joy from the stakeholders was infectious. Troy, the man at the head of the table, was the happiest among everyone in the room. He excitedly peppered his staff with follow up questions.

"Melissa, how's the People team doing with employee invites?" he asked.

"Well, as you know we're changing things up a bit this year," she said in her usual sunny disposition. "We set up the internal form for employees to submit their names for a chance to get in. Troy, we followed your lead on only giving tickets to people who got 'exceeds expectations' or higher on their performance reviews."

"The Myntors aren't going to know about that last part, right?" Troy asked under his breath. "That form is open to everybody?"

"Yes, sir," Melissa confirmed. "Sure is."

Elemynt needed its most enthusiastic internal supporters to applaud wildly at the key moments throughout the day's event. In doing so, the Myntors would unconsciously spur the rest of the room to see every announcement as a game-changing sensation. The underhanded play to keep possible dissenters out of the company's centerpiece event was the kind of trickery Kelsey came to expect from Elemynt.

If people outside of the room knew how Troy planned for a wide exclusion, the whole campus would be in an uproar. But it was Troy's company. He was well within his right to do what he wanted with it.

"Leon, how are we doing on security?" Troy asked. "No counterfeiters or gate crashers?"

"Absolutely not," Leon said with satisfaction. "We've added more guards than we had last year. San Francisco police officers will be stationed around the perimeter of the venue."

"We're getting in the weeds," Catherine said, halting the rundown. "We can circle back on the details in our next planning meeting. What's most important right now is that we finalize the lineup of speakers."

"I'm down with that," Troy smiled.

Troy's keynote speech would be the crown jewel of the immensely important event. His words of inspiration and optimism would set the tone for Elemynt's coming year and beyond. Tai and the Dream Team toiled for weeks on end to get the tone of the speech just right. Gary, a mainstay of E-Con, would kick off the subsequent round of presentations of upcoming products. Chief among them would be the announcement of pioneering facial recognition technology and the latest development in virtual reality.

Karla outlined the string of other speakers slated to present, including the VPs from marketing, engineering, and mobile.

"So we have all white guys going up there," Sarah said brazenly.

Sarah, always thinking from a media perspective, had a point. She also had the key responsibility of training each of the E-Con speakers on their delivery of company messaging in front of the worldwide audience. The burden would fall on her if the people onstage did not meet public expectations.

"I don't have to tell anyone that we already have issues with diversity at Elemynt," Sarah said. "Or that's what people still think. If we don't want to be in hot water again, we need a woman to speak on that stage."

"Cath will be up there for one of the presentations," Troy scoffed.

"And no one in this room appreciates that more than me. Love you, Catherine," Sarah said, acknowledging her boss. "But here's the thing... only two women have been onstage at E-Con since this company was founded. One of them was

Catherine and the other was me. We need another woman up there. Even better if it's someone in a technical role."

Sarah's assessment was both brusque and correct. Elemynt's diversity report was not so long ago that the company wouldn't face scrutiny for an issue that lingered in the minds of the public. Kelsey did her best not to let thoughts of the aftermath of the report's release shift her focus.

The Elemynt staffers at the table paused to think of suggestions for a female speaker. Catherine was contemplative as well, to Kelsey's surprise. She was undefeated in her track record of silencing people who stood up to her, a fact Kelsey was personally aware of.

"Get Zekiyah Johnson on board," Catherine said above the murmur. "She's a woman and also African-American."

"The manager in Research and Development?" Troy asked reservedly. "She's in engineering. She's not...um... camera ready."

"Most women in engineering aren't," a voice said from the doorway.

Jon, the man with no shame, entered the room and placed himself directly across from Kelsey. A tremendous fear welled inside her. It had been weeks since she had been in physical proximity to her manager. Her chest tightened and her breathing became alarmingly short. Kelsey's inclination to run out of the room and away from his presence was halted by her desire to not cause a scene in front of her peers. Instead, she looked away from her oppressor's glare.

Jon smiled viciously before turning his attention to Troy. "People are more likely to buy products when they're sold to them by an attractive woman. Does she fit the bill?"

Sarah sucked her teeth. "A stylist is a phone call away."

The conversation continued but Kelsey was not listening to a word that was said. Jon knew exactly what he was doing by sitting across from her. He was asserting his power as her manager and a vice president at Elemynt. Jon would not be defeated. No matter what Kelsey did or how much she tried to block him out, she could not escape his dominance over her life.

"My best hope and I'm sure that of everyone in this room..." Kelsey heard Catherine say in her assertive tone. "Is that E-Con will realign the public's perception of the good that Elemynt stands for. We also have to think about making the board and our investors happy with the results."

Catherine's pronouncement shifted the conversation to the real point of that year's E-Con and every E-Con before it — the coming IPO. The Elemynt initial public offering was expected to be one of the biggest in history by a technology company.

Wall Street was already salivating over the moneymaking machine set to be valued at tens of billions of dollars. The elevated excitement in the meeting room matched the anticipation of the soon to be landmark moment in the company's existence. The stakeholders involved — from employees to the board of directors to early investors — stood to make a whopping profit from touching the hem of Elemynt.

Reporters, eager to get crumbs of information they could publish, sent Kelsey and Sarah hundreds of emails about the coming payday. The ladies forwarded them to the IPO comms team without comment as previously instructed.

Elemynt would not make a formal announcement at E-Con of its planned move from public to private. It didn't have to. For a Silicon Valley company of its size and upward trajectory, an IPO was an inevitability.

"Becoming a public company is our goal, but it's not our mission," Troy said to the room. "Remember, the reason we're here is to make the world better and more connected."

Kelsey's heart thawed hearing Troy's moving note. He articulated the reason she came to Elemynt.

"And if we make tons of cash while we do it, even better!" he grinned from ear to ear.

The room thundered with applause. Kelsey's jaw dropped in astonishment. If the primary goal of the company wasn't earning ridiculous profit, their leader's point of view surely did not reflect that. Her disillusionment returned as quickly as it left.

Kelsey was well aware that the outcome of the IPO process was a tantalizing proposition for Troy. As the company's top stakeholder, Troy's hundreds of millions of shares stood to be worth $10 billion or more. The CEO would also retain control of just over half of the voting power of the board of directors. Change of that magnitude was certainly enticing for a man in his position.

Catherine, the traitorous bitch, would also be an instant billionaire. She, alongside Troy, built Elemynt into a technology powerhouse and soon to be Wall Street darling. With one ring of the stock market bell, they would reap the financial rewards of years of nonstop growth.

If Kelsey stuck around the company for a while, she could at least receive monetary compensation for the series of troubles they put her through. Kelsey couldn't kid herself...no amount of money could take away the mental scars inflicted on her by Elemynt.

Kelsey was the lone person in the room burdened by thoughts of Elemynt's tragic past year. The meeting's attendees were ecstatic that their hard work and dedication would pay off in extraordinary ways. Brand new cars would fill the garages of newly-purchased homes and condos. Yachts and vacations and wealth that most people would never see in their lifetime were within reach. But first, business.

Ravi outlined the next steps before the IPO, the most important of which was conducting the "roadshow" before the offering as required by the SEC. In cities across the nation, Elemynt executives would stand in front of large rooms packed with hundreds of representatives from investment firms and powerful mutual funds. Their pitch was simple. Elemynt was the smart move for every investor. Purchasing $100 million or more in company stock would be an honor and a privilege.

Unlike previous IPO roadshows by other companies, Elemynt's undertaking would be a Hollywood production. Instead of the usual PowerPoint slide deck others utilized to hawk their company, Elemynt would create a 15-minute piece of cinema for the money-saturated rooms. The high-energy video would detail the history of the company and its path toward profitability through glossy graphics and testimonies from the Dream Team. The underlying message throughout would be that Elemynt was committed to building a better platform for the people. Putting money into the company was investing in the future of society.

To top off the candy-coated roadshow, Troy, one of the world's youngest billionaires would arrive in his trademark T-shirt and jeans. A CEO wearing colorful sneakers rather than the spiffy dress shoes of a common industry executive would add to the novelty.

Troy was a literal genius to his infinite admirers. What began as an experiment during his university days had become a universally successful, internationally-renowned business. The starstruck crowds at the roadshow would shower him with money to get a piece of the action.

The planned presence of Catherine and Ravi at every stop of the roadshow would communicate that even with the fantastical aura that surrounded Elemynt, it was indeed a serious business.

Compared to the Congressional hearings, the roadshow would be a breeze. Catherine knew the business better than anyone and, most importantly, how to communicate it to investors. She knew every question that would be asked and prepared variations on the same answer for each one. The Elemynt roadshow would be the ultimate one-two punch — the Boy Wonder and the Boss Lady wooing investors to pour millions into Elemynt.

Kelsey desperately wanted to feel the same excitement for upcoming events that her colleagues did. Working on the Comms team for a notable institution beloved by the public was the ultimate goal for a public relations professional. The problem: Jon stole her joy.

Jon's overbearing presence in the meeting room was amplified by his boastful proclamations of what Elemynt could be post-IPO. How the right media strategies could accelerate growth beyond their imagination. Kelsey did not want to see Jon, let alone hear him talk. He was a predator and a liar and he deserved no place in her life.

Kelsey's mind drifted while the team dived deeper into the details of E-Con. Chaotic recollections of her history at Elemynt clouded her ability to care about the topics under discussion. Kelsey was shaken from her daze when Melissa quietly stepped into the room. She was so wrapped up in her thoughts she hadn't noticed that Melissa left.

Melissa's face was uncharacteristically solemn. Her usual effervescent charm was nowhere to be seen. Kelsey watched as the Head of People whispered in Jon's ear. He followed her out of the door leaving Kelsey to wonder what was happening.

Sarah looked around, also confused by the sudden departure. Something was amiss. Neither woman on the External Comms team could comprehend why Jon would exit one of the most important meetings they'd ever have. Catherine and Troy knew. Both executives glanced at the door every so often as they spoke about the agenda at hand.

The door swung open again to reveal a visibly flushed Melissa. She walked straight toward Kelsey and Sarah and crouched between their seats.

"Can you come with me for a sec?" she whispered to the pair.

The two Myntors dutifully followed Melissa around a corner into a small conference room that required special access to enter. Kelsey's mind raced thinking of the possible reasons for the extraction. They stood in awkward silence for a moment while Melissa formulated her words. No more surprises, Kelsey pleaded silently.

"Jon will no longer be working at this company, effective immediately,"

Melissa said. "We've asked him to step down from his position."

Kelsey let out an audible gasp of disbelief. Sarah furrowed her brow in confusion. What Melissa said couldn't be true. Jon was just sitting across from them. He was just talking about his vision for the team. The Comms women were floored by an announcement that came out of nowhere.

"Is this a joke or something?" Sarah asked incredulously. "Where did he go?"

In an even-toned voice befitting the Head of People, Melissa detailed the series of harassment allegations reported to Elemynt HR by female employees. An unspecified number of women accused Jon of unwanted sexual advances and assault over the course of his time at the company. An internal investigation revealed that Jon had a pattern of taking female Myntors on work trips with the intent of coercing them into sexual relations with him. The repeated abuse of power went unchecked for several years.

Kelsey and Sarah stood with their mouths agape as Melissa listed the charges that led to his dismissal. Kelsey was astounded that Jon's predatory behavior extended beyond his one-night encounter with her in Tokyo. She became angry. Her nostrils flared. Her manager's transgression was far from the isolated incident that HR led her to believe. Kelsey was called a liar when the company was fully aware that Jon was exerting authority over female Myntors to satisfy his sexual desires. Kelsey was one hundred percent sure that it was Jon's high standing in the company that kept him safe from dismissal.

"After video of him touching the employee at the holiday party came out, there was no other choice but to ask him to go," Melissa said.

"Why was he in the meeting if you already fired him?" Sarah fumed.

"Jon told us he was going to leave this morning, but I guess he showed up anyway. Don't worry, his badge was deactivated and Security took his phone and laptop."

Kelsey was dumbfounded as to why Melissa made no mention that she was one of the women to report Jon's behavior. It could be because they were in front of Sarah and Melissa was, in a warped way, protecting Kelsey's privacy. Or possibly that the exec team was satisfied with his exit and the details that led to it were no longer a top-of-mind concern. Whatever the reason behind the omission, knowing that she was one in a line of women subjected to his actions enraged Kelsey to no end.

"Sarah, you'll be leading External Comms while we search for a replacement," Melissa said.

"You're making me a VP?" Sarah asked in surprise.

"Interim. In the meantime, Jon wrote a statement you can send to reporters if they ask for it. Troy's going to make an announcement on Commynt thanking him for his service."

"What if that leaks?" Sarah emphasized. "We've had enough of those."

"Tai wrote the statement keeping that in mind," Melissa said. "It should be good. You two have any other questions I can answer?"

Kelsey and Sarah shook their heads no. They were still processing the sudden news.

"Feel free to reach out if you need to talk," Melissa said politely.

The messenger walked away. Sarah and Kelsey were left alone to process the gargantuan mess.

"I mean, can you believe it?" Sarah paced the room. "Did you ever think Jon would do something like that?"

"No," Kelsey lied. "You've known him for longer than I have."

"Which is what makes it so crazy! It's sad to see Jon go but I guess I'm happy they handled the situation?"

Kelsey had no plans to let Sarah in on her involvement in Jon's eviction. No need to prolong the pain by sharing it with her co-worker.

Kelsey did her best to eke out some semblance of visible remorse for their former manager's departure. Nothing materialized. Sarah was now the VP of Communications. Kelsey intended to fully support the woman who always supported her.

Jon would be on his own to create a statement for the press that covered his ass. Kelsey couldn't imagine what his excuse would be. Spending more time with family? He didn't have one. Devoting his life to charitable causes? Jon didn't have a philanthropic bone in his body.

None of it mattered in the slightest because Jon was gone and Kelsey was there to stay. Good luck and good riddance.

"This might sound weird…" Sarah mused. "But we have too much to focus on to spend time thinking about Jon and his ridiculousness. Am I right?"

"For sure," Kelsey said numbly.

"Okay, it's you and me now," Sarah said. "Let's do what we need to do to keep this train moving."

Sarah would hear no arguments from Kelsey.

* * *

When the newly-minted VP and her surviving colleague returned to their workspaces, Jon's area had been cleared out. There was no laptop, no notebooks, or framed photos of him with dignitaries in exotic locations. The lone reminder of his bygone employment was a gravestone-sized computer monitor stretched across a barren white desk.

Kelsey readjusted the vibrant pink orchids on her desk and unfolded her laptop. As Melissa promised, Jon had emailed his statement to External Comms and the Dream Team. Two sentences.

"My time at Elemynt has been deeply rewarding, both personally and professionally. I thank my colleagues and the leadership of the company for some of the best years of my career."

Jon's final declaration said nothing of the charges against him. No acknowledgment of the excruciating mental pain he put Kelsey and others through. Jon was simply a Silicon Valley careerist whose path led him away from Elemynt.

In the inevitable Commynt post from Troy, the CEO praised Jon and his contributions to Elemynt.

He told of how Jon fostered the company's presence in new markets and how without the extraordinarily talented VP, Elemynt would not be the leader in social media it became. The statement went out of its way to make it appear as if Jon's departure was a personal choice. Zero mention of the accusations that were his undoing.

"I wish Jon the best with his future endeavors," Troy concluded.

Reactions from Myntors to the post were mostly sterile. A growing collection of comments congratulated Jon on a superb tenure at Elemynt. For someone who was fairly behind the scenes at the company, it was a head-scratcher that Jon would be lavished with such fond adulation. However, he was a VP and a member of the Dream Team. More importantly, it was a post from Troy. If the CEO deemed Jon's exit as important, Myntors would treat it as such.

On a whim, Kelsey logged into the Mask app to see if there were discussions regarding Troy's post. Rumors of Jon being fired for sexual harassment were traded back and forth. Anonymous employees stated that they personally knew Myntors who he assaulted. Other users countered with attacks that accused the commenters of making up fake stories to take down a powerful man. The dismissive retorts were supported by an increasing number of likes.

As usual, employees had conversations on Mask that not even the boldest Myntor would say in an internal thread. Reading through the exchanges wasn't helping Kelsey's state of agitation. Before she returned her attention to her email, one comment in particular jumped out at her. "I'd leave too if they offered me a $30 million exit package."

Kelsey instinctively dismissed it as hearsay. There was no way Elemynt would fork over that ridiculous sum when Jon was completely in the wrong and their investigation confirmed as much. Kelsey paused. Thought it over. It was very much possible. Jon knew the power he held over Elemynt. He knew its secrets. He knew where the bodies were hidden. Elemynt was already estimated to be worth tens of billions of dollars or more ahead of the IPO. $30 million was pennies in comparison.

It wasn't hard for Kelsey to believe that a disgusting jerk like Jon would negotiate on his way out of the door so that he would never have to work again. He would live a luxurious lifestyle for the remainder of his days on earth thanks to a payday from a company whose name he nearly tarnished.

Jon didn't come to the executive meeting because he had a burning desire to talk about E-Con or the IPO. He intended to assert that though he may no longer have been an executive at Elemynt, but he would always be a man in charge. Kelsey refused to let his last attempt at relevance in her life take hold.

As the comments on the Mask threads began to spiral into flame wars, people questioned where Catherine was in the matter. If Jon was fired for sexual harassment as the testimonies suggested he was, the company's biggest advocate for women should have been the first to make a statement in support of female employees. Kelsey reeled as she read men virulently placing the blame Catherine for Jon's ousting. The woman at the top who wanted to see all the men in her path done away with had to have made the decision.

Their speculations about who did the firing meant nothing in the end. Jon was gone and he wasn't coming back.

It wouldn't be long before news of Jon's departure reached the press. Kelsey had no desire to be in the position of defending Jon to reporters. On the other hand, if handing out Jon's meager statement put an end to his influence in her life, she was all for it. Kelsey gave herself a pep talk before she set about diving into the coming influx of Jon related emails. This was a temporary task, she told herself. Better days were on the way. Stay calm. Choose happiness.

Kelsey and her new boss Sarah sat side by side waiting for the onslaught of messages from reporters. A trickle of pings came in. Mostly bloggers, not much else.

Kelsey drummed her fingers on the desk. "Am I missing something? The media loves stories like this."

"I think we have a bigger problem on our hands," Sarah said wide-eyed.

She was aghast watching something on her phone. Kelsey waited for her colleague to say what it was.

"Something I can help with?" Kelsey said.

"Dammit!" Sarah shouted, startling the Myntors scattered about the open office.

Before Kelsey could ask her what was wrong, Sarah dashed out of the workspace and, from what Kelsey could tell, out of the building. Where her teammate was running off to, she had no idea. The reason for her sudden departure was extremely worrying.

A message from Jade via Commynt brought Kelsey's attention back to her computer screen.

"Hey are you okay luv?" it read.

"Handing this Jon thing," Kelsey wrote back. "Sarah just ran out of the room. Literally."

"Oh," Jade replied. "It was probably the shooting."

"What are you talking about?" Kelsey asked warily.

No response.

"Jade??"

A web address appeared in the chat window. No context.

Kelsey clicked on the link to find a livestream from a random Elemynt account. The progress bar in the app indicated it had been underway for roughly twenty minutes. The puzzling video on Kelsey's screen was the first-person perspective of blood-spattered hands gripping the steering wheel of a moving car. An imposingly large gun sat atop the dashboard.

"This world will be made right!" a male voice said proudly.

The unnamed man laughed heartily as he drove toward blinding sunlight. Sirens sounded in the distance.

With great hesitation, Kelsey restarted the live video to the very beginning.

The young man, now visible with the phone camera in selfie mode, was dressed in a black T-shirt and military vest that contrasted with his pale white skin. He boastfully held up assault rifles nearly as long as his body to the camera. He described in troubling detail their destructive firepower.

The man yelled angrily into his phone, calling for the demise of "dangerous" immigrants that were infiltrating the United States and render whites a minority. Mexicans were rapists, animals, and drug dealers, he raged. They had to be stopped before they further infected the purity of the country.

"Hunt them down and kill them!" he roared. "In the name of all that is good and righteous!"

Kelsey was confused by his rambling and concerned by the guns in his possession. Jade's warning in eChat indicated that he planned to use them, but with nothing but the bright, blue sky in the background it was hard to tell where exactly he was located. She hoped that what she thought he might have in mind was just her nerves getting the better of her.

The brazen young man secured his phone in the chest pocket of his vest so that the camera could share his view. Directly in front of him was a large church with "La Iglesia Católica" emblazoned above the doorway. What sounded like hymnal singing in Spanish could be heard in the background.

"Showtime!" the man crowed.

The camera shook violently in his speedy run toward the church. The singing coming from inside grew louder. A mechanical clack sounded from the automatic weapon in his hands. Kelsey's heart stopped realizing that her worst fears were materializing in the palm of her hands. Her alarm was echoed in the horrified comments surging past the bottom of her screen.

"Someone stop him!"

"You're crazy wtf!!"

Crying emojis flashed through the comments. Call for someone to notify the police were scattered throughout. Then there were the messages egging him on.

"These illegals are out of control!"

"You rock dude!"

"Time to take out the trash!"

The young man burst through the church doors greeting the congregation with a violent spray of bullets from his semiautomatic rifle. Within seconds, rows of unsuspecting parishioners were struck down in bloody warfare while others stampeded for shelter. The horrific screaming in indistinguishable Spanish was drowned out by the rattle of open gunfire. Unceasing rounds of ammunition rang through the church as a frenzy of people leaped behind pews and ran frantically in every direction away from the scope of the heavily armed madman. The killer wasted no time unloading clips into the crowds shoving their way through the exits.

At the front of the church, the pastor waving from the raised steps tried to reason with the gunman.

"Stop! Have mercy!" he screamed in broken English.

His impassioned plea was returned with a blast of bullets to his raised hand that exploded it into a bloody mess. Several shots to his chest and the man of God was silenced.

A younger man hiding in the recesses of the church rushed toward the attacker in an attempt to take him down. He never stood a chance. A river of bullets slashed through his body from his neck to his heart.

The gunman continued his reign of terror down the center aisle of the church toward the altar, stepping over the piling corpses and the lifeless body of the pastor. Worshippers seeking refuge in the first few rows had their lives ripped from them in a hailstorm of bullets. A desperate mother cowered underneath a crucifix with her arms wrapped around her two young children. Her desperate cries for mercy were unheeded. In a flash of gunfire, all three were rendered lifeless, their blood spilling onto the stone tiles beneath them.

Kelsey trembled watching the horrendous carnage unfold on her screen. She along with thousands of others witnessed the slaughter on their smartphones, unable to stop the man on a murderous spree. A flurry of unsettling comments continued to cheer him on.

The video was the most horrendous thing she ever witnessed and somehow she could not tear herself away from watching. She told herself that surely someone in the church would take him down in a heroic effort. But there was no end in sight. The killer only paused to reload the clip of his weapon. More flecks of blood pooled on his camera lens until the image was barely visible. He wiped it clean. His viewers needed to see the vicious handiwork for themselves.

The killer continued his rampage into the fluorescent-lit hallways in the rear of the church, methodically moving from room to room, opening fire until bodies slumped in the corridors. The screams of crying children in a banquet hall faded into nothing. Praying souls shielding each other from the destruction were turned into limp gatherings of flesh.

The young man stopped. There was a surreal silence. He ran out of living targets.

He unleashed a continuous spread of bullets into the already dead victims as he ran back toward the entrance of what was once a pastoral house of worship.

He drove off in his car, gun on the dashboard, proudly congratulating himself on his vile accomplishment.

Sirens could again be heard in the distance. The screen went dark.

Kelsey's phone slipped out of her hand. She felt bile rising in her throat. She wracked her brain in an attempt to convince herself that what she saw was not real. It was a prank. An internet hoax. It had to be. Those people. Their lives.

Kelsey's daze was disrupted by the frantic commotion of Myntors yelling to each other and rushing into meeting rooms with doors slammed behind them. Frenzied instructions on how to respond to the deadly shooting were hurled across the open office. It was real. Kelsey had to move. Now.

Kelsey commandeered one of the campus bikes outside the building, slammed her heels and laptop into the front basket, and pedaled as fast as she could toward the executive conference room where the Dream Team was undoubtedly gathered.

* * *

A jarring array of high-level Myntors scrambled in sheer panic to get on one page. The heads of Security, Comms, the People team, and a host of important higher-ups loudly raised their voices above each other to arrive at a solution to clean up after the worst possible, unimaginable use of Elemynt. Every department would be held accountable for their role in the perpetuation of the brutal crime carried out on their app.

Troy flung the glass door open with so much force it rattled the walls of the conference room.

"I have the goddamn White House on the phone asking me what the hell is going on!" he yelled angrily. "Somebody tell me how the hell we let this happen."

Leon was ready with an explanation. "We moved as fast as we could to shut down the guy's account, but by the time we got to it, it was too late. My team is estimating almost two hundred thousand people saw the original video. That doesn't include other accounts who copied and reposted it."

The staffers around Kelsey recoiled at the inconceivable number. People were willingly watching the horrific video. The anarchy was made worse by individuals reposting clips to their feeds, subjecting their unsuspecting followers to the violence too. Kelsey could barely stomach the first minute, let alone find reason to share it with family and friends.

Representatives from the Community Safety team spoke urgently about the deluge of reports from users flagging the thousands of replicas of the video. Elemynt's moderators were working as fast as they could to take them down, but more were appearing every minute. Daniela, who sat off to the side, shook her head in pained frustration.

Kelsey wondered if Daniela was okay. Like the victims, she was Hispanic too. Seeing people gunned down because of their race had to be next-level traumatic.

"I have to point out this isn't the first time someone's posted a murder," Leon said to the anxious room. "There was that incident a few months after Elemynt Live launched."

"I never heard of that," Troy said.

"I sent it an internal email, but at the time it wasn't high priority. Less than fifty people saw that one. There's also been a few live suicides. But we've never seen anything on this scale."

On a TV in the corner of the room with closed captions enabled, Kelsey watched South Florida police make their updated statement on the tragedy. The police chief stepped to a podium crowded with news crew microphones.

"Thirty-five victims were pronounced dead on arrival at the local hospital," he said. "Another sixteen suffered from gunshot wounds and are, as of now, in critical condition. The alleged assailant traveled to the neighborhood to specifically target the Mexican population…"

The news channel cut to footage of uniformed police officers escorting the alleged killer away in a bulletproof vest. His face was blank. No remorse. A hint of a smirk crept over his face until it exploded into a full-blown smile. He winked at the cameras trained on him.

The police chief described how officers seized several weapons from his home. They found two fully automatic assault rifles, each with an extra magazine taped to it so that he could reload quickly. The attacker acquired the weapons online and had no criminal history.

An interview with an elderly neighbor came up onscreen.

"He was always a quiet boy," the closed caption below her read. "He wouldn't hurt a soul."

While the teams around her barking orders at each other, Kelsey navigated to the shooter's profile on the Elemynt app. The sounds of the meeting faded into a blur as Kelsey delved into the account's history. Photos of a stash of military-grade weapons, graphics with racist language, and crudely doctored images of supposed Mexican terrorists filled her screen.

Kelsey was sickened by the vast collection of posts filled with reckless hate. He declared that violence was the only way to take back the country from the "invasion of illegals." He encouraged others to join the war against the erasure of the white man.

"We have to prevent white genocide," he wrote in one post. "We need to protect the future of our people. Anyone who doesn't support me is a traitor against their race."

Kelsey was disgusted that such a human being could exist and that hordes of others agreed with him. The comments under the posts were similarly vicious. Kelsey clicked on the corresponding accounts to find profile photos containing Nazi swastikas, American stars and stripes, and Confederate flag insignia.

Those with actual faces in them were mostly younger white men. Kelsey was subjected to a rabbit hole of racist accounts saying awful things. Somehow the posts from the shooter and others like them went unchecked by Elemynt's moderators. Kelsey was sure most of it crossed the line of Elemynt's terms of service that banned calling for violence on the platform.

"Why are these posts still up?" Kelsey interjected shakily.

"The moderators aren't catching them," Leon said to the room. "Or they're in the backlog of reports they have to get through."

Gary cleared his throat to speak. "We have technology on deck that uses content-matching to delete posts similar to what's been flagged as hate speech before. My team built the system two years ago, I think. It can detect white nationalist language that our keyword filters might miss. It's based on the same algorithms we use to analyze photos and contextual language for ad targeting."

"And why didn't we deploy it?" Troy seethed.

"You told us not to," Gary said defensively. "You nixed it because you said it would trigger a drop in engagement. We were at a 91 percent success rate."

Troy stewed in frustration thinking over his past decision. The worst-case scenario he chose to overlook came to life in the most twisted way possible.

Wyatt, who was listening carefully, jumped in to soothe his boss' anger.

"It's not just engagement we have to worry about," he said. "If people get the idea that we're banning free speech, the civil liberties advocates will be all over us. There's no way we'd win if that got out there."

"So, we're doing nothing?" Daniela asked appalled. "We're supposed to let people say whatever they want because of free speech?"

"This is a sensitive topic and we can worry about Gary's idea later," Troy said. "We're putting a pin in it until we figure out how to deal with this guy going nuts on the app."

Tai suggested that a member of the Dream Team post on Commynt to intercede in the tense conversations among employees.

"No. this will die out," Troy said, asserting his authority.

Daniela, visibly upset by the apathy on Troy's part, was not done. "Our black and brown employees are upset about how other Myntors are responding to the shooting. They're being completely insensitive. There was a racial attack on our platform and we're not saying a word about it."

"These are my decisions and it's what we're sticking to," Troy said firmly.

The harrowing discussion was going in circles. Kelsey stepped out into an adjacent room while her co-workers debated the fine line between hate speech and free speech. Sarah was at the table representing External Comms. If the team was to get a jump on a media response, they also needed to know what the news was saying.

Flipping through the channels, every network covered the shooting with a line of outspoken pundits. Prominent civil rights groups condemned both the shooter and Elemynt for giving him a platform to broadcast his spree. The news intercut their panels of experts with footage of surviving victims pleading through tears for an end to gun violence in the country.

Several politicians took to the air to call for more stringent gun control laws. Others blamed mental health or video games as the reason for the young man's behavior. More invoked the second amendment of the U.S. Constitution and their right to bear arms.

"I'd argue that this is exactly why we shouldn't be taking guns away," a conservative pundit said. "Those people would've been able to defend themselves. This was one guy who happened to misuse his weapons."

On another channel, Tomás, the ever-vocal spokesperson for La Bandera, stood in front of a crowd of reporters broadcasting his every word.

"We are heartbroken by the senseless killing," he said boldly. "We speak for our brothers and sisters, our mothers and fathers, and the young innocent lives who were taken today in an act of senseless violence by a terrorist. These were people whose only crime was that they gathered to pray. No one should enter a house of worship in fear that their life could be taken at any moment."

Kelsey found herself agreeing with him. The parishioners in no way deserved to die in what was supposed to be their sanctuary.

"Elemynt provides a space for white supremacists to organize and to spread their message," Tomás continued. "People are watching violence live because of this app and the man who built it."

Kelsey noted his points and also the possible counterpoints that the company could deploy. To say that Troy created a digital monster that amplified the rottenness of society was misguided. Yes, it was a tragedy, but one that could have occurred with or without the Elemynt app.

"Their promises are empty words," Tomás said directly into the camera. "This isn't the first tragedy to happen. If the company doesn't enforce its own policies, it won't be the last."

Kelsey scrunched her nose. It wasn't Elemynt's responsibility to police human behavior. The company made a hefty financial contribution to La Bandera so they could do the work to prevent the racially-charged incidents from occurring.

Catherine's friend turned frenemy Senator Layne appeared on the screen with yet another press conference promoting her anti-Elemynt agenda.

"This is not who we are as Americans," the Congresswoman said, pounding her fist on the dais. "Elemynt must put every resource it has toward making sure that this despicable video does not inspire the next act of violence. The company should be combating hate with the same energy that they use to chase growth."

After jotting down a round of notes, Kelsey took a moment to scroll through her Elemynt feed. Photos of praying hands and glowing hearts and pleas to "Pray for Florida" were abound. A stream of sentimental captions and hashtags commemorated the lives of the victims and denounced the tragic event. By committing his act of terror, the killer unfortunately accomplished what he set out to gain — the attention of the world.

Commynt was itself rife with impassioned discussions among employees as Daniela pointed out. A string of commenters decried the violence and shared messages of love and support. Many questioned what Elemynt could do to remedy the situation. A small faction defaulted to logical problem-solving which sparked the ire of their fellow Myntors.

"Will taking down the video change that it happened? No. Should we do something? Yes, but we have to be smart about it."

"Just playing devil's advocate here... we can't stop people who have already planned to commit a crime."

"That doesn't mean we have to keep giving violent people a platform to carry it out."

"What if we put a one-minute delay when accounts go live? Like they do on TV to cut swear words."

"You misunderstand the purpose of 'live'. And are we not considering free speech?"

"Tell me you're not seriously saying that people have a right to kill people on the app because of free speech?"

"Maybe we can help police do better background checks?"

"We shouldn't be taking the video down because it's evidence of a crime. We're blocking information and public records and that's not what we're about as a company."

"We suspend Black people who talk about Black issues almost immediately, yet you want to keep up the video of a guy killing people in cold blood??"

"Some of you all might be smart, but the ignorance is out of control."

The more Myntors worked to offer what they saw as reasonable solutions, the more frantic the internal threads became. Employees attacked each other over the perceived lack of empathy for minorities deeply affected by the tragedy. They debated whether certain ideas were meaningless gestures. The digital space became a venue for Myntors to act out their rage and sorrow in the wake of the event.

The back and forth would persist until the Myntors' fingers were tired. Kelsey didn't have the time to sit back and wait for the conversation to peter out. Her patience was thin. Her responsibilities were in the executive conference room.

When Kelsey returned, Daniela was missing. She couldn't imagine why her co-worker would leave the crucial meeting, especially considering her central role in the discussion. The meeting went on without her.

Catherine had taken control. With Jon gone, the COO would take no chances with Elemynt's public relations strategy. Sarah and Kelsey were to follow her lead in order to get them out of the mess they found themselves in. Their boss rattled off the public statement she wanted External Comms to issue.

"Our thoughts and prayers are with the victims, their families, and the community affected by the attack," Catherine recited. "We remain committed to countering violent behavior on our platform… and so on and so on."

Sarah and Kelsey typed rapidly to keep up. It would be their job to make sure the statement was tightly written and press-ready.

"Add a note that we are working with a coalition of civil rights groups to determine how to prevent these attacks in the future," Catherine said.

"Who are the groups we're working with?" Kelsey asked.

"The ones you met with in New York, of course."

"They don't like us," Kelsey protested. "I don't see them signing off on participating."

Sarah whispered sternly for Kelsey to do as she was told. With Daniela missing in action and Scott not at the table for some reason, there was no one there to suggest the obvious — someone from the Diversity team should read over the statement too. Also, there wasn't a single person in the meeting room who wasn't white or Asian.

It's what Daniela would have pushed for. Kelsey found herself advocating on behalf of minorities not represented at the table.

Catherine roundly ignored the suggestion and pointed her finger at Kelsey and Sarah. "We send that statement as is to whoever who asks. No individual responses. No phone calls. We'll have it lawyered before it goes up on the company blog."

Wyatt perked up at the opportunity to contribute to Catherine's directive. Since his epic screwup at the hearing, he had been sidelined indefinitely.

Catherine dashed his hopes. "Not you, Wyatt. A member of your team."

Wyatt readjusted his posture to deflect the embarrassment of being shut down.

"Catherine, should we put your name in the byline to give it a more authentic feel?" Sarah asked.

"I do not want this tied to me or Troy," she said. "Have it come from the Head of the Community team."

"I don't think we should put up a blog post right now," Wyatt interjected again. "We need to keep things close to our chest—"

"Thank you, Wyatt," Catherine interrupted. "As I was saying…"

"From a legal perspective, if we—"

"I said thank you, Wyatt. If I haven't made myself incredibly clear, you are general counsel in name only. Any words you have to say were no longer valuable the moment you decided to embarrass this company in front of the United States Congress, not to mention embarrassing yourself."

Wyatt opened his mouth to reply to Catherine's rebuke.

Catherine shifted to face him directly. "Before you speak, know that our Comms team is not too busy to put together a press release outlining in detail how your presence at this company is no longer required. Make your next decision wisely."

Wyatt's first inclination was to storm out of the room and away from Catherine's presence. He was halted by the indisputable fact that his chance at a continued career in the legal field rested in her hands. He would sit silently in his place and watch the resolution of the crisis play out in front of him.

The room turned their attention back to Catherine. She was unfazed by Wyatt's interruption.

"If everyone carries out what I've said to a tee we can get through this together," she implored.

Kelsey and the staff had no choice but to follow through with Catherine's instructions. It was the same empty apologies... whatever would get them through the press cycle. "Spokesperson could not be reached for comment" would be at the tail end of every news story.

The company would make no specific promises on how it would eradicate inflammatory speech on its platform. A routine comment. That's all the public would get. Kelsey was distraught knowing that the company that she worked for tirelessly was failing the world it claimed to support.

* * *

Kelsey texted Daniela repeatedly. No reply.

Daniela was missing in action with no explanation of why. Kelsey's frustrations with current events evolved into worry. A Comms person going dark during an all hands on deck controversy meant something was seriously wrong.

Several hours went by before Kelsey received a text message back from Daniela. Kelsey was happy to know that her friend was okay.

The two agreed to meet at the organic vegetable garden in one of the furthest corners of campus. Kelsey found Daniela there sitting solemnly on a bench amidst the perfectly manicured plants.

"Where did you go?" Kelsey asked impatiently.

"I couldn't take it anymore," Daniela said. "I had to get out of there."

"What do you mean?"

"Kelsey, I have worked so hard to promote diversity inside of Elemynt and to the media like I'm supposed to. But I constantly feel like I'm defending a company that's more concerned with looking like it cares about diversity than actually making it happen."

"I get it," Kelsey said sincerely. "You said it was a problem when I first met you."

"Yes, and it's gotten so much worse. I don't understand why I'm going up against the executive team to do the thing they hired for. Real diversity and inclusion are never going to happen if they keep treating it like a 'nice to have' instead of an actual priority. They're so worried about pissing off the White and Asian Myntors that everyone else has to suffer because of it."

Daniela's frustrations were valid. As the company's external representative for diversity, she had to mask the divisiveness around the issue. Kelsey witnessed on several occasions her prescient attempts to correct the internal climate that ended in her getting shut down. The majority ruled. Troy and Catherine always had the final say.

"You've been doing awesome so far!" Kelsey said, reassuring her. "What makes you think you aren't making a difference?"

"Did you see the threads in Commynt?" Daniela bristled. "People rationalizing violence?"

"They're just talking," Kelsey said. "They don't mean half of it."

"You know I wish that was true? They don't care that people who look like me are being gunned down because of the color of their skin. People are carrying out these atrocious acts using the platform we work for and nothing's being done about it. Everyone's carrying on like these are anomalies we can just skip over."

Daniela was speaking truths about the current state of Elemynt that Kelsey opted to look past. She held onto the notion that her colleagues were doing great work and were genuinely good people. They were just operating in frayed times. Tensions were at a high. People weren't perfect.

"Kelsey, there's something else I wanted to tell you," Daniela said with a heavy heart.

"What is it?" Kelsey asked.

"I'm leaving Elemynt," Daniela said sadly. "I've put in my two weeks' notice."

"Wait, why?" Kelsey recoiled. "I'm so sorry you're going through it, but I really don't think you should go! The company *needs* you."

"Trust me when I say I'm not alone in this. Most of the Black and brown people at Elemynt are leaving a year or two after we get here for the same reason. The situations like the ones in Commynt are proof of what we have to go through all. the. time. Being made to feel like we're less than. Like our opinions don't matter. Microaggressions constantly. We are tired and torn up inside deciding whether we want to stay and deal with it or move on. Personally, I've had enough."

Kelsey winced at her colleagues' assessment of the internal discourse. She couldn't understand how Daniela would let the comments of a few employees hurt her as much as they did.

"I wanted you to know that when I leave, I'm not going out quietly," Daniela said.

"What's that supposed to mean?"

"Well, the last few months, the only way I've been able to deal with this hurt is by writing it down so I don't have to keep thinking about it over and over. I have a hidden note on my phone that I add to and then I put it away. My plan is to organize my thoughts and publish a post on Commynt before I go. You're my friend so I didn't want you to be surprised when it lands."

Kelsey was alarmed by Daniela's plan to land a potentially destructive critique of the company in its open forums. Kelsey believed that Elemynt could be saved. Her colleagues were already underwater with the negative public attention. Putting the magnifying glass on the company's ills would only serve to undercut it further.

"You know you don't have to do this," Kelsey pleaded. "If you want to leave you could just go. If you write a memo and it gets out, you'll get blacklisted at pretty much every tech company in the country. No one's going to want to hire a whistleblower."

Kelsey hoped to sway Daniela without revealing that she too had been through a similar situation, one that she was still trying to bury in her past. She called attention to Jon's behavior by reporting him to HR and it blew up in her face astronomically. She didn't see how much more helpful a public memo would be other than to rain down shame on Daniela.

"What about your RSUs?" Kelsey asked frantically. "You've only been at the company for two years. If you quit now, you'll have to give up the rest of your stock options. That's money you and Ro can use to buy a house together in Oakland or travel the world or something."

"Waiting two more years for full vesting is two more years of me being absolutely miserable," Daniela said. "My sanity is not worth a million-dollar check."

Kelsey pulled out a variety of reasons she could to get her friend to stay. Nothing was working. Her friend was resolute in her decision.

"Elemynt needs a wakeup call," Daniela said. "This isn't just about me or what my role is. It's so that people on the app who don't come from the same background as the majority of employees are given the respect they deserve."

"You think they don't get that? Myntors are looking out for everyone."

"And that's the problem," Daniela said. "Too many employees see Elemynt users as a singular group with the same needs and experiences. They ignore what we go through on the app because they can't empathize. Caring about helping people of color and women is part of the bigger picture and someone has to remind them of that."

Kelsey's eyes slowly began to water. Despite her best efforts, there was no way she could convince Daniela to not write her memo. It was clear from the moment they first met that Daniela was the type of person to stand up for what she believed in, even if it came at great personal expense. Still, Kelsey couldn't help but worry for her. Daniela was one woman taking on a whole company. She was opening up her motives and who she was as a person for debate. Inviting that kind of attention would take extraordinary resolve.

* * *

True to her word, Daniela published her missive in Commynt the Tuesday of her last week at the company. Kelsey nervously eyed the post sitting at number one in that day's trending posts. A surefire PR nightmare was on the other side of the click.

"Elemynt did not become one of the most popular social media platforms on the planet by doing the bare minimum," Daniela wrote. "So why does the company continue to take that approach when it comes to diversity?"

Kelsey cringed. Right out of the gate, Daniela did not plan to hold back.

"Elemynt has stood by while hundreds of millions of people on the app are subjected to racial slurs, threats of violence, and targeted harassment. Our users are reporting these violations of our terms of service, but instead of getting to the root of the widespread issue, we let algorithms decide each person's fate. We can say we never intend to profit from extremism, but the fact is we do every day. Ignoring the concerns of large groups of people in favor of servicing advertisers is against what Elemynt claims to stand for. The same dismissive attitude toward users of color also plays out against employees of color as well."

With great sincerity, Daniela told of how Hispanic and African-American Myntors in particular struggled to deal with aggressions from their white counterparts, both subtle and overt. She shared how they were often referred to as "diversity hires" regardless of having equal or better credentials than their colleagues. She highlighted the overrepresentation of people of color in contract roles with lesser pay and benefits who did the same work as their neighboring co-workers. Daniela spoke of how many black and brown employees, both full-time and contractors, were driven to leave the company altogether by ongoing discrimination.

"People of color across the company shouldn't feel afraid to voice their opinions for fear of being seen as a disruptor or aggressive. When Elemynt pushes out diverse workers, it ignores varied points of view that are valuable to the overall growth of the company. Thinking differently is what makes us great."

Because Daniela shared her frustrations with Kelsey throughout their time knowing each other, she empathized with her friend on a personal level. However, Kelsey could not ignore that Daniela was further upsetting the normally harmonious work environment at Elemynt by exposing what she saw as its most significant flaws. Kelsey continued to read the post, bracing herself for whatever other deep cuts Daniela would unleash on her colleagues.

"I know so many of you like me care about making sure the company is moving toward the future in a responsible way. We need to hold each other accountable. We need to stop thinking about our users as one monolithic group, but rather a spectrum of cultures with different needs that deserve our respect and attention. We can't change the world for the good if we ignore the world outside of Silicon Valley."

Daniela's memo was extraordinarily well crafted. It was that precision that worried Kelsey to an immense degree.

The memo was designed to go viral. It was a given that her internal post would leak and Daniela knew it. Every line was a quote that reporters could easily include in their stories. If Daniela wanted to publish an explosive screed that would shake the foundations of Elemynt, she accomplished her goal.

Kelsey didn't know whether to be upset or impressed that Daniela technically didn't violate company protocols in her writing. Daniela sidestepped Elemynt's nondisclosure agreements she was made to sign by not specifically mentioning any of the company's trade secrets.

There was no mention of how plans to curtail harassment were derailed by Troy. Not a peep of the study of women and their overall hatred for the platform. Nothing about private meetings or email exchanges or backdoor deals with external stakeholders. The data and comments Daniela could have included that would back up her assertions and offer concrete evidence of Elemynt's ills were omitted.

If she had planned to stay at the company, it was likely Daniela would not have been fired for her post. She was protected under the freedoms of the company's open culture. Kelsey suspected from the beginning that the openness Elemynt prided itself on would eventually have negative ramifications that would spill out into public view.

Kelsey truly loved her friend. However, that fondness could not erase Kelsey's dread of the dramatic run of events that would inevitably follow the memo. Daniela wrote it and would be long gone in a few days. Kelsey was the one who would be burdened with the fallout from the press. So far, she was committed to not letting Elemynt force her out of the company and a role that would lead her to the great career she imagined for herself. Kelsey never thought it would be Daniela who was jeopardizing her plans.

As Kelsey expected, a civil war was underway on Commynt. Total meltdown. Employees across the board had mighty opinions on Daniela's memo and weren't afraid to share them in increasingly contentious threads and posts. One side saw her writing as an all-out attack on the company. Others regarded her reflections as a common sentiment among minorities finally vocalized in an open forum.

The responses ranged from timid agreements to fervent denials that teetered on the line of outright hate. Kelsey sat at her desk reading with trepidation the volley of opinionated comments.

"If you can't handle this company, go back to where you come from."

"We only have winners here."

"Not all white people are racists!"

"Discrimination at Elemynt is real and we're not just making this up to make white folks feel bad."

"They don't ask you if you're a bigot on the job application."

Daniela's warnings regarding internal racial tension were ironically realized and on display. Combative Myntors who diminished the pleas of their minority coworkers didn't seem to grasp that experiences at Elemynt and on the app were not universal. More minorities, as she said, than Kelsey expected defended the company against Daniela's characterization of it. A few African American and Hispanic employees indicated that they never experienced racism at Elemynt and the idea that it happened on campus was ludicrous.

Daniela was surely happy to see that there were many more messages from employees of all stripes speaking in support of her and their colleagues from diverse backgrounds. The few white employees with hostile dissenting views were met with hundreds of responses calling out their prejudice. Kelsey wouldn't kid herself. There were likely many more employees who saw minorities as a plague but kept their incendiary opinions to themselves. Being racist in front of the whole company was a mighty bold move.

The most virulent hate for Daniela was unleashed by anonymous commenters in Mask. The Elemynt threads were packed with Myntors decrying her post as a racist rant.

"Another social justice warrior playing the race card!!"

"She should be grateful to white men who made Elemynt possible!"

"I've seen too many qualified white males passed over for promotions in favor of a woman or minority. Qualifications don't matter these days just your gender and your race."

"If they want to act like oh poor us we're slaves on a plantation let's do 'em a favor and treat them that way."

It wasn't that difficult to discern that there were very few minorities in the comments on Mask. The conversations mostly agreed with each other's pro-white, anti-diversity sentiment.

Kelsey to some degree wanted to empathize with them. As a white woman, she understood what it felt like to be discriminated against because of who she was. However, the comments were cloaked in misogyny and dripping with disdain for not just people of color but women in general.

As Kelsey predicted, several anonymous users questioned Daniela's motives for writing the post. They accused her of being an attention seeker or unfairly projecting her experiences on the entire company.

What Kelsey longed to tell them was that Daniela's intentions came from a good place. Behind the scenes, she was fighting to make sure everyone at Elemynt felt included. It took an enormous amount of courage for her to publish her candid analysis knowing the criticism that would arise from it. The post wasn't the writings of a disgruntled employee but rather an individual who wanted purposeful change for those who were maligned by the company's culture.

Back on the raging Commynt boards, there was still no statement from Troy or Catherine. Their absence hadn't gone unnoticed. Myntors on both sides of the argument called out their lack of contribution at a time when they needed the voice of leadership.

Finally, after what seemed like forever, Scott posted a short statement as a comment under Daniela's post.

"We thank everyone for the feedback," he wrote. "We'll talk privately with the Latin+ and Black+ group to find ways to resolve the issues."

"It's not our fault this is going on," wrote a Myntor with a Spanish sounding name. "Why is it always the minorities that have to be the ones solving diversity?"

"Our people have these conversations all the time," a woman added. "You should be speaking to everyone in the company about these issues, not just us."

Scott's response set off a fresh wave of bitter dialogue regarding the company's deferment of responsibility. Scott was likely in shambles because of the renewed spotlight on the Diversity team. He was in a tough position. He couldn't deny the failings Daniela outlined because he, more than anyone, knew them to be true. And it was likely that the exec team wouldn't let him admit as much.

Scott was always of the mind that his team was doing their very best. A few people trying to change the culture of a 20,000-employee company was more difficult than most people cared to recognize. Despite his efforts, Scott would likely be the face of the coming media storm.

To no one's surprise, Daniela's memo reached the press within an hour of its publishing. News stories were published en masse about the latest incarnation of Elemynt's issue with diversity.

Incendiary blog posts and unceasing analyses from tech reporters were rushed online. Scores of thinkpieces from both conservative and liberal commentators instantly went viral. Anchor after news anchor crowed to their viewers of another nail in the coffin for a turbulent company. At that point, Kelsey was used to the inflamed media circus that surrounded yet another Elemynt scandal.

Most concerningly, fake accounts began to pop up on Elemynt that used Daniela's name and pictures stolen from her actual account. They were packed with posts containing anti-white rants that were designed to look like they came from the author of the memo.

The series of impersonators angered Kelsey to no end. She was appalled knowing that a news outlet not paying attention could pick up on a fake account and attribute its hateful posts to Daniela. The storm surrounding her friend was growing at an accelerated rate beyond what she anticipated. Kelsey didn't expect to be fearing for Daniela's safety. Also, her texts weren't being returned.

Kelsey called Jade up immediately. As head of Media Partnerships, she held the keys to a resolution.

"I'll never understand the audacity of people on social media," Jade said.

"Can you verify her real account?" Kelsey pleaded. "She has enough press coverage to qualify."

"The rules are I'm supposed to get her permission first," Jade said. "But I haven't been able to reach her since she posted on Commynt."

"Me either, but can we make an exception this one time?" Kelsey said. "These accounts are going to make the situation so much worse."

"What am I saying?" Jade paused. "I'm the boss and she's our girl."

The phase of intense media scrutiny was Troy's worst nightmare come true again. Quotes from anonymous employees emboldened by Daniela's memo appeared in articles published by the most prolific news publishers in the country. The Myntors told of their long-standing grievances with the company, how many of Daniela's claims were instances they experienced personally. They lambasted Troy and the executive team as ineffectual leaders when it came to diversity at the company and on the app. They claimed that they didn't feel supported and how Elemynt would continue to be a hostile workplace for employees of color.

Dissenting internally was one thing but speaking publicly, anonymous or not, was considered treason. The Security team was likely already deploying its resources to root out the vocal employees. Every email would be searched, and every text message combed through until they found the culprits and had them fired on the spot. Elemynt would make an example of any employee who dared speak to the media. Speak up and be thrown out — the two options. The only comments from Elemynt were to come from the Comms team.

Sarah had been busy too. A post crafted by her, but bearing Scott's name, was published to the company blog. The headline: "Elemynt's Commitment to Diversity."

"Diversity and inclusion are part of who we are as a company," it read. "Together, we're building an inclusive culture where differences are valued. We will continue to advocate for diverse voices and support the discourse that makes Elemynt an outstanding place to work."

The missive praised the company's diversity efforts but said nothing of the specific criticisms Daniela made.

The proclamation intended to ward off media inquiries would not be enough to reverse the course of the escalating coverage. Between the anonymous quotes and the past reporting on the company, newsrooms had all the fodder they needed to issue stories that raked Elemynt across the coals. If anything, the vacant words of the blog post opened the door for more speculation around Elemynt's ineffectual efforts.

An email from Tim of the Washington Chronicle pushed through Kelsey and Sarah's inbox at the same time.

"I have info on the company that I want to discuss with you," the email read.

Kelsey's hopes of the snowballing issue dying out soon were dashed. A message from the stalwart reporter meant more trouble was brewing.

"We can ignore it, right?" Kelsey asked shakily. "Give him a general statement and he'll go away?"

"No, he won't," Sarah said crossly. "If we don't meet with him, he'll keep talking to our employees. We need to shut it down. Whatever it takes to get that awful man off our back."

"What do you think about inviting him to meet on campus?" Kelsey suggested earnestly. "The thing is we don't usually bring reporters inside HQ. He'll feel like he's won because he got what he thinks is exclusive access. Then we hit him with our regular talking points."

"You know what, that's not a bad idea," Sarah said thoughtfully. "We can have security stay on him so he can't talk to employees or go anywhere we say he can't go. I love it."

"You'll reach out to him?" Kelsey asked.

"He likes you more," Sarah said as she moved on to other matters. "Make it happen."

Kelsey arranged the meeting with Tim because she was instructed to, not because she had a strong desire to do so or had a stake in the results. Kelsey's will to support the company may have taken a swan dive, but her work ethic was very much still intact. Kelsey would go with the flow until she could figure out for herself how she wanted to leave. She stood strong in her resolve that a forced departure would not be her legacy.

Kelsey's conference with Tim was another hurdle to overcome, but one that she would execute with the least effort possible. Nip it in the bud, clear the thing out, move on.

* * *

The room Kelsey and Tim occupied was outfitted with Elemynt's signature effervescent décor. However, it was a glorified isolation cell from which Tim would not escape unless Security let him which they wouldn't until the scheduled meeting time was over. The reporter would not overhear a single employee conversation or see anything remotely proprietary. The two uniformed security guards posted outside the door would make sure of it as would the plain-clothes guards patrolling the immediate vicinity.

Tim stared Kelsey down, eager to riddle her with questions. His recorder sat on the table between them waiting for Kelsey to deliver his next headline. She intended to do nothing of the sort. Her private suspension of loyalty to the company did not translate to support for his crusade.

Kelsey calmly sipped from her cup of jasmine tea.

"How can I help you today?" she asked.

Tim wasted no time bombarding Kelsey with questions regarding the myriad of issues facing Elemynt. They came rushing at her one by one.

"How are your staff feeling now that this memo is out?" Tim said.

"We have no comment on that at this time," she replied.

"You don't think discrimination is an ongoing issue at Elemynt?" Tim pressed.

"No comment."

Tim's beady eyes scanned Kelsey's face analyzing what he could say to elicit a usable quote from her. He droned on asking questions she would not answer. The Comms rep had no motivation to make things worse for the company than they already were. Each silent sip of her tea was another "no comment."

"For a company that plays fast and loose with your users' information, you sure do value protecting your own," Tim said.

"That sounds like a personal opinion," Kelsey said undisturbed.

"My reporting is in the best interest of the people," he said.

"And so is Elemynt's mission," she heard Troy say.

Troy swaggered through the conference room doorway with his glare locked squarely on the reporter. How he found out about their meeting, let alone the location of it, Kelsey did not know. She suspected the calendar entry was flagged by the Security team because it included a known reporter's email. Never mind that she was a member of the Comms team.

Troy's vendetta against the journalist who hammered his company with negative press meant that if Tim was on campus, the CEO would hunt him down. A face-off between the two was inevitable. Kelsey was agitated that it would occur while she was present. She shifted her attention away from Tim and resigned herself to let The Troy Show unfold.

Tim was delighted to be in the unexpected presence of Troy. He could drill the head of the company with the questions that he'd been yearning to ask the top executive since he began covering Elemynt for his newsroom.

"Do you think the way employees are treated at Elemynt like Daniela

Vasquez's memo says they are correlate to the harassment and false information issues on your platform?" Tim asked.

Troy folded his hands. "Mister...what's your name?"

Troy knew his name.

"It's Tim Westbrook."

"Tim, do you use Elemynt?"

"Not personally, no."

"You're missing out!" Troy smiled proudly. "Elemynt is bringing the world closer together! People can connect with anyone in the world to discuss ideas, share memories...the list of ways we've improved lives around the world is a mile long."

Troy spoke in sanitized language that to the casual listener sounded like he was responding in the sincerest of ways. In reality, he was spouting fluff intended to numb the recipient with his charisma. Troy built the company by getting people to buy into his vision and ignore their misgivings. He had become quite good at doing so.

"That's cool, but you haven't answered my question," Tim pressed.

"I'm here talking with you so you can get an accurate representation of what we're doing here," Troy said with a smile.

"Let's move on," Tim said. "Tell me about this study of your female users that you conducted."

Troy froze. "I have no idea what you're talking about."

"You don't know about a team of your researchers doing focus groups and traveling to different cities to interview women about how their lives are affected by your app? Offering gift cards for their participation and making them sign long NDAs?"

"Nope, I haven't heard about that."

Kelsey was defending a liar.

Troy was in several meetings with Leon and his teams about the report, many of which Kelsey sat across from him. The truth was that Troy didn't like the scathing results, so he made several calls to bury it. The documentation of hundreds of women criticizing the company would never be seen outside of the walls of the executive conference room.

Troy effectively silenced the voices that cried out to Elemynt for help. That wasn't what he would say to the reporter. Whatever lie Troy needed to tell to protect himself and his company, he would do so and deliver it with a smile.

"I have several anonymous sources who've told me about this in detail," Tim said. "Not answering my questions doesn't mean I won't write a story."

"This is a free country," Troy smirked. "You can write whatever you want. And don't quote me on that."

"I'll make a note of it," Tim said with a hint of amusement.

Troy was increasingly incensed at the reporter's smug reaction to his responses.

"You might want to think twice and get your facts straight before you write your stories," he said.

"I'm a journalist," Tim countered. "That's what we do. You can either give me a quote that I can use, or it'll be my sources' word against yours."

Troy reached across the desk and turned off the recorder. "You want a statement? Here it is. Off the record, just for you. I can't stand you reporters. You're pricks who write whatever you want, but you've never created anything in your life. You make your living destroying things while I have worked to build. I won't let you tear my company apart."

"You don't need my help with that," Tim said. "You're doing a pretty good job of it yourself. If you don't like reporters, maybe it's because you have something to hide?"

Kelsey stood up sharply. "Thank you for your time Mr. Westbrook."

She would not let the cockfight continue on her watch. Troy's bravado threatened to do more damage that he would later blame someone else for. Kelsey escorted her angered boss out of the room before he could trade more barbs with Tim. The two security guards stood firmly by the door to continue sequestering the reporter to the room.

Stepping away from Tim did not do much to lessen Troy's surging aggravation.

"How did that zit bomb hear about the study?" he growled. "That was confidential information that no one should have their hands on besides me and The Dream Team!"

"It had to be someone in the company," Kelsey offered.

She honestly did not care.

"I want Leon to track down whoever it was and fire them right now!"

"Oh hey, Troy?" Tim called to them from the doorway. "Good luck with the employee walkout. This zit bomb will be watching."

Troy and Kelsey traded alarmed stares. Neither had heard about a walkout. Troy raced away from Tim's detestable presence at full speed toward his office, cursing every step of the way with Kelsey following his quickened footsteps.

NINETEEN

Kelsey was sick and tired of the executive conference room. She was tired of its ticking clocks, the sleek white walls, the panicked Myntors who populated it, and the streak of emergency discussions, each of which was a call to arms before the next potential downfall of the company.

In her haste to make Tim evaporate, Kelsey missed a text message from an unknown number with nothing in it except a link to an Elemynt account. At the top of its feed was a commandment in glaring words: "Myntors, Walkout now!" Following that were posts with phrases like "Raise Your Voice" and "Real Myntors use their Minds" in stark black and white letters. The captions declared that Elemynt had lost its moral compass in its quest to grow users at any cost. Another post written in bold lettering blasted Elemynt for letting racism and harassment flourish on the platform. Written underneath every post were the words "Be Ready."

There was no name on the account. However, in its short existence, it accrued thousands of followers. Each post received hundreds of responses of support in the comments below. Tim wasn't kidding.

She longed for the days when the room was a space of gladness and cheer and good news. Those were hard to come by anymore.

The walkout was the latest in an interminable series of catastrophic events to rattle the foundation of Elemynt. Yet another disastrous corporate scandal. This time it was an obstacle that Kelsey could not begin to conjure a solution for. Kelsey's ambition had been drained for her and she no longer cared to be at the forefront of a rescue mission for the company.

According to the heated discussions in Commynt, every employee, full-time or contractor, received the same text message she did on either their work or personal phone.

Before she arrived in the cursed room, Kelsey received an alert for a new post from the mysterious account. In it were five demands of company executives:

1. *Set accountability standards for harassment and false news on the platform.*
2. *Conduct a transparent investigation of HR's handling of employee complaints.*
3. *Diversify and increase the number of moderators.*
4. *Transition contract workers to full-time roles.*
5. *Set diversity goals for every manager.*

At the bottom of the post: "BE READY." Should Elemynt not meet the demands preemptively, a global walkout would commence. Date and time to come.

The emotions of the stakeholders at the meeting ranged from startled to dismayed to outright furious.

"The media is already picking up on this," Sarah warned the room. "Every time the account sends an update, journalists are on top of it and pushing out new stories."

"Who the hell is writing these posts?!" Troy demanded to know. "Are we even sure they're Myntors?"

"I don't know what you all think but maybe it's Daniela?" Sarah suggested. "I mean, she wrote the memo. That could've been her first threat and this is her follow-up."

Sarah and Daniela weren't exactly best friends, but Kelsey was perturbed to see her colleague throw the now ex-Myntor under the bus so quickly. It was true Daniela published a controversial internal post but that wasn't enough reason to believe she was also organizing a massive protest against Elemynt.

"Kelsey and Daniela were close," Tai said bitterly. "Maybe she knows something."

Tai's remark was less of an observation and more of a direct accusation. Kelsey was guilty by association for an offense they couldn't say for sure that Daniela committed. Her friend told her about the memo but she never mentioned plans for a walkout.

Tai was frazzled from the uproar that overtook her normal responsibilities as Internal Comms lead. Daniela's absence and Kelsey's proximity to her left Kelsey to be Tai's punching bag. Of course, all eyes in the room turned to Kelsey, waiting for her to explain herself.

"She's my friend, yeah, but I didn't have anything to do with this," Kelsey said defensively. "I haven't talked to her since before she posted the note."

"Your bestie is tearing down this company and you know nothing about it?" Catherine bristled.

"I know as much as anyone else at this table does," Kelsey recoiled.

Kelsey sensed the alarming signs of an oncoming panic attack. Heart thumping. Clouded thoughts. She did the breathing exercises Dr. Jill walked her through. She would not lose her cool in front of Elemynt's top executives.

Exhale. Inhale.

Exhale.

"I don't think this was Daniela," Leon interrupted. "Whoever's coordinating this has serious tech knowledge and they're working from the inside. Someone hacked into our internal database to access the phone number for every employee. The message was sent from a burner number that we can't trace."

Troy was livid at the revelation. The thought of his employees rising against him filled him with fiery rage fueled by the transgressions of the last few months. The comments and faves on the anonymous account's posts showed that it was not alone in its anti-Elemynt views. That his Myntors would consider biting the hand that fed them was cause for mass retribution.

"These people feel like because they get a check with Elemynt's name on it, they own it!" he yelled. "This is my company! They work for me."

"We have to handle this delicately," Melissa said in her calmest tone. "If employees don't feel like the company is listening to them, we're going to see more people leaving, productivity's going to go down, and our recruiting efforts will tank.

"Myntors...they trust you, Troy," Tai said. "You gotta keep 'em motivated."

"How am I supposed to do that when they have the media feeding them lies and a fake account telling them to leave?" Troy bellowed. "I should fire all of them and just start over!"

"Are you done grandstanding?" Catherine interrupted. "Your little ranting isn't getting us anywhere."

"Your job is to support me!" Troy erupted. "The CEO of this company!"

"My job is to make Elemynt successful and perhaps save it from you," Catherine said resolutely. "How about you focus on your toys and let me take care of the business."

The quietest hush fell over the room. No one, Troy included, moved a millimeter. Catherine had asserted her authority. They would be wise to fall in line. She was the company's best hope for recovery and the person closest to the top still in their right mind.

"Employees would be foolish to risk their jobs here," Catherine said. "But if a walkout does happen, we'll be ready. For now, there will be no internal statements. Do not respond to reporters' requests for comment. There will be *no more* leaks. Leon, can we flag employee phones and emails for conversations with journalists?"

"I have the perfect solution," Sarah said.

Sarah told of how for months she worked on a plan to thwart employee communication with outside media organizations. Together with Leon and the Global Security team, she developed a database of the domain names of every major news site and tech publication. If an email was sent from an Elemynt employee to an email address containing a domain on the blacklist, a red alert was triggered for Security to review.

It didn't matter if the message was sent from the employee's personal or Elemynt account. If they logged into an email system even once on a piece of company property, their email address and password were stored and their communication was tracked without their knowledge. The system was Sarah's way of limiting leaks and strengthening the messages External Comms imparted to the media. By eliminating voices of dissension, the work the team did would shine brighter than ever. She just needed approval from Troy to deploy.

"I want that system rolled out right away," Troy hammered his fist on the table. "Also, if this walkout happens, Leon, I want your team to set up cameras so we can record it from multiple angles. We're putting that plan I talked about in motion."

Troy readied for a counterattack against staff who dared defy the company in public view. He directed the Security team to pair the video with facial recognition technology to identify every Myntor who participated in the protest. Their names would be flagged to their direct managers who would be instructed to monitor the individuals closely.

Employees found to be continued dissenters would be given a negative review by their manager in their next PRA and set on track for termination. To protect the company, the managers could chalk the negative assessment up to whatever reason they chose. Poor performance. Lack of teamwork. The reason was of no consequence. The point was that if they were at the protest, they were on a fast track toward dismissal.

Kelsey found the solution to be incredibly distasteful. Stopping leaks was undoubtedly in the company's best interests. However, the surveillance and consequences of participation seemed unnecessarily punitive. Troy intended to use the product his teams labored over for years against them. However, as he said, it was his company.

* * *

The oversized Elemynt logo at the gateway to campus was off-limits. Campus security barricaded the area to shield Elemynt HQ from the crush of reporters angling to document the coming walkout. The tourists who normally flocked to take pictures in front of the landmark were turned away.

Elemynt employees around the world — from London to Singapore to Mumbai — received the same text message from the unknown number. The official time and place to gather for the global protest were again accompanied by the words "BE READY." The identity of the crafty organizers remained a mystery. It was impossible to tell how many people would show. There were more than ten thousand employees at headquarters alone.

Kelsey and Jade arrived early to witness the event from its inception. They wanted to see firsthand what they would be burdened with in their duty to represent the company publicly. The despondent twosome stood a safe distance from the crowd of reporters and broadcasters capturing the scene. The last thing Kelsey wanted was to end up in pictures or worse, to be asked for comment.

Jade was shaken that the company she championed loyally was at the center of an employee uprising.

"A walkout...that's what it's come to?" Jade said with hurt in her voice. "This is not what I signed up for when I moved my family all the way from L.A."

Kelsey squeezed her hand. "Literally no one takes a job thinking they're going to protest their company. But this is happening and here we are."

At ten a.m. on the dot, crowds of Myntors poured out of the various corners of the campus and through its main gateway. They hoisted homemade signs with messages like "Support People of Color!" and "The Future is Female" written across them. Chants of "Stand up!" and "Do more! Be better!" shone a spotlight on Elemynt's deficiencies. Employees raised their phones above their heads, capturing video or going live to share the important moment with the world.

Fists pumped in the air as Myntors made their voices heard.

"Enough is enough!" they shouted.

"Inclusivity now!"

The high-energy assembly marched toward the assigned meeting point — nearby Mitchell Park in the center of Palo Alto. A trail of journalists followed closely behind them. Jade and Kelsey walked a few steps behind the procession in awe of their audacious colleagues.

The scale of the walkout was more extensive than Kelsey anticipated. The thousand or more protestors crowded into the park's grassy expanse. News cameras on tripods trained their lenses on the speakers atop the makeshift stage. Helicopters hovered overhead to secure aerial shots of the demonstration. Elemynt employees were in full display of the public, their every move under scrutiny.

A large portion of Myntors wisely stowed away their badges before stepping outside the Elemynt cocoon. Sadly, even if reporters didn't catch their names, the facial recognition tech covertly deployed in the area gave company brass the power to easily identify participants from its ranks. The workers were being surveilled en masse in ways they wouldn't believe.

An African-American woman wielding a megaphone yelled to the impassioned crowd.

"For people who have been harassed or mistreated, we are here for you!" she shouted. "Inside the company, on the app, we support you! It is unacceptable that people are being attacked just because of who they are. It's time for Elemynt leadership to stop making empty promises and to start changing the policies that negatively impact employees and our users!"

The crowd roared in response and followed the proclamations with chants that echoed their core demands.

More staffers took their turn with the megaphone to vocalize their message of change to the crowd and onlookers. Kelsey could not discern if the speakers were also the organizers or simply employees with something to say.

"We've had enough of Elemynt being used as a tool for promoting hate," another woman shouted to the restless crowd. "We're not gonna sit by while Elemynt is used for lies! More people are will get hurt if Elemynt does nothing."

"They're choosing money over what's right!" someone yelled in response.

"And that has to stop now!" she yelled back.

A chain of speakers took to the stage, one speech after the other. Each with the same call for Elemynt to make positive change.

"We build the greatest product in the world. I shouldn't have to worry about it being used for evil and misinformation!"

"Elemynt should be a place of equality for all people, not just the people who look like Troy."

"We have to make our voices heard! Elemynt must be held accountable!"

After each message of protest, the crowd issued thunderous cheers fueled by pent up anger at Elemynt's controversial policies.

Elemynt's open culture backfired on the company in an astounding display of resistance. Thousands of employees at across multiple levels had a sense of ownership in their company and were unburdened by fear of retaliation. They convinced themselves that they could make a difference by speaking up. They were no longer content to be pacified with flowery words from Troy and the Dream Team.

No amount of free meals or on-site gyms would make up for their work being used as a divisive tool for violence against women and ethnic minorities. They called out the lack of inclusivity for diverse Myntors and the sexual harassment happening on the app and on the campus. Kelsey never foresaw that the conversation surrounding Daniela's internal memo would extend past the confines of the threads on Commynt.

Through all the chaos, Daniela was nowhere to be found. No calls. No texts. Kelsey knew her friend. She may not have been there in person but she was certainly somewhere watching.

Though a mass of employees was gathered in protest before her, Kelsey was acutely aware that there were more at their desks silently harboring resentment at the uprising. They were happy to work for the most important company in the world. Elemynt was an unassailable testament to innovation. The company had its flaws, but it was always a champion of the people.

According to Elemynt loyalists, the protestors were ungrateful, disgruntled employees who should leave if they were so bothered by their workplace. Myntors in Commynt called for unwavering support for Troy and the executive leadership team during the crisis.

Kelsey was torn between agreeing with the demands of the protestors and carrying out the duties of her role. She didn't need to look at her phone to know the walkout was making headlines in news media around the world.

It was possible that the high visibility of the walkout would embarrass senior execs into action. Kelsey was doubtful though. The only way Elemynt would make meaningful change is if they lost money, users or both.

Jade gripped her cell phone in exasperation watching as her inbox was slammed with messages from partners. Her anxiety rose with each passing second.

"Did you see this?" Jade said, handing Kelsey her phone. "La Bandera is calling for a boycott of Elemynt. Can you believe it?"

"I guess the donation didn't work," Kelsey sighed heavily. "A hundred thousand dollars for nothing."

Kelsey clicked play on a video in the top spot of the CNN News website.

"We stand with the employees of Elemynt," Tomás said to a crowd of reporters. "Latinos have a right to be protected from violent propaganda and misinformation. That starts with having diverse voices inside the company."

Tomás continued his condemnation by announcing La Bandera's launch of its "#DeleteElemynt" campaign. He maintained that the only way Elemynt would heed their demands was for people to cease their use of the platform in large numbers. Profiting off hate would not stand if there was no one for advertisers to sell to.

So far, the campaign was working. Thousands of posts included the #DeleteElemynt hashtag and hordes of people announced they were shutting down their accounts. The trouble for the company was piling up exponentially.

"Wouldn't it be lovely if there was a pharmacy on campus?" Jade said with her stare fixed on the PR disaster. "I could use a Xanax right now. A Valium. Tylenol and a whiskey sour. Something."

"Maybe the protestors can add it to the list of demands," Kelsey said in a daze.

From across the way, just behind a line of photographers, Tim waved at Kelsey. She eyed him in disgust. Kelsey was in no mood to entertain the man who stood to gain the most from documenting the public protests.

Recognizing that Kelsey would not come his way, Tim waved his phone wildly and tapped on the screen. His self-righteous smile told her that something was up. Kelsey navigated to the Washington Chronicle mobile site. The featured article with the bold headline would make Troy's head explode.

An exposé with Tim's byline displayed proudly at the top contained dozens of quotes from current and former employees, many more than the few that dotted prior stories.

Women shared how they were treated unfairly by their managers and ridiculed by their coworkers because of their gender. African American and Hispanic employees told of the racist comments and behaviors they were subjected to as part of their work environment. Myntors of varying races, genders, and sexual orientations told of how they were silenced when they spoke up about decisions that were harmful to users from underrepresented backgrounds.

The article also included a statement from the nameless organizers of the protests. They reiterated their desire for quantifiable diversity goals and accountability for the vile behavior and rampant misinformation on the platform. They stood up for the rights of contract workers and against HR's history of dismissing employee complaints.

Kelsey was weary from the constant turns for the worse. She also couldn't ignore her continued duties as a member of the Comms team. For Kelsey, bearing witness to the uprising would not change its trajectory. She had to think about her well-being and that of the company she intended to go far in. If the protest worked, that would be awesome. Either way, she wanted to be in the room while change was up for discussion.

Kelsey excused herself to head back to campus, leaving Jade to watch the unrest solo.

* * *

Kelsey needed more tea from the micro-kitchen.

The reaction in Commynt to the Chronicle story was what Kelsey expected it would be — a collective rage decrying the actions of leakers. She took deep breaths while reading through the many messages from employees angered at what they saw as an act of betrayal from their fellow Myntors.

"You hate this company!"

"Why would you attack your coworkers who are trying to make the world a better place?"

"If you have a problem take it to HR!"

A host of replies called for the traitors who dared leak information to the media to be hunted down and expelled from the campus grounds. Several responders defended the leakers as concerned employees who cared deeply about the company, but felt they had no internal channel in which they could affect cultural change.

The pleas for empathy were drowned out by employees framing news media as antagonists hellbent on tearing Elemynt down. Myntors who violated their implicit oath of solidarity were contributing to the company's destruction by outside forces.

The sentiment was buoyed by an inevitable warning from Leon and the Security team in an email sent to the entire staff.

"When employees share internal information with outside forces, they are intentionally putting the future of Elemynt at risk," it read. "They are also violating the conditions of their employment and may be subject to penalty under the law and termination of their position. Please consider the diligent work of your colleagues and the overall mission of the company before betraying the trust Elemynt has in you. Thank you for your cooperation in maintaining a safe workplace for everyone."

The thinly-veiled threat was intended to strike fear in anyone who further dared to speak out of turn. The message came too late though. The damage was already done and employees were at each other's throats.

Throughout the escalating ordeal, there was no internal or external statement from Troy or Catherine themselves. Their words could restore a sense of peace to the atmosphere on campus. Kelsey refreshed her Commynt feed in vain, hoping that one of the execs posted a statement and that she somehow missed it. She had not.

All of the top trending posts on Commynt were regarding the walkout. The thread with the link to the Chronicle story was at number one with hundreds of comments on it. Number two stopped Kelsey in her tracks. A post entitled "The Bigger Picture" authored by Wyatt.

It was a strange choice for the disgraced Myntor to write a post for mass internal consumption considering he was all but excommunicated from the company. Catherine ensured he was general counsel in name only.

In what had become an unfortunate routine for her, Kelsey inhaled deeply before beginning her read of the Commynt post.

"Our mission at Elemynt is to connect people," Wyatt wrote. "Sometimes those people have bad intentions. That's a part of life and we can't change who they are."

Kelsey felt the bile rising in her throat. She read on, hoping the post wasn't going in the direction she thought it was.

"Some people are going to have their feelings hurt or make comments people think are sexist or racist," Wyatt continued. "If someone waves a gun for the camera, they would do that whether or not our platform existed. We can't regulate human nature. As Myntors, we have to be thinking about the bigger picture. To get to our next billion users, we're going to have to take some of the bad with the good."

Wyatt went on, weighing the costs of the company's quest for growth. He excused many of the questionable practices the protestors were pushing back on. His words made it seem as if Elemynt prioritized gaining users over all else. Kelsey was in disbelief that he would frame the company's priorities in such a way.

Wyatt pleaded his case like a courtroom lawyer convincing the jury not to convict his client. Kelsey saw the public declaration for what it was—an attempt to get back in the good graces of Troy. How Wyatt arrived at writing a shaky memo as the means to do that was illogical. His judgment was clouded by desperation. Wyatt seized the moment in the wrong way.

"Now is the time for you to stand up for the company," Wyatt rounded out his post. "Believe in the company like it believes in you."

First, his disastrous hearing and now this load of crap. What made the proclamation worse was that Wyatt was known to be a part of Troy's small inner circle. It wasn't much of a stretch to believe that the thoughts in his post were reflective of Troy's views. Which would actually be true.

The musings mirrored Troy's disdain for criticism and his belief that creating a platform was a war that incurred casualties along the way. However, no one outside of the executive conference room was supposed to know that. Troy was a visionary. An innovator. A good guy.

Kelsey watched the faves accumulate on the post. The comments accrued at an even faster rate. 239. 410. 602.

Wyatt's aim to get Myntors back on track with a reminder of Elemynt's mission had the opposite effect. The internal conversations were more polarizing than before. Employees who agreed with him found themselves in a bitter battle with those who saw the post as a myopic disregard for human decency. Kelsey restrained her desire to smash her computer with a hammer, exit the building, and never look back.

Kelsey found herself longing for the days when she only had to deal with one crisis at a time. The result of Daniela's memo was a pile-on of scandals with no end in sight.

Wyatt's internal post was circulated outside of the company almost immediately. News stories quoted the writing in its entirety. Screenshots appeared on the web of the memo as well as employee comments below it, minus identifying information. Kelsey could not begin to rationalize how Wyatt thought that wouldn't be the result of his magnum opus.

The press accompanied their coverage with details of Wyatt's disastrous performance in front of Congress. They characterized his latest controversial action as a further devastating blow to Elemynt. Twenty-four news channels fanned the flames by citing his comments as proof that the leaders of the company were indeed the greedy degenerates the public imagined them to be.

Kelsey was so furious about Wyatt's post and the resulting media attention that her brain didn't have the capacity to have a panic attack. It was a complete public relations disaster that the best PR rep in the world could not recover from. Whatever good reputation Kelsey possessed before joining Elemynt was completely demolished. She was broken in ways that she would never recover from. All because of one stupid little memo from Daniela.

Kelsey was through with holding back. She needed to talk to the woman most responsible for the catastrophe. Friend or no friend, Daniela would not escape Kelsey's wrath.

* * *

If it had been up to Kelsey, she would have met Daniela in a wide, open space where she could scream out her frustrations with no witnesses. Instead, she journeyed to the selection Daniela insisted on — a small coffee shop tucked away in a shopping center, away from the pandemonium at headquarters. The space was sparsely populated with Stanford University students shrouded by headphones and hunched over laptops. Kelsey selected a table near the rear so she and her rogue colleague could have some semblance of privacy.

Daniela walked in looking confident. Relaxed. Not like a woman whose name was on the lips of everyone in the company and possibly the whole world. The fact that her presence was in direct contrast to Kelsey's distressed state of mind made Kelsey more resentful.

"Congratulations," Kelsey said bitterly. "You got what you wanted."

Daniela folded her arms, unmoved by the attack. "Are you at least going to have the decency to ask me if I organized the walkout?"

"Well? Did you?"

"I may be good at what I do but organizing tens of thousands of employees after the hell the company put me through is more than I would ever want to put on myself. The answer is no. I did not."

Kelsey refused to believe Daniela. She couldn't fathom that anyone but the martyr in front of her led the charge to unravel the fabric of the company. Even if

Daniela wasn't directly responsible for the walkout, she was certainly the catalyst.

"If it wasn't the woman who went all Rosa Parks on us, who was it?" Kelsey asked.

"Like I said when you asked me five seconds ago, it wasn't me," Daniela said steadfastly. "But I know who it was."

"And let me guess? You aren't going to tell me."

Daniela sipped her chamomile tea. She said nothing. The hanging silence was punctuated by the sounds of steam from the nearby espresso machine.

In the time Kelsey had known her, Daniela was nothing but loyal and supportive of her friends. Caring deeply about other people and their happiness was what drove her to be a strong advocate for inclusion. Daniela was one of the most genuinely selfless people Kelsey had ever met. If Daniela said she didn't organize the walkout, Kelsey was compelled to believe her.

The wearied Myntor slumped in her chair. "Thanks to whoever it is, we have a big mess on our hands. I don't know what I'm supposed to do with this."

Daniela stared directly into her clouding eyes. "This is your moment, Kelsey. You're going to have to decide what you want to stand up for. You can either fight for Elemynt or fight for what you believe in. But you know better than I do that it's impossible to do both."

People had been telling Kelsey since her first day at the company what she should or shouldn't be doing. Yes, Elemynt was terrible, yes the system needed to be changed but when and how that was supposed to happen was beyond Kelsey's brainpower at the moment. The last thing Kelsey wanted after the tumultuous day was for Daniela to force her in a corner.

"Daniela, great seeing you," Kelsey said, standing up to shake her hand. "Good luck with everything."

* * *

Kelsey returned to her office building mentally drained from the day's events. Her mind still swirled from Daniela's challenge. Kelsey couldn't comprehend what taking a stand would look like. She was, after all, the mouthpiece of Elemynt. That was her job. Kelsey's ambitions of heading her own company one day rested on her performance during Elemynt's darkest times.

Kelsey's pondering was interrupted by a loud fuss on the other side of the building. It sounded weirdly like a one-man protest.

"Get your hands off me!" she heard the voice yell.

Wyatt.

Kelsey strode over to his desk to find the pompous jackhole surrounded by two imposing security officers. A growing crowd of Myntors watched as he petulantly stuffed a bankers box with his personal belongings.

"This company doesn't deserve me!" he shrieked. "I'm the one who helped build up this place! Elemynt won't survive without me!"

Wyatt's sweat-drenched hair flung wildly in his face as he grabbed for items that didn't belong to the company — photos with D.C. politicos, plaques of recognition, gifts from Troy. The officers stood unblinking at his ridiculous display. Wyatt's badge remained tightly gripped in one of their hands.

His sudden discharge had to be because of his crap of a post on Commynt. Wyatt was so steeped in his hubris that he didn't see that the desperate writing, however well-intentioned, would be the final nail in his rapidly lowering coffin. Wyatt brought negative attention to the company. A cardinal sin. Being a friend of Troy wouldn't save him. It was likely his trusted buddy that signed his death warrant.

Wyatt grimaced at Kelsey who stood with contempt in front of him.

"I guess you got what you wanted, huh?" he seethed. "For me to be fired."

"I didn't write the stupid post," Kelsey replied curtly. "You didn't need my help to be an idiot. That's all you."

"You wouldn't still be in this job if it wasn't for me!"

"Did you need help packing?" Kelsey laughed in his twisting face.

One of the security officers took the last memento out of Wyatt's hand and shoved it in the box. "Time to go, Mr. Schumacher."

The two hulking men firmly escorted Wyatt and his effects out of the building amid gasps from witnessing Myntors. Kelsey trailed behind the moving fiasco.

"You all can kiss this company goodbye!" he yelled before getting one last polite shove out of the building and into the street.

TWENTY

The Elemynt account from the anonymous organizers was updated again. The latest post congratulated the thousands of Myntors who raised their voices for good in the global walkout. By speaking up publicly and in large numbers they sent a message to the executive team that Elemynt needed to change for the better or risk losing its workforce.

What was happening behind closed doors, however, would infuriate every person who protested. A meeting of executives was indeed underway, but the goal was not to address the issues employees complained about. The strategy meeting centered on how to move past the dramatic uproar with the least change possible.

The Dream Team let employees have the opportunity to air grievances by not interrupting their protest. Their primary task though was to make sure a few vocal dissensions didn't affect the company's bottom line.

Kelsey dialed into the video conference from a small meeting room in a remote building on campus, far from her desk or anyone with a "Chief" or "VP" in their title. She needed to distance herself from the chaos, if only physically. Sarah would want to do most of the talking anyway. The new head of communications was positioned squarely in the middle of the room where the executives gathered. Kelsey watched the screen intently.

"I'm just going to say it," Sarah looked around the room. "We need to postpone E-Con this year or there's a huge possibility that it's going to backfire on us."

"Not an option," Troy said, furrowing his brow. "E-Con is our chance to save our reputation. We need to remind people why Elemynt is the best. We have new products to get out there."

"Besides, it's too late to delay it," Catherine said. "May I remind you that aside from the obvious damage to the company, the reputation of senior leadership is at stake as well."

The attendees in the room knew Catherine was referring to herself in particular. Catherine's high-profile role at a company accused of spreading hate speech and discrimination was devastating to her "Boss Lady" brand.

Criticisms of the COO in the press had intensified over the past few weeks. Devotees who once idolized Catherine and her female empowerment beliefs identified her as a central part of the problem. Shared concerns about how much Catherine knew about the lack of action on harassment complaints at Elemynt cast her legitimacy as a role model for women into doubt.

And rightfully so, Kelsey thought. After how Catherine treated her and countless other female employees, the criticisms were, unbeknownst to the general public, completely justified. By always putting Elemynt first, Catherine empowered the company to look past bad behavior in the name of growing the business.

Kelsey did her best to hide her deepening sadness. She was on video. Her every move was visible on the excessively large television screen in the room where the back and forth was underway.

Catherine was both defensive of her reputation and aggressive in leading the charge to protect it.

"The accusations are a pain," she said. "That doesn't mean this business stops running."

"I agree 110 percent," Troy confirmed. "We keep going with the plans for E-Con. Now what I wanna know is how do we get our Myntors back on track?"

"The employees who protested made their decision," Catherine said unequivocally. "Collect the names of those who participated from the facial recognition software and alert their managers immediately. They'll know what to do."

The callousness of the execs in the room was wholly unnerving to Kelsey. Their response to valid criticism was severe punishment. There was no consideration in the slightest of Myntors' demands or Daniela's pivotal memo. The selfishness of the leaders devoted to preserving the status quo would continue unchecked.

"If we don't create a space for Myntors to speak up they're going to keep talking to the media," Kelsey found herself saying. "Have we thought about that?"

Kelsey was mentally fried but the punitive train of thought needed to be derailed.

"How about we do a town hall?" Tai jumped in. "We get feedback from Myntors like in all-hands. This time we do it with an open mic. Let them get it off their chests."

Kelsey was taken aback by Tai's idea, mostly because they were in sync for once. Tai's recommendation was different from her usual approach of funneling carefully written messaging into speeches or Commynt posts or other channels that did not require more than a scripted response.

Troy wasn't convinced. "Won't having people telling us why they're upset in front of the whole company make the problem worse? Why would we do that? We have people send their questions in advance for a reason."

"It'll make people feel like we're listening with no filter," Tai said. "Either do it this way or it's going to get worse. I dunno. That's my take."

"Whatever," Troy said. "Go ahead and do it. They get to talk, E-Con is still on...everybody's happy."

Kelsey watched as the corresponding team members in the room sent off emails to move forward on Tai's idea and the direction Troy set for them. Catherine relaxed somewhat, also satisfied with the post-walkout resolution.

"Also, Kelsey…" Troy looked into the camera. "I want you to call your celebrity friend...Grace Oliver. Have her onstage with Catherine at E-Con to talk about our new features. We have her behind us and we can get the media back on our side."

Tasking his employee with carrying out a pure media play that did not care at all about Grace's cause or her defense of women on the app was an unquestionable compromise of Kelsey's morals. There had to be another way to shed a positive light on Elemynt.

"I don't know if I feel comfortable with that," Kelsey said meekly. "After the thing with the Emmys—"

"Kelsey, you work for me," Troy said coldly. "This is my company and obviously what I say goes. If you can't handle a simple request, you can start looking for a new job."

Kelsey looked to her former hero with one last plea for help. "Catherine, can I get your input on this?"

"Perhaps you didn't hear Troy correctly," Catherine said. "If you are silly enough to let your personal feelings cloud your judgment, you are welcome to return to Boston where you can rot at a third-rate startup praying that the company doesn't close down before your next paycheck. Are we clear? Or do you need me to repeat that?"

The onlookers in the room, including Sarah, waited for Kelsey's response.

"I'll make it work," she said.

Kelsey had no other words.

Troy, satisfied with her answer, brought the video call to an end.

"Give this a few days and I'm telling you the excitement for E-Con will make people forget about the walkout," he said. "We pull off a successful IPO and that's big money in the pockets of our Myntors. They've been waiting a long time for this and so have I. Let's do what we need to do."

Kelsey shut off the meeting just as a stream of uncontrollable tears down her face. She couldn't stand the dirty manipulation...the outright lies. Employees couldn't be so naive that they'd be distracted by a pile of cash or the shiny words that their CEO hurled at them regularly. The most brilliant minds in the world were so blinded by their cocoons of comfort that they couldn't see Elemynt for what it really was. Kelsey's sobbing intensified as she thought through the sequence of crippling issues that her employer put her through since her start.

Kelsey buried her head on the table in an attempt to make the hurt and sadness go away. She was tired of constantly crying and, more importantly, having reasons to cry.

Kelsey heard the meeting room door open obtrusively behind her.

"Go away!" she commanded the intruder.

There was no response. The door did not close. Kelsey lifted her head and wiped her flushed cheeks.

In the doorway stood Sarah shaking her head at Kelsey with the utmost condescension.

"What are you doing here?" Kelsey stammered.

"I saw you on the video call and I recognized this room," Sarah said. "I've been in here too, you know. To cry or to get myself together away from everybody else. It gets hard, doesn't it? The long nights... constantly protecting the company."

"It's been hell," Kelsey choked. "I don't know what I'm supposed to do about it."

"Play your role."

"Excuse me?"

"I know what happened in Tokyo...with Jon," Sarah stared at her.

"You have no idea," Kelsey shivered.

"Oh, I do. Because it happened to me too. On one of those 'work trips' he loves. We were at a bar in Amsterdam after a day at the local office. A couple of glasses of whiskey and he decided it was okay to put his grubby hands on my body. He told me that we'd work better as a team if I was to let him have his way with me. He said that *I* wanted it too."

Kelsey's eyes widened hearing Sarah retell a story similar to her own. She was horrified that Jon's despicable pattern of behavior extended to her closest teammate.

"When I got back from the trip, I reported him to HR but guess what? No one would take me seriously. Jon was a perfect manager and an essential member of the team. They said I was trying to bring him down because I was passed over for his role. Catherine? She laughed at me in my face."

"I thought you were okay working under Jon?" Kelsey sniffled. "That's what you told me."

Sarah dug her hands into Kelsey's trembling shoulders. "I've been at this company for five very long years, three of them leading external communications at Elemynt by myself. And what do I get for doing the best comms work this company's ever seen? Troy decided to put his friend Jon in the role that was supposed to be mine. He gave him a VP title, doubled his pay, and left me to follow orders that I should've been the one giving."

"Those are your problems Sarah, not mine," Kelsey huffed.

"See that's where you're wrong. I saw Jon playing the same 'let's go on a work trip' game with other girls in the company. He told them how special they were and how they should work closely together. He was a VP and their career was in his hands."

"So why didn't you tell me about this if you knew what was going on?" Kelsey winced.

"Because I needed you to stay," Sarah said. "You don't get it, do you?"

Kelsey shook her head no. She genuinely did not understand why her trusted colleague was suddenly so full of venom. Sarah exhaled in disgust.

"When I met you in your interview for the job, I knew that you were the pretty blonde that was exactly Jon's type. But there was something different about you. You had this... fire. You were a workhorse. If Jon made a move like I knew he would eventually, you wouldn't stop until you got justice. Jon had his reservations about you, but I made sure that Kelsey Pace was sitting in that seat next to him. It wouldn't be long before he invited you on one of his trips."

Kelsey recoiled in horror at the startling confirmation coming from her co-worker's lips. Sarah used her as a pawn from the moment they first met and acted as if she was the most sincere, nurturing teammate who wanted the new recruit to do her best at the company. Kelsey questioned every bit of support Sarah ever offered her. The pep talks and the guidance on making impact were all bullshit motivated by her sick agenda. Sarah doomed Kelsey to fail from the beginning.

"As it turns out, you aren't the woman I thought you were," Sarah seethed. "You're weak and because of that Jon would've gotten away with his filth again. Except who knew the low-life couldn't keep his hands to himself at the holiday party? I told HR that they could either fire him or I would leak the video of Jon with his dirty paws all over that girl to the press. And you'll love this... for extra insurance, I sent Catherine a list of names of other girls he assaulted."

"How did you even get access to that information?" Kelsey said with her mouth agape.

"That part was easy," Sarah smiled. "I checked his calendar to see what long trips he took with just himself and one female employee. Turns out the names matched up pretty well with the list of HR reports against him."

Kelsey shook her head in stunned disbelief. "You ratted out assault victims so you could force your boss out and move up in the company?"

"I did what I had to do!" Sarah yelled defensively.

"By making me a part of your sick game?" Kelsey yelled back.

The revelation loosened another stream of tears within her.

"I am your manager and you will do what I tell you to do!" Sarah commanded. "Jon is gone, I am the VP of External Communications, and right now we have an internal uprising that we have to put a stop to. I want you out there writing me some goddamn press releases, or I will tell Troy that you lied about Jon and have your name in the press as the girl who cried rape."

Kelsey cowered in Sarah's despicable presence. There was no doubt her certifiably insane manager would make good on the threats. Kelsey sat glued to the conference room chair unsure of what to say or do next.

"One more thing, Kelsey," Sarah said as she opened the door to leave. "I noticed you haven't been posting on Elemynt lately. Go ahead and step that up. We don't want anybody thinking you don't support this company."

Sarah exited the room, leaving Kelsey to clean up the pool of tears on the table.

* * *

In the less than 24 hours after Tai posted the announcement of the emergency town hall on Commynt, the hastily put together, internal-only event was underway. No one told Kelsey she had to be there in person. Sequestering herself in a small meeting room on the far side of campus was Kelsey's silent protest. She watched the live video stream of the packed room from a building that was thankfully nearly empty.

Troy and Catherine sat at the head of the stage in the auditorium in front of an audience of thousands, with many more watching at their desks. No contractors. Full-time employees only. A lengthy queue of Myntors waited their turn in front of a mic placed in the aisle of the auditorium.

The employees in line fidgeted in anticipation of asking questions of their leaders. The other senior executives flanking Catherine and Troy also showed signs of unease. A showdown was about to commence.

Kelsey was surprised that the town hall was allowed to happen at all. Personal reservations aside, the attendees at the executive meeting knew Tai was right. Without the open forum, more leaks from dissatisfied Myntors were inevitable.

Troy began the tense meeting with his signature thoughtful pace across the stage. He lowered his head at what was likely a pre-approved angle, followed by a gaze of radiant optimism toward the audience.

"This is a challenging time," he spoke slowly. "There's been a lot of ups and downs these past few months. What's most important to me and to our team here is that Myntors have a platform to make their voices heard at this company."

There was a smattering of applause from those in the room. Kelsey rolled her eyes.

"I believe that we can move forward together through honest conversations like what we're hoping for today. Thank you everybody for being a part of this process with us."

Troy gestured for the first person in the line to begin her question. A mousy woman in an oversized hoodie tapped the mic.

"Hi, my name is Claudia. I work in Sales Engineering," she cracked. "I wasn't sure if I wanted to say anything today. There's a lot of pressure for Myntors to act like everything is fine and that we always love working here. We can't talk about how terrible the company can be sometimes."

Her heartfelt remark was met with supportive applause. Kelsey could also hear an undercurrent of boos from unseen faces in the auditorium. A sense of despair rose from within Claudia. She second-guessed her decision to speak. Revealing her true feelings while the whole company watched was enormously brave of her. Troy smiled through gritted teeth.

"Don't boo," Troy instructed the crowd. "Elemynt is great because we listen to each other. Please go on."

"What I'm saying is a lot of the women I talk to here feel like we're second-class citizens," Claudia said. "Our co-workers harass us or put us down. They make us feel like we're not welcome. If we tell our managers, a lot of times they'll say we're being troublemakers. These things are happening on the app too. Women are being harassed and it feels like Elemynt doesn't care."

Troy was silent. Kelsey cringed at the awkwardness in the room in the face of an undeniably true statement.

"We hear your concerns," Troy said to Claudia. "We know we need to do better and I promise that we will."

The two stared at each other. Troy moved on.

Claudia's opener was followed by a long line of employees critiquing the company culture and the emotional pain that resulted from it.

"I'm constantly being talked over in meetings and having my work mansplained to me."

"My team members have told me to my face that I'm only here because I'm Latino and they needed diversity."

"I've been here for almost four years now. My male co-workers who I helped train are getting promotions over me."

"I love this company very much. But I'm tired of being called 'honey' or 'girl' or 'sweetie' every day."

A succession of agitated Myntors shared accounts of their struggles with colleagues. They spoke of how uncomfortable it made them feel to be subjected to a culture that favored white males and where their ideas were undervalued. They shared stories of avoiding conversations with family and friends who held them responsible for Elemynt's faults. Pent up anguish and despair came to light in the normally joyous auditorium.

A young African-American woman with a curly afro hairstyle approached the mic. "A big part of the reason I came to Elemynt is because I wanted to represent for my community," she said. "The app is how, I'd say, most of us communicate. However, it's hard to want to stay here when I find out my co-workers were taking bets on how soon they could make me leave. Instead of them being held accountable for what they did, I was the one who got moved to another team."

Troy again issued a reassuring response sorely lacking in substance.

More minority women lamented being referred to as "articulate" or "hostile," having to perform menial tasks not asked of their male colleagues, or repeatedly being called the name of another co-worker of the same race. Employees across a wide spectrum of race, age, and gender talked about the depression and mental anxiety the "microaggressions" caused. Some spoke about having to go to therapy or the health problems they incurred because of the additional stress being a minority at Elemynt caused.

The harrowing stories continued for hours while execs squirmed in their seats. It was time to wrap up and no solution to address the myriad of issues was proposed by the figureheads at the front of the room.

Troy stepped back from his center spot to let Catherine take the stage in his place. She delicately held the microphone in her hand.

"I'm grateful to employees who shared feedback," Catherine said to the assembly. "I apologize for any frustration we may have caused as the leadership of this company. From your comments, we recognize that we may not be doing the best job in supporting all of you. What I can tell you is that we will review how we can change that. We always welcome your input."

Catherine spoke with the emotional depth of a child reciting their ABCs. Kelsey struggled with the lingering pain of watching Myntors bravely telling their stories, not knowing they were falling on deaf ears. There would be no follow-ups or plans put in place as a result of the town hall. It was all a show.

Catherine may have convinced everyone watching of her sincerity, but Kelsey saw her for what she was — a company spokeswoman using her training to win over the room. Catherine hadn't reached the Chief Operating Officer level without softening her adept communication or scaling back behavior that could be seen as aggressive, the opposite of the advice her "Boss Lady" book offered. Overt kindness was how she asserted dominance and disarmed her adversaries.

"We are a family and these are issues we have to work on together internally," Catherine said, essentially admonishing current and future leakers. "I encourage you as Myntors to continue to root for our company and champion our values. We're not perfect, but we will always strive to be our best."

After Catherine's trite statement concluded, the auditorium was doused in the upbeat music that signaled the end of staff-wide gatherings. The emotionally spent employees filed out of the venue. Most looked satisfied with Troy and Catherine's pacifying words and extolled their honesty. Those who voiced their concerns in front of their peers reset their emotions before returning to their respective buildings. The townhall idea worked. The mass revolt was extinguished. Troy's billion-dollar company would live to see another day.

* * *

Kelsey dialed Grace's number with urgency. Troy had a request for the star. To not at least ask her would be an infraction against the company. If Kelsey did not go out on her own terms, she would never be able to forgive herself.

"Troy? He flew to L.A. last week to apologize to me in person," Grace said with a lingering trace of sadness. "He said he wants to partner with me on a tool you guys are building?"

"You already talked?" Kelsey gasped.

"Yeah, he asked me to make a big announcement at E-Con with him about this feature I inspired. I haven't given him an answer yet."

The way Troy implored Kelsey to reach out to Grace never suggested that he spoke with her already. Kelsey was being played again. She was his way to seal the deal, to use someone close to Grace to convince her to follow through with his commands. And he hadn't bothered to tell the unsuspecting celebrity that the security feature they were supposedly collaborating on had been languishing in a digital dustbin for months.

"I want to say that Troy has the best intentions but... I can't," Kelsey confessed. "They're going to use you for the great PR. Having the woman who stood up to Elemynt onstage at E-Con is how they make themselves look great in front of the press."

A silent pause on the other end of the line was followed by sighs of distress. Grace had been through enough Elemynt-inflicted cruelty. Having the company take advantage of a woman who went through unfathomable hell as a result of their product was a twist of the knife.

"He also told me he'd donate to my charity if I did it," Grace said mournfully. "He never asked me if I was okay. What I got was a smile and a seven-figure check dangled in front of me."

"Grace, are you okay?" Kelsey asked earnestly.

"I wish I was," she replied. "I stopped using the app when the death threats started coming in. Now, these guys are showing up outside my house and threatening my family..."

Grace recounted somberly how an anonymous account posted her home address on Elemynt. The revelation was accompanied by promises to rape her violently and kill each of her loved ones. She continued to receive outrageous letters, phone calls, and emails with descriptions of how she would be murdered or encouraging her to commit suicide. Bomb threats were called on her office and to her mother's home. She faced a constant barrage of evil, all because she was vocal on her Elemynt account about the issues women were up against.

Kelsey tried her best to keep her composure. She didn't want to relay to Grace that the resolution to the horrors she faced teetered on hopeless, though that would have been the truth.

Elemynt's thin plans to resolve online harassment were limited to the announcement of a feature that was not likely to be deployed in a meaningful way. The system developed by the engineers could identify bad actors, but there was nothing to suggest the moderation process would be more stringent following its implementation. Like many other systems at Elemynt, it was a tool to project ambitions of change that was a purely symbolic gesture.

Troy had no incentive to alter his practices because no one from the outside could see into the inner workings of his product. No one knew the scale of the app's problems or even its successes other than those who worked at the highest level at Elemynt.

The knowledge of the Myntors who made up the company's workforce was limited to the scope of their work. Small pieces of a greater puzzle. They had no concrete understanding of the overall direction of the company other than what Troy and the Dream Team told them.

The future of Elemynt was Troy's game to win or lose. There was no way he'd let the company fail because the experiences of what he saw as a small fraction of users did not match the contentedness of the majority. Grace and the many women and minorities run amok by Elemynt stood no chance.

Kelsey could only comfort Grace.

"There's so many more people out there that love you than these dickheads hiding behind their phones," she said, restraining her emotions.

"Of course, there are," Grace said. "I get messages from women everywhere who say they love what I do and support me. But I had to hire bodyguards and put extra security on my house because I don't know which of these wackos is going to follow through with their comments."

Kelsey was mortified that she was one of the precious few that knew the full scope of the problems women faced on Elemynt. The study of female users Troy commissioned revealed that more than seventy percent said they had been sexually harassed on the platform at some point. A whopping 93 percent said they had a negative encounter with another user on the app related to their gender, race, or sexual orientation. And that was just the women the researchers were in contact with. The team surmised that many more quit the app because of the atrocious behavior and thus were no longer reachable through social media.

Like Grace, a considerable number of the women surveyed said that they continued using the app despite the negativity. They felt Elemynt was their sole way of staying connected with the world. Deleting Elemynt meant cutting themselves off from cherished family and friends.

Kelsey wanted to believe that Elemynt, the legendary tech institution she supported so strongly, was working to help those hundreds of millions of people. However, those at the top of the company did not care enough about their troubles to take lasting action.

Troy's response to the damaging data was to bury the study to make sure it wasn't seen by anyone outside of the executive conference room. In doing so, the CEO silenced the voices of more than half of Elemynt's users. As long as advertisers could keep putting ads for chocolate candy and pink razor blades in women's feeds, the Dream Team would take no major step to correct the "engagement" on the app.

"I know you said this security feature was already built," Grace said. "But I think it could help a lot of women who want to keep using Elemynt. I need your honest opinion. Should I go onstage with him?"

Kelsey thought carefully.

* * *

Just as Troy predicted, the noise surrounding the walkout evaporated within a criminally short time. A trickle of comments in the internal threads calling for change was the sole evidence that it was once a dominating cause for concern. Employees returned their focus to work, content that senior leadership was working diligently on their demands. In reality, they were doing the complete opposite.

Melissa and members of the People team met with every manager at the company in top-secret, mandatory workshops. They shared tactics for alleviating concerns among their direct reports.

When speaking to small groups, the managers were to point out individual employees whose recent accomplishments reflected the spirit of Elemynt. Lavish them with praise. Hold them up as shining examples for others to follow.

They were instructed to conduct open Q&As with their team but take a long time to answer each question to limit the number that could be asked. Trail off. Digress. Bring every question back to the company's pre-written lines. Say "I hear you." Listen with feigned sincerity. Offer up nothing.

The public would not escape the carefully crafted tactics either.

Under the direction of Troy, each high-level executive took to their Elemynt accounts for a collective charm offensive. They posted photos of their darling children. Pics of dogs at sunset were deployed. Glowing images of grandmothers, nature walks, weddings, and their favorite people to follow were shared in a hardly subtle tribute to the company.

Each caption was some variation of "Elemynt is the best and this is why. Keep using it."

Commercials featuring swaying fields and happy moms and groups of people whose lives were made better through the app played in constant rotation on television and video sites. The company plastered major transportation centers in Washington, D.C., New York, and Los Angeles with banners that announced how Elemynt was and would always be "people first."

In a post on his personal account, Troy promised to "keep working to make Elemynt better" but made no mention of the actual walkout. What he did offer was a special treat for the public...a tease of the grand spectacle of E-Con. He cleverly inferred that the long-awaited IPO was coming soon.

The post was the breadcrumbs the media needed to completely forget about the employee protests. The rumor machine about the soon to be biggest news story to ever hit the tech industry was in full effect.

The excitement surrounding the pronouncements flooded the Elemynt campus as well. Myntors talked in the halls, over free coffee and kombucha, and at the thirteen food service locations on campus about the coming IPO. No one knew exactly how much money they stood to make. What they did know is many more zeros would be added to their bank accounts. The promise of a big financial haul was enough to let the spirit of the protests against Elemynt fade into a distant memory.

If Kelsey were to bring up the continued ills of the company to a fellow Myntor, she would have been instantly attacked. Critiques of Elemynt at that point were considered treason.

Kelsey desperately wanted legitimate change at the company that was in the best interests of its employees and its users. She felt alone in that desire.

After weeks of lost sleep, Kelsey knew she had a phone call to make. Someone deserved an apology.

* * *

Kelsey and Jade were miles away from Silicon Valley. They braced the cold, early morning air of Jack London Square in Oakland. The sole movement in the empty plaza were ships bobbing silently in the water. Metal shipping cranes from the nearby Port of Oakland towered over the skyline. The restaurants that lined the area were vacant and uncomfortably quiet. A train rumbled in the distance.

They remained in place to talk to the person standing across from them.

Daniela, the woman who was always brimming with confidence, said nothing. She was burdened by her long-simmering disappointment in the two women.

"Your friend tries to make the world a better place and you turn on her," Daniela shook her head. "Thanks for that."

"I promise that's not what happened," Kelsey said.

"You were too wrapped in yourself to realize the company was treating you and other people like dirt," Daniela said. "When you finally figured that out you came running to the person who called them out on it. That pretty much sum it up?"

Her assessment was true. For those transgressions and more, Kelsey owed Daniela several apologies. Kelsey's self-centered behavior didn't allow her to empathize with Daniela's efforts to uplift the people around her. To Kelsey, Daniela was needlessly taking the company off track with her calls for inclusion. Kelsey did not make the isolating task any easier for her friend.

"I'm sorry for how I treated you," Kelsey said. "Honestly, you didn't deserve that. I should have been listening more instead of talking over you all the time."

"I'm glad you came to that realization," Daniela said softly. "Are you still blaming me for organizing the walkout?"

Jade reeled from Daniela's loaded assertion. She, like many other Myntors, believed Daniela was at the center of the unrest. The anonymous organizers never surfaced so people held on to the assumption that the departed employee was behind it. Daniela's bold calls to action in her memo gave them every reason to believe that was so.

"Daniela, sweetie, if you didn't call the walkout who did?" Jade asked exhaustedly.

"She's right behind you," Daniela pointed.

Tai stood casually under an unlit lamp post. She walked toward them. "Sup."

Kelsey wanted to slap Tai across her face. Her scheming co-worker accused her in front of a room of executives of being complicit in the orchestration of the protest. Why Tai would do that knowing that she was the mastermind the whole time was unfathomable.

"You have got to be kidding me!" Kelsey groaned.

"No joke," Tai shrugged. "All me."

"I should've known it was you!" Kelsey said. "You have access to every employee's phone number because Internal Comms has their contact information. You could easily send a message to everybody at the same time."

"And do it with a fake number so nobody knows it was me, yeah," Tai said. "I might know a thing or two about getting around the Security team's systems. Setting up an anonymous Elemynt account was the easiest part. Piece of cake."

"But, hun, why would you want to encourage Myntors to go against the company?" Jade asked. "You love Elemynt more than any of us. You've been at the company for almost a decade now."

"Bingo," Tai said. "That's exactly why. I've been working at Elemynt for the longest. I've watched it go downhill. When we started, we had this vision that we were going to change the world for good by connecting people. Now it's all about making money and getting more data from more users so we can sell their lives to advertisers. That shady stuff and letting people get harassed is not what I signed up for. So I did what I had to do."

Tai regarded her colleagues with defeat rather than her usual defiance. Each of the women could understand her position, Kelsey chief among them. She traveled the same turbulent roller coaster of emotions in a fraction of the time.

Tai backed away from Kelsey and Jade. "If you want to hit me just try not to do it in the face? I have a 9 a.m. meeting tomorrow."

"No one's punching anyone," Daniela said.

Despite Tai's attempt to trash her career, Kelsey could not hold her at fault. Her methods were suspect, but her intentions were pure. If a die-hard loyalist like Tai could turn against Elemynt, Kelsey wondered why she had for so long been needlessly devoted to her oppressor.

"I can't believe I thought Elemynt would support me," Kelsey said, hanging her head in shame. "This is…"

"Kelsey, what's wrong?" Jade asked. "What happened?"

"You know how I was avoiding you all?" Kelsey asked.

"Yes, we pretty much stalked your calendar to find you," Jade said.

An emotional floodgate burst open from deep within Kelsey's soul. She recounted to her colleagues Jon's assault in Tokyo and her subsequent ordeal with HR. She shared the heartbreak of her lowest moments and how Sarah deliberately engineered the tragic chain of events to happen. Jon stepped into Sarah's trap and ruined Kelsey's life in the process.

Kelsey once believed that powering forward was the best way to go. But she didn't have it in her to continue.

The ladies swooped in to give their friend the hug she desperately needed.

"I take it you heard the news about Jon?" Jade said.

"No, what did he do now?" Kelsey said, wiping away the beginning of a tear. "I thought he disappeared with his money."

"He just landed a job as Chief Marketing Officer at LunaTech," Jade sighed. "He's basically in a bigger role at a new company."

"With a nicer salary too," Tai added.

Kelsey's heart slipped out of her chest and crashed to the brick-paved ground. Jon's ability to level up within a few weeks of his ousting from Elemynt was sickening. His behavior had minimal consequences on his career and it nearly tore hers apart. What burned Kelsey deeper was the gigantic, undeserved payday on his way out courtesy of Elemynt. Jon didn't ever have to work again. He had tens of millions of dollars in hush money in the bank. Accepting the new role was a power play to assert his dominance in the industry. Jon was gone but made sure he would never be forgotten by his former colleagues.

"If Elemynt let HR silence you...a person telling the truth," Daniela thought aloud. "Think about how far they'll go to protect the company."

Jade stood ardently in the company's defense to the shock of her friends.

"I'm not saying it excuses what they did to Kelsey, but come on. Every business looks out for its best interests. Elemynt's not the worst place in the world."

The ladies stared at Jade blankly.

It was easy for her to feel that way. Jade operated within the most gilded bubble of anyone. Her proximity to the glamour of celebrity culture was an indulgent treat few Myntors had the pleasure of experiencing. Jade really did believe that Elemynt was a virtuous company caught up in undeserved scandal. She was the last of their group to feel that way.

Kelsey hoped that her friend hadn't been brainwashed like herds of other

Myntors. If so, her world needed to be shattered with the hammer of truth.

"Did you know that Troy is using one of your celebrity partners as a pawn?" Kelsey asked insistently. "He wants Grace Oliver to speak at E-Con so she and the other famous influencers will stop telling people how terrible we are."

"Kelsey's not lying," Tai shrugged.

"Holy crap," Daniela said, shaking her head. "Just when I thought this couldn't get worse."

Jade stood motionless staring at the ground beneath her. The news was more of a gut punch to her than Kelsey expected. The facade of joy Jade put up to shield her sadness from outsiders weakened.

"This role has become the absolute worst," Jade said dejectedly. "I can't get anyone to partner with me. Talent is leaving the platform left and right because they're either dealing with harassment themselves or they're watching the news and seeing it happen to their friends in the industry. I keep making excuses for Elemynt but they're starting to see through it and nothing I'm saying matters."

"They're seeing the truth," Kelsey said.

"It'll get better though," Jade smiled weakly. "We just need to give it time."

Daniela was not convinced. "Jade, why did you delete your daughters' Elemynt account?"

Jade was unsettled by Daniela's pointed question. She tripped over her words. She tried to formulate a proper excuse.

Kelsey was unsure of what Daniela was talking about. Kelsey hadn't used the app in months so she didn't know who was posting or when.

"These are little girls and people are leaving disgusting comments about them on their photos," Jade said. "The most awful language! I log in and see people calling them whores or saying how they can't wait for them to turn 18. My girls can't read the comments on their own posts."

Jade's which that were always clear and full of life dulled with tears of anguish. She loved her daughters dearly. She would forever go to great lengths to protect them.

"I report the accounts myself so of course it gets fast-tracked because I'm the head of media partnerships..." Jade said.

"And you're aware not everyone has the same privilege," Daniela said.

"I know, I know," Jade said as she stemmed the trail of blurring mascara. "Most of my team's time has become helping our partners deal with the same kind of issues. I did not sign up to be an on-demand therapist."

"Troy's priority isn't people, it's non-stop growth for his baby," Daniela emphasized. "Elemynt treats the problems women and black and brown people are up against as no big deal."

"People are miserable," Kelsey said in agreement. "And the company is making a lot of money off of it which is insane."

"It's time for Elemynt to make real changes to its policies," Daniela stated. "That's not going to happen if employees don't speak up."

"Ahem, we did a whole walkout," Tai said. "You saw how that went."

"The walkout worked," Daniela insisted. "It got the attention of the executive team and lots of people outside of Elemynt. The problem is employees got suckered by more empty promises we know the company has no intentions of keeping."

"Or they'll do the bare minimum," Tai said.

"We have to do something bigger," Daniela thought hard.

"What's bigger than a global employee protest?" Kelsey asked skeptically.

A lightbulb went off in Daniela's head. "People out there know Elemynt is up to no good, but they can't prove it. They go off guesses and suspicions. And reporters will keep writing whatever Elemynt feeds them. On top of that, the company knows Congress has no clue what they're supposed to be regulating, so there's no change happening there. The public can't hold Elemynt accountable unless they have hard evidence of how bad things are. We're going to give it to them."

Kelsey thought about the tons of documents that would expose Elemynt's villainous ways. The studies they killed. The email exchanges. The analyses of racist content and false information on the platform and the plans they made to ignore them. It was all there.

"If people outside of Elemynt see the secrets that the company hides from them, they'll lose their entire minds," Kelsey said.

"So we make it all public at E-Con," Daniela said fearlessly. "It's one of the biggest online events ever. Millions of people watch the livestream, not to mention the TV news coverage and the reporting on it."

"Are you crazy?!" Tai said exclaimed. "Because you sound like you're crazy. This is internal-only documentation we're talking about releasing."

"Elemynt's lawyers will be kicking down our front doors," Jade said.

"They'd tie us up and bury our bodies under the campus," Tai added. "Being escorted away by security on national television? Not a good look."

"There has to be a way to do this without being caught," Daniela said unswayed.

"Anything's possible at Elemynt," Kelsey offered meekly.

The words escaped Kelsey's lips because she knew them to be true. Still, the idea of a reconnaissance mission against her current employer was quite a leap.

Tai rolled her eyes in a dramatic display. "Let's say I was to consider getting access to this documentation that proves how shitty Elemynt is without anyone noticing. Who are we supposed to send it to?"

"If there's a way to do it anonymously, I could share with my reporter contacts," Kelsey found herself saying. "But come on, this is seriously dangerous stuff we're talking about. Taking on one of the most influential companies in the world?"

"It's become very necessary, don't you think?" Daniela said. "We have to get Elemynt to slow down and think about their impact on society. They have to build products with accountability in mind, not just what gets them the most users."

An awkward silence. The faint crank of metal cranes in the distance, but no one saying a word. Charting a new course for Elemynt was a daring proposal. One that could alter their lives forever. They couldn't make the decision on a whim.

"If we don't take this step, who will?" Daniela pleaded. "Would you rather be loyal to a company that puts you through hell and doesn't give a damn about it or fight for the billion-plus people out there? They need us."

Kelsey had nothing to lose. She already had her eye on the door for longer than she cared to admit. The people in whom she entrusted her career were the ones setting her up for failure. Catherine, Troy, Jon, and Sarah. The groups who she previously regarded as aggressors — the protesting Myntors, the civil rights organizations in NYC, Congress — were just people standing up for what they believed in. Kelsey couldn't recognize that because their goals were in contrast to hers. In retrospect, it was the detractors were on the right side of history.

Looking back at their time together, Kelsey knew that Daniela hoped she would challenge herself to be a better version of the woman she had come to know. Instead, Kelsey went off on a nebulous quest for "impact" thinking it would be the secret to her success. She shut down the friend who was guiding her toward a better path.

When Kelsey was busy looking to Sarah in admiration, she should have taken lessons from Jade, a mentor and a friend. The guide to a successful life and career was right in front of Kelsey's eyes. Stay strong and be the boss without losing sight of who you are.

Tai had been a pain in the ass since Kelsey first met her. She now understood it was because Tai was passionate about the mission of her work. She consistently stood in defense of it. Her approach may have been more aggressive than

Kelsey's, but they were two sides of the same coin.

Kelsey's fear of retribution from Elemynt was outweighed by her desire for fairness and justice. For women, people of color, and those at the intersections of underrepresented backgrounds. No one should feel like a second-class citizen on an app meant for everyone. If Elemynt was truly a platform for connecting the whole world, the company needed to start acting like it. The enchantment of Elemynt would keep pulling Kelsey back in if she didn't take a stand.

"I'm in," Kelsey said.

"You're game?" Daniela said with surprise.

"You told me to find my voice and stand up for what I believe in," Kelsey said. "I'll follow your lead. Tell me what you need."

Daniela looked to the remaining ladies. "Tai? Jade?"

The two stared off in the distance. No response from either.

"You think I want to go through the effort of doing this?" Daniela said asked earnestly. "I don't. But I want to walk away from Elemynt knowing my time there meant something. Giving voice to the voiceless is what we're about. We know that"

Her pleas again went unanswered.

"I can't believe I have to convince the woman who organized a campus-wide walkout," Daniela chuckled.

"I did it secretly," Tai frowned.

"Which means you can do it again."

"Are you challenging me?"

"Yes, I am."

"Well..." Tai smirked. "I guess I'm down for a little anarchy. You're on, sister!"

Jade, the final link in the chain, was hesitant to show the same enthusiasm.

"I'm not sure I'm comfortable with this, loves," Jade said reluctantly. "Can't we just go to E-Con and enjoy it?"

"Are you really going to enjoy it though?" Daniela challenged. "After all that's happened?"

"Your celebrity partners are leaving the platform and it's tanking your reputation," Kelsey said.

"It's not my reputation I care about," Jade said defensively.

"You came here because you wanted to help people," Kelsey pressed.

"We all did."

"And you want Sophie and Stella to grow up in a world that doesn't treat them like target practice. Their mommy has always had their back. She's their hero."

"That's true, but..." Jade said.

"I'm telling you we can do this without people knowing it's us," Tai implored. "Troy's not the only one who can keep secrets."

"We're not talking about revealing business plans or proprietary technology," Daniela assured Jade. "Show the people the truth that's hiding in the cracks and let them decide for themselves if they want to stay on the app."

Jade flipped her hair and smiled mischievously. "So, darling...what did you have in mind?"

* * *

Two short days left until E-Con. The teams normally seated in Kelsey's corner of the office were either at the venue or scattered in large conference rooms. There were rehearsals to be done, post-event marketing campaigns to launch. The grand event required the attention of a wide range of staff to focus on the details that would make it a massive success. If there was ever an opportunity to tap into Elemynt's systems unnoticed, this was it.

Kelsey tried not to let her nerves get the best of her. She had to remember the mission at hand. Download everything they could and do it quickly.

There may not have been people around, but Kelsey and Tai were not alone.

The security cameras affixed in nearly every corner of the campus buildings meant someone was always watching. On the way to her workspace the day before, Kelsey counted 14 total. Three pointed at the building entrance, five in the lobby, four more in the hallway, and two with her desk in clear sight. There was no escaping the heavy surveillance. As if she needed more reasons to be terrified.

Daniela drove the formulation of the plan, however, as much as she wanted to, she could not be on campus to carry it out. Daniela was a marked woman. Her presence on campus would result in a prompt call to Security thanks to the results of her notorious memo.

To stay connected with their friend and co-conspirator, Tai and Kelsey equipped themselves with Bluetooth earbuds to remain on a three-way phone call. They wouldn't talk above a whisper. Too much was at stake.

Tai took extra measures to make sure that she and Kelsey would not be found out. Tai used technical wizardry Kelsey didn't quite understand to log in with other random employees' usernames and passwords on burner laptops.

IP address rerouting would make it appear to Security as if the files were being accessed by those employees at their assigned workspaces. If the other Myntors were apprehended, a quick analysis would show they never touched the important files during the time frame.

Tai and Kelsey, meanwhile, would be sitting pretty at Kelsey's desk in plain view of the security cameras. If by chance they were suspected of pulling off a heist, video would show the two were working as normal in their space. Nothing to see there.

Tai crossed her fingers that the plan would work. "A bunch of random hackers on the other side of the world got backdoor access without anybody knowing. I can pull this off too."

She didn't sound 100 percent sure. Which made Kelsey exceptionally nervous.

Kelsey tried to ignore her racing pulse and pounding heartbeat. She was in too deep to turn back. She needed to believe in herself and remember why she was taking the risk in the first place. The terrible secrets and lies contained in the files would be exposed for the world to consume. With knowledge came change.

"You wanna look calm like you're doing your regular job," Tai whispered.

"Got it," Kelsey said. Her fingers hovered over the laptop waiting for Tai's signal.

Tai logged into the Security team's hidden communication channel to monitor the chatter.

"If they suspect something big, they'll say it in here," she said.

Kelsey took a breath.

"You've got this, ladies," Daniela said in their ear.

With a few keystrokes and clicks, the downloading of documents began. Analysis of the amount of violent and divisive content on the platform. Email exchanges that showed how the company buried technology that would curb it. Details of the hundreds of data points Elemynt kept on each of its users. Presentations, PDFs, Excel files, emails. The laptops were turned at an angle so the spree couldn't be viewed by the cameras. The progress bar ticked upwards as the pair loaded file after file.

Seconds felt like hours. At any minute, security could round the corner and yank the laptops away and their badges along with it.

"How're we doing over there?" Daniela asked.

"Peachy keen," Kelsey said shakily.

"There's something else I want you to do."

"Kinda busy here, Daniela," Tai said without moving her fingers from her keyboard.

"There are going to be too many people cheering Elemynt on at E-Con," Daniela said through their earbuds. "We need to change the dynamic. Kelsey, do you have access to the E-Con guest list?"

"Yeah, why?"

"When are they printing registration badges?"

"Tomorrow. No last-minute changes after that."

"Tai, do you have the names of the Myntors who participated in the walkout?" Daniela asked.

Tai thought it over. "Not really. I sent the info to every employee at the company. That's not gonna help."

"What about the facial recognition database?" Kelsey suggested. "Troy told Security to analyze the video from the protest to identify all the Myntors who were there."

"You're kind of a genius, Kelsey," Tai grinned. "I can find that no problem."

Kelsey smiled warmly. But there was no time to appreciate Tai's kind words.

A new plan was set in motion. Together, Kelsey and Tai worked to swap out the employee guest list for E-Con with the names of people who protested during the walkout. The batch of Myntors who received the last-minute invitation wouldn't know why or how they made the list nor would they care. They scored a coveted seat at E-Con. No questions necessary.

Those employees who were on the original list would receive an email update that they were "waitlisted." Because of the switch, the would-be guests could show up to the venue if they wanted to, but they would not receive a badge. No confirmed invitation, no credentials.

Kelsey did her best to lower her quickening heartbeat. Their task escalated from downloading a bunch of files to an intricate plot with many moving parts.

"Is there a way to make sure they don't know who made the changes?" Kelsey asked.

"Already on it," Tai said. "We change the name that last accessed the list to another employee account."

"Brilliant," Daniela said. "Who though?"

Security would surely be on the doorstep of whomever they selected.

"Put Sarah's name on there," Kelsey said without hesitation.

"Whoa, we got a dangerous woman here!" Tai grinned slyly.

"Sarah loves being in charge," Kelsey said. "Let's give her more responsibility."

How about that?"

Daniela and Tai praised Kelsey's bold move in excited whispers. For someone to set their manager up for failure took nerve. Kelsey didn't bat an eyelash. She stopped caring about Sarah's professional well-being a long time ago.

"Tai, add the name Brad Smith on the list if you can," Kelsey said.

"Who's that?"

"Big fan of Elemynt."

Tai made the change without question. She and Kelsey continued to download the mass of files in their crosshairs.

Daniela's voice piped into their earbuds. "Can you put my name on the guestlist too? I don't want to miss the fireworks."

"Nope. Uh uh. Big red flag," Tai said. "Everybody from Maine to California knows who you are. We can't put you on unless the plan is to ruin what we got going."

Daniela sucked her teeth at the exclusion. The ladies were right. If the infamous Myntor was seen walking through the doors of the auditorium, she'd be at best escorted very far away from the venue. At worse, she'd be jailed for trespassing. Or be the victim of whatever vindictive plan Troy could cook up.

"We'll find another way, Daniela," Kelsey assured her.

Footsteps.

Kelsey and Tai froze. Someone was walking up behind them. Their plan was discovered. They were done, it was a wrap. Kelsey's life and career flashed before her eyes.

To the pair's great relief, the shuffling was from two random Myntors making their way through the adjacent walkway. The startled twosome turned their attention back to the laptops. They needed to be more selective about which files to obtain. Time was a factor.

"How are the files coming?" Daniela pressed.

"Smooth as silk," Kelsey said in an attempt to convince herself she had the situation under control.

Kelsey was keen on getting the study that Troy commissioned of female Elemynt users. The damaging one he successfully made disappear. The file folder contained video interviews, datasets, notes from the researchers, and presentations outlining the harm Elemynt unleashed on the lives of women everywhere. The study was also emblematic of the problems other people from diverse backgrounds faced on the app.

The size of it was so massive that Kelsey was hesitant to make it one of the first files they grabbed. She didn't want to set off alarms. However, she wouldn't walk away without it. Kelsey's conscience wouldn't allow her to let the critical information remain hidden away.

Kelsey fought against her nerves. She clicked the download button.

Twenty percent.

Thirty percent.

The eyes of the cameras overhead bore into Kelsey's back.

Kelsey nearly swiped the laptop into the trash can under her desk at the sight of a hulking Elemynt security officer who appeared out of nowhere. The burly uniformed enforcer was walking the path toward them. There was nowhere to run.

"Look, Tai," Kelsey gulped.

"Routine sweep," Tai said without moving her lips. "He's going to turn left at the next hallway."

Sure enough, the polo-wearing official disappeared down an adjacent corridor.

"We have to hurry up," Tai said. "If we see another one, they're definitely headed this way."

The two renegades were in the clear. At least Kelsey thought so until Tai sat back in panicked disbelief.

"Holy hell...we're on their radar," she said in a muted panic.

Kelsey watched with dread as Tai scrolled through the security team's private communication channel. Messages were being traded back and forth in a flurry.

"Security is trying to detect the source of the reroute," Tai shuddered. "We have to go. If they find us, it's two minutes max before the closest person on the team makes it here."

"How much do you have left to download?" Daniela asked through the earbuds.

The enormous file for the study of women trailed at a sluggish 80 percent. It was without question the document that most represented that Elemynt was not the advocate for people it heralded itself to be. Kelsey refused to walk away from the laptop without having a copy of it in her possession. She willed the ticking number to reach completion.

"Put some speed on it, sister!" Tai warned. "If we download any more, they'll shut everything down."

"Almost there, I swear!"

After what seemed like an eternity, the download finally reached 100 percent. Kelsey and Tai promptly snatched the burner laptops from their desk in a controlled dash to the exit. The two frantic employees rounded the maze of conference rooms, avoiding the most direct path security could take to Kelsey's desk. One whiz through the micro-kitchen, past the smiling receptionist at the building's front desk and they were out of the door.

"Have a nice day!" the desk clerk called after them.

TWENTY-ONE

E-Con, the event that was supposed to be Elemynt's yearly crowning achievement, would instead be a day of reckoning the company would never forget.

In order for the upheaval to occur, Kelsey had to keep herself together. Rattled nerves hindered her ability to think straight. This was not the time for Kelsey to lose her cool. The ladies were counting on their friend.

The Events team spared no expense making sure the grandeur of the San Francisco venue matched the spectacular announcements to come. A several stories-tall recreation of Elemynt's iconic green logo at the entrance proclaimed the company's greatness to guests entering the auditorium. Inside, electrifying neon lighting systems and interactive exhibits featuring the latest technology wowed the exhilarated attendees. An electronic map the size of a billboard glowed with tens of thousands of tiny dots representing Elemynt Live streams happening around the world.

The massive flock of creators, influencers, and business owners crowded the lobby of the auditorium waiting for the start of the auspicious event. Watching tech titan Troy McCray deliver the keynote that would define the future of social communication was an honor. Hearing firsthand about the latest line of Elemynt products to launch was a privilege.

The registration lines packed with merry Elemynt fans stretched the perimeter of the building. Luscious spreads of artisanal pastries, pressed juices, and exotic coffees brewed on-3site by a squadron of baristas were abound. The excitement reverberating throughout the space obscured the presence of uniformed security officers stationed at every door and gathering point of the lobby. The atmosphere was classic Elemynt: chaos cloaked in a cheery veneer.

Hosts in pristine, mint green T-shirts welcomed guests waiting to secure a badge for entry. Imprinted on the back of each one was the password to the fastest Wi-Fi network money could buy. Elemynt needed praise for their announcements to get out as fast as possible.

The hot-topic event was going to be exponentially more newsworthy when Kelsey and her colleagues were through. No one appreciated the fast Wi-Fi more than them.

There was an increased commotion as more people made their way to the front of the registration line. Many, many employees were being denied badges. Their names, which were definitely supposed to be on the list, were nowhere to be found. The unsuspecting casualties of war frantically pulled up confirmation messages in their emails as proof of their claims.

"Sorry, we don't have a badge for you," the hosts repeated over and over.

The registration staff was not prepared for the mounting uproar. The teams were given specific instructions by the organizers. An email — even from an Elemynt employee — was not enough to gain entry into the prized event. Absolutely no gate crashers were allowed. The desk workers' only option was to smile politely.

In contrast, the employees whose names were on the replacement list the ladies concocted were greeted warmly. The former protestors were handed badges with wide smiles and hearty welcomes. The Myntors — who still had no idea how they managed to snag the last-minute credentials — could not believe their luck. Without a second thought, they squeezed into the queue forming at the doors of the auditorium to get the best seat possible.

Mission accomplished. The next step would be infinitely harder.

Kelsey was scheduled to be backstage with the rest of the Comms team. She had a task to complete first. She had to hurry before they noticed she wasn't there.

Kelsey stood in the lobby clutching her badge in one hand and her phone in the other. The clamor for credentials was reaching near-riot status. Extra security officers were called in from the auditorium to aid the panicked registration workers.

Kelsey nervously dialed Sarah. She stepped closer to the roar of the crowd so it would hang prominently in the background of the call. Sarah picked up.

"There's an issue with the passes," Kelsey said into the phone. "Everyone's freaked. We need you to come to the lobby ASAP."

"That's not my department," Sarah replied tersely. "The Events team handles the guest list, not me. And you're supposed to be backstage right now anyway."

Kelsey thought quickly. "There's VIP media out here. They need your clearance."

"Fine," Sarah groaned heavily. "I'll be there in five minutes."

Seconds later, a figure walked toward Kelsey that was not Sarah. Timothy. Of course.

"Big day!" he said as he made his way closer to the uneasy Myntor.

Tim held his laptop and recorder tightly in his arms with his press credentials dangling from his neck. The line of stories her would write about E-Con would go on for weeks. Kelsey was quite through with the unrelenting reporter interrupting her at critical times. His presence was already a distraction from the plan underway.

"Comment on the record before you all get started?" Tim asked.

"It's kind of a busy day," Kelsey said, gesturing to the liveliness in the lobby. "Wouldn't you be more comfortable in the designated media area like the other journalists?"

"I need to know what's going on behind the scenes," Tim said brightly. "How is the Elemynt team feeling about their big moment? Are your people still hoping these announcements will make up for what you've done in the past?"

Before she could respond to the reporter's grating questions, Kelsey spotted Sarah swiftly walking their way. Her badge swung wildly from her hip.

Sarah wagged her phone in Tim's face. "First of all, it's me who you should be talking to and you of all people should know this isn't the time."

Sarah motioned for Kelsey to move along to her designated post. Tim's eyes darted away from Kelsey toward her perturbed manager.

"I just have a few questions for you," he said unwaveringly to Sarah.

"Oh, give it a rest, will you?" she snapped. "You're lucky we let you in the building. And another thing..."

Tim might have been good for something after all. While Sarah shouted down her opponent, Kelsey casually bumped against her colleague. With a practiced sleight of hand, Sarah's badge was in Kelsey's possession and tucked under her laptop. She had it. Time to make a quick departure.

"I'm going to head inside," Kelsey said as she backed away.

"I'm right behind you," Sarah said in a huff.

Tim stood in Sarah's path. "One second. Just one more question."

"Excuse me!" Sarah shouted. "Please move away from my presence or I will have security escort you directly to your car or scooter or whatever dingy vehicle you rode here on."

Kelsey didn't pause to see the outcome of the fraught exchange. The two could argue amongst themselves. Too much at stake to slow down.

Brad was thankfully right where he was supposed to be. Kelsey asked him to meet in the furthest corner of the venue's atrium and there he was, waiting in anticipation for the woman he loved. Brad's fresh tan from his time cruising the Mediterranean made him look especially handsome. She kept herself from swooning.

"I can't believe you got me an invitation," Brad beamed. "This means the world to me. And so do you."

Kelsey interrupted her guy before he could gush further. Time was of the essence.

"Brad, I need you to do me a favor," Kelsey said. "A woman is going to come up to you in a few minutes... give her this badge for me?"

Kelsey slid Sarah's all-access pass from under her laptop and into his hand.

"What's this about?" he asked curiously. "Who is it?"

"You said you wanted to be there for me. I need you to do this one thing. Get her the badge, okay?"

"Yeah no problem, babe," he assured her. "What's going on? Something I should know about?"

Kelsey placed a kiss on his tanned cheek. "Official Elemynt business. Gotta run."

Kelsey sped toward the auditorium's staff entrance and flashed her pass to the security officer. The true magnitude of E-Con sunk in the moment she entered.

Rows of seats for more than a thousand attendees were waiting to be filled. Millions more would watch from the comfort of their home thanks to the efforts of the Elemynt production crew. Stagehands and technicians hustled through the striking venue, testing microphones, running through scripts, and double and triple-checking important details, big and small. A floor-to-ceiling presentation screen dominated the expansive stage. Every speech, presentation, and announcement would be streamed to devices from Silicon Valley to Shanghai.

More than a dozen or so TV news cameras packed into the media riser in the rear of the auditorium. The question that was top of mind for both journalists and the executive team was whether Elemynt would be able to move forward in the wake of a year plagued by scandal. That was quite the mountain to overcome considering the issues that lingered in the minds of the public — a major security breach, accusations of harassment, profiting from racial hatred, plus three Congressional hearings with varied results. Elemynt would have to pull off a spectacularly game-changing event if the company had any hope of rolling out a successful IPO.

With a slate of killer product announcements at E-Con, Elemynt could drive up its engagement and growth numbers in a snap. Investors would throw cash by the fistful at a company bulldozing its way toward phenomenal profits. Elemynt would be the star of Wall Street because of technology that raided people's personal information and put lives at stake.

Kelsey had no doubts Elemynt's disregard for the safety of its users would increase more as intrusion translated to increased revenue. There was little thought given to how people were engaging or how controversial the content on the app may have been. Numbers were numbers. Troy and investors would make sure that the growth of Elemynt was on a constant upward swing, by any means necessary.

That trajectory began with the critical moment scheduled to start in less than thirty minutes. Kelsey, Daniela, Tai, and Jade chose to take a stand against the compromised morality of Elemynt. If their plan was executed successfully, the company's moment of triumph would never come.

The backstage area behind the curtain was categorical madness. Workers ran to test sound equipment, arrange cables, put last-minute touches on this and that, and, in general, make sure that the year's most significant event went off without a hitch. Kelsey was profoundly overwhelmed by the hysteria of it all. With an untold number of eyes on her and her co-conspirators, one slip and their plot would be instantly unraveled.

Troy shouted orders to those staff who, in his eyes, appeared to be lagging.

"Come on, peeps!" he yelled. "If we don't nail this, we're disappointing a whole lot of people! Let's go!"

Troy's overexcited antics were spawning chaos rather than confidence. The stakeholders involved were well-aware of how their individual responsibilities would help drive a successful E-Con. The scramble to carry out remaining duties in the short time left was proof of that.

Catherine was unfazed by the ongoing commotion. The legendary COO sat coolly in front of a vanity mirror looking over her notes. Her makeup artist applied camera-ready blush to her cheeks. A hairdresser beautified her locks. The stage manager reached in between the two to apply a lavalier mic to the lapel of her tailored jacket. Kelsey walked swiftly in the opposite direction of the conniving executive.

Kelsey watched as the production team tested a row of backstage monitors available for the staff to view the event. The live video feeds from the cameras trained on the stage were piped into each one. A second set of screens mirrored the slideshow and the monitor from which they were to read the scripts prepared for them.

Each staffer that would appear onstage rehearsed endlessly under Sarah's watchful eye in the weeks leading up to E-Con. The delivery of their announcements had to be perfect. They didn't stand a chance of it if the renegade ladies had their way.

Kelsey spotted Sarah's laptop in its fake marble case on a table reserved for the Comms team. With no laptop and no badge, Sarah was at a significant disadvantage for what lay ahead.

Zekiyah, the engineering manager at the center of previous discussions, stood at the edge of the backstage curtain looking more nervous than Kelsey was. The soon to be speaker fumbled with the notes in her hand.

"You're going to be fine," Kelsey said, standing by her side. "The monitor will be right there in front of you."

"Oh? No, it's not that," Zekiyah said. "Four years at this company and they've never asked me to speak at an event before. Not even a team offsite meeting. All of a sudden, they're putting me on a stage in front of a million people."

"It's a lot to handle but it'll be over before you know it," Kelsey said caringly.

"Speaking in public is no problem for me," she said. "I'm actually pretty good at it. Hey, didn't I see you at the walkout?"

Kelsey wasn't sure how to respond. She hadn't shared details of her official Comms role at Elemynt with Zekiyah and how she was compelled to be at the park that day. But there was solidarity in having attended the protest, regardless of the capacity.

"Yeah, it's a day I'll never forget," Kelsey sighed.

"Funny thing is I was supposed to be one of the speakers there," Zekiyah said wistfully. "I backed out last minute and just hung out in the crowd instead. Didn't want to risk losing my job. It's crazy that a couple of months ago, I was out there protesting this place. Now they have me at E-Con speaking on behalf of the company."

"Only two other women have been on that stage and of them was Catherine," Kelsey said. "That's an honor."

"And I'm the first black woman," Zekiyah said. "I don't want to think they picked me to do this because of that. But there's plenty of other people who the company is always putting in front of the mic."

Zekiyah was inching closer to a truth they both knew, but Kelsey was reticent to speak aloud.

"I was in that meeting when they picked speakers and… um…" she trailed off.

Kelsey's hesitant fumbling told Zekiyah everything she needed to know. She was a capable woman but yes, she was selected to be the event's token minority. Despite the circumstances, Kelsey was committed to supporting Zekiyah in her debut rather than serve as a distraction. It was the manager's turn to speak.

"Somebody who I care about a lot always told me that representation can change lives," Kelsey said with sincerity. "Other people from your background are going to appreciate seeing someone who looks like them on that big stage. It's so important."

"Yeah, I guess," Zekiyah said as she stared off into the distance.

Kelsey wanted badly to tell Zekiyah of the crew's plan for turning the tables on Elemynt. She wanted to say that they were fighting on behalf of women, people of color, and other marginalized people wronged through Elemynt's actions or lack thereof. Instead, Kelsey politely excused herself to the green room, leaving Zekiyah to ponder her coming presentation.

Kelsey's phone would not stop ringing. Sarah was still stuck outside in the lobby. With no badge and no one to vouch for her, she would remain there for the foreseeable future. Kelsey was absolutely fine with that.

Sarah's pleas for assistance continued to go unanswered. A series of text messages that started as urgent requests — "Please come get me" — escalated to anger — "You better not ruin this!" If Sarah had a clue of what was to come next, she would have likely broken down the auditorium doors. She would know soon enough.

In the private green room deeper in the recesses of the backstage area, Grace and Jade were having last-minute discussions about their role in what was to come. The mega-star had happily accepted Kelsey and Jade's suggestion to speak onstage at E-Con. She was even more enthusiastic upon hearing that the original purpose Troy and Catherine wanted her to fulfill was not what the duo had in mind.

Despite her initial encouragement, Jade was herself beginning to have doubts.

"Are we sure we want to do this?" Jade asked. "Corporate takedowns are usually not my thing."

"Hey, Elemynt has wrecked plenty of lives already," Kelsey said. "Let's not forget that."

"And people deserve to know what's going on behind the scenes, don't they?" Grace added.

"I can't ignore that I'm risking my job here…" Jade said.

"You're taking a stand," Kelsey said supportively.

"I'll never work in entertainment again."

"Not true," Grace interjected. "I might be on television, but *you* are the real star. Jade, do you know how many of us in the industry look up to you? You've made so many smart decisions that have taken you to the top. You've changed people's lives with your work. You gotta believe in yourself. Let's do what needs to be done."

"I'm in," Jade said. "But I do have one regret."

"What's that?" Kelsey asked.

"It's Elemynt's funeral and I'm not wearing all black," she joked nervously. "How gauche."

"We're going to be dead too if we don't take our places," Kelsey said. "They're starting soon."

Moments before the event was scheduled to start, the doors to the auditorium flew open to the delight of the anxious crowd. The peppy corporate music that was a trademark of all-hands meetings welcomed them as they filed into every available seat.

Kelsey watched the activity from the monitors backstage. Her post for the day. The cameras made a grand sweep over the audience. Kelsey spotted Brad sitting gleefully in the fourth row. A small part of her was sad he wasn't going to get the Elemynt lovefest he came for. However, she would not stop the plan for one ex-boyfriend.

The sea of heads in the room bowed over the soft glow of their phones and laptops. Attendees came expecting surprise announcements from Elemynt, the world's most influential social media app. They were ready.

10:00 AM.

The lights dimmed.

Curtains swept open.

Showtime.

* * *

Troy McCray, king of Silicon Valley, strode from his perch backstage into the center spotlight to deliver his official greetings to the people.

He was met with mostly tepid applause.

The reception from the audience came as a slight shock to the CEO and the

Myntors observing backstage. It wasn't the response they were expecting. Not for the biggest day in Elemynt's history. Had the original guest list been intact, Troy would have received the over-the-top, thunderous, earth-shaking applause he was used to receiving at E-Con. That would not be the case this year.

The range of cameras trained on Troy captured his perceptible stumble following the lack of feedback. He straightened himself up. This was his moment. He would dole out his charisma in its highest dose to win the hearts and minds in the venue.

"Eight years ago, I had a dream," Troy said with head held high. "I wanted to build a social network that put people first and allowed them to shape how they connect with the world. My plan was always to create a product with innovation in mind that would constantly evolve. Many of you believe in my ideas too and that's what brings us here today."

The usual surge of energy in response to his opening words was noticeably absent.

Troy continued to read from the monitor the prepared notes that the various communications teams toiled over to perfect. He gesticulated to imbue each word with power. He spoke with radiant confidence of the company's progress. His speech was expertly designed to convince news organizations to write of how the revered CEO was ushering in a new era of Elemynt.

"At Elemynt, we keep our ambitions high to bring you the best product possible," Troy said proudly. "Every day, we turn imagination into reality. Now, we're taking it further than we ever have before."

A few sporadic cheers. Something was indeed amiss.

Daniela's plan to alter the guest list had its primary effect. Take away the cheering section and see what Troy does in front of people who don't particularly care for him.

Troy pressed on.

"The advances in social technology Elemynt has made over the years have been out of this world. This is just the beginning. I can't wait for you to see what we have in store for you today."

Neither could Kelsey. She nodded to Tai who sat stoically in the production booth across the way. Jade and Grace remained stationed in the green room.

Troy exited the stage to a smattering of handclaps. He grumbled to himself before disappearing backstage.

Gary stepped in for his turn in front of the audience. His chest puffed with pride as he teed up his introduction to Elemynt's newest outstanding product.

"How many of you have played VR games before?" Gary asked brightly. "I see those hands out there!"

There were very few raised hands. Any demonstrations of support from the audience were lukewarm at best.

The screen behind Gary lit up with a montage of fresh-faced people of all ages using Elemynt-branded virtual reality headsets. Their broad smiles and laughter indicated that the product filled their lives with abundant joy and happiness.

The people in the seats who should have been oohing and aahing in anticipation of the product debut were mostly stone-faced.

"At Elemynt, we believe virtual reality is more than gaming," Gary said with pre-determined levels of enthusiasm. "Our latest gear will take real-life experiences to the next level. I'm proud to announce the future of VR!"

A flashy 3-D image of the latest edition of Elemynt's shiny headset filled the screen. It spun in place to show every angle of the new toy. The music swelled to a laudatory crescendo.

"If you're like me you hate having to go to the store to buy new clothes," Gary said with a laugh. "And if you order them online, you're taking a gamble on whether they'll be the right fit. You have to pack them back up, ship them... who has the time? My wife doesn't. She still drags me to the department store when it's time to buy new shirts so we can try them on in person."

Amused laughs circulated through the auditorium, mostly from listeners picturing the stout executive being dragged unwillingly into a clothing store.

"I'm excited to share with you that Elemynt is taking physical shopping into the virtual world. Now, when you log in to the headset with your Elemynt account, our new system will analyze your social media profile to determine what kind of clothes you like. It can tell what brands are your favorites and suggest to you new ones you might want to try. It can also, using only your photos, analyze your body measurements with close to one hundred percent accuracy. Then, using a 360-degree, crystal-clear virtual mirror, you can try on clothes and spin like you were in a real dressing room using a virtual model that looks just like you."

Several overly thrilled consumers appeared in a video sequence on the screen behind him, each selecting outfits in the virtual world. The exhilarated gasps from watchers and the media in the auditorium were warranted. The technology was stunning.

"Here's the best part," Gary crowed. "When you're ready, you can buy the clothes in VR using your credit or debit card on file and have them shipped to you within 48 hours! How does that sound?"

The warm applause he received was less muted than before, but far from the hearty cheers a product with incredibly forward-thinking innovation would normally reap. Kelsey was not a fan and neither were a considerable number of people in the crowd. The technology was intrusive in a way that was not immediately obvious. Just how Elemynt liked their products.

The spectators in the venue may have been less than enthused, but Gary was satisfied that the watchers at home were surely over the moon at the announcement.

Gary continued, excitedly announcing more of the novel features of the new VR headset.

"Want to find the perfect car for you?" he asked rhetorically. "Our unique algorithms will analyze your personality based on your social media posts and suggest the ride of your dreams. Through VR, you can test drive the car before it leaves the lot. Then when you're ready to buy, you'll have it delivered to your front door with all the custom additions you want! We'd like to thank our selected manufacturers for their collaboration on this."

Gary talked through the price of the headset, the specs, and the available colors — silver, steel, and rose gold. What was supposed to be the most anticipated moment of his portion of the program arrived. The proclamation fans and the media would go crazy for.

"And it's available..." Gary said looking at his glistening watch. "Now."

Sarah was supposed to hit send on a blog post announcing the VR headset as soon as Gary gave the important verbal cue. However, Sarah had still not managed to work her way into the venue. It was very likely that Sarah, like the hundreds of others unexpectedly stranded in the lobby, was watching the milestone event on her phone. Her sob stories to the security officers of how she was slated to be inside would be indistinguishable from those of other would-be gate crashers. Sarah had no badge and no hope of getting one.

Having her phone in her hand wouldn't help Sarah fulfill her duties either. For security reasons, she was required to send the post from her company-issued laptop. The very same laptop that sat idly on the table in front of Kelsey. She was happy to offer the same level of "help" Sarah gave her. The laptop would go untouched.

Catherine was the first to finally ask about Sarah's presence.

"Come to think of it, I haven't seen her since we started," Catherine said warily. "Kelsey, where is she?"

Kelsey shrugged, conjuring every bit of innocence she could project.

"Are you pushing out the post?" Catherine asked.

"It's taken care of," Kelsey responded.

Catherine and Troy had bigger problems to worry about than a blog post not being published.

Zekiyah, now adorned with a face full of exaggerated makeup courtesy of the staff glam squad, found a low-trafficked area backstage to ready herself. She looked pensive as she waited her turn. Unlike other speakers, Zekiyah wasn't going over her notes. She simply stared out at the stage. Kelsey was curious to know what was going on in her head.

"Ladies and gentlemen..." an unseen announcer said pleasantly. "Please welcome Senior Manager of Research and Development, Zekiyah Johnson."

The next presenter stepped onto the stage with a beautiful, full smile and a heartfelt wave. The crowd gave Zekiyah the most rousing applause for anyone all day, Troy included. Most of the backstage staff watching the monitors was perplexed by the lively reception.

"We love you, Zekiyah!" a yell came from the audience.

"Get 'em, girl!"

Catherine and Troy were confounded that a random engineering manager they plucked from obscurity would warrant the welcome response. They failed to realize that the speaker walking onto the stage was a prominent figure at the employee walkout and one of the most vocal and well-loved advocates for diversity in the Commynt threads. In their rush to secure an African-American woman for E-Con, her background somehow escaped the critical eye of the Dream Team. Kelsey was tickled by their oversight.

The script written for Zekiyah appeared on the monitor before her.

"Hey, everybody," Zekiyah said into the mic. "I'm supposed to talk with you about the latest facial recognition technology at Elemynt. My team built features that let you go to restaurants or check into hotels with your face and the business knows who you are based on your Elemynt account. They know your preferences, what you like, that sort of thing..."

The audience was intrigued by the demo that Zekiyah was on deck to debut. The use of facial recognition technology was growing in new and creative ways. What Elemynt planned to release would be the next evolution of a rapidly evolving field.

"We also have the technology for you to get money from an ATM with your face, if that's your thing," Zekiyah said. "No pin or card required. The machine learning systems we built can recognize faces better than humans do. Which is pretty cool."

A corresponding slide of happy people using the cutting-edge tech appeared on the screen behind her.

"You know what's not cool?" Zekiyah said. "Elemynt squeezing as much personal information out of people as they can to make insane profits."

Gasps of incredulity ricocheted throughout the auditorium. The audience was thrown back into their seats by the daring assertion. Something was definitely off about this year's E-Con. There was no way Zekiyah was saying the lines that were written for her. Kelsey was also taken aback by the unexpected switch.

"You're kidding yourself if you think Elemynt is building these systems out of charity," Zekiyah continued. "The company's priority isn't making it easier to do basic tasks, even though that's what they'll tell you. What Elemynt really cares about is ripping off people's identities and selling it to advertisers. The more it knows about you, the more money it makes off you."

"What is this garbage?!" Catherine asked in alarm. "Where is her script??"

"Maybe she's adding personal touches," said Jim, the technical director overseeing the cameras in the venue. "Let's hold on her."

"This facial recognition can be used to track you the moment you step outside of the house," Zekiyah continued. "If the information got in the wrong hands, people would lose their privacy forever. Elemynt has to stop pretending it cares about our lives. Helping people connect is just a side effect of what it does."

Zekiyah calmly explained herself in a manner free from the calculated hand movements and select phrasing that was the hallmark of the other E-Con speakers. She bore her soul to the captivated audience. The courageous woman spoke of the concerns of people from underrepresented backgrounds. She decried the exclusion of minority voices from internal decision-making. In an even tone, she conveyed both her love for her job and issued a plea for Elemynt to make decisions in the interest of all users.

"Get her off that stage!" Troy yelled adamantly to the backstage crew.

"Hey, we're live!" Jim said from his station. "We do that in the middle of her talking and you've got a bigger problem on your hands."

Kelsey, for one, was thrilled with Zekiyah's statement. The ladies' plans to shed light on the company's misdeeds were enriched by the speaker's heartfelt solicitation. Zekiyah's words reinforced that Daniela was right. Minorities at Elemynt were tired of the unjust treatment forced upon them.

"Where the hell is Sarah?!" Catherine asked through gritted teeth.

Catherine was out for blood. Sarah, the freshly anointed VP of Comms was asked directly responsible for coaching the speakers. The narrative Zekiyah shared with the eagerly listening attendees was nowhere near what she was slated to say. In Catherine's mind, if Sarah caught wind that the speaker planned to make the slightest of changes, she should have notified higher-ups of the infraction right away.

Catherine frantically wrangled production assistants, harassed the technical director, and did everything short of pulling the wires right out of the wall to cut off Zekiyah. Troy was livid that the cameras that were supposed to capture his glorious moment were trained on Zekiyah's dissent.

"Why don't you fucking fix this!" Troy growled at Catherine. "What is wrong with you people!"

Catherine lashed out in return. "If you would do me the kind favor of backing off and stop acting like a maniac, we can figure out what to do!"

Troy stalked off to find someone else to unleash his fury on.

"Where is Grace Oliver?" Catherine yelled at the P.A.s. "We're doing our presentation together right now!"

"She's still in the green room," one replied shakily.

"Well go get her!"

Kelsey couldn't help but laugh to herself at the commotion Zekiyah's spot of honesty caused among the company's top ranks. The contrast in her calm delivery and the scrambling behind the scenes was a delight to witness.

"Elemynt is special because it gives individuals a voice," Zekiyah said to the engaged crowd. "People of color deserve to be heard too. Our concerns should be everybody's concerns."

A standing ovation rang throughout the auditorium in support of Zekiyah's sincere sentiment. The journalists stationed in the riser behind the audience were in awe of the response. The mutiny onstage was unexpectedly well received.

Exceedingly loyal E-Con audiences from previous years would have drowned Zekiyah in hostile boos. However, her petition rang true. For the employees that filled the seats, Zekiyah encapsulated many of their frustrations. She would rightly be regarded as a champion for the people.

"Thanks for listening," Zekiyah said. "God bless."

The Myntor happily exited the stage in the opposite direction of the fuming staff up in arms around Kelsey.

Phones across the venue flickered on like strobe lights to share Zekiyah's message of care of integrity with the outside world. Troy angrily directed the official cameras to pan away from shots of the audience. The news camera crews responded in turn by shifting focus to the attendees posting to their Elemynt accounts, invigorated by what they just witnessed.

The buzz of disbelief in the auditorium grew to deafening levels. If Catherine planned to salvage the event, she needed to move quickly.

"Catherine, go!" Troy bellowed. "Get out there right now!"

Effervescent music rang out as Catherine and Grace made their way to the stage armed with handheld mics and broad smiles. The volume of the music was at a high enough level to drown out the residual reactions to Zekiyah's disruptive speech.

"Thank you for joining us for this year's E-Con," Catherine said to Grace with forced pleasantness.

The words "It's an honor to be here" appeared on the monitor before them. It was Grace's line. She hesitated. Looked around.

Kelsey was struck by sudden panic. If Grace didn't follow through with the plan, all the work and sacrifices the group made to change the course of Elemynt would be for nothing. Her fate and that of the company was in her hands.

"It's a pleasure to have you here," Catherine prompted the star guest. "We're thrilled to introduce Elemynt's new safety and security features."

"You mean the tools to fight harassment that you've been holding onto for more than a year now?" Grace said accusatorily. "The features you didn't roll out because you didn't want to stop the growth of your company?"

Catherine choked on her words. The COO was shaken that Grace was aware of the true timeline of the project and that she would broadcast it publicly in front of the murmuring audience.

"Some things in tech require time," Catherine hedged. "As I was saying…"

"You're a boss lady," Grace said with a smile. "I'm sure everyone's as curious as I am to know what you've done personally to stand up for the women being threatened on your app."

"Well, there are many factors that go into these things," Catherine hissed without breaking face. "That's why we're proud to debut this new feature together with you."

"So you've known about this behavior on Elemynt for a long time and you're just now doing something about it? That's really interesting."

Catherine could barely contain how furious she was that her planned remarks were co-opted into a tense back and forth with Grace. The consummate professional would not lose her cool in front of a crowd of gawking onlookers.

"We thank you for voicing your concerns about a unique situation that you experienced," Catherine said.

"It's just me?" Grace smiled to the camera. "Sure, okay."

"In fact, we have a video we'd like to share that showcases how Elemynt is enriching the lives of women everywhere," Catherine brightened.

"Can't wait to see it!" Grace said with affected cheer.

The lights on the stage dimmed. The confused faces in the rows of seats before them faded into the darkness. Grace stood by Catherine's side, barely visible in the shadowy venue.

The 60-foot high screen transitioned from the company logo to a video montage.

"Elemynt doesn't care about women," an unnamed voice said declaratively.

The audience nearly screamed out in shock. The statement sounded like an attack on the company, but it was coming from an Elemynt-produced presentation. The spectators rumbled with questions of whether Elemynt was trying to prove something about itself with the opener. Cutting remarks did not align with the company's usual presentation style. E-Con was known for gushing testimonies about how great Elemynt was.

Unbeknownst to anyone working behind the scenes, Tai replaced the saccharine video Catherine spoke of with something far more interesting — footage pulled from the study of female users that Troy commissioned. One after the other, women interviewed by the researchers spoke of the deep trauma they incurred while using Elemynt. The succession of clips with blurred faces told stories of the vile comments and offline consequences they were subjected to in the course of their use of the app.

"One of my friends from school killed herself last summer because someone hacked her account and put her private pics and messages on the internet."

"I'm just trying to live my life and keep in touch with people. I shouldn't have to deal with random men calling me a whore or saying I should be murdered or gang-raped."

"Someone created a fake account pretending to be my mother to harass me. She died three years ago."

"I used to post pictures of my family but not anymore. Too many people in the comments calling us illegals or telling me to go back to my country. I was born here in the States."

"Aren't the security features supposed to help me? I keep reporting abuse in the app and nothing happens. If they do respond, I get messages saying the filth doesn't violate the rules when it clearly does."

"Troy McCray doesn't care about black people. You think he cares about us? If he did I wouldn't see someone calling me the n-word every time I post."

Women of various ages and races told of how the digital interactions that the company brushed off as harmless caused emotional and psychological harm to them or to other people they knew. The problem wasn't limited to one gender either. The history of Elemynt showed that people who others perceived as different - LGBTQ+, users with disabilities, people of different nationalities, and more — were subjected to similar abuse and little recourse.

Tears were shed in the audience watching the women tell of the grievances they faced in their time on Elemynt. The negative effects of the company's idle response to their concerns were on full display.

"Why should I have to be the one to leave the app?" one woman said dejectedly. "Kick those other people off. They're the ones making people's lives hell."

While Catherine was distracted by the commentary playing out on the screen, a shadowy figure slipped onto the stage.

At the conclusion of the video, the spotlights again shone on the platform. There standing in the very center at Catherine's side was Daniela with Grace's mic in her hand.

"Thank you, Catherine," Grace waved. "For being there for women when they needed you most. Daniela, you had something you wanted to share with everybody?"

The audience nearly lost their minds seeing Catherine face to face with her most vocal critic. Every attendee in the room knew who Daniela was. It was hard not to. Daniela's face and her message of inclusivity at Elemynt was splashed on major news sites and television news channels worldwide since her memo leaked to the public. Their astounded gasps were no match for Catherine's horror. The color drained from the executive's face until she was a pale white.

"Where did she come from?!" Catherine mouthed to Troy who was standing behind the curtain.

Grace politely exited the stage. While Troy and Catherine traded silent signals of confusion with each other, Daniela delivered her message to the stunned onlookers in the auditorium and beyond.

"You can see Elemynt values women, don't they?" Daniela said wryly. "What you just saw were the results of a study commissioned by Troy himself. He didn't like what came back so guess what his next move was? That's right, he killed it."

The audience drowned the room in an upheaval of boos. Catherine wrung her hands in fright at the incredible response. A stagehand waved for her to return to the backstage area so she could triage the brutal condemnation with the rest of the staff. Catherine instinctively stayed in place. The event was live with millions of people watching. She couldn't dart off while Daniela was shining a light on the company's true priorities.

Ever the camera-ready show woman, Catherine waited with a pained smile for a pause in the criticism. She intended to snatch the mic into her possession. Daniela wouldn't give her a chance.

"The world deserves better than how Elemynt is treating us," Daniela said. "By avoiding its responsibility to the greater good, Elemynt has supported the spread of false information and violence, on and off the platform. They've sold our personal details to the highest bidder. We have to ask ourselves how much of our privacy, our lives, and our basic human rights we will sacrifice for faves and shares."

Daniela continued only to find that her mic was shut off by the production crew backstage. That would not stop her from speaking her truth. Daniela raised her voice until it filled every nook and crevice of the auditorium.

"Elemynt is obsessed with harvesting other people's secrets and yet they'll tell any lie they have to so they can protect their own," Daniela said to the room. "The company has to pay more attention to not just connecting communities, but to the concerns of the communities it connects."

Tim sat squarely in the middle of the theater blown away by the events playing out in front of him. The reporter worked through his awe to document what was in all likelihood the beginning of Elemynt's demise.

Tai, Jade, and Kelsey stood in their respective spots backstage doing their best to mirror the aghast responses of the people around them. Their plan to turn E-Con on its head was so far executed flawlessly. The women had to keep their cool so they would not be found out. Also, there was one more component left. The cherry on top.

"Elemynt will keep working in ways that fail the people who use its products until we make them care," Daniela said with vigor. "I believe information is power. To the media in the room, please check your emails to see the truth Elemynt has fought hard to hide."

Tai discreetly hit send on a link to the cache of incriminating files they procured to every credentialed reporter in attendance. It was all the evidence the media needed of Elemynt's wrongdoing.

Leon's detailed report of the breach with the true numerical impact and a timeline that contradicted Troy's congressional testimony. The hundreds of data points Elemynt collected on each person without their knowledge. The development of "shadow profiles" created to track people who had never used the app. The deployment of facial recognition technology to identify participants in the walkout. The memo to managers directing them to keep employees who protested under close watch and potentially punish them in their reviews. Anonymized complaints from female employees to HR and the severance packages offered in response to shut them up. Threads on Commynt after the first hearing in which employees with redacted names openly mocked members of Congress. The racially insensitive threads after Luke Schultz's post. The comments on Wyatt's memo in agreement with his encouragement to overlook ongoing bad behavior. The absence of executives who let the rotten comments fester and allowed for a culture of rampant discrimination.

The online folder containing the files, the email address they were sent from, and the IP address would be traced by the Security team back to Sarah, thanks to Tai's diligent work. If Sarah wanted to play a vicious game to get to the top, the ladies would outmatch her at every turn.

Reporters stationed in the media riser scrambled to access the damning info in their inbox. The click-clack of typing on laptops and phones echoed through the vast space. The disastrous Elemynt event would be the headline at the top of news sites within minutes. The restless audience swapped guesses of what other chaos E-Con had in store for its crumbling showcase.

"Troy, your speech... do it now!" Catherine yelled. "We need to move past this! Cue the monitor!"

The technical director gave Catherine a thumbs up. The mood in the venue turned chilly as Troy shooed Daniela off the stage.

"Thank you for that insight," Troy said with his legendary charisma intact. "We love passion!"

Chants of "Let her speak!" rang through the vast space. Troy straightened himself and launched into his remarks despite the antagonistic audience. Daniela disappeared into the shadows of the auditorium as quickly as she entered.

"This has been an intense year," Troy said, reading the monitor in defiance of loud boos and hisses. "It takes courage to move forward when the odds are stacked against you. We believe the products and features we've announced today will change lives around the globe. This is the beginning of an outstanding new future for Elemynt."

Troy continued to talk and pace thoughtfully across the open stage as he practiced many times over. He did not care that hardly anyone in the room was listening to him. He leaned on the words of the monitor to convey his message to the cameras trained on him. The people at home and watching on their phones would not see him falter.

"We've caused society… to fall apart?" Troy read with confusion.

Kelsey peered over at the monitor on which Troy's speech scrolled. Someone changed the subsequent words on the prompter into a scathing self-critique of the company. The tech director was bewildered at how the change could have happened under his watch. Kelsey caught the eye of Tai who was visibly bemused. Her faux innocent shrug said what Kelsey needed to know.

"No wonder we can't find Sarah!" Catherine screeched. "She's the one causing this mess! I will not let us be the subject of her revenge! Call Leon right now!"

Catherine threatened to fire the production team and the entire backstage crew if they didn't get Troy's correct speech on the monitor.

The CEO of Elemynt struggled without his scripted words. Troy's polished veneer cracked. His "everything will be awesome" demeanor he perfected while heading one of the most powerful companies in tech was stripped away. What was left was a petulant child chastising the audience for attempting to torpedo the social media giant he created from the ground up.

"Elemynt is not your enemy!" Troy shouted back at the outraged crowd. "You want privacy? You want to feel safe? Go live out in the middle of the woods somewhere! Or better yet, start your own damn company."

"By hacking into people's personal lives and letting them get dumped on?" someone yelled back.

"A few bad things happen and you want to cry about it?" Troy continued his tirade. "If you didn't want your information out there, you wouldn't upload it in the first place."

"People are dead because of you and you don't care!" a voice in the crowd retorted.

The opinionated audience would not relent in their ferocious criticism. They refused to allow Troy to feed them his half-truths and outright lies. The huddle of staffers near Kelsey watched in complete disbelief. Their prized event was collapsing and they had no idea why or how. Kelsey, Daniela, Tai, and Jade knew. Together, the ladies succeeded in showing the world Elemynt's true colors.

"Cut the cameras!" Catherine screamed.

The COO could barely be heard over the frenzy in the theater. The spectators mocked and jeered Troy which further enraged him. They snapped photos of his reddened face to post to their Elemynt accounts. Tech journalists watching the disruption were beside themselves with astonishment. They furiously typed away on their laptops to capture the riotous event.

Troy attempted to speak louder over the din but to no avail. The smooth operator persona vanished completely.

"You ungrateful twats!" he screamed. "We're building something good for you! You should be grateful for what we've done."

The CEO who was rarely told "no" or had his ideas shut down by others found himself smack dab in the middle of unfamiliar territory. For the majority of his career, he was shielded from criticism by rooms full of yes men whose primary goal was to carry out his wishes.

In fairness, Troy didn't set out to develop an app that would be a chink in the armor of moral decency. However, he did create a platform without consideration of the worst-case scenarios of its use. When the issues presented themselves, he did not care to fix them. Troy's initial motivation for building the app aside, his continued dismissals of its evils would be the cause of its downfall.

"This is my company and I will run it however I want," Troy yelled out. "You don't like Elemynt? Stop using it."

"We will!"

"Unbelievable!" a reporter said in amazement.

Troy's piercing diatribe only served to provoke the audience more. Shouting with unrestrained rage was backfiring in the worst possible way. Reciprocal anger flooded the room and it grew more elevated by the second. The protests in the venue were captured live on camera and broadcasted to an infinite number of watchers. The more Troy ranted, the more he caused his company's multibillion-dollar worth to evaporate.

"We will not be silenced!" the audience railed.

Troy finally stopped speaking long enough to notice the production assistants desperately beckoning him to leave the stage. When he didn't heed their call, Catherine commanded them to physically usher Troy away from the platform. The crowd cheered as Troy stalked off, leaving an uproarious revolution in his wake. Catherine shoved her manicured finger into his chest.

"Are you happy, Troy?" she howled. "This company is on fire and you handed people the matches. Well, guess what? I will not be standing by your side while you watch it burn."

Neither would Kelsey. Her time at Elemynt had come to an end.

Pandemonium erupted in the crowd. Commands from security officers to disperse went unheeded. Attendees who once sat dutifully in their seats rushed the stage loudly chanting "Delete Elemynt" on repeat. Signs with the hashtag call to action #DeleteElemynt were hoisted in the air. The employees who once used a neighborhood park as their arena for protest seized their chance to be heard on a global platform.

Spectators and the vocal Myntors snapped photos and recorded video of the unrest to share with everyone they knew. For some, it would be the last time they ever used the Elemynt app.

Journalists documenting the melee in the room untethered themselves from the riser that separated them from attendees. News crews repositioned their cameras in the theater so reporters could go on-air live in the thick of the demonstration. Other members of the media seized the opportunity to rush the backstage area where they angled to get a comment from Troy or Catherine. Kelsey stepped back to let them have their moment.

Troy, the closest person to the curtain, was the first to incur the onslaught of questions.

A TV reporter thrust a mic in his face. "Troy, what do you think about what your employees said today?"

"Can you speak to the validity of the information we received?" another asked.

"I have nothing to say to you people!" he yelled in a strong rebuke. "Catherine, you talk to them!"

Troy shoved Catherine in between him and the reporters, clearing the way for the CEO to bolt towards the exit. Catherine was left solo to fend off the unrelenting crowd of journalists.

"Catherine, is Elemynt not protecting women?"

"What was your role in the suppression of information?"

Catherine, for once, was speechless. No pacifying language. No crushing retorts. Her lips quivered trying to formulate a response to the barrage of criticism.

"Our communication team will get back to you," Catherine replied shakily.

She could not have been more wrong. There would be no spokespeople to come through for Catherine as they had before. The Comms teams that months ago would have supported the revered executive through thick and thin were worn out. They could no longer blindly support a woman whose moral compass was compromised by her loyalty to Elemynt.

The reporters chased after Catherine as she darted toward the first exit door she could find.

One by one, Kelsey, Tai, and Jade calmly filed out of the backstage area along with the other staffers abandoned by the leaders of Elemynt.

A separate crowd of journalists gathered around Grace who stood in an aisle of the theater. In a makeshift press conference, she shared her reasons for shedding light on Elemynt's controversial actions.

"This was for all the women and people of color out there who feel like they're alone in dealing with online harassment," Grace said. "You don't have to take it anymore. If you're thinking about staying on the app, I would say consider if you want to support a company that's not supporting you."

Throughout the commotion, Brad had not moved from his seat. Kelsey caught a glimpse of him waiting dutifully for her to emerge from behind the curtain. He looked at her with love in his eyes. She nodded in his direction. The ex-boyfriend came through for her. The title could change in the future. Possibly. That was a decision Kelsey would make for herself a later time. She mouthed a thank you.

The women reconvened as planned in a far corner of the lobby away from the chaos in the auditorium. Daniela emerged from a hidden VIP exit to join them. The attendees running in every direction were too busy to notice that the woman who crashed Elemynt's party in epic fashion was within speaking distance.

"Hey ladies!" Daniela smiled. "What've you been up to? Anything interesting?"

"I have no idea what you're talking about," Jade laughed. "That was a lovely E-Con, don't you think?"

"Probably the best year ever," Kelsey joked.

"And who knows…" Tai shrugged. "We might've caught the last one."

The four women congratulated each other on an extraordinary job well done. The long stretch of anguish that each of them endured at the hands of Elemynt and the days spent rectifying it were finally over. The company would finally be held accountable for its actions. The ladies could walk away with satisfaction knowing they changed the world for the better.

Out of nowhere, Sarah burst through the crowd to confront the cheerful group.

"You took my badge!" she yelled in fiery anger.

"We did what now?" Kelsey replied coyly.

"Oh dear, maybe you dropped your badge on the floor?" Jade grinned. "Have you looked around for it?"

Sarah did not deserve a single, solitary breath of a response. The Myntor chased her career ambitions relentlessly at the expense of the welfare of other people. Enabling sexual assault, undercutting the walkout, setting up her colleagues for failure, and continually working in her own warped interests was detestable behavior. She cast into the fire whoever stood in the way of her ascension to the top.

"I know you all had something to do with this...mess!" Sarah barked.

"Us? No, that was you," Tai said with a smirk. "Congrats on sending those files to the reporters."

"I knew you were terrible but taking down the company?" Daniela shook her head. "That was some kind of choice."

"Yeah, nice touch, Sarah," Kelsey said.

"I didn't do any of that!" Sarah raged. "Do you know how connected I am? I'll make sure you four never work in Silicon Valley again."

Tai scoffed at her tirade. "More threats to destroy people's careers? Classic Sarah. Have fun with that."

Leon marched through the lobby and toward the group with wrath in his eyes. Kelsey feared that the security chief was on his way to apprehend Daniela. The ladies instinctively created a protective circle around their friend.

Leon forcefully held out his palm. "Sarah, I need your phone."

"This was *not* my fault!" Sarah shrieked in protest.

"Then explain why the changes to the employee guest list were traced to your computer," Leon said firmly. "Or why your login was used to switch out Troy's speech on the monitors. My officers also told me Daniela was given your badge to get inside the event."

Sarah writhed away from Leon in disgust at the accusations.

"Get your hands off me!" she screamed. "It wasn't me, I swear!"

Leon was unmoved by her histrionics. "We've already confiscated your work laptop that you kept backstage. Your company email and the service on your phone have been disabled. Your access to the campus buildings has been revoked too."

"I can't believe this!" Sarah said incredulously. "What about the stuff on my desk? How am I supposed to get that?"

"My team will arrange for you to pick up your belongings at the main lobby at a scheduled time. We'll let you know when after we conclude our investigation."

Sarah angrily returned her attention to the group. "I don't know who you bitches think you are, but I'm not going to let you force me out of my company."

Sarah lashed out and ranted about how she was set up and had nothing to do with the collapse of the event. However, Sarah had no proof it was anyone but her. Her fingerprints were on the corpse of E-Con and the smoking gun was in her hand.

Sarah threw her phone at Leon's feet and stormed off in a rampage.

"Enjoy your long vacation!" Tai yelled after her. "Have fun on the yacht!"

Leon excused himself. "Ladies, you might want to get back to HQ. It's going to be all hands on deck. Daniela, good seeing you again."

The crew of four sighed in collective relief as he walked away. Daniela was apparently in the clear. The release of documents that followed her speech and the question of how she made it onto the stage in the first place were not the Security team's immediate concerns. Elemynt couldn't undo her words and would not seek to provoke her further. It was highly unlikely the company would not go after Zekiyah or Grace either. Doing so would inevitably result in more backlash from the already incensed public.

"Changing the words on the monitor... that's such a smart idea," Kelsey smiled.

"Jade came up with it," Tai said.

"Who me?" Jade laughed it off. "Wasn't it Sarah who hacked into the system?"

"I don't know what that woman does in her free time," Tai chuckled. "Seriously though, she'll be fine. They'll trace her computer. There's no evidence on it that it was her."

"Hold on, everybody," Kelsey halted the conversation. "Quiet a sec."

Timothy Westbrook, chronicler of all things Elemynt including the corporate disaster he would write endless stories about, walked purposefully in Kelsey's direction. Daniela swiftly escorted the rest of the group to the side to watch the exchange from afar.

"Hey so... I'm pretty sure I saw you swipe Sarah's badge earlier," Tim said.

"No, you didn't," Kelsey responded casually.

"You sure? Right at the beginning when we were talking?"

"You must have me confused with somebody else," Kelsey said.

"Okay, let me ask you this..." Tim said without stumbling. "Did you have something to do with what went on in there? That was some kinda show."

"As an employee of Elemynt, I stand behind the company 100 percent."

"And these files... you didn't have anything to do with that either? Do you think they'll change how people see the platform?"

"You're the journalist, Tim. Write it up and let the people make their choice."

"Can I quote you on that?" he perked up.

Kelsey scrunched her face.

"I'll take that as a no," he said.

"Tim, this has been an awesome meeting," Kelsey said. "I think there are more free snacks left if you want."

"Hmm, gotcha," he said, glancing at her sideways. "If you think there's more newsworthy events coming...you know where to find me."

Kelsey would not be looking for him. She was thoroughly done with media circuses and press fires or events directly or tangentially related to Elemynt. Her three friends also felt the same. The group offered each other looks of comfort under the dimming Elemynt signage.

"Daniela, don't you want to go back in there and do interviews?" Jade asked. "This is your moment, darling."

"What we did speaks for itself, don't you think?" she said.

The women were in agreement. Together they took on what seemed impossible days prior. Kelsey, Jade, and Tai appreciated Daniela for encouraging them to push for change in ways they were reticent to do on their own.

"I just want to say thank you," Daniela said humbly. "The last year has been a huge challenge. I wouldn't have made it through it without you three."

"Life's better when we support each other," Kelsey smiled.

"Damn straight," Jade said. "Whoops, I mean 'gay'. Damn inclusive."

The group shared a laugh that Kelsey hoped wouldn't be their last. The ladies moved in for a sisterly embrace that said more to each other than a thank you ever could. Tai, however, wanted no part of the display of affection.

"Come in here, Tai," Jade said.

"Hugs?" she recoiled. "Gross."

"You helped make this possible," Daniela said. "You're getting a hug."

Tai reluctantly accepted the love from her friends.

The masses emptied out of the auditorium and journeyed back into the world. Elemynt's fate would be determined not by crafted speeches and dazzling demos, but by the billion individuals who together made the company into the success it was. Kelsey could not wait to see what happened next.

TWENTY-TWO

Kelsey sat on her couch watching a cable news channel with more personal investment than she ever had in the last year. Troy was due to speak at noon from outside Elemynt headquarters.

Three weeks had passed since E-Con and the day Kelsey officially retreated from the campus. Her apartment was in disarray from packing. He needed to hurry soon. Her suitcases sat ready beside her.

The epic event that should have been a climactic moment for Elemynt instead became a wild blow the business would never recover from. The #DeleteElemynt movement accelerated instantly and led to a flurry of account deletions by more than 300,000 people in 24 hours. The company's plot to harvest private data on each user in detrimental ways they couldn't imagine previously was more than enough reason for them to leave the app. People would find other avenues to connect with their communities. They didn't have to completely hand over their privacy to be able to keep in touch with others.

The internal documents that revealed in detail how the company misled the public were the largest factor in its descent into demise. Elemynt executives were vocal in their rebuttal, calling the documents misleading. The U.S. Justice Department thought otherwise. The company was placed under criminal investigation for data collection that exceeded consumer expectations and the promotion of nefarious activity by foreign actors. Congresswoman Layne and the House and Senate committees backed the Department's efforts the full resources of their offices.

Congress and the American public had the evidence to make their own assessments of Elemynt's intentions free from Troy's idealistic proclamations or Catherine's behind the scenes machinations.

The astonishing turn of events sent shockwaves through the Elemynt workforce. Employees who strongly opposed the actions of the company left in a mass exodus and took positions at other Silicon Valley companies. The vesting stock in Elemynt that incentivized Myntors to stay no longer held its power over them.

The promise of an IPO and the big payday that would result from it was gone. The likelihood that the company would recover enough to become the profitable unicorn it sought to be was unlikely. For those employees who did stay behind, the massive cohort of ride-or-die Elemynt cheerleaders dwindled to a few ardent supporters.

Behind the scenes, Elemynt officially withdrew all plans for its IPO weeks before it was set to file the official paperwork. The company cites "market conditions" as the reason for the change. Industry observers of course saw right through the excuse.

An IPO at a later stage may have been possible for Elemynt, but no time in the near future. Fewer people on the platform translated to fewer eyeballs for advertisers to throw cash toward. Convincing investors to hand over money in light of the increasingly troubling circumstances surrounding the company would be extremely difficult. Without the instant infusion of capital an IPO would bring, the question of how the company would continue its growth trajectory had yet to be answered.

Troy stepped into the frame of Kelsey's television. The campus' famous Elemynt logo that was a beacon for travelers to Silicon Valley served as his backdrop. Troy's usual T-shirt and sneakers were replaced by a fitted black suit and tie that reflected the seriousness of the moment. A gaggle of news cameras and reporters huddled around him to capture the would-be billionaire who fell from grace.

"To say that I am ashamed is an extreme understatement," Troy read from his pre-written statement. "I should've used better judgment and constructed the app to better reflect the needs and concerns of the people who use it. That's why I am announcing today that I plan to step down from my position as CEO of Elemynt."

The startled murmur from the reporters digesting Troy's words of resignation overwhelmed his ability to continue. Kelsey saw the statement for what it was: inevitable.

"The company needs new leadership and I don't want to be a distraction while Elemynt works to build a more inclusive culture and reimagines the inner workings of the product."

What Troy failed to mention was that several days prior, he received a letter signed by the company's board of directors demanding he vacate his post. His departure was not the generous gesture he would have people believe. It was a mandate from which he intended to save face. The billion-dollar company he founded teetered at the edge of financial ruin. His ousting was a last-ditch effort to save it.

Catherine's fate was less certain. The COO bailed on the company as she promised behind the curtains at E-Con. In an effort to continue her legacy as one of tech's most revered executives, she embarked on a press tour to rehabilitate her image. However, instead of the media portraying her as a victim of corporate circumstance as she intended, Catherine was grilled mercilessly about her role in the breakdown of Elemynt's morality. After a few days under the microscope, she disappeared from public view.

Catherine's influential friends refused to advocate on her behalf in the press. She attempted to make a sizable donation to Code XX, the women's charity that honored her less than a year prior. They refused the gift. It was revealed that before E-Con Catherine pitched a TV network on a "Boss Lady" talk show centered on her feminist teachings. It fell through due to her soured reputation.

Catherine became a pariah who people went out of their way to disassociate themselves from.

Troy's exit would not be without some last-minute changes. He told the gathered media of his appointment of a roundtable composed of a diverse range of managers and employees. Myntors that represented all levels of the company would guide its next steps.

"I've encouraged my teams to rethink Elemynt's workplace culture," he said. "There are ideas under discussion to tie manager pay to efforts to build more diverse and inclusive teams. Also to roll out more aggressive measures to permanently bar bad actors and better filter out potentially abusive content. Plans are underway to triple the number of moderators on staff and create a path for more than half of the company's contractor workers to transition into full-time positions. It's a start but it's something. I hope that the new CEO of Elemynt will follow through with these initiatives in their leadership."

It was hard for Kelsey to tell if Troy's turnaround on the issues was the result of goodwill or an effort to save face and the financial future of the company. Either way, the results of the proposed ideas would be an ethical improvement.

Moving forward, Elemynt could build products with not just innovation in mind, but also accountability. People from diverse backgrounds would have the opportunity to use Elemynt in the way Troy originally intended. The app would be a more welcoming place for all.

Together with her group of extraordinary women, Kelsey succeeded in changing the course of history. Success to her meant more than just her standing in the company. Giving voice to the voiceless was more rewarding than any raise, promotion, or benefit that Elemynt could offer.

* * *

The warm Costa Rican sun smiled on Kelsey. The fresh-faced traveler peered from her private chartered boat out at the expanse of crystal blue ocean off the shores of the coast.

The trip would be a do-over of Kelsey's last visit. The one where she was crippled by a panic attack and at the brink of exhaustion. There would be none of that this time around. She journeyed to the beautiful destination along with her friends to celebrate their iconic accomplishment.

Together, Kelsey, Jade, Daniela, and Tai basked in the glow of the afternoon rays. Kelsey was overjoyed that she could take an actual vacation without the burden of a morally questionable company on her back.

Relaxation was that day's number one priority. In the days to come, they would go for a dip in the area's cooling waterfalls, go birdwatching amid the lush foliage, or experience whatever tropical adventure their hearts desired.

In the meantime, the ladies were content to lay out on the boat deck enjoying their favorite refreshing drinks. Tai, in cargo shorts, made headway on her favorite beer. Daniela was healthy and rested after her storied departure from the company.

"There's nothing more freeing than leaving a job that's wearing you out," Daniela said as she sipped from a fresh coconut.

"Tell us, Daniela.... is your life destroyed forever?" Jade said jokingly.

Daniela shook her head no. "Would you believe I got a ton of job offers after E-Con? My email inbox was out of control! For good, this time. Senator Layne offered me a position on her staff as press secretary. I'm thinking about taking it."

"How wonderful is that!" Jade exclaimed.

"I couldn't believe it when she asked me," Daniela said. "The Congresspeople want to know how they should stay on top of tech companies and they liked how passionate I was about the issue. Either way, Ro is happy for me because she says I'm not as high strung as I was this past year."

"So, you're saying you want to ditch us for the East Coast so you can be happy," Tai deadpanned. "Cool, cool."

"D.C. is a flight away!" Daniela laughed. "You'll have a reason to come visit the place that has nothing to do with Congressional hearings."

"Focusing on yourself and stepping away from other people's chaos is always a good way to go," Kelsey affirmed.

"I'll say," Jade raised her glass. "And guess who's starting their own foundation?"

"Our favorite glamour girl," Daniela cheesed.

"The one and only, darling," Jade said. "I'm building a program to match women and people of color who are leaders in their community with high-profile partners interested in similar causes. If these big stars are going to stay on Elemynt, which a lot of them are, we want to make sure they're using the app for more than selfies and backstage photos. There's so much good that can be done when they use their platforms to raise awareness. And — you'll love this — Grace is coming on as the lead investor."

"Fantastic!" Kelsey exclaimed. "You're going to change so many lives."

"That's the plan!" Jade beamed.

The ladies lavished Jade with a round of congratulations on her next step. It took a significant amount of nerve for an executive that was well regarded in her industry to strike out on her own. Jade did so with a firm belief that her calling was much more than shepherding celebrities at Elemynt.

Jade took a sly sip of her cocktail. "I'm also trying to bring Tai on board to be our head of communications."

"Ah, I don't know..." Tai dragged. "I kinda need a break from the Comms life."

"What if I promised you a matching salary, free lunch every week, and a mani-pedi every Friday?"

"Scratch the spa days and give me a beer fridge. Then I'll consider it."

Kelsey secretly hoped that Tai would accept Jade's offer. Joining her foundation may have been the change in scenery that Tai needed following her front-row seat for Elemynt's decline. Truthfully, Tai would be a wonderful talent where she chose to spend her time. Any company would be lucky to have her brilliant mind on board.

"I have this idea I've been thinking about," Daniela said, propping herself up in her seat. "How about *I* write a 'boss lady' book? But a realistic one. It could be for the woman of color with limited professional connections who wants to push through the male-dominated workplace."

"I'm seeing best-selling author!" Jade lit up. "Okay, pretend I'm Oprah. I'll ask you a few questions. Daniela, what would you recommend to working women?"

"Don't let men define who you are," Daniela held her head high. "When they get you to stop speaking up, that's when you're defeated. Find your allies... your good girlfriends who can support you and encourage you. Ignorant men at your job can't break you down if you don't let them. Also, document everything just in case!"

"You're ready for a world tour!" Jade said with delight.

"Oh, and have another job lined up before you decide to leave," Daniela added. "The light bills won't pay themselves!"

The ladies applauded Daniela's honest answer and poised delivery. There were many women from underrepresented backgrounds whose lives could be transformed by her firsthand career insight. Kelsey imagined a great life ahead for her outstanding friend.

"How about a toast?" Daniela said, lifting a glass of champagne. "To my lovely ladies who have gone on this journey together and are better for it. Cheers and... as they say in Costa Rica...pura vida!"

"A pure life!" Kelsey smiled.

The frosty drinks clinked against each other under the azure sky. The women soaked in the sound of velvet waves gliding alongside the boat and into the twinkling blue expanse. The peacefulness of the moment was what they long hoped for after the reign of turmoil unleashed on them by their employer.

"Kelsey, you never told us where you're off to after Elemynt," Daniela said with curiosity.

"I never said I was leaving..." Kelsey raised an eyebrow.

The ladies gasped with such disbelief that they nearly turned the boat over. Kelsey was surprised by their appalled reaction.

"I go back to the office next week," she said.

"Kelsey, no!" Jade yelped.

"All that work to pull off our E-Con thing and you're staying?" Tai stared quizzically.

"After everything they've put you through?" Daniela said in shock.

"Jon's gone, Troy and Catherine are gone, and so is Sarah," Kelsey explained.

"There's no more hearings and they're tightening up security on the app. All the things that were bringing me down are out of the way. This is an opportunity for me to step up and possibly be a real boss. I'm totally next in line for the VP of communications role."

Jade was unconvinced. "Are you sure, love? There are a thousand jobs out there that you could land instead. And what if they find out you were part of the reason those documents leaked?"

"What are they going to do?" Kelsey asked. "Murder me?"

"They might..." Tai said.

"It wouldn't surprise me at all," Jade added. "I'd hate to see your picture on the cover of the Washington Chronicle."

"I thought you said you were packing up your apartment?" Daniela asked firmly.

"Um no, I was packing my luggage to come here..." Kelsey said. "Listen, ladies. I could just throw my phone in the ocean and walk away from the company. But I can do more good inside than I can from the outside. Somebody has to keep those guys in check."

"You cannot be serious," Daniela winced.

"One hundred percent," Kelsey said confidently. "The reason why I came to Elemynt in the first place is because there were these incredible moments happening on the platform all the time. And there still are. I wanted to promote the good ways the app was being used. Now that Elemynt is getting its act together, it's time to show the world the positivity the app can bring into their lives."

Jade was overcome with worry. "Kelsey, how about you take a new position with me at the foundation? We're going to be doing the kind of work you're talking about."

"I appreciate it so much, Jade," Kelsey said. "But this is my decision and I'm sticking with it."

Kelsey ran her fingers through the warm water on the side of the boat as the other ladies murmured to themselves. They may not have been convinced that what Kelsey was doing was right, but it was her life to lead.

The worst possible trials of her career were brought on by people no longer at the company. It was time to rebuild. With new leadership and a new direction, there was nowhere to go but up.

* * *

After the sun set on the horizon and the boat docked on the shore, Kelsey returned to her hotel room full of joy and optimism for the future of her career. Her restorative vacation was off to a beautiful start. Kelsey slipped into bed to indulge in the most relaxing sleep she had in a very long time.

A loud buzzing.

Kelsey's phone shook incessantly on the nightstand.

She shot up in the dark. The time. She had only been asleep for an hour.

Five missed calls.

At the top of her notifications was an email in her Elemynt inbox marked with a red flag. Sent by Leon.

The subject line flashed three words. "EMERGENCY MEETING NOW."